Matters of Life and Death

Matters
of
Life and Death
New American Stories

Edited and
with an Introduction by
Tobias Wolff

W
A WAMPETER PRESS / GEORGE MURPHY BOOK

Typesetting and design by Coastal Composition, Box 2600, Ocean Bluff, MA 02065

Cover Design by George Murphy

First Edition, January 1983.

All rights reserved.

Copyright © 1983, Wampeter Press
    Introduction and selection Copyright © 1983, Tobias Wolff

Printed in the U.S.A.

The publication of this book is supported by grants from the National Endowment for the Arts and the Massachusetts Council on the Arts & Humanities.

Library of Congress Catalog Card Number: 82-70441
ISBN: 0-931694-14-0 paperbound
ISBN: 0-931694-17-5 clothbound

Wampeter Press, Box 512, Green Harbor, MA 02041

This book is dedicated to John Cheever

1912–1982

"I wish I could say that a kindly lion had set me straight, or an innocent child, or the strains of distant music from some church, but it was no more than the rain on my head – the smell of it flying up to my nose – that showed me the extent of my freedom from the bones in Fontainebleau and the works of a thief. There were ways out of my trouble if I cared to make use of them. I was not trapped. I was here on earth because I chose to be."

from "The Housebreaker of Shady Hill"

ACKNOWLEDGEMENTS

The author and the publisher would like to thank David Allender, Melanie Fleishman, Seymour Lawrence, Gordon Lish, Tia Maytag, Rosemary Murphy, Mitch Rose, Amanda Urban, and Catherine Wolff for their encouragement, assistance and support.

CONTENTS

Introduction

Tobias Wolff

"Almighty God," says an Isak Dinasen character, "as the heavens are higher than the earth, so are Thy short stories higher than our short stories."

This is the truth, as any subscriber to the *Syracuse Herald-Journal* will immediately recognize. We read here not long ago of a commercial fisherman who was lost in a storm near Mendicino, California. Pieces of his boat were found. Some three weeks later he himself washed up in the surf off the coast of Oregon -- alive, on Christmas Eve.

And there was a story about a woman in Prague who discovered that her husband was cheating on her. She pleaded with him to stop, but he refused. In a fit of despair she threw herself out the window of her flat and fell four stories before landing on her husband, who at that moment was walking below. She lived, he died.

Soul claps its hands and sings.

No lesson is too obvious, no sentiment too coarse, no plot too intricate or tidy or preposterous to actually happen. And it all, as we say in creative writing classes, "works."

We are tempted, in the face of such reckless, prodigal invention, to fall silent. This temptation is made all the more compelling by the awesome foulness of our recent history, and the possibility of extinction that we wake to every morning. We live, more or less consciously, with some very discouraging prospects -- so discouraging as to make the essentially optimistic act of writing seem, at times, absurd.

The other temptation is for us to become ironists. Irony offers us a way of talking about the unspeakable. In the voices of Swift and Nabokov and Jane Austen we sometimes hear what would have been a scream if irony had not subdued it to eloquence, and translated it from the private to the public world.

Irony is also a way of not talking about the unspeakable. It can be used to deflect or even to deny what is difficult, painful, dangerous -- that is, consequential. Whatever its merits or shortcomings as entertainment, television is ironical in this sense. You aren't really expected to take what you see seriously, because if you did you would be too distracted and miserable to watch the other three shows you're supposed to watch. Something in the set is forever winking at us. Between the treatment of a given question and its possibilities, between our complacency and our fears, we are always aware of a calculated distance. Television has made a deal with us: it won't take us too seriously if we won't take it too seriously.

This shouldn't surprise us. The same ironical distance gives American life its distinctive spaciousness, its robust innocence of the timidity brought on by soul-searching, its freedom from the restraints of logic. Everyone jogs now. If we are to believe one of the stories in this book, travelling salesmen jog in Holiday Inn parking lots. Having little interest in our souls, we have turned with religious ardor to the perfection of our bodies, but we have omitted to pass a law preventing our neighbor from buying a pistol on a whim and plugging us as we run by. The other experience most of us share in addition to jogging -- marriage -- has become a supreme exercise in irony. In San Mateo County, California, there were more divorces last year than weddings.

In short, there is something about the way we live that makes it hard for us to take ourselves seriously.

The arts reflect this problem in their general preoccupation with method at the expense of their interest in the human. Movies, for example, are increasingly about technique, and technology, rather than people, and draw their inspiration from other movies rather than from any special passion or insight of the director. Literature is in danger of becoming similarly stylized and self-absorbed. There is a vast and growing body of fiction that takes as its subject the process of inventing fiction, or the conventions of fiction in this or that form, or the nature of fictional structures. This work is considered experimental by those who produce and admire it, generally the same people, but in practice most of it has become so ritualized and predictable that it is, in effect, simply another form of silence: white noise.

For that matter, most of the noise that fills our lives is white noise. We live in a great silence where what frightens us and moves us and sustains us is rarely given voice. But when that silence is broken we bend forward and listen.

That was how I came to choose the stories in this anthology. In the voices that tell them I heard something that I couldn't ignore, some note of menace or hope or warning or appeal or awe; and in the matter of the stories themselves, the people who inhabit them and what they do, I saw something that I couldn't look away from.

The writers included here represent no school. They see things in different, even contradictory ways. Taken together, their stories express a variety of responses not only to the lives that they record, but also to the possibilities of language and form. Some of these pieces present us with apparently simple visions of life which somehow turn mysterious, strange, both unfamiliar and too familiar -- plain doors that open on a maze. Others proceed through antic, visionary complications. The voices alter from story to story, ranging from the severely colloquial to the outrageously figurative. The one thing that all these writers have in common beyond the fact of their talent is that however they go about their business, they do mean business.

They speak to us, without flippancy, about things that matter. They write about what happens between men and women, parents and children. They write about fear of death, fear of life, the feelings that bring people together and force them apart, the costs of intimacy. They remind us that our house is built on sand. They are, every one of them, interested in what it means to be human.

Which is not to say that these stories are grave. They aren't. Some of them are funny. Nor are they particularly instructive morally, or spiritually uplifting. There are a few stories in here that I would positively disapprove of if they weren't so good, and so honest. The truth is not always uplifting.

Tolstoy's Ivan Ilyich, lying on his deathbed, finally can tolerate only the company of his servant Gerasim, because Gerasim is the one person in the house who does not pretend that Ivan Ilyich "is simply ill, and that he only need keep quiet and undergo a treatment and then something very good would result." Gerasim alone does not reduce "the dreadful act of his dying to the level of a casual, unpleasant, and almost indecorous incident."

There is something of Gerasim in every good writer -- the willingness to say that unspeakable thing which everyone else in the house is too coy, or too frightened, or too polite to say.

Tobias Wolff
Syracuse, New York

Ann Beattie

The Burning House

Freddy Fox is in the kitchen with me. He has just washed and dried an avocado seed I don't want, and he is leaning against the wall, rolling a joint. In five minutes, I will not be able to count on him. However: he started late in the day, and he has already brought in wood for the fire, gone to the store down the road for matches, and set the table. "You mean you'd know this stuff was Limoges even if you didn't turn the plate over?" he called from the dining room. He pretended to be about to throw one of the plates into the kitchen, like a Frisbee. Sam, the dog, believed him and shot up, kicking the rug out behind him and skidding forward before he realized his error; it was like the Road Runner tricking Wile E. Coyote into going over the cliff for the millionth time. His jowls sank in disappointment.

"I see there's a full moon," Freddy says. "There's just nothing that can hold a candle to nature. The moon and the stars, the tides and the sunshine—and we just don't stop for long enough to wonder at it all. We're so engrossed in ourselves." He takes a very long drag on the joint. "We stand and stir the sauce in the pot instead of going to the window and gazing at the moon."

"You don't mean anything personal by that, I assume."

"I love the way you pour cream in a pan. I like to come up behind you and watch the sauce bubble."

"No, thank you," I say. "You're starting late in the day."

"My responsibilities have ended. You don't trust me to help with the cooking, and I've already brought in firewood and run an

1

errand, and this very morning I exhausted myself by taking Mr. Sam jogging with me, down at Putnam Park. You're sure you won't?"

"No, thanks," I say. "Not now, anyway."

"I love it when you stand over the steam coming out of a pan and the hairs around your forehead curl into damp little curls."

My husband, Frank Wayne, is Freddy's half brother. Frank is an accountant. Freddy is closer to me than to Frank. Since Frank talks to Freddy more than he talks to me, however, and since Freddy is totally loyal, Freddy always knows more than I know. It pleases me that he does not know how to stir sauce; he will start talking, his mind will drift, and when next you look the sauce will be lumpy, or boiling away.

Freddy's criticism of Frank is only implied. "What a gracious gesture to entertain his friends on the weekend," he says.

"Male friends," I say.

"I didn't mean that you're the sort of lady who doesn't draw the line. I most certainly did not mean that," Freddy says. "I would even have been surprised if you had taken a toke of this deadly stuff while you were at the stove."

"O.K.," I say, and take the joint from him. Half of it is left when I take it. Half an inch is left after I've taken two drags and given it back.

"More surprised still if you'd shaken the ashes into the saucepan."

"You'd tell people I'd done it when they'd finished eating, and I'd be embarrassed. You can do it, though. I wouldn't be embarrassed if it was a story you told on yourself."

"You really understand me," Freddy says. "It's moon-madness, but I have to shake just this little bit in the sauce. I have to do it."

He does it.

Frank and Tucker are in the living room. Just a few minutes ago, Frank returned from getting Tucker at the train. Tucker loves to visit. To him, Fairfield County is as mysterious as Alaska. He brought with him from New York a crock of mustard, a jeroboam of champagne, cocktail napkins with a picture of a plane flying over a building on them, twenty egret feathers ("You cannot get them anymore—strictly illegal," Tucker whispered to me), and, under his black cowboy hat with the rhinestone-studded chin strap, a toy frog that hopped when wound. Tucker owns a gallery in SoHo, and Frank keeps his books. Tucker is now stretched out in the living room, visiting with Frank, and Freddy and I are both listening.

2

" . . . so everything I've been told indicates that he lives a purely Jekyll-and-Hyde existence. He's twenty years old, and I can see that since he's still living at home he might not want to flaunt his gayness. When he came into the gallery, he had his hair slicked back—just with water; I got close enough to sniff—and his mother was all but holding his hand. So fresh-scrubbed. The stories I'd heard. Anyway, when I called, his father started looking for the number where he could be reached in the Vineyard—very irritated, because I didn't know James, and if I'd just phoned James I could have found him in a flash. He's talking to himself, looking for the number, and I say, 'Oh, did he go to visit friends or—' and his father interrupts and says, 'He was going to a gay pig roast. He's been gone since Monday.' *Just like that*."

Freddy helps me carry the food out to the table. When we are all at the table, I mention the young artist Tucker was talking about. "Frank says his paintings are really incredible," I say to Tucker.

"Makes Estes look like an Abstract Expressionist," Tucker says. "I want that boy. I really want that boy."

"You'll get him," Frank says. "You get everybody you go after."

Tucker cuts a small piece of meat. He cuts it small so that he can talk while chewing. "Do I?" he says.

Freddy is smoking at the table, gazing dazedly at the moon centered in the window. "After dinner," he says, putting the back of his hand against his forehead when he sees that I am looking at him, "we must all go to the lighthouse."

"If only *you* painted," Tucker says. "I'd want you."

"You couldn't have me," Freddy snaps. He reconsiders. "That sounded halfhearted, didn't it? Anybody who wants me can have me. This is the only place I can be on Saturday night where somebody isn't hustling me."

"Wear looser pants," Frank says to Freddy.

"This is so much better than some bar that stinks of cigarette smoke and leather. Why do I do it?" Freddy says. "Seriously—do you think I'll ever stop?"

"Let's not be serious," Tucker says.

"I keep thinking of this table as a big boat, with dishes and glasses rocking on it," Freddy says.

He takes the bone from his plate and walks out to the kitchen, dripping sauce on the floor. He walks as though he's on the deck of a wave-tossed ship. "Mr. Sam!" he calls, and the dog springs up from the living-room floor, where he had been sleeping; his toenails on the bare wood floor sound like a wheel spinning in gravel.

"You don't have to beg," Freddy says. "Jesus, Sammy—I'm just giving it to you."

"I hope there's a bone involved," Tucker says, rolling his eyes to Frank. He cuts another tiny piece of meat. "I hope your brother does understand why I couldn't keep him on. He was good at what he did, but he also might say just *anything* to a customer. You have to believe me that if I hadn't been extremely embarrassed more than once I never would have let him go."

"He should have finished school," Frank says, sopping up sauce on his bread. "He'll knock around a while longer, then get tired of it and settle down to something."

"You think I died out here?" Freddy calls. "You think I can't hear you?"

"I'm not saying anything I wouldn't say to your face," Frank says.

"I'll tell you what I wouldn't say to your face," Freddy says. "You've got a swell wife and kid and dog, and you're a snob, and you take it all for granted."

Frank puts down his fork, completely exasperated. He looks at me.

"He came to work once this stoned," Tucker says. *"Comprenez-vous?"*

"You like me because you feel sorry for me," Freddy says.

He is sitting on the concrete bench outdoors, in the area that's a garden in the springtime. It is early April now—not quite spring. It's very foggy out. It rained while we were eating, and now it has turned mild. I'm leaning against a tree, across from him, glad it's so dark and misty that I can't look down and see the damage the mud is doing to my boots.

"Who's his girlfriend?" Freddy says.

"If I told you her name, you'd tell him I told you."

"Slow down. What?"

"I won't tell you, because you'll tell him that I know."

"He knows you know."

"I don't think so."

"How did you find out?"

"He talked about her. I kept hearing her name for months, and then we went to a party at Andy's, and she was there, and when I said something about her later he said, 'Natalie who?' It was much too casual. It gave the whole thing away."

He sighs. "I just did something very optimistic," he says. "I came out here with Mr. Sam and he dug up a rock and I put the avocado seed in the hole and packed dirt on top of it. Don't say it—I know: can't grow outside, we'll still have another snow, even if it grew, the next year's frost would kill it."

"He's embarrassed," I say. "When he's home, he avoids me. But it's rotten to avoid Mark, too. Six years old, and he calls up his friend Neal to hint that he wants to go over there. He doesn't do that when we're here alone."

Freddy picks up a stick and pokes around in the mud with it. "I'll bet Tucker's after that painter personally, not because he's the hottest thing since pancakes. That expression of his—it's always the same. Maybe Nixon really loved his mother, but with that expression who could believe him? It's a curse to have a face that won't express what you mean."

"Amy!" Tucker calls. "Telephone."

Freddy waves goodbye to me with the muddy stick. " 'I am not a crook,' " Freddy says. "Jesus Christ."

Sam bounds halfway toward the house with me, then turns and goes back to Freddy.

It's Marilyn, Neal's mother, on the phone.

"Hi," Marilyn says. "He's afraid to spend the night."

"Oh, no," I say. "He said he wouldn't be."

She lowers her voice. "We can try it out, but I think he'll start crying."

"I'll come get him."

"I can bring him home. You're having a dinner party, aren't you?"

I lower my voice. "Some party. Tucker's here. J.D. never showed up."

"Well," she says. "I'm sure that what you cooked was good."

"It's so foggy out, Marilyn. I'll come get Mark."

"He can stay. I'll be a martyr," she says, and hangs up before I can object.

Freddy comes into the house, tracking in mud. Sam lies in the kitchen, waiting for his paws to be cleaned. "Come on," Freddy says, hitting his hand against his thigh, having no idea what Sam is doing. Sam gets up and runs after him. They go into the small downstairs bathroom together. Sam loves to watch people urinate. Sometimes he sings, to harmonize with the sound of the urine going into the water. There are footprints and pawprints everywhere. Tucker is shrieking with laughter in the living room. "...he says, he says to the other one, 'Then, dearie, have you ever played *spin* the bottle?' " Frank's and Tucker's laughter drowns out the sound of Freddy peeing in the bathroom. I turn on the water in the kitchen sink, and it drowns out all the noise. I begin to scrape the dishes. Tucker is telling another story when I turn off the water: " . . . that it was Onassis in the Anvil, and nothing would talk him out of it. They told him Onassis was dead, and he thought they were trying to make him think he was crazy. There was nothing to do but go along with him, but, God—he was trying to goad this poor old fag into fighting about Stavros Niarchos. You know—Onassis's *enemy*. He thought it was *Onassis*. In the *Anvil*." There is a sound of a glass breaking. Frank or Tucker puts "John Coltrane Live in Seattle" on the stereo and turns the volume down low. The bathroom door opens. Sam runs into the kitchen and begins to lap water from his dish. Freddy takes his little silver case and his rolling papers out of his shirt pocket. He puts a piece of paper on the kitchen table and is about to sprinkle grass on it, but realizes just in time that the paper has absorbed water from a puddle. He balls it up with his thumb, flicks it to the floor, puts a piece of rolling paper where the table's dry and shakes a line of grass down it. "You smoke this," he says to me. "I'll do the dishes."

"We'll both smoke it. I'll wash and you can wipe."

"I forgot to tell them I put ashes in the sauce," he says.

"I wouldn't interrupt."

"At least he pays Frank ten times what any other accountant for an art gallery would make," Freddy says.

Tucker is beating his hand on the arm of the sofa as he talks, stomping his feet. " . . . so he's trying to feel him out, to see if this old guy with the dyed hair knew *Maria Callas*. Jesus! And he's so out of it he's trying to think what opera singers are called, and instead of coming up with *'diva'* he comes up with *'duenna.'* At this point, Larry Betwell went up to him and tried to calm him down, and he breaks into song—some aria or something that Maria Callas was famous for. Larry told him he was going to lose his *teeth* if he didn't get it together, and . . ."

"He spends a lot of time in gay hangouts, for not being gay," Freddy says.

I scream and jump back from the sink, hitting the glass I'm rinsing against the faucet, shattering green glass everywhere.

"What?" Freddy says. "Jesus Christ, what is it?"

Too late, I realize what it must have been that I saw: J.D. in a goat mask, the puckered pink plastic lips against the window beside the kitchen sink.

"I'm sorry," J.D. says, coming through the door and nearly colliding with Frank, who has rushed into the kitchen. Tucker is right behind him.

"Ooh," Tucker says, feigning disappointment, "I thought Freddy smooched her."

"I'm sorry," J.D. says again. "I thought you'd know it was me."

The rain must have started again, because J.D. is soaking wet. He has turned the mask around so that the goat's head stares out from the back of his head. "I got lost," J.D. says. He has a farmhouse upstate. "I missed the turn. I went miles. I missed the whole dinner, didn't I?"

"What did you do wrong?" Frank asks.

"I didn't turn left onto 58. I don't know why I didn't realize my mistake, but I went *miles*. It was raining so hard I couldn't go over twenty-five miles an hour. Your driveway is all mud. You're going to have to push me out."

"There's some roast left over. And salad, if you want it," I say.

"Bring it in the living room," Frank says to J.D. Freddy is holding out a plate to him. J.D. reaches for the plate. Freddy pulls it back. J.D. reaches again, and Freddy is so stoned that he isn't quick enough this time—J.D. grabs it.

"I thought you'd know it was me," J.D. says. "I apologize." He dishes salad onto the plate. "You'll be rid of me for six months, in the morning."

"Where does your plane leave from?" Freddy says.

"Kennedy."

"Come in here!" Tucker calls. "I've got a story for you about Perry Dwyer down at the Anvil last week, when he thought he saw Aristotle Onassis."

"Who's Perry Dwyer?" J.D. says.

"That is not the point of the story, dear man. And when you're in Cassis, I want you to look up an American painter over there. Will you? He doesn't have a phone. Anyway—I've been tracking him, and I know where he is now, and I am *very* interested, if you would stress that with him, to do a show in June that will be *only* him. He doesn't answer my letters."

"Your hand is cut," J.D. says to me.

"Forget it," I say. "Go ahead."

"I'm sorry," he says. "Did I make you do that?"

"Yes, you did."

"Don't keep your finger under the water. Put pressure on it to stop the bleeding."

He puts the plate on the table. Freddy is leaning against the counter, staring at the blood swirling in the sink, and smoking the joint all by himself. I can feel the little curls on my forehead that Freddy was talking about. They feel heavy on my skin. I hate to see my own blood. I'm sweating. I let J.D. do what he does; he turns off the water and wraps his hand around my second finger, squeezing. Water runs down our wrists.

Freddy jumps to answer the phone when it rings, as though a siren just went off behind him. He calls me to the phone, but J.D. steps in front of me, shakes his head no, and takes the dish towel and wraps it around my hand before he lets me go.

"Well," Marilyn says. "I had the best of intentions, but my battery's dead."

J.D. is standing behind me, with his hand on my shoulder.

"I'll be right over," I say. "He's not upset now, is he?"

"No, but he's dropped enough hints that he doesn't think he can make it through the night."

"O.K.," I say. "I'm sorry about all of this."

"Six years old," Marilyn says. "Wait till he grows up and gets that feeling."

I hang up.

"Let me see your hand," J.D. says.

"I don't want to look at it. Just go get me a Band-Aid, please."

He turns and goes upstairs. I unwrap the towel and look at it. It's pretty deep, but no glass is in my finger. I feel funny; the outlines of things are turning yellow. I sit in the chair by the phone. Sam comes and lies beside me, and I stare at his black-and-yellow tail, beating. I reach down with my good hand and pat him, breathing deeply in time with every second pat.

"*Rothko?*" Tucker says bitterly, in the living room. "Nothing is great that can appear on greeting cards. Wyeth is that way. Would "Christina's World" look bad on a cocktail napkin? You know it wouldn't."

I jump as the phone rings again. "Hello?" I say, wedging the phone against my shoulder with my ear, wrapping the dish towel tighter around my hand.

"Tell them it's a crank call. Tell them anything," Johnny says. "I miss you. How's Saturday night at your house?"

"All right," I say. I catch my breath.

"Everything's all right here, too. Yes indeed. Roast rack of lamb. Friend of Nicole's who's going to Key West tomorrow had too much to drink and got depressed because he thought it was raining in Key West, and I said I'd go in my study and call the National Weather Service. Hello, Weather Service. How are you?"

J.D. comes down from upstairs with two Band-Aids and stands beside me, unwrapping one. I want to say to Johnny, "I'm cut. I'm bleeding. It's no joke."

It's all right to talk in front of J.D., but I don't know who else might overhear me.

"I'd say they made the delivery about four this afternoon," I say.

"This is the church, this is the steeple. Open the door, and see all the people," Johnny says. "Take care of yourself. I'll hang up and find out if it's raining in Key West."

"Late in the afternoon," I say. "Everything is fine."

"Nothing is fine," Johnny says. "Take care of yourself."

He hangs up. I put the phone down, and realize that I'm still having trouble focusing, the sight of my cut finger made me so light-headed. I don't look at the finger again as J.D. undoes the towel and wraps the Band-Aids around my finger.

"What's going on in here?" Frank says, coming into the dining room.

"I cut my finger," I say. "It's O.K."

"You did?" he says. He looks woozy—a little drunk. "Who keeps calling?"

"Marilyn. Mark changed his mind about staying all night. She was going to bring him home, but her battery's dead. You'll have to get him. Or I will."

"Who called the second time?" he says.

"The oil company. They wanted to know if we got our delivery today."

He nods. "I'll go get him, if you want," he says. He lowers his voice. "Tucker's probably going to whirl himself into a tornado for an encore," he says, nodding toward the living room. "I'll take him with me."

"Do you want me to go get him?" J.D. says.

"I don't mind getting some air," Frank says. "Thanks, though. Why don't you go in the living room and eat your dinner?"

"You forgive me?" J.D. says.

"Sure," I say. "It wasn't your fault. Where did you get that mask?"

"I found it on top of a Goodwill box in Manchester. There was also a beautiful old birdcage—solid brass."

The phone rings again. I pick it up. "Wouldn't I love to be in Key West with you," Johnny says. He makes a sound as though he's kissing me and hangs up.

"Wrong number," I say.

Frank feels in his pants pocket for the car keys.

J.D. knows about Johnny. He introduced me, in the faculty lounge, where J.D. and I had gone to get a cup of coffee after I registered for classes. After being gone for nearly two years, J.D. still gets mail at the department—he said he had to stop by for the mail anyway, so he'd drive me to campus and point me toward the registrar's. J.D. taught English; now he does nothing. J.D. is glad that I've gone back to college to study art again, now that Mark is in school. I'm six credits away from an M.A. in art history. He wants me to think about myself, instead of thinking about Mark all the time. He talks as though I could roll Mark out on a string and let him fly off, high above me. J.D.'s wife and son died in a car crash. His son was Mark's age. "I wasn't prepared," J.D. said when we were driving over that day. He always says this when he talks about it. "How could you be prepared for such a thing?" I asked him. "I am now," he said. Then, realizing he was acting very hardboiled, made fun of himself. "Go on," he said, "punch me in the stomach. Hit me as hard as you can." We both knew he isn't prepared for anything. When he couldn't find a parking place that day, his hands were wrapped around the wheel so tightly that his knuckles turned white.

Johnny came in as we were drinking coffee. J.D. was looking at his junk mail—publishers wanting him to order anthologies, ways to get free dictionaries.

"You are so lucky to be out of it," Johnny said, by way of greeting. "What do you do when you've spent two weeks on 'Hamlet' and the student writes about Hamlet's good friend Horchow?"

He threw a blue book into J.D.'s lap. J.D. sailed it back.

"Johnny," he said, "this is Amy."

"Hi, Amy," Johnny said.

"You remember when Frank Wayne was in graduate school here? Amy's Frank's wife."

"Hi, Amy," Johnny said.

J.D. told me he knew it the instant Johnny walked into the room—he knew that second that he should introduce me as somebody's wife. He could have predicted it all from the way Johnny looked at me.

For a long time J.D. gloated that he had been prepared for what happened next—that Johnny and I were going to get together. It took me to disturb his pleasure in himself—me, crying hysterically on the phone last month, not knowing what to do, what move to make next.

"Don't do anything for a while. I guess that's my advice," J.D. said. "But you probably shouldn't listen to me. All I can do myself is run away, hide out. I'm not the learned professor. You know what I believe. I believe all that wicked fairy-tale crap: your heart will break, your house will burn."

Tonight, because he doesn't have a garage at his farm, J.D. has come to leave his car in the empty half of our two-car garage while he's in France. I look out the window and see his old Saab, glowing in the moonlight. J.D. has brought his favorite book, "A Vision," to read on the plane. He says his suitcase contains only a spare pair of jeans, cigarettes, and underwear. He is going to buy a leather jacket in France, at a store where he almost bought a leather jacket two years ago.

In our bedroom there are about twenty small glass prisms hung with fishing line from one of the exposed beams; they catch the morning light, and we stare at them like a cat eyeing catnip held above its head. Just now, it is 2 A.M. At six-thirty, they will be filled with dazzling color. At four or five, Mark will come into the bedroom and get in bed with us. Sam will wake up, stretch, and shake, and the tags on his collar will clink, and he will yawn and shake again and go downstairs, where J.D. is asleep in his sleeping bag and Tucker is asleep on the sofa, and get a drink of water from his dish. Mark has been coming into our bedroom for about a year. He gets onto the bed by climbing up on a footstool that horrified me when I first saw it—a gift from Frank's mother: a footstool that says "Today Is the First Day of the Rest of Your Life" in needlepoint. I kept it in a closet for years, but it occurred to me that it would help Mark get up onto the bed, so he would not have to make a little leap and possibly skin his shin again. Now Mark does not disturb us when he comes into the bedroom, except that it bothers me that he has reverted to sucking his thumb. Sometimes he lies in bed with his cold feet against my leg. Sometimes, small as he is, he snores.

Somebody is playing a record downstairs. It's the Velvet Underground—Nico, in a dream or swoon, singing "Sunday Morning." I can barely hear the whispering and tinkling of the record. I can only follow it because I've heard it a hundred times.

I am lying in bed, waiting for Frank to get out of the bathroom. My cut finger throbs. Things are going on in the house even though I have gone to bed; water runs, the record plays, Sam is still downstairs, so there must be some action.

I have known everybody in this house for years, and as time goes by I know them all less and less. J.D. was Frank's adviser in college. Frank was his best student, and they started to see each other outside of class. They played handball. J.D. and his family came to dinner. We went there. That summer—the summer Frank decided to go to graduate school in business instead of English—J.D.'s wife and son deserted him in a more horrible way, in that car crash. J.D. has quit his job. He has been to Las Vegas, to Colorado, New Orleans, Los Angeles, Paris twice; he tapes postcards to the walls of his living room. A lot of the time, on the weekends, he shows up at our house with his sleeping bag. Sometimes he brings a girl. Lately, not. Years ago, Tucker was in Frank's therapy group in New York and ended up hiring Frank to work as the accountant for his gallery. Tucker was in therapy at the time because he was obsessed with foreigners. Now he is also obsessed with homosexuals. Before the parties he does TM and yoga, and during the parties he does Seconals and isometrics. When I first met him, he was living for the summer in his sister's house in Vermont while she was in Europe, and he called us one night, in New York, in a real panic because there were wasps all over. They were "hatching," he said—big, sleepy wasps that were everywhere. We said we'd come; we drove all through the night to get to Brattleboro. It was true: there were wasps on the undersides of plates, in the plants, in the folds of curtains. Tucker was so upset that he was out behind the house, in the cold Vermont morning, wrapped like an Indian in a blanket, with only his pajamas on underneath. He was sitting in a lawn chair, hiding behind a bush, waiting for us to come.

And Freddy—"Reddy Fox," when Frank is feeling affectionate toward him. When we first met, I taught him to ice-skate and he taught me to waltz; in the summer, at Atlantic City, he'd go with me on a roller coaster that curved high over the waves. I was the one—not Frank—who would get out of bed in the middle of the night and meet him at an all-night deli and put my arm around his shoulders, the way he put his arm around my shoulders on the roller coaster, and talk quietly to him until he got over his latest anxiety attack. Now he tests me, and I retreat: this man he picked up, this man who picked him up, how it feels to have forgotten somebody's name when your hand is in the back pocket of his jeans and you're not even halfway to your apartment. Reddy Fox— admiring my new red silk blouse, stroking his fingertips down the front, and my eyes wide, because I could feel his fingers on my chest, even though I was holding the blouse in front of me on a hanger to be admired. All those moments, and all they meant was that I was fooled into thinking I knew these people because I knew the small things, the personal things.

Freddy will always be more stoned than I am, because he feels comfortable getting stoned with me and I'll always be reminded that he's more lost. Tucker knows he can come to the house and be the center of attention; he can tell all the stories he knows, and we'll never tell the story we know about him hiding in the bushes like a frightened dog. J.D. comes back from his trips with boxes full of postcards, and I look at all of them as though they're photographs taken by him, and I know, and he knows, that what he likes about them is their flatness—the unreality of them, the unreality of what he does.

Last summer, I read "The Metamorphosis" and said to J.D., "Why did Gregor Samsa wake up a cockroach?" His answer (which he would have toyed over with his students forever) was "Because that's what people expected of him."

They make the illogical logical. I don't do anything, because I'm waiting, I'm on hold (J.D.); I stay stoned because I know it's better to be out of it (Freddy); I love art because I myself am a work of art (Tucker).

Frank is harder to understand. One night a week or so ago, I thought we were really attuned to each other, communicating by telepathic waves, and as I lay in bed about to speak I realized that the vibrations really existed: they were him, snoring.

Now he's coming into the bedroom, and I'm trying again to think what to say. Or ask. Or do.

"Be glad you're not in Key West," he says. He climbs into bed.

I raise myself up on one elbow and stare at him.

"There's a hurricane about to hit," he says.

"What?" I say. "Where did you hear that?"

"When Reddy Fox and I were putting the dishes away. We had the radio on." He doubles up his pillow, pushes it under his neck. "Boom goes everything," he says. "Bam. Crash. Poof." He looks at me. "You look shocked." He closes his eyes. Then, after a minute or two, he murmurs, "Hurricanes upset you? I'll try to think of something nice."

He is quiet for so long that I think he has fallen asleep. Then he says, "Cars that run on water. A field of flowers, none alike. A shooting star that goes slow enough for you to watch. Your life to do over again." He has been whispering in my ear, and when he takes his mouth away I shiver. He slides lower in the bed for sleep. "I'll tell you something really amazing," he says. "Tucker told me he went into a travel agency on Park Avenue last week and asked the travel agent where he should go to pan for gold, and she told him."

"Where did she tell him to go?"

"I think somewhere in Peru. The banks of some river in Peru."

"Did you decide what you're going to do after Mark's birthday?" I say.

He doesn't answer me. I touch him on the side, finally.

"It's two o'clock in the morning. Let's talk about it another time."

"You picked the house, Frank. They're your friends downstairs. I used to be what you wanted me to be."

"They're your friends, too," he says. "Don't be paranoid."

"I want to know if you're staying or going."

He takes a deep breath, lets it out, and continues to lie very still.

"Everything you've done is commendable," he says. "You did the right thing to go back to school. You tried to do the right thing by finding yourself a normal friend like Marilyn. But your whole life you've made one mistake—you've surrounded yourself with men. Let me tell you something. All men—if they're crazy, like Tucker, if they're gay as the Queen of the May, like Reddy Fox, even if they're just six years old—I'm going to tell you something about them. Men think they're Spider-Man and Buck Rogers and Superman. You know what we all feel inside that you don't feel? That we're going to the stars."

He takes my hand. "I'm looking down on all of this from space," he whispers. "I'm already gone."

Raymond Carver

The Calm

I was getting a haircut. I was in the chair and three men were sitting along the wall across from me. Two of the men waiting I'd never seen before. But one of them I recognized, though I couldn't exactly place him. I kept looking at him as the barber worked on my hair. The man was moving a toothpick around in his mouth, a heavyset man, short wavy hair. And then I saw him in a cap and uniform, little eyes watchful in the lobby of a bank.

Of the other two, one was considerably the older, with a full head of curly gray hair. He was smoking. The third, though not so old, was nearly bald on top, but the hair at the sides hung over his ears. He had on logging boots, pants shiny with machine oil.

The barber put a hand on top of my head to turn me for a better look. Then he said to the guard, "Did you get your deer, Charles?"

I liked this barber. We weren't acquainted well enough to call each other by name. But when I came in for a haircut, he knew me. He knew I used to fish. So we'd talk fishing. I don't think he hunted. But he could talk on any subject. In this regard, he was a good barber.

"Bill, it's a funny story. The damndest thing," the guard said. He took out the toothpick and laid it in the ashtray. He shook his head. "I did and I didn't. So yes and no to your question."

I didn't like the man's voice. For a guard, the voice didn't fit. It wasn't the voice you'd expect.

The two other men looked up. The older man was turning the

15

pages of a magazine, smoking, and the other fellow was holding a newspaper. They put down what they were looking at and turned to listen to the guard.

"Go on, Charles," the barber said. "Let's hear it."

The barber turned my head again, and went back to work with his clippers.

"We were up on Fikle Ridge. My old man and me and the kid. We were hunting those draws. My old man was stationed at the head of one, and me and the kid were at the head of another. The kid had a hangover, goddamn his hide. The kid, he was green around the gills and drank water all day, mine and his both. It was in the afternoon and we'd been out since daybreak. But we had our hopes. We figured the hunters down below would move a deer in our direction. So we were sitting behind a log and watching the draw when we heard this shooting down in the valley."

"There's orchards down there," said the fellow with the newspaper. He was fidgeting a lot and kept crossing a leg, swinging his boot for a time, and then crossing his legs the other way. "Those deer hang out around those orchards."

"That's right," said the guard. "They'll go in there at night, the bastards, and eat those little green apples. Well, we heard this shooting and we're just sitting there on our hands when this big old buck comes up out of the underbrush not a hundred feet away. The kid sees him the same time I do, of course, and he throws down and starts banging. The knothead. That old buck wasn't in any danger. Not from the kid, as it turns out. But he can't tell where the shots are coming from. He doesn't know which way to jump. Then I get off a shot. But in all the commotion, I just stun him."

"Stunned him?" the barber said.

"You know, stun him," the guard said. "It was a gut shot. It just like stuns him. So he drops his head and begins this trembling. He trembles all over. The kid's still shooting. Me, I felt like I was back in Korea. So I shot again but missed. Then old Mr. Buck moves back into the brush. But now, by God, he doesn't have any oompf left in him. The kid has emptied his goddamn gun all to no purpose. But I hit solid. I'd rammed one right in his guts. That's what I meant by stunned him."

"Then what?" said the fellow with the newspaper, who had rolled it and was tapping it against his knee. "Then what? You must have trailed him. They find a hard place to die every time."

"But you trailed him?" the older man asked, though it wasn't really a question.

"I did. Me and the kid, we trailed him. But the kid wasn't good for much. He gets sick on the trail, slows us down. That chucklehead." The guard had to laugh now, thinking about that situation. "Drinking beer and chasing all night, then saying he can hunt deer. He knows better now, by God. But, sure, we trailed him. A good trail, too. Blood on the ground and blood on the leaves. Blood everywhere. Never seen a buck with so much blood. I don't know how the sucker kept going."

"Sometimes they'll go forever, " the fellow with the newspaper said. "They find them a hard place to die every time."

"I chewed the kid out for missing his shot, and when he smarted off at me, I cuffed him a good one. Right here." The guard pointed to the side of his head and grinned. "I boxed his goddamn ears for him, that goddamn kid. He's not too old. He needed it. So the point is, it got too dark to trail, what with the kid laying back to vomit and all."

"Well, the coyotes will have that deer by now," the fellow with the newspaper said. "Them and the crows and the buzzards."

He unrolled the newspaper, smoothed it all the way out, and put it off to one side. He crossed a leg again. He looked around at the rest of us and shook his head.

The older man had turned in his chair and was looking out the window. He lit a cigarette.

"I figure so," the guard said. "Pity too. He was a big old son of a bitch. So in answer to your question, Bill, I both got my deer and I didn't. But we had venison on the table anyway. Because it turns out the old man has got himself a little spike in the meantime. Already has him back to camp, hanging up and gutted slick as a whistle, liver, heart, and kidneys wrapped in waxed paper and already setting in the cooler. A spike. Just a little bastard. But the old man, he was tickled."

The guard looked around the shop as if remembering. Then he picked up his toothpick and stuck it back in his mouth.

The older man put his cigarette out and turned to the guard. He drew a breath and said, "You ought to be out there right now looking for that deer instead of in here getting a haircut."

"You can't talk like that," the guard said. "You old fart. I've seen you someplace."

"I've seen you too," the old fellow said.

"Boys, that's enough. This is my barbershop," the barber said.

"I ought to box *your* ears," the old fellow said.

"You ought to try it," the guard said.

"Charles," the barber said.

The barber put his comb and scissors on the counter and his

hands on my shoulders, as if he thought I was thinking to spring from the chair into the middle of it. "Albert, I've been cutting Charles's head of hair, and his boy's too, for years now. I wish you wouldn't pursue this."

The barber looked from one man to the other and kept his hands on my shoulders.

"Take it outside," the fellow with the newspaper said, flushed and hoping for something.

"That'll be enough," the barber said. "Charles, I don't want to hear anything more on the subject. Albert, you're next in line. Now." The barber turned to the fellow with the newspaper. "I don't know you from Adam, mister, but I'd appreciate if you wouldn't put your oar in."

The guard got up. He said, "I think I'll come back for my cut later. Right now the company leaves something to be desired."

The guard went out and pulled the door closed, hard.

The old fellow sat smoking his cigarette. He looked out the window. He examined something on the back of his hand. He got up and put on his hat.

"I'm sorry, Bill," the old fellow said. "I can go a few more days."

"That's all right, Albert," the barber said.

When the old fellow went out, the barber stepped over to the window to watch him go.

"Albert's about dead from emphysema," the barber said from the window. "We used to fish together. He taught me salmon inside out. The women. They used to crawl all over that old boy. He's picked up a temper, though. But in all honesty, there was provocation."

The man with the newspaper couldn't sit still. He was on his feet and moving around, stopping to examine everything, the hat rack, the photos of Bill and his friends, the calendar from the hardware showing scenes for each month of the year. He flipped every page. He even went so far as to stand and scrutinize Bill's barbering license, which was up on the wall in a frame. Then he turned and said, "I'm going too," and out he went just like he said.

"Well, do you want me to finish barbering this hair or not?" the barber said to me as if I was the cause of everything.

The barber turned me in the chair to face the mirror. He put a hand to either side of my head. He positioned me a last time, and then he brought his head down next to mine.

We looked into the mirror together, his hands still framing my head.

I was looking at myself, and he was looking at me too. But if the barber saw something, he didn't offer comment.

He ran his fingers through my hair. He did it slowly, as if thinking about something else. He ran his fingers through my hair. He did it tenderly, as a lover would.

That was in Crescent City, California, up near the Oregon border. I left soon after. But today I was thinking of that place, of Crescent City, and of how I was trying out a new life there with my wife, and how, in the barber's chair that morning, I had made up my mind to go. I was thinking today about the calm I felt when I closed my eyes and let the barber's fingers move through my hair, the sweetness of those fingers, the hair already starting to grow.

Stanley Elkin

The Conventional Wisdom

Ellerbee had been having a bad time of it. He'd had financial reversals. Change would slip out of his pockets and slide down into the crevices of other people's furniture. He dropped deposit bottles and lost money in pay phones and vending machines. He over-tipped in dark taxicabs. He had many such financial reversals. He was stuck with Super Bowl tickets when he was suddenly called out of town and with theatre and opera tickets when the ice was too slick to move his car out of his driveway. But all this was small potatoes. His portfolio was a disgrace. He had gotten into mutual funds at the wrong time and out at a worse. His house, appraised for tax purposes at many thousands of dollars below its replacement cost, burned down, and recently his once flourishing liquor store, one of the largest in Minneapolis, had drawn the attentions of burly, hopped-up and armed deprivators, ski-masked, head-stockinged. Two of his clerks had been shot, one killed, the other crippled and brain damaged, during the most recent visitation by these marauders, and Ellerbee, feeling a sense of responsibility, took it upon himself to support his clerks' families. His wife reproached him for this, which led to bad feeling between them.

"Weren't they insured?"

"I don't know, May. I suppose they had some insurance but how much could it have been? One was just a kid out of college."

"Whatshisname, the vegetable."

"Harold, May."

"What about whosis? He was no kid out of college."

20

"George died protecting my store, May."

"Some protection. The black bastards got away with over fourteen hundred bucks." When the police called to tell him of the very first robbery, May had asked if the men had been black. It hurt Ellerbee that this should have been her first question. "Who's going to protect you? The insurance companies red-lined that lousy neighborhood a year ago. We won't get a penny."

"I'm selling the store, May. I can't afford to run it anymore."

"Selling? Who'd buy it? *Selling!*"

"I'll see what I can get for it," Ellerbee said.

"Social Security pays them benefits," May said, picking up their quarrel again the next day. "Social Security pays up to the time the kids are eighteen years old, and they give to the widow, too. Who do you think you are, anyway? We lose a house and have to move into one not half as good because it's all we can afford, and you want to keep on paying the salaries not only of two people who no longer work for you, but to pay them out of a business that you mean to sell! Let Social Security handle it."

Ellerbee, who had looked into it, answered May. "Harold started with me this year. Social Security pays according to what you've put into the system. Dorothy won't get three hundred a month, May. And George's girl is twenty. Evelyn won't even get that much."

"Idealist," May said. "Martyr."

"Leave off, will you, May? I'm responsible. I'm under an obligation."

"Responsible, under an obligation!"

"Indirectly. God damn it, yes. Indirectly. They worked for me, didn't they? It's a combat zone down there. I should have had security guards around the clock."

"Where are you going to get all this money? We've had financial reverses. You're selling the store. Where's this money coming from to support three families?"

"We'll get it."

"*We'll* get it? There's no we'll about it, Mister. *You'll.* The stocks are in joint tenancy. You can't touch them, and I'm not signing a thing. Not a penny comes out of my mouth or off my back."

"All right, May," Ellerbee said. "I'll get it."

In fact Ellerbee had a buyer in mind—a syndicate that specialized in buying up businesses in decaying neighborhoods—liquor and drugstores, small groceries—and then put in ex-convicts as personnel, Green Berets from Vietnam, off-duty policemen, experts in the martial arts. Once the word was out, no one ever attempted to rob these places. The syndicate hiked the price of each item at least 20 percent—and got it. Ellerbee was fascinated and appalled by their strong-arm tactics. Indeed, he more than a little suspected that it was the syndicate itself which had been robbing him—all three times his store had been held up he had not been in it—to inspire him to sell, perhaps.

"We read about your trouble in the paper," Mr. Davis, the lawyer for the syndicate, had told him on the occasion of his first robbery. The thieves had gotten away with $300 and there was a four-line notice on the inside pages. "Terrible," he said, "terrible. A fine old neighborhood like this one. And it's the same all over America today. Everywhere it's the same story. Even in Kansas, even in Utah. They shoot you with bullets, they take your property. Terrible. The people I represent have the know-how to run businesses like yours in the spoiled neighborhoods." And then he had been offered a ridiculous price for his store and stock. Of course he turned it down. When he was robbed a second time, the lawyer didn't even bother to come in person. "Terrible. Terrible," he said. "Whoever said lightning doesn't strike twice in the same place was talking through his hat. I'm authorized to offer you ten thousand less than I did the last time." Ellerbee hung up on him.

Now, after his clerks had been shot, it was Ellerbee who called the lawyer. "Awful," the lawyer said. "Outrageous. A merchant shouldn't have to sit still for such things in a democracy."

They gave him even less than the insurance people had given him for his underappraised home. Ellerbee accepted, but decided it was time he at least hint to Davis that he knew what was going on. "I'm selling," he said, "because I don't want anyone else to die."

"Wonderful," Davis said, "wonderful. There should be more Americans like you."

He deposited the money he got from the syndicate in a separate account so that his wife would have no claims on it and now, while he had no business to go to, he was able to spend more time in the hospital visiting Harold.

"How's Hal today, Mrs. Register?" he asked when he came into the room where the mindless quadraplegic was being cared for. Dorothy Register was a red-haired young woman in her early twenties. Ellerbee felt so terrible about what had happened, so guilty, that he had difficulty talking to her. He knew it would be impossible to visit Harold if he was going to run into his wife when he did so. It was for this reason, too, that he sent the checks rather than drop them off at the apartment, much as he wanted to see Hal's young son, Harold, Jr., in order to reassure the child that there was still a man around to take care of the boy and his young mother.

"Oh, Mr. Ellerbee," the woman wept. Harold seemed to smile at them through his brain damage.

"Please, Mrs. Register," said Ellerbee, "Harold shouldn't see you like this."

"Him? He doesn't understand a thing. You don't understand a thing, do you?" she said, turning on her husband sharply. When she made a move to poke at his eyes with a fork he didn't even blink. "Oh, Mr. Ellerbee," she said, turning away from her husband, "that's not the man I married. It's awful, but I don't feel anything for him. The only reason I come is that the doctors say I cheer him up. Though I can't see how. He smiles that way at his bedpan."

"Please, Mrs. Register," Ellerbee said softly. "You've got to be strong. There's little Hal."

"I know," she moaned, "I know." She wiped the tears from her eyes and sniffed and tossed her hair in a funny little way she had which Ellerbee found appealing. "I'm sorry," she said. "You've been very kind. I don't know what I would have done, what *we* would have done. I can't even thank you," she said helplessly.

"Oh don't think about it, there's no need," Ellerbee said quickly. "I'm not doing any more for you than I am for George Lesefario's widow." It was not a boast. Ellerbee had mentioned the older woman because he didn't want Mrs. Register to feel compromised. "It's company policy when these things happen," he said gruffly.

Dorothy Register nodded. "I heard," she said, "that you sold your store."

He hastened to reassure her. "Oh now listen," Ellerbee said, "you mustn't give that a thought. The checks will continue. I'm getting another store. In a very lovely neighborhood. Near where we used to live before our house burned down."

"Really?"

"Oh yes. I should be hearing about my loan any time now. I'll probably be in the new place before the month is out. Well," he said, "speaking of which, I'd better get going. There are some fixtures I'm supposed to look at at the Wine and Spirits Mart." He waved to Harold.

"Mr. Ellerbee?"

"Mrs. Register?"

The tall redhead came close to him and put her hands on his shoulders. She made that funny little gesture with her hair again and Ellerbee almost died. She was about his own height and leaned forward and kissed him on the mouth. Her fingernails grazed the back of his neck. Tears came to Ellerbee's eyes and he turned away from her gently. He hoped she hadn't seen the small lump in his trousers. He said goodbye with his back to her.

The loan went through. The new store, as Ellerbee had said, was in one of the finest neighborhoods in the city. In a small shopping mall, it was flanked by a good bookstore and a fine French restaurant. The Ellerbees had often eaten there before their house burned to the ground. There was an art cinema, a florist, and elegant haberdashers and dress shops. The liquor store, called High Spirits, a name Ellerbee decided to keep after he bought the place, stocked, in addition to the usual gins, Scotches, bourbons, vodkas, and blends, some really superior wines, and Ellerbee was forced to become something of an expert in oenology. He listened to his customers—doctors and lawyers, most of them—and in this way was able to pick up a good deal.

The business flourished—doing so well that after only his second month in the new location he no longer felt obliged to stay open on Sundays—though his promise to his clerks' families, which he kept, prevented him from making the inroads into his extravagant debt that he would have liked. Mrs. Register began to come to the store to collect the weekly checks personally. "I thought I'd save you the stamp," she said each time. Though he enjoyed seeing her—she looked rather like one of those splendid wives of the successful doctors who shopped there—he thought he should discourage this. He made it clear to her that he would be sending the checks.

Then she came and said that it was foolish, his continuing to pay her husband's salary, that at least he ought to let her do something to earn it. She saw that the suggestion made him uncomfortable and clarified what she meant.

"Oh no," she said, "all I meant was that you ought to hire me. I was a hostess once. For that matter I could wait on trade."

"Well, I've plenty of help, Mrs. Register. Really. As I may have told you, I've kept on all the people who used to work for Anderson." Anderson was the man from whom he'd bought High Spirits.

"It's not as though you'd be hiring additional help. I'm costing you the money anyway."

It would have been pleasant to have the woman around, but Ellerbee nervously held his ground. "At a time like this," he said, "you ought to be with the boy."

"You're quite a guy," she said. It was the last time they saw each other. A few months later, while he was examining his bank statements, he realized that she had not been cashing his checks. He called her at once.

"I can't," she said. "I'm young. I'm strong." He remembered her fierce embrace in her husband's hospital room. "There's no reason for you to continue to send me those checks. I have a good job now. I can't accept them any longer." It was the last time they spoke.

And then he learned that George's widow was ill. He heard about it indirectly. One of his best customers—a psychiatrist—was beeped on the emergency Medi-Call he carried in his jacket, and asked for change to use Ellerbee's pay phone.

"That's not necessary, Doc," Ellerbee said, "Use the phone behind my counter."

"Very kind," the psychiatrist said, and came back of the counter. He dialed his service. "Doctor Potter. What have you got for me, Nancy? What? She did *what*? Just a minute, let me get a pencil.—Bill?" Ellerbee handed him a pencil. "Lesefario, right. I've got that. Give me the surgeon's number. Right. Thanks, Nancy."

"Excuse me, Doctor," Ellerbee said. "I hadn't meant to listen, but Lesefario, that's an unusual name. I know an Evelyn Lesefario."

"That's the one," said the medical man. "Oh," he said, "you're *that* Ellerbee. Well, she's been very depressed. She just tried to kill herself by eating a mile of dental floss."

"I hope she dies," his wife said.

"*May!*" said Ellerbee, shocked.

"It's what she wants, isn't it? I hope she gets what she wants."

"That's harsh, May."

"Yes? Harsh? You see how much good your checks did her? And another thing, how could she afford a high-priced man like Potter on what *you* were paying her?"

He went to visit the woman during her post-operative convalescence, and she introduced him to her sister, her twin she said, though the two women looked nothing alike and the twin seemed to be in her seventies, a good dozen years older than Mrs. Lesefario. "This is Mr. Ellerbee that my husband died protecting his liquor store from the niggers."

"Oh yes?" Mrs. Lesefario's sister said. "Very pleased. I heard so much about you."

"Look what she brought me," Mrs. Lesefario said, pointing to a large brown paper sack.

"Evelyn, don't. You'll strain your stitches. I'll show him." She opened the sack and took out a five-pound bag of sugar.

"Five pounds of sugar," the melancholic woman said.

"You don't come empty-handed to a sick person," her sister said.

"She got it at Kroger's on special. Ninety-nine cents with the coupon," the manic-depressive said gloomily. "She says if I don't like it I can get peach halves."

Ellerbee, who did not want to flaunt his own gift in front of her sister, quietly put the dressing gown, still wrapped, on her tray table. He stayed for another half hour, and rose to go.

"Wait," Mrs. Lesefario said. "Nice try but not so fast."

"I'm sorry?" Ellerbee said.

"The ribbon."

"Ribbon?"

"On the fancy box. The ribbon, the string."

"Oh, your stitches. Sorry. I'll get it."

"I'm a would-be suicide," she said. "I tried it once, I could try it again. You don't bring dangerous ribbon to a desperate, unhappy woman."

In fact Mrs. Lesefario did die. Not of suicide, but of a low-grade infection she had picked up in the hospital and which festered along her stitches, undermining them, burning through them, opening her body like a package.

The Ellerbees were in the clear financially, but his wife's reactions to Ellerbee's efforts to provide for his clerks' families had soured their relationship. She had discovered Ellerbee's private account and accused him of dreadful things. He reminded her that it had been she who had insisted he would have to get the money for the women's support himself—that their joint tenancy was not to be disturbed. She ignored his arguments and accused him further. Ellerbee loved May and did what he could to placate her.

"How about a trip to Phoenix?" he suggested that spring. "The store's doing well and I have complete confidence in Kroll. What about it, May? You like Phoenix, and we haven't seen the folks in almost a year."

"Phoenix," she scoffed, "The *folks*. The way you coddle them. Any other grown man would be ashamed."

"They raised me, May."

"They raised you. Terrific. They aren't even your real parents. They only adopted you."

"They're the only parents I ever knew. They took me out of the Home when I was an infant."

"Look, you want to go to Phoenix, go. Take money out of your secret accounts and go."

"Please, May. There's no secret account. When Mrs. Lesefario died I transferred everything back into joint. Come on, sweetheart, you're awfully goddamn hard on me."

"Well," she said, drawing the word out. The tone was one she had used as a bride, and although Ellerbee had not often heard it since, it melted him. It was her signal of sudden conciliation, cute surrender, and he held out his arms and they embraced. They went off to the bedroom together.

"You know," May said afterwards, "it *would* be good to run out to Phoenix for a bit. Are you sure the help can manage?"

"Oh, sure, May, absolutely. They're a first-rate bunch." He spoke more forcefully than he felt, not because he lacked confidence in his employees, but because he was still disturbed by an image he had had during climax. Momentarily, fleetingly, he had imagined Mrs. Register beneath him.

In the store he was giving last-minute instructions to Kroll, the man who would be his manager during their vacation in Phoenix.

"I think the Californias," Ellerbee was saying. "Some of them beat several of even the more immodest French. Let's do a promotion of a few of the better Californias. What do you think?"

"They're a very competitive group of wines," Kroll said. "I think I'm in basic agreement."

Just then three men walked into the shop.

"Say," one called from the doorway, "you got something like a Closed sign I could hang in the door here?" Ellerbee stared at him. "Well you don't have to look at me as if I was nuts," the man said. "Lots of merchants keep them around. In case they get a sudden toothache or something they can whip out to the dentist. All right, if you ain't you ain't."

"I want," the second man said, coming up to the counter where Ellerbee stood with his manager, "to see your register receipts."

"What is this?" Kroll demanded.

"No, don't," Ellerbee said to Kroll. "Don't resist." He glanced toward the third man to see if he was the one holding the gun, but the man appeared merely to be browsing the bins of Scotch in the back. Evidently he hadn't even heard the first man, and clearly he could not have heard the second. Conceivably he could have been a customer. "Where's your gun?" Ellerbee asked the man at the counter.

"Oh gee," the man said, "I almost forgot. You got so many things to think about during a stickup—the traffic flow, the timing, who stands where—you sometimes forget the basics. Here," he said, "here's my gun, in your kisser," and he took an immense handgun from his pocket and pointed it at Ellerbee's face.

Out of the corner of his eye Ellerbee saw Kroll's hands fly up. It was so blatant a gesture Ellerbee thought his manager might be trying to attract the customer's attention. If that was his idea it had worked, for the third man had turned away from the bins and was watching the activity at the counter. "Look," Ellerbee said, "I don't want anybody hurt."

"What's he say?" said the man at the door who was also holding a pistol now.

"He don't want nobody hurt," the man at the counter said.

"Sure," said the man at the door, "it's costing him a fortune paying all them salaries to the widows. He's a good businessman all right."

"A better one than you," the man at the counter said to his confederate sharply. "He knows how to keep his mouth shut."

Why, they're white, Ellerbee thought. They're *white* men! He felt oddly justified and wished May were there to see.

"The register receipts," the man at the counter coaxed. Ellerbee's cash register kept a running total on what had been taken in. "Just punch Total Tab," the man instructed Kroll. "Let's see what we got." Kroll looked at Ellerbee and Ellerbee nodded. The man reached forward and tore off the tape. He whistled. "Nice little place you got here," he said.

"What'd we get? What'd we get?" the man at the door shouted.

Ellerbee cleared his throat. "Do you want to lock the door?" he asked. "So no one else comes in?" He glanced toward the third man.

"What, and have you kick the alarm while we're fucking around trying to figure which key opens the place?" said the man at the door. "You're cute, you're a cutie. What'd we get? Let's see." He joined the man at the counter. "Holy smoke! Jackpot City! We're into four figures here." In his excitement he did a foolish thing. He set his revolver down on top of the appetizer table. It lay on the tins of caviar and smoked oysters, and imported cheeses and roasted peanuts. The third man was no more than four feet from the gun, and though Ellerbee saw that the man had caught the robber's mistake and that by taking one step toward the table he could have picked up the pistol and perhaps foiled the robbery, he made no move. Perhaps he's one of them, Ellerbee thought, or maybe he just doesn't want to get involved. Ellerbee couldn't remember ever having seen him. (By now, of course, he recognized all his repeat customers.) He still didn't know if he were a confederate or just an innocent bystander, but

Ellerbee had had enough of violence and hoped that if he *were* a customer he wouldn't try anything dumb. He felt no animus toward the man at all. Kroll's face, however, was all scorn and loathing.

"Let's get to work," the man said who had first read the tape, and then to Kroll and Ellerbee, "Back up there. Go stand by the aperitifs."

The third man fell silently into step beside Ellerbee.

"Listen," Ellerbee explained as gently as he could, "you won't find that much cash in the drawer. A lot of our business is Master Charge. We take personal checks."

"Don't worry," the man said who had set his gun down (and who had taken it up again). "We know about the checks. We got a guy we can sell them to for—what is it, Ron, seventeen cents on the dollar?"

"Fourteen, and why don't you shut your mouth, will you? You want to jeopardize these people? What do you make it?"

Ellerbee went along with his sentiments. He wished the big-mouth would just take the money and not say anything more.

"Oh, jeopardize," the man said. "How jeopardized can you get? These people are way past jeopardized. About six hundred in cash, a fraction in checks. The rest is all credit card paper."

"Take it," Ron said.

"You won't be able to do anything with the charge slips," Kroll said.

"Oh yeah?" Ron's cohort said. "This is modern times, fellow. We got a way we launder Master Charge, BankAmericard, all of it."

Ron shook his head and Ellerbee glanced angrily at his manager.

The whole thing couldn't have taken four minutes. Ron's partner took a fifth of Chivas and a bottle of Lafitte '47. He's a doctor, Ellerbee thought.

"You got a bag?"

"A bag?" Ellerbee said.

"A bag, a paper bag, a doggy bag for the boodle."

"Behind the counter," Ellerbee said hopelessly.

The partner put the cash and the bottle of Chivas into one bag and handed it to Ron, and the wine, checks, and credit charges into a second bag which he held on to himself. They turned to go. They looked exactly like two satisfied customers. They were almost at the door when Ron's partner nudged Ron. "Oh, yeah," Ron said, and turned back to look at them. "My friend, Jay Ladlehaus, is right," he said, "you know too much."

Ellerbee heard two distinct shots before he fell.

When he came to, the third man was bending over him. "You're not hurt," Ellerbee said.

"Me? No."

The pain was terrific, diffuse, but fiercer than anything he had ever felt. He saw himself covered with blood. "Where's Kroll? The other man, my manager?"

"Kroll's all right."

"He is?"

"There, right beside you."

He tried to look. They must have blasted Ellerbee's throat away, half his spinal column. It was impossible for him to move his head. "I can't see him," he moaned.

"Kroll's fine." The man cradled Ellerbee's shoulders and neck and shifted him slightly. "There. See?" Kroll's eyes were shut. Oddly, both were blackened. He had fallen in such a way that he seemed to lie on both his arms, retracted behind him into the small of his back like a yogi. His mouth was open and his tongue floated in blood like meat in soup. A slight man, he seemed strangely bloated, and one shin, exposed to Ellerbee's vision where the trouser leg was hiked up above his sock, was discolored as thundercloud.

The man gently set Ellerbee down again. "Call an ambulance," Ellerbee wheezed through his broken throat.

"No, no. Kroll's fine."

"He's not conscious." It was as if his words were being mashed through the tines of a fork.

"He'll be all right. Kroll's fine."

"Then for *me*. Call one for *me*."

"It's too late for you," the man said.

"For Christ's sake, will you!" Ellerbee gasped. "I can't move. You could have grabbed that hoodlum's gun when he set it down. All right, you were scared, but some of this is your fault. You didn't lift a finger. At least call an ambulance."

"But you're dead," he said gently. "Kroll will recover. You passed away when you said 'move.'"

"Are you crazy? What are you talking about?"

"Do you feel pain?"

"What?"

"Pain. You don't feel any, do you?" Ellerbee stared at him. "Do you?"

He didn't. His pain was gone. "Who are you?" Ellerbee said.

"I'm an angel of death," the angel of death said.

"You're—"

"An angel of death."

Somehow he had left his body. He could see it lying next to Kroll's. "I'm dead? But if I'm dead—you mean there's really an afterlife?"

"Oh boy," the angel of death said.

They went to Heaven.

Ellerbee couldn't have said how they got there or how long it took, though he had the impression that time had passed, and distance. It was rather like a journey in films—a series of quick cuts, of montage. He was probably dreaming, he thought.

"It's what they all think," the angel of death said, "that they're dreaming. But that isn't so."

"I could have dreamed you said that," Ellerbee said, "that you read my mind."

"Yes."

"I could be dreaming all of it, the holdup, everything."

The angel of death looked at him.

"Hobgoblin . . . I could . . ." Ellerbee's voice—if it was a voice—trailed off.

"Look," the angel of death said, "I talk too much. I sound like a cabbie with an out-of-town fare. It's an occupational hazard."

"What?"

"*What?* Pride. The proprietary air. Showing off death like a booster. Thanatopography. 'If you look to your left you'll see where . . . Julius Caesar de dum de dum . . . Shakespeare da da da . . . And dead ahead our Father Adam heigh ho—' The tall buildings and the four-star sights. All that Baedeker reality of plaque place and high history. The Fields of Homer and the Plains of Myth. Where whosis got locked in a star and all the Agriculture of the Periodic Table—the South Forty of the Universe, where Hydrogen first bloomed, where Lithium, Berylium, Zirconium, Niobium. Where Lead failed and Argon came a cropper. The furrows of gold, Bismuth's orchards . . . . Still think you're dreaming?"

"No."

"Why not?"

"The language."

"Just so," the angel of death said. "When you were alive you had a vocabulary of perhaps seventeen or eighteen hundred words. Who am I?"

"An eschatological angel," Ellerbee said shyly.

"One hundred percent," the angel of death said. "Why do we do that?"

"To heighten perception," Ellerbee said, and shuddered.

The angel of death nodded and said nothing more.

When they were close enough to make out the outlines of Heaven, the angel left him and Ellerbee, not questioning this, went on alone. From this distance it looked to Ellerbee rather like a theme park, but what struck him most forcibly was that it did not seem—for Heaven—very large.

He traveled as he would on Earth, distance familiar again, volume, mass, and dimension restored, ordinary. (*Quotidian*, Ellerbee thought.) Indeed, now that he was convinced of his death, nothing seemed particularly strange. If anything, it was all a little familiar. He began to miss May. She would have learned of his death by this time. Difficult as the last year had been, they had loved each other. It had been a good marriage. He regretted again that they had been unable to have children. Children—they would be teenagers now—would have been a comfort to his widow. She still had her looks. Perhaps she would remarry. He did not want her to be lonely.

He continued toward Heaven and now, only blocks away, he was able to perceive it in detail. It looked more like a theme park than ever. It was enclosed behind a high milky fence, the uprights smooth and round as the poles in subway trains. Beyond the fence were golden streets, a mixed architecture of minaret-spiked mosques, great cathedrals, the rounded domes of classical synagogues, tall pagodas like holy vertebrae, white frame churches with their beautiful steeples, even what Ellerbee took to be a storefront church. There were many mansions. But where were the people?

Just as he was wondering about this he heard the sound of a gorgeous chorus. It was making a joyful noise. "Oh dem golden slippers," the chorus sang, "Oh dem golden slippers." It's the Heavenly Choir. He went toward the fence and put his hands on the smooth posts and peered through into Heaven. He heard laughter and caught a glimpse of the running heels of children just disappearing around the corner of a golden street. They all wore shoes.

Ellerbee walked along the fence for about a mile and came to gates made out of pearl. The Pearly Gates, he thought. There are actually Pearly Gates. An old man in a long white beard sat behind them, a key attached to a sort of cinch that went about his waist.

"Saint Peter?" Ellerbee ventured. The old man turned his shining countenance upon him. "Saint Peter," Ellerbee said again, "I'm Ellerbee."

"I'm Saint Peter," Saint Peter said.

"Gosh," Ellerbee said, "I can't get over it. It's all true."

"What is?"

"Everything. Heaven. The streets of gold, the Pearly Gates. You. Your key. The Heavenly Choir. The climate."

A soft breeze came up from inside Heaven and Ellerbee sniffed something wonderful in the perfect air. He looked toward the venerable old man.

"Ambrosia," the Saint said.

"There's actually ambrosia," Ellerbee said.

"You know," Saint Peter said, "you never get tired of it, you never even get used to it. He does that to whet our appetite."

"You eat in Heaven?"

"We eat manna."

"There's actually manna," Ellerbee said. An angel floated by on a fleecy cloud playing a harp. Ellerbee shook his head. He had never heard anything so beautiful. "Heaven is everything they say it is," he said.

"It's Paradise," Saint Peter said.

Then Ellerbee saw an affecting sight. Nearby, husbands were reunited with wives, mothers with their small babes, daddies with their sons, brothers with sisters—all the intricate blood loyalties and enlisted loves. He understood all the relationships without being told—his heightened perception. What was most moving, however, were the old people, related or not, some just lifelong friends, people who had lived together or known one another much the greater part of their lives and then had lost each other. It was immensely touching to Ellerbee to see them gaze fondly into one another's eyes and then to watch them reach out and touch the patient, ancient faces, wrinkled and even withered but, Ellerbee could tell, unchanged in the loving eyes of the adoring beholder. If there were tears they were tears of joy, tears that melded inextricably with tender laughter. There was rejoicing, there were Hosannas, there was dancing in the golden streets. "It's wonderful," Ellerbee muttered to himself. He didn't know where to look first. He would be staring at the beautiful flowing raiments of the angels—There are actually raiments, he thought, there are actually angels—so fine, he imagined, to the touch that just the caress of the cloth must have produced exquisite sensations not matched by anything in life, when something else would strike him. The perfectly proportioned angels' wings like discrete Gothic windows, the beautiful halos—There are actually halos—like golden quoits, or, in the distance, the lovely green pastures, delicious as fairway—all the perfectly banked turns of Heaven's geography. He saw philosophers deep in conversation. He saw kings and heroes. It was astonishing to him, like going to an exclusive restaurant one has only read about in columns and spotting, even at first glance, the celebrities one has read about, relaxed, passing the time of day, out in the open, up-front and sharing their high-echelon lives.

"This is for keeps?" he asked Saint Peter. "I mean it goes on like this?"

"World without end," Saint Peter said.

"Where's . . ."

"That's all right, say His name."

"God?" Ellerbee whispered.

Saint Peter looked around. "I don't see Him just . . . Oh, wait. *There!*" Ellerbee turned where the old Saint was pointing. He shaded his eyes. "There's no need," Saint Peter said.

"But the aura, the light."

"Let it shine."

He took his hand away fearfully and the light spilled into his eyes like soothing unguents. God was on His throne in the green pastures, Christ at His right Hand. To Ellerbee it looked like a picture taken at a summit conference.

"He's beautiful. I've never . . . It's ecstasy."

"And you're seeing Him from a pretty good distance. You should talk to Him sometime."

"People can talk to Him?"

"Certainly. He loves us."

There were tears in Ellerbee's eyes. He wished May no harm, but wanted her with him to see it all. "It's wonderful."

"We like it," Saint Peter said.

"Oh, I do too," Ellerbee said. "I'm going to be very happy here."

"Go to Hell," Saint Peter said beatifically.

Hell was the ultimate inner city. Its stinking sulfurous streets were unsafe. Everywhere Ellerbee looked he saw atrocities. Pointless, profitless muggings were commonplace; joyless rape that punished its victims and offered no relief to the perpetrator. Everything was contagious, cancer as common as a cold, plague the quotidian. There was stomachache, headache, toothache, earache. There was angina and indigestion and painful third-degree burning itch. Nerves like a hideous body hair grew long enough to trip over and lay raw and exposed as live wires or shoelaces that had come undone.

There was no handsomeness, no beauty, no one walked upright, no one had good posture. There was nothing to look at—although it was impossible to shut one's eyes—except the tumbled kaleidoscope variations of warted deformity. This was one reason, Ellerbee supposed, that there was so little conversation in Hell. No one could stand to look at anyone else long enough. Occasionally two or three—lost souls? gargoyles? devils? demons?—of the damned, jumping about in the heat first on one foot then the other, would manage to stand with their backs to each other and perhaps get out a few words—a foul whining. But even this was rare and when it happened that a sufferer had the attention of a fellow sufferer he could howl out only a half-dozen or so words before breaking off in a piercing scream.

Ellerbee, constantly nauseated, eternally in pain, forever be-fouling himself, longed to find something to do, however tedious or make-work or awful. For a time he made paths through the smoldering cinders, but he had no tools and had to use his bare feet, moving the cinders to one side as a boy shuffles through fallen leaves hunting something lost. It was too painful. Then he thought he would make channels for the vomit and excrement and blood. It was too disgusting. He shouted for others to join him in work details—"Break up the fights, pile up the scabs"—and even ministered to the less aggravated wounds, using his hands to wipe away the gangrenous drool since there was no fabric in Hell, all clothing consumed within minutes of arrival, flesh alone incon-sumable, glowing and burning along the bones slow as phosphor. Calling out, suggesting in screams which may have been incoher-ent, all manner of pointless, arbitrary arrangements—that they organize the damned, that they count them. Demanding that their howls be synchronous.

No one stopped him. No one seemed to be in charge. He saw, that is, no Devil, no Archfiend. There were demons with cloven feet and scaly tails, with horns and pitchforks—They actually have horns, Ellerbee thought, there are actually pitchforks—but these seemed to have no more authority than he had himself, and when they were piqued to wrath by their own torment the jabs they made at the human damned with their sharp arsenal were no more painful—and no less,—than anything else down there.

Then Ellerbee felt he understood something terrible—that the abortive rapes and fights and muggings were simply a refinement of his own attempts to socialize. They did it to make contact, to be friendly.

He was free to wander the vast burning meadows of Hell and to scale its fiery hills—and for many years he did—but it was much the same all over. What he was actually looking for was its Source, Hell's bright engine room, its storm-tossed bridge. It had no engine room, there was no bridge, its energy, all its dreadful combustion coming perhaps from the cumulative, collective agony of the in-mates. Nothing could be done.

He was distracted, as he was sure they all were—"Been to Heaven?" he'd managed to gasp to an old man whose back was on fire and the man had nodded—by his memory of Paradise, his long-distance glimpse of God. It was unbearable to think of Heaven in his present condition, his memory of that spectacular place poisoned by the discrepancy between the exaltation of the angels and the plight of the damned. It was the old story of the disappointment of rising expectations. Still, without his bidding, thoughts of Paradise force-fed themselves almost constantly into his skull. They induced sadness, rage.

He remembered the impression he'd had of celebrity when he'd stood looking in at Heaven from beyond the Pearly Gates, and he thought to look out for the historic bad men, the celebrated damned, but either they were kept in a part of Hell he had not yet seen or their sufferings had made them unrecognizable. If there were great men in Hell he did not see them and, curiously, no one ever boasted of his terrible deeds or notoriety. Indeed, except for the outbursts of violence, most of the damned behaved, considering their state, in a respectable fashion, even an exemplary one. Perhaps, Ellerbee thought, it was because they had not yet abandoned hope. (There was actually a sign: "Abandon Hope, All Ye Who Enter Here." Ellerbee had seen it.)

For several years he waited for May, for as long, that is, as he could remember her. Constant pain and perpetual despair chipped away at most of the memories he had of his life. It was possible to recall who and what he had been, but that was as fruitless as any other enterprise in the dark region. Ultimately, like everything else, it worked against him—Hell's fine print. It was best to forget. And that worked against him too.

He took the advice written above Hellgate. He abandoned hope, and with it memory, pity, pride, his projects, the sense he had of injustice—for a little while driving off, along with his sense of identity, even his broken recollection of glory. It was probably what they—whoever they were—wanted. Let them have it. Let them have the straight lines of their trade wind, trade route, through street, thrown stone vengeance. Let them have everything. Their pastels back and their blues and their greens, the recollection of gratified thirst, and the transient comfort of a sandwich and beer that had hit the spot, all the retrospective of good weather, a good night's sleep, a good joke, a good tune, a good time, the entire mosaic of small satisfactions that made up a life. Let them have his image of his parents and friends, the fading portrait of May he couldn't quite shake, the pleasure he'd had from work, from his body. Let them have all of it, his measly joy, his scrapbook past, his hope, too.

Which left only pure pain, the grand vocabulary they had given him to appreciate it, to discriminate and parse among the exquisite lesions and scored flesh and violated synapses, among the insulted nerves, joints, muscle and tissue, all the boiled kindling points of torment and the body's grief. That was all he was now, staggering Hiroshima'd flesh—a vessel of nausea, a pail of pain.

He continued thus for several years, his amnesia willed— There's Free Will, Ellerbee thought—shuffling Hell in his rote aphasia, his stripped self a sealed environment of indifference. There were years he did not think the name Ellerbee.

And even *that* did not assuage the panic of his burning theater'd, air raid warning'd, red-alert afterlife. (And that was what they wanted, and he knew it, wanting as much as they did for him to persist in his tornado-watch condition, fleeing from others through the crimped, cramped streets of mazy, refugee Hell, dragging his disaster poster avatar like a wounded leg.) He existed like one plugged into superb equipment, interminably terminal—and changed his mind and tried it the other way again, taking back all he had surrendered, Hell's Indian giver, and dredged up from where he had left them the imperfect memories of his former self. (May he saw as she had once been, his breast-less, awkward, shapeless childhood sweetheart.) And when that didn't work either—he gave it a few years—he went back to the other way, and then back again, shifting, quickly tiring of each tack as soon as he had taken it, changing fitfully, a man in bed in a hot, airless room rolling position, aggressively altering the surfaces of his pillow. If he hoped—which he came to do whenever he re-verted to Ellerbee—it was to go mad, but there was no madness in Hell—the terrific vocabulary of the damned, their poet's knack for rightly naming everything, which was the fail-safe of Reason—and he could find peace nowhere.

He had been there sixty-two years, three generations, older now as a dead man than he had been as a living one. Sixty-two years of nightless days and dayless nights, of aggravated pain and cumulative grief, of escalated desperation, of not getting used to it, to any of it. Sixty-two years of Hell's greenhorn, sixty-two years eluding the muggers and evading the rapists, all the joyless joy riders out for a night on his town, steering clear of the wild, stampeding, horizontal avalanche of the damned. And then, spin-ning out of the path of a charging, burning, screaming inmate, he accidentally backed into the smoldering ruin of a second. Ellerbee leaped away as their bodies touched.

"Ellerbee?"

Who? Ellerbee thought wildly. Who?

"Ellerbee?" the voice repeated.

How? Ellerbee wondered. How can he know me? In this form, how I look . . .

Ellerbee peered closely into the tormented face. It was one of the men who had held him up, not the one who had shot him but his accomplice, his murderer's accomplice. "Ladlehaus?" It was Ellerbee's vocabulary which had recognized him for his face had changed almost completely in the sixty-two years, just as Ellerbee's had, just as it was Ladlehaus's vocabulary which had recognized Ellerbee.

"It is Ellerbee, isn't it?" the man said.

Ellerbee nodded and the man tried to smile, stretching his wounds, the scars which seamed his face, and breaking the knitting flesh, lined, caked as stool, braided as bowel.

"I died," he said, "of natural causes." Ellerbee stared at him. "Of leukemia, stroke, Hodgkins's disease, arteriosclerosis. I was blind the last thirteen years of my life. But I was almost a hundred. I lived to a ripe old age. I was in a Home eighteen years. Still in Minneapolis."

"I suppose," Ellerbee said, "you recall how *I* died."

"I do," Ladlehaus said. "Ron dropped you with one shot. That reminds me," he said. "You had a beautiful wife. May, right? I saw her photograph in the Minneapolis papers after the incident. There was tremendous coverage. There was a TV clip on the Six O'Clock News. They interviewed her. She was—" Ellerbee started to run. "Hey," the accomplice called after him. "Hey, wait."

He ran through the steamy corridors of the Underworld, plunging into Hell's white core, the brightest blazes, Temperature's moving parts. The pain was excruciating, but he knew that it was probably the only way he would shake Ladlehaus so he kept running. And then, exhausted, he came out the other side into an area like shoreline, burning surf. He waded through the flames lapping about his ankles and then, humiliated by fatigue and pain, he did something he had never done before.

He lay down in the fire. He lay down in the slimy excrement and noxious puddles, in the loose evidence of their spilled terror. A few damned souls paused to stare at him, their bad breath dropping over him like an awful steam. Their scabbed faces leaned down toward him, their poisoned blood leaking on him from imperfectly sealed wounds, their baked, hideous visages like blooms in nightmare. It was terrible. He turned over, turned face down in the shallow river of pus and shit. Someone shook him. He didn't move. A man straddled and penetrated him. He didn't move. His attacker groaned. "I can't," he panted, "I can't—I can't see myself in his *blisters*." That's why they do it, Ellerbee thought. The man grunted and dismounted and spat upon him. His fiery spittle burned into an open sore on Ellerbee's neck. He didn't move. "He's dead," the man howled. "I think he's dead. His blisters have gone out!"

He felt a pitchfork rake his back, then turn in the wound it had made as if the demon were trying to pry foreign matter from it.

"Did he die?" Ellerbee heard.

He had Free Will. He wouldn't move.

"Is he dead?"

"How did he do it?"

Hundreds pressed in on him, their collective stench like the swamps of men dead in earthquake, trench warfare—though Ellerbee knew that for all his vocabulary there were no proper analogies in Hell, only the mildest approximations. If he didn't move they would go away. He didn't move.

A pitchfork caught him under the armpit and turned him over.

"He's dead. I think so. I think he's dead."

"No. It can't be."

"I think."

"How? How did he do it?"

"Pull his cock. See."

"No. Make one of the women. If he isn't dead maybe he'll respond."

An ancient harridan stooped down and rubbed him between her palms. It was the first time he had been touched there by a woman in sixty-two years. He had Free Will, he had Free Will. But beneath her hot hands his penis began to smoke.

"Oh God," he screamed. "Leave me alone. Please," he begged. They gazed down at him like teammates over a fallen player.

"Faker," one hissed.

"Shirker," said another scornfully.

"He's not dead," a third cried. "I told you."

"There's no death here."

"World without end," said another.

"Get up," demanded someone else. "Run. Run through Hell. Flee your pain. Keep busy."

They started to lift him. "Let go," Ellerbee shouted. He rolled away from a demon poking at him with a pitchfork. He was on his hands and knees in Hell. Still on all fours he began to push himself up. He was on his knees.

"Looks like he's praying," said the one who had told him to

run.

"No."

"Looks like it. I think so."

"How? What for?"

And he started to pray.

"Lord God of Ambush and Unconditional Surrender," he prayed. "Power Play God of Judo Leverage. Grand Guignol, Martial Artist—"

The others shrieked, backed away from him, cordoning Ellerbee off like a disaster area. Ellerbee, caught up, ignoring them, not even hearing them, continued his prayer.

"Browbeater," he prayed, "Bouncer Being, Boss of Bullies— this is Your servant, Ellerbee, sixty-two-year fetus in Eternity, tot, toddler, babe in Hell. Can You hear me? I know You exist because I saw You, avuncular in Your green pastures like an old man on a picnic. The angeled minarets I saw, the gold streets and marble temples and all the flashy summer-palace architecture, all the gorgeous glory locked in Receivership. Your zones Heaven in Holy Escrow. The miracle props—harps and Saints and popes at tea. All of it—Your manna, Your ambrosia, Your Heavenly Host in their summer whites. So can You *hear* me, pick out my voice from all the others in this din bin? Come on, come on, Old Terrorist, God the Father, God the Godfather! The conventional wisdom is we can talk to You, that You love us, that—"

"I can hear you."

A great awed whine rose from the damned, moans, sharp cries. It was as if Ellerbee alone had not heard. He continued his prayer.

"I hear you," God repeated.

Ellerbee stopped.

God spoke. His voice was pitchless, almost without timbre, almost bland. "What do you want, Ellerbee?"

Confused, Ellerbee forgot the point of his prayer. He looked at the others who were quiet now, perfectly still for once. Only the snap of localized fire could be heard. God was waiting. The damned watched Ellerbee fearfully. Hell burned beneath his knees. "An explanation," Ellerbee said.

"For openers," God roared, "I made the heavens and the earth! Were you there when I laid the foundations of the firmament? When I—"

Splinters of burning bone, incandescent as filament, glowed in the gouged places along Ellerbee's legs and knees where divots of his flesh had flared and fallen away. "An *explanation*," he cried out, "an *explanation!* None of this what-was-I-doing-when-You-pissed-the-oceans stuff, where I was when You colored the nigger and ignited Hell. I wasn't around when You elected the affinities. I wasn't there when you shaped shit and fashioned cancer. Were *You* there when I loved my neighbor as myself? When I never stole or bore false witness? I don't say when I never killed but when I never even raised a hand or pointed a finger in anger? Where were You when I picked up checks and popped for drinks all round? When I shelled out for charity and voted Yes on the bond issues? So no Job job, no nature in tooth and claw, please. An explanation!"

"You stayed open on the Sabbath!" God thundered.

"I what?"

"You stayed open on the Sabbath. When you were just getting started in your new location."

"You mean because I opened my store on Sundays? That's why?"

"You took My name in vain."

"I took . . ."

"That's right, that's right. You wanted an explanation, I'll give you an explanation. You wanted I/Thou, I'll give you I/Thou. You took It in vain. When your wife was nagging you because you wanted to keep those widows on the payroll. She mocked you when you said you were under an obligation and you said, 'Indirectly. G—d damn it, yes. Indirectly,' 'Come on, sweetheart,' you said, 'you're awfully g—ddamn hard on me.' "

"That's why I'm in Hell? *That's* why?"

"And what about the time you coveted your neighbor's wife? You had a big boner."

"I coveted no one, I was never unfaithful, I practically chased that woman away."

"You didn't honor your father and mother."

Ellerbee was stunned. "I did. I *always* honored my father and mother. I loved them very much. Just before I was killed we were planning a trip to Phoenix to see them."

"Oh, *them*. They only adopted you. I'm talking about your natural parents."

"I was in a Home. I was an *in*fant!"

"Sure, sure," God said.

"And *that's* why? *That's* why?"

"You went dancing. You wore zippers in your pants and drove automobiles. You smoked cigarettes and sold the demon rum."

"These are Your reasons? *This* is Your explanation?"

"You thought Heaven looked like a theme park!"

Ellerbee shook his head. Could this be happening? This pettiness signaled across the universe? But anything could happen, everything could, and Ellerbee began again to pray. "Lord," he prayed, "Heavenly Father, Dear God—maybe whatever is is right and maybe whatever is is right isn't, but I've been around now, walking up and down in it, and *every*thing is true. There is nothing that is not true. The philosopher's best idea and the conventional wisdom, too. So I am praying to You now in all humility, asking Your forgiveness and to grant one prayer."

"What is it?" God asked.

Ellerbee heard a strange noise and looked around. The damned, too, were on their knees—all the lost souls, all the gargoyles, all the demons, kneeling in fire, capitulate through Hell like a great ring of the conquered.

"What is it?" He asked.

"To kill us, to end Hell, to close the camp."

"Amen," said Ellerbee and all the damned in a single voice.

"Ha!" God scoffed and lighted up Hell's blazes like the surface of a star. Then God cursed and abused Ellerbee, and Ellerbee wouldn't have had it any other way. *He*'d damned him, no surrogate in Saint's clothing but the real McCoy Son of a Bitch God Whose memory Ellerbee would treasure and eternally repudiate forever, happily ever after, world without end.

But everything was true, even the conventional wisdom, perhaps especially the conventional wisdom—that which had made up Heaven like a shot in the dark and imagined into reality halos and Hell, gargoyles, gates of pearl, and the Pearl of Great Price, that had invented the horns of demons and cleft their feet and conceived angels riding clouds like cowboys on horseback, their harps at their sides like goofy guitars. Everything. Everything was. The self and what you did to protect it, learning the house odds, playing it safe—the honorable percentage baseball of existence.

Forever was a long time. Eternity was. He would seek out Ladlehaus, his murderer's accomplice, let bygones be bygones. They would get close to each other, close as family, closer. There was much to discuss in their fine new vocabularies. They would speak of Minneapolis, swap tales of the Twin Cities. They would talk of Ron, of others in the syndicate. And Ladlehaus had seen May, had caught her in what Ellerbee hoped was her grief on the Six O'Clock News. They would get close. And one day he would look for himself in Ladlehaus's glowing blisters.

Richard Ford

Rock Springs

Edna and I had started down from Kalispell heading for Tampa–St. Pete where I still had some friends from the old glory days who wouldn't put the police on me. I had managed to scrape with the law in Kalispell over several bad checks — which is a prison crime in Montana. And I knew Edna was already looking at her cards and thinking about a move, since it wasn't the first time I'd been in law scrapes in my life. She herself had already had troubles aplenty, losing her kids, and keeping her ex-husband Danny from breaking in her house and stealing her things while she was at work, which was really why I had moved in in the first place, that and needing to give my daughter Cheryl a better shake in things.

I don't know what was between Edna and me. Just beached by the same tides when you got down to it. But love has been built on frailer ground than that, as I well know. And when I came in the house that afternoon I just asked her if she wanted to go to Florida with me and she said "Why not."

Edna and I had been a pair eight months, more or less man and wife, some of which time I had been out of work, and some when I'd worked at the dog track as a hot handler and could help with the rent and talk sense to Danny when he came around. Danny was afraid of me because Edna had told him I'd been in prison in Florida for killing a man once, though that wasn't true. I had once been in jail in Tallahassee for stealing tires and had gotten into a fight on the county farm where a man had lost his eye. But I

43

hadn't done the hurting, and Edna just wanted the story worse than it was so Danny wouldn't act crazy and make her have to take her kids back, since she had made a good adjustment to not having them, and I already had Cheryl with me. I'm not a violent person and would never put a man's eye out, much less kill someone. My former wife Helen would come all the way from Waikiki Beach to testify to that. We never had violence, and I believe in crossing the street to stay out of trouble's way. Though Danny didn't know that.

But we were half down through Wyoming going toward I-80 and feeling good about things, when the oil light flashed on in the car I'd stolen, a sign I knew to be a bad one.

I'd gotten us a good car, a cranberry Mercedes I'd stolen out of an opthalmologist's lot in Whitefish, Montana. I stole it because I thought it would be comfortable over a long haul, because I thought it got good mileage, which it didn't, and because I'd never had a good car in my life, just old Chevy junkers and used trucks back from when I was a kid swamping citrus with Cubans.

The car made us all high that day. I ran the windows up and down and Edna told us some jokes and made faces. She could be lively. Her features would light up like a beacon and you could see her beauty, which wasn't ordinary. It all made me giddy, and I drove clear down to Bozeman, then straight on through the park to Jackson Hole. I rented us the bridal suite in the Quality Court in Jackson, and left Cheryl and Little Duke sleeping while Edna and I drove to a rib barn and drank beer and laughed till after midnight.

It felt like a whole new beginning for us, bad memories left behind and a new horizon to build on. I got so worked up I had a tattoo done on my arm that said, FAMOUS TIMES, and Edna bought a Bailey hat with an Indian feather band and a little turquoise and silver bracelet for Cheryl, and we made love on the seat of the car in the Quality Court parking lot just as the sun was burning up on the Snake River, and everything seemed then like the end of the rainbow.

It was that very enthusiasm in fact that made me keep the car one day longer instead of driving it in the river and stealing another one like I should have done and *had* done before.

Where the car went bad there wasn't a town in sight or even a house, just some low mountains maybe fifty miles away, or maybe a hundred, a barbed wire fence in both directions, hardpan prairie, and some hawks sailing through the evening air seizing insects.

I got out to look at the motor and Edna got out with Cheryl and the dog to let them have a pee by the car. I checked the water and checked the oil stick and both of them said perfect.

"What's that light mean, Earl?" Edna said. She had come and stood by the car with her hat on. She was just sizing things up for herself.

"We shouldn't run it," I said. "Something's not right in the oil."

She looked around at Cheryl and Little Duke who were peeing on the hardtop side-by-side like two little dolls, then out at the mountains which were becoming purple and lost in the distance. "What're we going to do?" she said. She wasn't worried yet, but she wanted to know what I was thinking about.

"Let me try it again," I said.

"That's a good idea," she said, and we all got back in the car.

When I tried the motor it turned over right away and the red light stayed off and there weren't any noises to make you think something was wrong. I let it idle a minute, then pushed the accelerator down and watched the red bulb, but there wasn't any light on, and I started wondering if maybe I hadn't dreamed I saw it, or that it had been the sun catching an angle off the window chrome, or maybe I was scared of something and didn't know it.

"What's the matter with it, Daddy?" Cheryl said from the back seat. I looked back at her and she had on her turquoise bracelet and Edna's hat set back on the back of her head. She looked like a little cowgirl in the movies.

"Nothing honey, everything's fine now," I said.

"Little Duke tinkled where I tinkled," Cheryl said and laughed.

"You're two of a kind," Edna said, not looking back. Edna was usually good with Cheryl, but I knew she was tired now. We hadn't had much sleep, and she had a tendency to get cranky when she didn't sleep. "We oughta ditch this damn car first chance we get," she said.

"What's the first chance we've got?" I said. I knew she'd been at the map.

"Rock Springs, Wyoming," Edna said with conviction. "Thirty miles down this road." She pointed out ahead. I had wanted all along to drive the car into Florida like a big success story. But I knew Edna was right about it, that we shouldn't take crazy chances. I had kept thinking of it as my car and not the opthalmologist's, and that was how you got caught in these things.

"Then my belief is we ought to go to Rock Springs and negotiate ourselves a new car," I said. I wanted to stay up-beat, like everything was panning out right.

"Great idea," Edna said, and leaned over and kissed me hard on the mouth.

"Now you're talking," Cheryl said. "Let's get on out of here right now."

The sunset that day I remember as being the prettiest I'd ever seen. Just as it touched the rim of the horizon it all at once fired the air into jewels and red sequins the precise likes of which I had never seen before and haven't seen since. The west has it all over everywhere for sunsets, even Florida where it's supposedly flat but where half the time trees block your view.

"It's cocktail hour," Edna said after we'd driven a while. "We ought to have a drink and celebrate something." She felt a lot better thinking we were going to get rid of the car. It certainly had dark troubles and was something you'd want to put behind you.

Edna had out a whiskey bottle and some plastic cups and was measuring levels on the glove box lid. She liked drinking, and she liked drinking in the car, which was something you got used to in Montana where it wasn't against the law, though strangely enough where a bad check would land you in Deer Lodge Prison for a year.

"Did I ever tell you I once had a monkey?" Edna said, setting my drink on the dashboard where I could reach it when I was ready. Her spirits were already picked up. She was like that, up one minute and down the next.

"I don't think you ever did tell me that," I said. "Where were you then?"

"Missoula," she said. She put her bare feet on the dash and rested the cup on her breasts. "I was waitressing at the Am–Vets. It was before I met you. Some guy came in one day with a monkey. A spider monkey. And I said, just to be joking, 'I'll roll you for that monkey.' And the guy said, 'Just one roll?' And I said sure. He put the monkey down on the bar, picked up the cup and rolled out box cars. I picked it up and rolled out three fives. And I just stood there looking at the guy. He was just some guy passing through, a vet. He got a strange look on his face —I'm sure not as strange as the one I had — but he looked kind of sad and surprised and satisfied all at once. I said, 'We can roll again.' But he said, 'No, I never roll twice for anything.' And he sat and drank a beer and talked about one thing and another for a while, about Nuclear War and building a strong-hold somewhere up in the Bitterroot, whatever it was, while I just watched the monkey, wondering what I was going to do with it when the guy left. And pretty soon he got up and said, 'Well good-bye, Chipper,' that was this monkey's name, of course. And then he left before I could say anything. And the monkey just sat on the bar all that night. I don't know what made me think of that, Earl. Just something wierd. I'm letting my mind wander."

"That's perfectly fine," I said. I took a drink of my drink. "I'd never own a monkey," I said after a minute. "They're too nasty. I'm sure Cheryl would like a monkey though, wouldn't you honey?" Cheryl was down on the seat playing with Little Duke. She used to talk about monkeys all the time then, which was when she was ten. "What'd you ever do with that monkey?" I said, watching the speedometer. We were having to go slower now because the red light kept fluttering on. And all I could do to keep it off was go slower. We were maybe going thirty-five and it was an hour before dark, and I was hoping Rock Springs wasn't far away.

"You really want to know?" she said. She gave me a quick sharp glance, then looked back at the empty desert as if she was brooding over it.

"Sure," I said. I was still up-beat. I figured *I* could worry about breaking down and let other people be happy for a change.

"I kept it a week," she said. She seemed gloomy all of a sudden, as if she saw some aspect of the story she had never seen before. "I took it home and back and forth to the Am-Vets on my shifts. And it didn't cause any trouble. I fixed a chair up for it to sit on back of the bar, and people liked it. It made a nice little clicking noise. We changed its name to Mary because Oscar figured out it was a girl. Though I was never really comfortable with it at home. I felt like it watched me too much. Then one day a guy came in, some guy who'd been in Viet Nam, still wore a fatigue coat. And he said to me, 'Don't you know that a monkey'll kill you? It's got more strength in its fingers than you got in your whole body." He said people had been killed in Viet Nam by monkeys, bunches of them marauding while you were asleep and killing you and covering you with leaves. I didn't believe a word of it, except that when I got home and got undressed I started looking over across the room at Mary on her chair in the dark watching me. And I got the creeps. And after a while I got up and went out to the car, got a length of clothesline wire, and came back in and wired her to the door knob through her little silver collar, and went back and tried to sleep. And I guess I must've slept the sleep of the dead —though I don't remember it — because when I got up I found Mary had tipped off her chair back and hanged herself on the wire line. I'd made it too short."

Edna seemed badly affected by that story and slid low in the seat so she couldn't see out over the dash. "Isn't that a shameful story, Earl, what happened to that poor little monkey?"

"I see a town! I see a town!" Cheryl started yelling from the back seat, and right up Little Duke started yapping and the whole car fell into a racket. And sure enough she had seen something I hadn't, which was Rock Springs, Wyoming, at the bottom of a long hill, a little glowing jewel in the desert with I-80 running on the north side and the black desert spread out behind.

"That's it, honey," I said. "That's where we're going. You saw it first."

"We're hungry," Cheryl said. "Little Duke wants some fish, and I want spaghetti." She put her arms around my neck and hugged me.

"Then you'll just get it," I said. "You can have anything you want. And so can Edna and so can Little Duke." I looked over at Edna smiling, but she was staring at me with eyes that were fierce with anger. "What's wrong?" I said.

"Don't you care anything about that awful thing that happened to me?" she said. Her mouth was drawn tight and her eyes kept cutting back at Cheryl and Little Duke, as if they had been tormenting her.

"Of course I do," I said. "I thought that was an awful thing." I didn't want her to be unhappy. We were almost there and pretty soon we could sit down and have a real meal without thinking somebody might be hunting us.

"You want to know what I did with that monkey?" Edna said.

"Sure I do," I said.

She said, "I put him in a green garbage bag, put it in the trunk of my car, drove to the dump and threw him in the trash." She was staring at me darkly, as if the story meant something to her that was real important but that only she could see and that the rest of the world was a fool for.

"Well that's horrible," I said. "But I don't see what else you could do. You didn't mean to kill it. You'd have done it differently if you had. And then you had to get rid of it, and I don't know what else you could do. Throwing it away seems unsympathetic to somebody, probably, but not to me. Sometimes that's all you can do, and you can't worry about what somebody else thinks." I tried to smile at her, but the red light was staying on if I pushed the accelerator at all, and I was trying to gauge if we could coast to the Interstate before the car gave out completely. I looked at Edna again. "What else can I say?" I said.

"Nothing," she said and stared back at the dark highway. "I should've known that's what you'd think. You've got a character that leaves something out, Earl. I've known that a long time."

"And yet here you are," I said. "And you're not doing so bad. Things could be a lot worse. At least we're all together here."

"Things could always be worse," Edna said. "You could go to the electric chair tomorrow."

"That's right," I said. "And somewhere somebody probably will. Only it won't be you."

"I'm hungry," said Cheryl. "When're we gonna eat. Let's find a motel. I'm tired of this, Little Duke's tired of it too."

Where the car stopped rolling was some distance from the Interstate, though you could see the clear outline of it in the dark with Rock Springs lighting up the sky behind. You could hear the big tractors hitting the spacers in the overpass, revving up for the climb to the mountains.

I shut off the lights.

"What're we going to do now?" Edna said irritably, giving me a bitter look.

"I'm figuring it," I said. "It won't be hard, whatever it is. You won't have to do anything."

"I'd hope not," she said and looked the other way.

Across the road and across a dry wash a hundred yards, was what looked like a huge mobile home town with a factory or a refinery of some kind lit up behind it, and in full swing. There were lights on in a lot of the mobile homes, and there were cars moving along an access road that ended near the freeway overpass a mile the other way. The lights in the mobile homes seemed friendly to me, and I knew right then what I should do.

"Get out," I said and opened my door.

"Are we walking?" Edna said.

"We're pushing," I said.

"I'm not pushing," Edna said and reached up and locked her door.

"All right," I said. "Then you just steer."

"You pushing us to Rock Springs, are you Earl? It doesn't look like it's more than about three miles," Edna said.

"I'll push," Cheryl said from the back.

"No, hon. Daddy'll push. You just get out with Little Duke and move out of the way."

Edna gave me a threatening look just as if I'd tried to hit her. But when I got out she slid into my seat and took the wheel, staring angrily ahead straight into the cottonwood scrub.

"Edna can't drive that car," Cheryl said from out in the dark. "She'll run it in the ditch."

"Yes she can, hon. Edna can drive it as good as I can. Probably better."

"No she can't," Cheryl said. "No she can't, either." And I thought she was about to cry but she didn't.

I told Edna to keep the ignition on so it wouldn't lock up, and to steer into the cottonwoods with the parking lights on so she could see. And when I started, she steered it straight off into the trees and I kept pushing until we were twenty yards into the cover and the tires sank in the soft sand, and nothing at all could be seen from the road.

"Now where are we?" she said, sitting at the wheel. Her voice was tired and hard, and I knew she would put a meal to use. She had a sweet nature, and I recognized this wasn't her fault, but mine. Only I wished she could be more hopeful like I was.

"You stay right here and I'll go over to that trailer park and call us a cab," I said.

"What cab?" Edna said, her mouth wrinkled as if she'd never heard anything like that in her life.

"There'll be cabs," I said and tried to smile at her. "There's cabs everywhere."

"What're you going to tell him when he gets here? Our stolen car broke down and we need a ride to where we can steal another one? That'll be a big hit, Earl."

"I'll talk," I said. "You just listen to the radio ten minutes then walk out to the shoulder. And you and Cheryl act nice. I don't want her making suspicions."

"Like we're not suspicious enough already, right?" Edna looked up at me out of the lighted car. "You don't think right, did you know that, Earl? You think the world's stupid and you're smart. But that's not how it is. I feel sorry for you. You might've *been* something, but things just went crazy someplace."

I had a thought about poor Danny. He was a vet, and crazy as a shithouse mouse, and I was glad he wasn't in for all this. "Just get the baby in the car," I said, trying to be patient. "I'm hungry like you are."

"I'm tired of this," Edna said. "I wish I'd stayed in Montana."

"Then you can go back in the morning," I said. "I'll buy the ticket and put you on the bus. But not till then."

"Just get on with it, Earl," she said slumping down in the seat, turning off the parking lights with one foot and the radio on with the other.

The mobile home community was as big as any I'd ever seen. It was attached in some way to the plant that was lighted up behind it, because I could see a car once in a while leave one of the trailer streets, turn in the direction of the plant, then go slowly into it. Everything in the plant was white, and you could see that all the trailers were painted white and looked exactly alike. A deep hum came out of the plant, and I thought as I got closer that it wouldn't be a location I'd ever want to work in.

I went right to the first trailer where there was a light and knocked on the metal door. Kids' toys were lying in the gravel around the little wood steps, and I could hear talking on t.v. that suddenly went off. I heard a woman's voice talking and then the door opened wide.

A large Negro woman with a wide friendly face stood in the doorway. She smiled at me and moved forward as if she was going to come out, but stopped at the top step. There was a little Negro boy behind her peeping out from behind her legs, watching me with his eyes half closed. The trailer had that feeling that no one else was inside, which was a feeling I knew something about.

"I'm sorry to intrude," I said. "But I've run up on a little bad luck tonight. My name's Earl Middleton."

The woman looked at me, then out into the night toward the freeway as if what I had said was something she was going to be able to see. "What kind of bad luck?" she said, looking down at me again.

"My car broke down out on the highway," I said. "I can't fix it myself, and I wondered if I could use your phone to call for help."

The woman smiled down at me knowingly. "We can't live without cars, can we?"

"That's the honest truth," I said.

"They're like our hearts," she said firmly, her face shining in the little bulb light that burned beside the door. "Where's your car situated?"

I turned and looked over into the dark, but I couldn't see anything because of where we'd put it. "It's over there," I said. "You can't see it in the dark."

"Who all's with you now?" the woman said. "Have you got your wife with you?"

"She's with my little girl and our dog in the car," I said. "My daughter's asleep or I would have brought them."

"They shouldn't be left in that dark by themselves," the woman said and frowned. "There's too much unsavoriness out there."

"The best I can do is hurry back," I said. I tried to look sincere, since everything except Cheryl being asleep and Edna being my wife was the truth. The truth is meant to serve you if you'll let it, and I wanted it to serve me. "I'll pay for the phone call," I said. "If you'll bring the phone to the door I'll call from right here."

The woman looked at me again as if she was searching for a truth of her own, then back out into the night. She was maybe in her sixties but I couldn't say for sure. "You're not going to rob me, are you Mr. Middleton?" she said, and smiled like it was a joke between us.

"Not tonight," I said and smiled a genuine smile. "I'm not up to it tonight. Maybe another time."

"Then I guess Terrel and I can let you use our phone with Daddy not here, can't we Terrel? This is my grandson, Terrel Junior, Mr. Middleton." She put her hand on the boy's head and looked down at him. "Terrel won't talk. Though if he did he'd tell you to use our phone. He's a sweet boy." She opened the screen for me to come in.

The trailer was a big one with a new rug and a new couch and a living room that expanded to give the space of a real house. Something good and sweet was cooking in the kitchen and the trailer felt like it was somebody's comfortable new home instead of just temporary. I've lived in trailers, but they were just snail-backs with one room and no toilet, and they always felt cramped and unhappy — though I've thought maybe it might've been me that was unhappy in them.

There was a big Sony t.v. and a lot of kid's toys scattered on the floor. I recognized a Greyhound Bus I'd gotten for Cheryl. The phone was beside a new leather recliner, and the Negro woman pointed for me to sit down and call, and gave me the phone book. Terrel began fingering his toys and the woman sat on the couch while I called, watching me and smiling.

There were three listings for cab companies, all with one number different. I called the numbers in order and didn't get an answer until the last one which answered with the name of the second company. I said I was on the highway beyond the Interstate and that my wife and family needed to be taken to town and I would arrange for a tow later. While I was giving the location, I looked up the name of a tow service to tell the driver in case he asked.

When I hung up the Negro woman was sitting looking at me with the same look she had been staring with into the dark, a look that seemed to want truth. She was smiling though, something pleased her and I reminded her of it.

"This is a very nice home," I said, resting in the recliner which felt like the driver's seat of the Mercedes, and where I'd have been happy to stay.

"This isn't *our* house, Mr. Middleton," the Negro woman said. "The company owns these. They give them to us for nothing. We have our own home in Rockford, Illinois."

"That's wonderful," I said.

"It's never wonderful when you have to be away from home, Mr. Middleton, though we're only here three months, and it'll be easier when Terrel Junior begins his special school. You see our son was killed in the war, and his wife ran off without Terrel Junior. Though you shouldn't worry. He can't understand us. His little feelings can't be hurt." The woman folded her hands in her lap and smiled in a satisfied way. She was an attractive woman and had on a blue and pink floral dress that made her seem bigger than she could've been, just the right woman to sit on the couch she was sitting on. She was good nature's picture, and I was glad she could be, with her little brain-damaged boy, living in a place where no one in his right mind would want to live a minute. "Where do you live, Mr. Middleton?" she said politely, smiling in the same sympathetic way.

"My family and I are in transit," I said. "I'm an opthalmologist, and we're moving back to Florida where I'm from. I'm setting up practice in some little town where it's warm year round. I haven't decided where."

"Florida's a wonderful place," the woman said. "I think Terrel would like it there."

"Could I ask you something," I said.

"You certainly may," the woman said. Terrel had begun pushing his Greyhound across the front of the t.v. screen, making a scratch that no one watching the set could miss. "Stop that, Terrel Junior," the woman said quietly. But Terrel kept pushing his bus on the glass, and she smiled at me again as if we both understood something sad. Except I knew Cheryl would never damage a television set. She had respect for nice things, and I was sorry for the lady that Terrel didn't. "What did you want to ask," the woman said.

"What goes on in that plant or whatever it is back there beyond these trailers, where all the lights are on?"

"Gold," the woman said and smiled.

"It's what?" I said.

"Gold," the Negro woman said, smiling as she had for almost all the time I'd been there. "It's a gold mine."

"They're mining gold back there?" I said, pointing.

"Every night and every day," she said, smiling in a pleased way.

"Does your husband work there?" I said.

"He's the assayer," she said. "He controls the quality. He works three months a year, and we live the rest of the time at home in Rockford. We've waited a long time for this. We've been happy to have our grandson, but I won't say I'll be sorry to have him go. We're ready to start our lives over." She smiled broadly at me and then at Terrel who was giving her a spiteful look from the floor. "You said you had a daughter," the Negro woman said. "And what's her name?"

"Irma Cheryl," I said. "She's named for my mother."

"That's nice," she said. "And she's healthy, too. I can see it in your face." She looked over at Terrel Junior.

"I guess I'm lucky," I said.

"So far you are," she said. "But children bring you grief, the same way they bring you joy. We were unhappy for a long time before my husband got his job in the gold mine. Now, when Terrel starts to school, we'll be kids again." She stood up. "You might miss your cab, Mr. Middleton," she said, walking toward the door, though not to be forcing me out. She was too polite. "If *we* can't see your car, the cab surely won't be able to."

"That's true," I said, and got up off the recliner where I'd been so comfortable. "None of us have eaten yet, and your food makes me know how hungry we probably all are."

"There are fine restaurants in town, and you'll find them," the Negro woman said. "I'm sorry you didn't meet my husband. He's a wonderful man. He's everything to me."

"Tell him I appreciate the phone," I said. "You saved me."

"You weren't hard to save," the woman said. "Saving people is what we were all put on earth to do. I just passed you on to whatever's coming to you."

"Let's hope it's good," I said, stepping back into the dark.

"I'll be hoping, Mr. Middleton. Terrel and I will both be hoping."

I waved to her as I walked out into the darkness toward the car where it was hidden in the night.

The cab had already arrived when I got there. I could see its little red and green roof lights all the way across the dry wash, and it made me worry that Edna was already saying something to get us in trouble, something about the car or where we'd come from, something that would create suspicion on us. I thought, then, how I never planned things well enough. There was always a gap between my plan and what happened, and that I only responded to things as they came along, and hoped I wouldn't get in trouble. I was an offender in the law's eyes. But I always *thought* differently, as if I weren't an offender and had no intention of being one, which was the truth. But as I read on a napkin once, between the idea and the act a whole kingdom lies. And I had a hard time with my acts, which were oftentimes offender's acts, and my ideas, which were as good as the gold they mined there where the bright lights were blazing.

"We're waiting for you, Daddy," Cheryl said when I crossed the road. "The taxicab's already here."

"I see, hon," I said and gave Cheryl a big hug. The cab driver was sitting in the driver's seat having a smoke with the lights on inside. Edna was leaning against the back of the cab between the tail lights, wearing her Bailey hat. "What'd you tell him?" I said when I got close.

"Nothin," she said. "What's there to tell?"

"Did he see the car?"

She glanced over in the direction of the trees where we had hid the Mercedes. Nothing was visible in the darkness, though I could hear Little Duke combing around in the underbrush tracking something, his little collar tinkling. "Where're we going?" she said. "I'm so hungry I could pass out."

"Edna's in a terrible mood," Cheryl said. "She already snapped at me."

"We're tired, honey," I said. "So try to be nicer."

"She's never nice," Cheryl said.

"Run go get Little Duke," I said. "And hurry back."

"I guess *my* questions come last here, right?" Edna said.

I put my arm around her. "That's not true," I said.

"Did you find somebody over there in the trailers you'd rather stay with? You were gone long enough."

"That's not a thing to say," I said. "I was just trying to make things look right, so we don't get put in jail."

"So *you* don't, you mean," Edna said and laughed a little laugh I didn't like hearing.

"That's right. So I won't," I said. "I'd be the one in Dutch." I stared out at the big lighted assemblage of white buildings and white lights beyond the trailer community, plumes of white smokes escaping up into the heartless Wyoming sky, the whole company of buildings looking like some unbelievable castle, humming away in a distorted dream. "You know what all those buildings are there?" I said to Edna, who hadn't moved, and who didn't really seem to care if she ever moved anymore ever.

"No. But I can't say it matters, cause it isn't a motel and it isn't a restaurant," she said.

"It's a gold mine," I said, staring at the gold mine, which I knew now from walking to the trailer was a greater distance from us than it seemed, though it seemed huge and near up against the cold sky. I thought there should've been a wall around it with guards, instead of just the lights and no fence. It seemed as if anyone could go in and take what they wanted, just the way I had gone up to that woman's trailer and used the telephone, though that obviously wasn't true.

Edna began to laugh then. Not the mean laugh I didn't like, but a laugh that had something caring behind it, a full laugh that enjoyed a joke, a laugh she was laughing the first time I laid eyes on her in Missoula in the East Gate Bar in 1979, a laugh we used to laugh together when Cheryl was still with her mother, and I was working steady at the track and not stealing cars or passing bogus checks to merchants. A better time all around. And for some reason it made me laugh just hearing her, and we both stood there behind the cab in the dark laughing at the gold mine in the desert, me with my arm around her and Cheryl out rustling up Little Duke and the cab driver smoking in the cab, and our stolen Mercedes Benz that I had such hopes for in Florida, stuck up to its axle in sand where I'd never get to see it again.

"I always wondered what a gold mine would look like when I saw it," Edna said, still laughing, wiping a tear from her eye.

"Me too," I said. "I was always curious about it."

"We're a couple of fools, ain't we Earl?" she said, unable to quit laughing completely. "We're two of a kind."

"It might be a good sign, though," I said.

"How could it be," she said. "It's not our gold mine. There aren't any drive-up windows." She was still laughing.

"We've seen it," I said, pointing. "That's it right there. It may mean we're getting closer. Some people never see it at all."

"In a pig's eye, Earl," she said. "You and me see it in a pig's eye."

And she turned and got in the cab to go.

The cab driver didn't ask anything about our car or where it was, to mean he'd noticed something queer. All of which made me feel like we had made a clean break from the car and couldn't be connected with it until it was too late, if ever. The driver told us a lot about Rock Springs while he drove, that because of the gold mine a lot of people had moved there in just six months, people from all over including New York, and that most of them lived out in the trailers. Prostitutes from New York City who he called "B–

girls" had come into town, he said, on the prosperity tide and Cadillacs with New York plates cruised the little streets every night full of Negroes with big hats who ran the women. He told us everybody who got in his cab now wanted to know where the women were, and that when he got our call he almost didn't come because some of the trailers were brothels operated by the mine for engineers and computer people away from home. He said he got tired of running back and forth out there just for vile business. He said that *Sixty Minutes* had even done a program about Rock Springs and that a blow-up had resulted in Cheyenne, though nothing could be done unless the prosperity left town. "It's prosperity's fruit," the driver said. "I'd rather be poor, which is lucky for me."

He said all the motels were sky high, but since we were a family he could show us a nice one that was affordable. But I told him we wanted a first-rate place where they took animals and the money didn't matter because we had had a hard day and wanted to finish on a high note. I also knew that it was in the little nowhere places that the police look for you and find you. People I'd known were always being arrested in cheap hotels and tourist courts with names you'd never heard of before. Never in Holiday Inns or Travel-Lodges.

I asked him to drive us to the middle of town and back out again so Cheryl could see the train station, and while we were there I saw a pink Cadillac with New York licenses and a t.v. aerial, being driven slowly by a Negro in a big hat, down a narrow street where there were just bars and a Chinese restaurant. It was an odd sight, nothing you could ever expect.

"There's your pure criminal element," the cab driver said, and seemed sad. "I'm sorry for people like you to see a thing like that. We've got a nice town here, but there're some that wants to ruin it for everybody. There used to be a way to deal with trash and criminals, but those days are gone forever."

"You said it," Edna said.

"You shouldn't let it get *you* down," I said to the cab driver. "There's more of you than them. And there always will be. You're the best advertisement this town has. I know Cheryl will remember you and not *that* man, won't you honey?" But Cheryl was asleep by then, holding Little Duke in her arms on the taxi seat.

The driver took us to the Ramada Inn on the Interstate, not far from where we'd broken down. I had a small pain of regret as we drove under the Ramada awning, that we hadn't driven up in a cranberry-colored Mercedes, but instead in a beat-up old Chrysler taxi driven by an old man full of complaints. Though I knew it was for the best. We were better off without that car, better really in any other car but that one, where the signs had turned bad.

I registered in under another name and paid for the room in cash so there wouldn't be any questions. On the line where it said *representing* I wrote opthalmologist and put M.D. after the name. It had a nice look to it, even though it wasn't my name.

When we got to the room, which was on the back where I'd asked for it, I put Cheryl on one of the beds and Little Duke beside her so they'd sleep. She'd missed dinner, but it only meant she'd be hungry in the morning, when she could have anything she wanted. A few missed meals don't make a kid bad. I'd missed a lot of them myself and haven't turned out completely bad.

"Let's have some fried chicken," I said to Edna when she came out of the bathroom. "They have good fried chicken at the Ramadas, and I noticed the buffet was still up. Cheryl can stay right here, where it's safe, till we're back."

"I guess I'm not hungry anymore," Edna said. She stood at the window staring out into the dark. I could see out the window past her some yellowish foggy glow in the sky. For a moment I thought it was the gold mine out in the distance lighting the night, though it was only the Interstate.

"We could order up," I said. "Whatever you want. There's a menu on the phone book. You could just have a salad."

"You go ahead," she said. "I've lost my hungry spirit." She sat on the bed beside Cheryl and Little Duke, and looked at them in a sweet way and put her hand on Cheryl's cheek just as if she'd had a fever. "Sweet little girl," she said. "Everybody loves you."

"What do you want to do?" I said. "I'd like to eat. Maybe *I'll* order up some chicken."

"Why don't you do that?" she said. "It's your favorite." And she smiled at me from the bed.

I sat on the other bed and dialed room service. I asked for chicken, garden salad, potato and a roll, plus a piece of hot apple pie and iced tea. I realized I hadn't eaten all day. When I put down the phone I saw that Edna was watching me from the other bed, not in a hateful way or a loving way, just in a way that seemed to say she didn't understand something and was going to ask me about it.

"How did watching me get so entertaining?" I said, and smiled at her. I was trying to be friendly. I knew how tired she must be. It was after nine o'clock.

"I was just thinking how much I hated being in a motel without a car that was mine to drive. Isn't that funny? I started feeling like that last night when that purple car wasn't mine. That purple car just gave me the willies, I guess, Earl."

"One of those cars *outside* is yours," I said. "Just stand right there and pick it out."

"I know," she said. "But that's different, isn't it?" She reached and got her blue Bailey hat, put it on her head, and set it way back like Dale Evans. She looked sweet. "I used to like to go to motels, you know," she said. "There's something secret about them and free — I was never paying, of course. But you felt safe from everything and free to do what you wanted because you'd made the decision to be here and paid that price, and all the rest was the good part. Fucking and everything, you know." She smiled at me in a good-natured way.

"Isn't that the way this is?" I said. I was sitting on the bed watching her, not knowing what to expect her to say next.

"I don't guess it is, Earl," she said and stared out the window. "I'm thirty-two and I'm going to have to give up on motels. I can't keep that fantasy going anymore."

"Don't you like this place?" I said and looked around at the room. I appreciated the modern paintings and the low-boy bureau and the big t.v. It seemed like a plenty nice enough place to me, considering where we'd been already.

"No, I don't," Edna said with real conviction. "There's no use in my getting mad at you about it. It isn't your fault. You do the best you can for everybody. But every trip teaches you something. And I've learned I need to give up on motels before some bad thing happens to me. I'm sorry."

"What does that mean?" I said, because I really didn't know what she had in mind to do, though I should've guessed.

"I guess I'll take that ticket you mentioned," she said, and got up and faced the window. "Tomorrow's soon enough. We haven't got a car to take me anyhow."

"Well that's a fine thing," I said, sitting on the bed, feeling like I was in a shock. I wanted to say something to her, to argue her, but I couldn' think what to say that seemed right. I didn't want to be mad at her, but it made me mad.

"You've got a right to be mad at me, Earl," she said, "but I don't think you can really blame me." She turned around and faced me and sat on the window ledge, her hands on her knees. Someone knocked on the door. I just yelled for them to set the tray down and put it on the bill.

"I guess I *do* blame you," I said. I was angry. I thought about how I could have disappeared into that trailer community and hadn't, had come back to keep things going, had tried to take control of things for everybody when they looked bad.

"Don't. I wish you wouldn't," Edna said, and smiled at me like she wanted me to hug her. "Anybody ought to have their choice in things if they can. Don't you believe that, Earl? Here I am out here in the desert where I don't know anything, in a stolen car, in a motel room under an assumed name, with no money of my own, a kid that's not mine, and the law after me. And I have a choice to get out of all of it by getting on a bus. What would you do? I know exactly what you'd do."

"You think you do," I said. But I didn't want to get into an argument about it and tell her all I could've done and didn't do. Because it wouldn't have done any good. When you get to the point of arguing, you're past the point of changing anybody's mind, even though it's supposed to be the other way, and maybe for some classes of people it is, just never mine.

Edna smiled at me and came across the room and put her arms around me where I was sitting on the bed. Cheryl rolled over and looked at us and smiled, then closed her eyes, and the room was quiet. I was beginning to think of Rock Springs in the way I knew I would always think of it, a low-down city full of crimes and whores and disappointments, a place where a woman left me, instead of a place where I got things on the straight track once and for all, a place I saw a gold mine.

"Eat your chicken, Earl," Edna said. "Then we can go to bed. I'm tired, but I'd like to make love to you, anyway. None of this is a matter of not loving you, you know that."

Sometime late in the night after Edna was asleep, I got up and walked outside into the parking lot. It could've been any time because there was still the light from the Interstate frosting the low sky, and the big red Ramada sign humming motionlessly in the night and no light at all in the east to indicate it might be morning. The lot was full of cars all nosed-in, most of them with suitcases strapped to their roofs and their trunks weighed down with belongings the people were taking someplace, to a new home or a vacation resort in the mountains. I had laid in bed a long time after Edna was asleep, watching the Atlanta Braves on cable television, trying to get my mind off how I'd feel when I saw that bus pull away the next day, and how I'd feel when I turned around and there stood Cheryl and Little Duke and no one to see about them but me all alone, and that the first thing I had to do was get hold of some automobile and get the plates switched, then get them some breakfast and get us all on the road to Florida, all in the space of probably two hours, since that Mercedes would certainly look less hid in the daytime than the night, and word travels fast. I've always taken care of Cheryl myself, as long as I've had her with me. None of the women ever did, most of them didn't even seem to like her, though they took care of me in a way so that I could take care of her. And I knew that once Edna left all that was going to get harder. Though what I wanted most to do was not think about it just for a little while, try to let my mind go limp so it could be strong for the rest of what there was. I thought that the difference between a successful life and an unsuccessful one, between me at that moment and all the people who owned the cars that were nosed-in to their proper places in the lot, maybe between me and that woman out in the trailers by the gold mine was how well you were able to put things like this out of your mind and not be bothered by them, and maybe too, by how many troubles like this one you had to face in a lifetime. Through luck or design they had all faced fewer troubles, and by their own characters, they forgot them faster. And that's what I wanted for me. Fewer troubles, fewer memories of trouble.

I walked over to a car, a Pontiac with Ohio tags, one of the ones with bundles and suitcases strapped to the top and a lot more in the trunk, by the way it was riding. I looked inside the driver's window. There were maps and paperback books and sunglasses and the little plastic holders for cans that hang on the window wells. And in the back there were kid's toys and some pillows and a cat box with a cat sitting in it staring up at me like I was the face of the moon. It all looked familiar to me, the very same things I would have in my car if I had a car. Nothing seemed surprising, nothing different. Though I had a funny sensation at that moment and turned and looked up at the windows along the back of the Ramada Inn. All were dark except two. Mine and another one. And I wondered, because it seemed funny, what would you think a man was doing if you saw him in the middle of the night, looking in the windows of cars in the parking lot of the Ramada Inn? Would you think he was trying to get his head cleared? Would you think he was trying to get ready for a day when trouble would come down on him? Would you think his girlfriend was leaving him? Would you think he had a daughter? Would you think he was anybody like you?

John Gardner

Redemption

One day in April—a clear, blue day when there were crocuses in bloom—Jack Hawthorne ran over and killed his brother, David. Even at the last moment he could have prevented his brother's death by slamming on the tractor brakes, easily in reach for all the shortness of his legs; but he was unable to think, or, rather, thought unclearly, and so watched it happen, as he would again and again watch it happen in his mind, with nearly undiminished intensity and clarity, all his life. The younger brother was riding, as both of them knew he should not have been, on the cultipacker, a two-ton implement lumbering behind the tractor, crushing new-ploughed ground. Jack was twelve, his brother, David, seven. The scream came not from David, who never got a sound out, but from their five-year-old sister, who was riding on the fender of the tractor, looking back. When Jack turned to look, the huge iron wheels had reached his brother's pelvis. He kept driving, reacting as he would to a half-crushed farm animal, and imagining, in the same stab of thought, that perhaps his brother would survive. Blood poured from David's mouth.

Their father was nearly destroyed by it. Sometimes Jack would find him lying on the cow-barn floor, crying, unable to stand up. Dale Hawthorne, the father, was a sensitive, intelligent man, by nature a dreamer. It showed in old photographs, his smile coded, his eyes on the horizon. He loved all his children and would not consciously have been able to hate his son even if Jack had indeed been, as he thought himself, his brother's murderer. But he could not help sometimes seeming to blame his son, though consciously he blamed only his own unwisdom and—so far as his belief held firm—God. Dale Hawthorne's mind swung violently at this time, reversing itself almost hour by hour, from desperate faith to the most savage, black-hearted atheism. Every sickly calf, every sow that ate her litter, was a new, sure proof that the religion he'd followed all his life was a lie. Yet skeletons were orderly, as were, he thought, the stars. He was unable to decide, one moment full of rage at God's injustice, the next moment wracked by doubt of His existence.

Though he was not ordinarily a man who smoked, he would sometimes sit up all night now, or move restlessly, hurriedly, from room to room, chain-smoking Lucky Strikes. Or he would ride away on his huge, darkly thundering Harley-Davidson 80, trying to forget, morbidly dwelling on what he'd meant to put behind him—how David had once laughed, cake in his fists; how he'd once patched a chair with precocious skill—or Dale Hawthorne would think, for the hundredth time, about suicide, hunting in mixed fear and anger for some reason not to miss the next turn, fly off to the right of the next iron bridge onto the moonlit gray rocks and black water below—discovering, invariably, no reason but the damage his suicide would do to his wife and the children remaining.

Sometimes he would forget for a while by abandoning reason and responsibility for love affairs. Jack's father was at this time still young, still handsome, well-known for the poetry he recited at local churches or for English classes or meetings of the Grange—recited, to loud applause (he had poems of all kinds, both serious and comic), for thrashing crews, old men at the V.A. Hospital, even the tough, flint-eyed orphans at the Children's Home. He was a celebrity, in fact, as much Romantic poet-hero as his time and western New York State could afford—and beyond all that, he was now so full of pain and unassuageable guilt that women's hearts flew to him unbidden. He became, with all his soul and without cynical intent—though fleeing all law, or what he'd once thought law—a hunter of women, trading off his sorrow for the sorrows of wearied, unfulfilled country wives. At times he would be gone from the farm for days, abandoning the work to Jack and whoever was available to help—some neighbor or older cousin or one of Jack's uncles. No one complained, at least not openly. A stranger might have condemned him, but no one in the family did, certainly not Jack, not even Jack's mother, though her sorrow was increased. Dale Hawthorne had always been, before the accident, a faithful man, one of the most fair-minded, genial farmers in the country. No one asked that, changed as he was, he do more, for the moment, than survive.

As for Jack's mother, though she'd been, before the accident, a cheerful woman—one who laughed often and loved telling stories, sometimes sang anthems in bandanna and blackface before her husband recited poems—she cried now, nights, and did only as much as she had strength to do—so sapped by grief that she could barely move her arms. She comforted Jack and his sister, Phoebe—herself as well—by embracing them vehemently whenever new waves of guilt swept in, by constant reassurance and extravagant praise, frequent mention of how proud some relative would be—once, for instance, over a drawing of his sister's, "Oh, Phoebe, if only your great-aunt Lucy could see this!" Great-aunt Lucy had been famous, among the family and friends, for her paintings of families of lions. And Jack's mother forced on his sister and himself comforts more permanent: piano and, for Jack, French-horn lessons, school and church activities, above all an endless, exhausting ritual of chores. Because she had, at thirty-four, considerable strength of character—except that, these days, she was always eating—and because, also, she was a woman of strong religious faith, a woman who, in her years of church work and teaching at the high school, had made scores of close, for the most part equally religious, friends, with whom she regularly corresponded, her letters, then theirs, half filling the mailbox at the foot of the hill and cluttering every table, desk, and niche in the large old house—friends who now frequently visited or phoned—she was able to move step by step past disaster and in the end keep her family from wreck. She said very little to her children about her troubles. In fact, except for the crying behind her closed door, she kept her feelings strictly secret.

But for all his mother and her friends could do for him—for all his father's older brothers could do, or, when he was there, his father himself—the damage to young Jack Hawthorne took a long while healing. Working the farm, ploughing, cultipacking, disking, dragging, he had plenty of time to think—plenty of time for the accident to replay, with the solidity of real time repeated, in his mind, his whole body flinching from the image as it came, his voice leaping up independent of him, as if a shout could perhaps drive the memory back into its cave. Maneuvering the tractor over sloping, rocky fields, dust whorling out like smoke behind him or, when he turned into the wind, falling like soot until his skin was black and his hair as thick and stiff as old clothes in an attic—the circles of foothills every day turning greener, the late-spring wind flowing endless and sweet with the smell of coming rain—he had all the time in the world to cry and swear bitterly at himself, standing up to drive, as his father often did, Jack's sore hands clamped tight to the steering wheel, his shoes unsteady on the bucking axlebeam—for stones lay everywhere, yellowed in the sunlight, a field of misshapen skulls. He'd never loved his brother, he raged out loud, never loved anyone as well as he should have. He was incapable of love, he told himself, striking the steering wheel. He was inherently bad, a spiritual defective. He was evil.

So he raged and grew increasingly ashamed of his raging, reminded by the lengthening shadows across the field of the theatricality in all he did, his most terrible sorrow mere sorrow on a stage, the very thunderclaps above—dark blue, rushing sky, birds crazily wheeling—mere opera set, proper lighting for his rant. At once he would hush himself, lower his rear end to the tractor seat, lock every muscle to the stillness of a statue, and drive on, solitary, blinded by tears; yet even now it was theater, not life—mere ghastly posturing, as in that story of his father's, how Lord Byron once tried to get Shelley's skull to make a drinking cup. Tears no longer came, though the storm went on building. Jack rode on, alone with the indifferent, murderous machinery in the widening ten-acre field.

When the storm at last hit, he'd been driven up the lane like a dog in flight, lashed by gusty rain, chased across the tracks to the tractor shed and from there to the kitchen, full of food smells from his mother's work and Phoebe's, sometimes the work of two or three friends who'd stopped by to look in on the family. Jack kept aloof, repelled by their bright, melodious chatter and absentminded humming, indignant at their pretense that all was well. "My, how you've grown!" the old friend or fellow teacher from high school would say, and to his mother, "My, what big *hands* he has, Betty!" He would glare at his little sister, Phoebe, his sole ally, already half traitor—she would bite her lips, squinting, concentrating harder on the mixing bowl and beaters; she was forever making cakes—and he would retreat as soon as possible to the evening chores.

He had always told himself stories to pass the time when driving the tractor, endlessly looping back and forth, around and around, fitting the land for spring planting. He told them to himself aloud, taking all parts in the dialogue, gesturing, making faces, discarding dignity, here where no one could see or overhear him, half a mile from the nearest house. Once all his stories had been of sexual conquest or of heroic battle with escaped convicts from the Attica Prison or kidnappers who, unbeknownst to anyone, had built a small shack where they kept their captives, female and beautiful, in the lush, swampy woods beside the field. Now, after the accident, his subject matter changed. His fantasies came to be all of self-sacrifice, pitiful stories in which he redeemed his life by throwing it away to save others more worthwhile. To friends and officials of his fantasy, especially to heroines—a girl named Margaret, at school, or his cousin Linda—he would confess his worthlessness at painful length, naming all his faults, granting himself no quarter. For a time this helped, but the lie was too obvious, the manipulation of shame to buy love, and in the end despair bled all color from his fantasies. The foulness of his nature became clearer and clearer in his mind until, like his father, he began to toy—dully but in morbid earnest now—with the idea of suicide. His chest would fill with anguish, as if he were dreaming some nightmare wide awake, or bleeding internally, and his arms and legs would grow shaky with weakness, until he had to stop and get down from the tractor and sit for a few minutes, his eyes fixed on some comforting object, for instance a dark, smooth stone.

Even from his father and his father's brothers, who sometimes helped with the chores, he kept aloof. His father and uncles were not talkative men. Except for his father's comic poems, they never told jokes, though they liked hearing them; and because they had lived there all their lives and knew every soul in the county by name, nothing much surprised them or, if it did, roused them to mention it. Their wives might gossip, filling the big kitchen with their pealing laughter or righteous indignation, but the men for the most part merely smiled or compressed their lips and shook their heads. At the G.L.F. feedstore, occasionally, eating an ice cream while they waited for their grist, they would speak of the weather or the Democrats; but in the barn, except for "Jackie, shift that milker, will you?" or "You can carry this up to the milk house now," they said nothing. They were all tall, square men with deeply cleft chins and creases on their foreheads and muscular jowls; all Presbyterians, sometimes deacons, sometimes elders; and they were all gentle-hearted, decent men who looked lost in thought, especially Jack's father, though on occasion they'd abruptly frown or mutter, or speak a few words to a cow, or a cat, or a swallow. It was natural that Jack, working with such men, should keep to himself, throwing down ensilage from the pitch-dark, sweet-ripe crater of the silo or hay bales from the mow, dumping oats in front of the cows' noses, or—taking the long-handled, blunt wooden scraper from the whitewashed wall—pushing manure into the gutters.

He felt more community with the cows than with his uncles

or, when he was there, his father. Stretched out flat between the two rows of stanchions, waiting for the cows to be finished with their silage so he could drive them out to pasture, he would listen to their chewing in the dark, close barn, a sound as soothing, as infinitely restful, as waves along a shore, and would feel their surprisingly warm, scented breath, their bovine quiet, and for a while would find that his anxiety had left him. With the cows, the barn cats, the half-sleeping dog, he could forget and feel at home, feel that life was pleasant. He felt the same when walking up the long, fenced lane at the first light of sunrise—his shoes and pants legs sopping wet with dew, his ears full of birdcalls—going to bring in the herd from the upper pasture. Sometimes on the way he would step off the deep, crooked cow path to pick cherries or red raspberries, brighter than jewels in the morning light. They were sweeter then than at any other time, and as he approached, clouds of sparrows would explode into flight from the branches, whirring off to safety. The whole countryside was sweet, early in the morning—newly cultivated corn to his left; to his right, alfalfa and, beyond that, wheat. He felt at one with it all. It was what life ought to be, what he'd once believed it was.

But he could not make such feelings last. *No*, he thought bitterly on one such morning, throwing stones at the dull, indifferent cows, driving them down the lane. However he might hate himself and all his race, a cow was no better, or a field of wheat. Time and again he'd been driven half crazy, angry enough to kill, by the stupidity of cows when they'd pushed through a fence and—for all his shouting, for all the indignant barking of the dog—they could no longer locate the gap they themselves had made. And no better to be grain, smashed flat by the first rainy wind. So, fists clenched, he raged inside his mind, grinding his teeth to drive out thought, at war with the universe. He remembered his father, erect, eyes flashing, speaking Mark Antony's angry condemnation from the stage at the Grange. His father had seemed to him, that night, a creature set apart. His extended arm, pointing, was the terrible warning of a god. And now, from nowhere, the black memory of his brother's death rushed over him again, mindless and inexorable as a wind or wave, the huge culti-packer lifting—only an inch or so—as it climbed toward the shoulders, then sank on the cheek, flattening the skull—and he heard, more real than the morning, his sister's scream.

One day in August, a year and a half after the accident, they were combining oats—Jack and two neighbors and two of his cousins—when Phoebe came out, as she did every day, to bring lunch to those who worked in the field. Their father had been gone, this time, for nearly three weeks, and since he'd left at the height of the harvest season, no one was sure he would return, though as usual they kept silent about it. Jack sat alone in the shade of an elm, apart from the others. It was a habit they'd come to accept as they accepted, so far as he knew, his father's ways. Phoebe brought the basket from the shade where the others had settled to the shade here on Jack's side, farther from the bright, stubbled field.

"It's chicken," she said, and smiled, kneeling.

The basket was nearly as large as she was—Phoebe was seven—but she seemed to see nothing unreasonable in her having to lug it up the hill from the house. Her face was flushed, and drops of perspiration stood out along her hairline, but her smile was not only uncomplaining but positively cheerful. The trip to the field was an escape from housework, he understood; even so, her happiness offended him.

"Chicken," he said, and looked down glumly at his hard, tanned arms black with oat-dust. Phoebe smiled on, her mind far away, as it seemed to him, and like a child playing house she took a dishtowel from the basket, spread it on the grass, then set out wax-paper packages of chicken, rolls, celery, and salt, and finally a small plastic thermos, army green.

She looked up at him now. "I brought you a thermos all for yourself because you always sit alone."

He softened a little without meaning to. "Thanks," he said.

She looked down again, and for all his self-absorption he was touched, noticing that she bowed her head in the way a much older girl might do, troubled by thought, though her not quite clean, dimpled hands were a child's. He saw that there was something she wanted to say and, to forestall it, brushed flying ants from the top of the thermos, unscrewed the cap, and poured himself iced tea. When he drank, the tea was so cold it brought a momentary pain to his forehead and made him aware once more of the grating chaff under his collar, blackening all his exposed skin, gritty around his eyes—aware, too, of the breezeless, insect-filled heat beyond the shade of the elm. Behind him, just at the rim of his hearing, one of the neighbors laughed at some remark from the younger of his cousins. Jack drained the cup, brooding on his aching muscles. Even in the shade his body felt baked dry.

"Jack," his sister said, "did you want to say grace?"

"Not really," he said, and glanced at her.

He saw that she was looking at his face in alarm, her mouth slightly opened, eyes wide, growing wider, and though he didn't know why, his heart gave a jump. "I already said it," he mumbled. "Just not out loud."

"Oh," she said, then smiled.

When everyone had finished eating she put the empty papers, the jug, and the smaller thermos in the basket, grinned at them all and said goodbye—whatever had bothered her was forgotten as soon as that—and, leaning far over, balancing the lightened but still-awkward basket, started across the stubble for the house. As he cranked the tractor she turned around to look back at them and wave. He nodded and, as if embarrassed, touched his straw hat.

Not till he was doing the chores that night did he grasp what her look of alarm had meant. If he wouldn't say grace, then perhaps there was no heaven. Their father would never get well, and David was dead. He squatted, drained of all strength again, staring at the hoof of the cow he'd been stripping, preparing her for the milker, and thought of his absent father. He saw the motorcycle roaring down a twisting mountain road, the clatter of the engine ringing like harsh music against shale. If what he felt was hatred, it was a terrible, desperate envy, too; his father all alone, uncompromised, violent, cut off as if by centuries from the warmth, chatter, and smells of the kitchen, the dimness of stained glass where he, Jack, sat every Sunday between his mother and sister, looking toward the pulpit where in the old days his father had sometimes read the lesson, soft-voiced but aloof from the timid-eyed flock, Christ's sheep.

Something blocked the light coming in through the cowbarn window from the west, and he turned his head, glancing up.

"You all right there, Jackie?" his uncle Walt said, bent forward, near-sightedly peering across the gutter.

He nodded and quickly wiped his wrist across his cheeks. He moved his hands once more to the cow's warm teats.

A few nights later, when he went in from chores, the door between the kitchen and livingroom was closed, and the house was unnaturally quiet. He stood a moment listening, still holding the milk pail, absently fitting the heel of one boot into the bootjack and tugging until the boot slipped off. He pried off the other, then walked to the icebox in his stocking feet, opened the door, carried the pitcher to the table, and filled it from the pail. When he'd slid the pitcher into the icebox again and closed the door, he went without a sound, though not meaning to be stealthy, toward the livingroom. Now, beyond the closed door, he heard voices, his sister and mother, then one of his aunts. He pushed the door open and looked in, about to speak.

Though the room was dim, no light but the small one among the pictures on the piano, he saw his father at once, kneeling by the davenport with his face on his mother's lap. Phoebe was on the davenport beside their mother, hugging her and him, Phoebe's cheeks stained, like her mother's, with tears. Around them, as if reverently drawn back, Uncle Walt, Aunt Ruth, and their two children sat watching, leaning forward with shining eyes. His father's head, bald down the center, glowed, and he had his glasses off.

"Jackie," his aunt called sharply, "come in. It's all over. Your dad's come home."

He would have fled, but his knees had no strength in them and his chest was wild, churning as if with terror. He clung to the door-knob, grotesquely smiling—so he saw himself. His father raised his head. "Jackie," he said, and was unable to say more, all at once sobbing like a baby.

"Hi, Dad," he brought out, and somehow managed to go to him and get down on his knees beside him and put his arm around his back. He felt dizzy now, nauseated, and he was crying like his father. "I hate you," he whispered too softly for any of them to hear.

His father stayed. He worked long days, in control once more, though occasionally he smoked, pacing in his room nights, or rode off on his motorcycle for an hour or two, and seldom smiled. Nevertheless, in a month he was again reciting poetry for schools and churches and the Grange, and sometimes reading Scripture from the pulpit Sunday mornings. Jack, sitting rigid, hands over his face, was bitterly ashamed of those poems and recitations from the Bible. His father's eyes no longer flashed, he no longer had the style of an actor. Even his gestures were submissive, as pliant as the grass. Though tears ran down Jack Hawthorne's face—no one would deny that his father was still effective, reading carefully, lest his voice should break. "Tomorrow's Bridge" and "This Too Will Pass"—Jack scorned the poems' opinions, scorned the way his father spoke directly to each listener, as if each were some new woman, his father some mere suffering sheep among sheep, and scorned the way Phoebe and his mother looked on smiling, furtively weeping, heads lifted. Sometimes his father would recite a poem that Jack himself had written, in the days when he'd tried to write poetry, a comic limerick or some maudlin piece about a boy on a hill. Though it was meant as a compliment, Jack's heart would swell with rage; yet he kept silent, more private than before. At night he'd go out to the cavernous haymow or up into the orchard and practice his French horn. One of these days, he told himself, they'd wake up and find him gone.

He used the horn more and more now to escape their herding warmth. Those around him were conscious enough of what was happening—his parents and Phoebe, his uncles, aunts, and cousins, his mother's many friends. But there was nothing they could do. "That horn's his whole world," his mother often said, smiling but clasping her hands together. Soon he was playing third horn with the Batavia Civic Orchestra, though he refused to play in church or when company came. He began to ride the Bluebus to Rochester, Saturdays, to take lessons from Arcady Yegudkin, "the General," at the Eastman School of Music.

Yegudkin was seventy. He'd played principal horn in the orchestra of Czar Nikolai and at the time of the Revolution had escaped, with his wife, in a dramatic way. At the time of the purge of Kerenskyites, the Bolsheviks had loaded Yegudkin and his wife, along with hundreds more, onto railroad flatcars, reportedly to carry them to Siberia. In a desolate place, machine guns opened fire on the people on the flatcars, then soldiers pushed the bodies into a ravine, and the train moved on. The soldiers were not careful to see that everyone was dead. Perhaps they did not relish their work; in any case, they must have believed that, in a place so remote, a wounded survivor would have no chance against wolves and cold weather. The General and his wife were among the few who lived, he virtually unmarked, she horribly crippled. Local peasants nursed the few survivors back to health, and in time the Yegudkins escaped to Europe. There Yegudkin played horn with all the great orchestras and received such praise—so he claimed, spreading out his clippings—as no other master of French horn had received in all history. He would beam as he said it, his Tartar eyes flashing, and his smile was like a thrown-down gauntlet.

He was a barrel-shaped, solidly muscular man, hard as a boulder for all his age. His hair and moustache were as black as coal except for touches of silver, especially where it grew, with majestic indifference to ordinary taste, from his cavernous nostrils and large, dusty-looking ears. The sides of his moustache were carefully curled, in the fashion once favored by Russian dandies, and he was one of the last men in Rochester, New York, to wear spats. He wore formal black suits, a huge black overcoat, and a black fedora. His wife, who came with him and sat on the long maple bench outside his door, never reading or knitting or doing anything at all except that sometimes she would speak unintelligibly to a student—Yegudkin's wife, shriveled and twisted, watched him as if worshipfully, hanging on his words. She looked at least twice the old man's age. Her hair was snow white and she wore lumpy black shoes and long black shapeless dresses. The two of them would come, every Saturday morning, down the long marble hall-way of the second floor of Killburn Hall, the General erect and imperious, like some sharp-eyed old Slavonic king, moving slowly, waiting for the old woman who crept beside him, gray claws on his coat sleeve, and seeing Jack Hawthorne seated on the bench, his books and French horn in its tattered black case on the floor beside him, the General would extend his left arm and boom, "Goot mworning!"

Jack, rising, would say, "Morning, sir."

"You have met my wife?" the old man would say then, bowing and taking the cigar from his mouth. He asked it each Saturday.

"Yes, sir. How do you do?"

The old man was too deaf to play in orchestras anymore. "What's the difference?" he said. "Every symphony in America, they got Yegudkins. I have teach them all. Who teach you this? *The General!*" He would smile, chin lifted, triumphant, and salute the ceiling.

He would sit in the chair beside Jack's and would sing, with violent gestures and a great upward leap of the belly to knock out the high B's and C's—*Tee! Tee!*—as Jack read through Kopprasch, Gallay, and Kling, and when it was time to give Jack's lip a rest, the General would speak earnestly, with the same energy he put into his singing, of the United States and his beloved Russia that he would nevermore see. The world was at that time filled with Russophobes. Yegudkin, whenever he read a paper, would be so enraged he could barely contain himself. "In all my age," he often said, furiously gesturing with his black cigar, "if the Russians would come to this country of America, I would take up a rifle and shot at them—*boof!* But the newspapers telling you lies, all lies! You think them dumb fools, these Russians? You think they are big, fat bush-overs?" He spoke of mile-long parades of weapon-ry, spoke of Russian cunning, spoke with great scorn, a sudden booming laugh, of Napoleon. Jack agreed with a nod to whatever the General said. Nevertheless, the old man roared on, taking great pleasure in his rage, it seemed, sometimes talking like a rabid communist, sometimes like a fascist, sometimes like a citizen helplessly caught between mindless, grinding forces, vast, idiot herds. The truth was, he hated both Russians and Americans about equally, cared only for music, his students and, possibly, his wife.

In his pockets, in scorn of the opinions of fools, he carried condoms, dirty pictures, and grimy, wadded-up dollar bills.

One day a new horn he'd ordered from Germany, an Alexander, arrived at his office—a horn he'd gotten for a graduate student. The old man unwrapped and assembled it, the graduate student looking on—a shy young man, blond, in a limp gray sweater—and the glint in the General's eye was like madness or at any rate lust, perhaps gluttony. When the horn was ready he went to the desk where he kept his clippings, his tools for the cleaning and repair of French horns, his cigars, photographs, and medals from the Czar, and pulled open a wide, shallow drawer. It contained perhaps a hundred mouthpieces, of all sizes and materials, from raw brass to lucite, silver, and gold, from the shallowest possible cup to the deepest. He selected one, fitted it into the horn, pressed the rim of the bell into the right side of his large belly—the horn seemed now as much a part of him as his arm or leg—clicked the shining keys to get the feel of them, then played. In that large, cork-lined room, it was as if, suddenly, a creature from some other universe had appeared, some realm where feelings become birds and dark sky, and spirit is more solid than stone. The sound was not so much loud as large, too large for a hundred French horns, it seemed. He began to play now not single notes but, to Jack's astonishment, chords—two notes at a time, then three. He began to play runs. As if charged with life independent of the man, the horn sound fluttered and flew crazily, like an enormous trapped hawk hunting frantically for escape. It flew to the bottom of the lower register, the foundation concert F, and crashed below it, and on down and down, as if the horn in Yegudkin's hands had no bottom, then suddenly changed its mind and flew upward in a split-second run to the horn's top E, dropped back to the middle and then ran once more, more fiercely at the E, and this time burst through it and fluttered, manic, in the trumpet range, then lightly dropped back into its own home range and, abruptly, in the middle of a note, stopped. The room still rang, shimmered like a vision.

"Good horn," said Yegudkin, and held the horn toward the graduate student, who sat, hands clamped on his knees, as if in a daze.

Jack Hawthorne stared at the instrument suspended in space and at his teacher's hairy hands. Before stopping to think, he said, "You think I'll ever play like that?"

Yegudkin laughed loudly, his black eyes widening, and it seemed that he grew larger, beatific and demonic at once, like the music; overwhelming. "Play like *me*?" he exclaimed.

Jack blinked, startled by the bluntness of the thing, the terrible lack of malice, and the truth of it. His face tingled and his legs went weak, as if the life were rushing out of them. He longed to be away from there, far away, safe. Perhaps Yegudkin sensed it. He turned gruff, sending away the graduate student, then finishing up the lesson. He said nothing, today, of the stupidity of mankind. When the lesson was over he saw Jack to the door and bid him goodbye with a brief half-smile that was perhaps not for Jack at all but for the creature on the bench. "Next Saturday?" he said, as if there might be some doubt.

Jack nodded, blushing.

At the door opening on the street he began to breathe more easily, though he was weeping. He set down the horn case to brush away his tears. The sidewalk was crowded—dazed-looking Saturday-morning shoppers herding along irritably, meekly, through painfully bright light. Again he brushed tears away. He'd been late for his bus. Then the crowd opened for him and, with the horn cradled under his right arm, his music under his left, he plunged in, starting home.

Barry Hannah

Testimony of Pilot

When I was ten, eleven and twelve, I did a good bit of my play in the backyard of a three-story wooden house my father had bought and rented out, his first venture into real estate. We lived right across the street from it, but over here was the place to do your real play. Here there was a harrowed but overgrown garden, a vine-swallowed fence at the back end, and beyond the fence a cornfield which belonged to someone else. This was not the country. This was the town, Clinton, Mississippi, between Jackson on the east and Vicksburg on the west. On this lot stood a few water oaks, a few plum bushes, and much overgrowth of honey-suckle vine. At the very back end, at the fence, stood three strong nude chinaberry trees.

In Mississippi it is difficult to achieve a vista. But my friends and I had one here at the back corner of the garden. We could see across the cornfield, see the one lone tin-roofed house this side of the railroad tracks, then on across the tracks many other bleaker houses with rustier tin roofs, smoke coming out of the chimneys in the late fall. This was niggertown. We had binoculars and could see the colored children hustling about and perhaps a hopeless sow or two with her brood enclosed in a tiny boarded-up area. Through the binoculars one afternoon in October we watched some men corner and beat a large hog on the brain. They used an ax and the thing kept running around, head leaning toward the ground, for several minutes before it lay down. I thought I saw the men laughing when it finally did. One of them was staggering,

75

plainly drunk to my sight from three hundred yards away. He had the long knife. Because of that scene I considered Negroes savage cowards for a good five more years of my life. Our maid brought some sausage to my mother and when it was put in the pan to fry, I made a point of running out of the house.

I went directly across the street and to the back end of the garden behind the apartment house we owned, without my breakfast. That was Saturday. Eventually, Radcleve saw me. His parents had him mowing the yard that ran alongside my dad's property. He clicked off the power mower and I went over to his fence, which was storm wire. His mother maintained handsome flowery grounds at all costs; she had a leaf mold bin and St. Augustine grass as solid as a rug.

Radcleve himself was a violent experimental chemist. When Radcleve was eight, he threw a whole package of .22 shells against the sidewalk in front of his house until one of them went off, driving lead fragments into his calf, most of them still deep in there where the surgeons never dared tamper. Radcleve knew about the sulfur, potassium nitrate and charcoal mixture for gunpowder when he was ten. He bought things through the mail when he ran out of ingredients in his chemistry sets. When he was an infant, his father, a quiet man who owned the Chevrolet agency in town, bought an entire bankrupt sporting-goods store, and in the middle of their backyard he built a house, plain-painted and neat, one room and a heater, where Radcleve's redundant toys forevermore were kept—all the possible toys he would need for boyhood. There were things in there that Radcleve and I were not mature enough for and did not know the real use of. When we were eleven, we uncrated the new Dunlop golf balls and went on up on a shelf for the tennis rackets, went out in the middle of his yard, and served new golf ball after new golf ball with blasts of the rackets over into the cornfield, out of sight. When the strings busted we just went in and got another racket. We were absorbed by how a good smack would set the heavy little pills on an endless flight. Then Radcleve's father came down. He simply dismissed me. He took Radcleve into the house and covered his whole body with a belt. But within the week Radcleve had invented the mortar. It was a steel pipe into which a flashlight battery fit perfectly, like a bullet into a muzzle. He had drilled a hole for the fuse of an M-80 firecracker at the base, for the charge. It was a grand cannon, set up on a stack of bricks at the back of my dad's property, which was the free place to play. When it shot, it would back up violently with thick smoke and you could hear the flashlight battery whistling off. So that morning when I ran out of the house protesting the hog sausage, I told Radcleve to bring over the mortar. His ma and dad were in Jackson for the day, and he came right over with the pipe, the batteries and the M–80 explosives. He had two gross of them.

Before, we'd shot off toward the woods to the right of nigger-town. I turned the bricks to the left; I made us a very fine cannon carriage pointing toward niggertown. When Radcleve appeared, he had two pairs of binoculars around his neck, one pair a newly plundered German unit as big as a brace of whiskey bottles. I told him I wanted to shoot for that house where we saw them killing the pig. Radcleve loved the idea. We singled out the house with heavy use of the binoculars.

There were children in the yard. Then they all went in. Two men came out of the back door. I thought I recognized the drunk-ard from the other afternoon. I helped Radcleve fix the direction of the cannon. We estimated the altitude we needed to get down there. Radcleve put the M–80 in the breech with its fuse standing out of the hole. I dropped the flashlight battery in. I lit the fuse. We backed off. The M–80 blasted off deafeningly, smoke rose, but my concentration was on that particular house over there. I brought the binoculars. We waited six or seven seconds. I heard a great joyful wallop on tin. "We've hit him on the first try, the first try!" I yelled. Radcleve was ecstatic. "Right on his roof!" We bolstered up the brick carriage. Radcleve remembered the correct height of the cannon exactly. So we fixed it, loaded it, lit it and backed off. The battery landed on the roof, blat, again, louder. I looked to see if there wasn't a great dent or hole in the roof. I could not understand why niggers weren't pouring out distraught from that house. We shot the mortar again and again, and always our battery hit the tin roof. Sometimes there was only a dull thud, but other times there was a wild distress of tin. I was still looking through the binoculars, amazed that the niggers wouldn't even come out of their house to see what was hitting their roof. Radcleve was on to it better than me. I looked over at him and he had the huge German binocs much lower than I did. He was looking straight through the cornfield, which was all bare and open, with nothing left but rotten stalks. "What we've been hitting is the roof of that house just this side of the tracks. White people live in there," he said.

I took up my binoculars again. I looked around the yard of that white wooden house on this side of the tracks, almost next to the railroad. When I found the tin roof, I saw four significant dents in it. I saw one of our batteries lying in the middle of a sort of crater. I took the binoculars down into the yard and saw a

77

blond middle-aged woman looking our way.

"Somebody's coming up toward us. He's from that house and he's got, I think, some sort of fancy gun with him. It might be an automatic weapon."

I ran my binoculars all over the cornfield. Then, in a line with the house, I saw him. He was coming our way but having some trouble with the rows and dead stalks of the cornfield.

"That is just a boy like us. All he's got is a saxophone with him," I told Radcleve. I had recently got in the school band, playing drums, and had seen all the weird horns that made up a band.

I watched this boy with the saxophone through the binoculars until he was ten feet from us. This was Quadberry. His name was Ard, short for Arden. His shoes were foot-square wads of mud from the cornfield. When he saw us across the fence and above him, he stuck out his arm in my direction.

"My dad says stop it!"

"We weren't doing anything," says Radcleve.

"Mother saw the smoke puff up from here. Dad has a hangover."

"A what?"

"It's a headache from indiscretion. You're lucky he does. He's picked up the poker to rap on you, but he can't move further the way his head is."

"What's your name? You're not in the band," I said, focusing on the saxophone.

"It's Ard Quadberry. Why do you keep looking at me through the binoculars?"

It was because he was odd, with his hair and its white ends, and his Arab nose, and now his name. Add to that the saxophone.

"My dad's a doctor at the college. Mother's a musician. You better quit what you're doing . . . . I was out practicing in the garage. I saw one of those flashlight batteries roll off the roof. Could I see what you shoot 'em with?"

"No," said Radcleve. Then he said: "If you'll play that horn."

Quadberry stood out there ten feet below us in the field, skinny, feet and pants booted with black mud, and at his chest the slung-on, very complex, radiant horn.

Quadberry began sucking and licking the reed. I didn't care much for this act, and there was too much desperate oralness in his face when he began playing. That was why I chose the drums. One had to engage himself like suck's revenge with a horn. But what Quadberry was playing was pleasant and intricate. I was sure it was advanced, and there was no squawking, as from the other eleven-year-olds on sax in the band room. He made the end with a clean upward riff, holding the final note high, pure and unwavering.

"Good!" I called to him.

Quadberry was trying to move out of the sunken row toward us, but his heavy shoes were impeding him.

"Sounded like a duck. Sounded like a girl duck," said Radcleve, who was kneeling down and packing a mudball around one of the M-80s. I saw and I was an accomplice, because I did nothing. Radcleve lit the fuse and heaved the mudball over the fence. An M-80 is a very serious firecracker; it is like the charge they use to shoot up those sprays six hundred feet on July Fourth at country clubs. It went off, this one, even bigger than most M-80s.

When we looked over the fence, we saw Quadberry all muck specks and fragments of stalks. He was covering the mouthpiece of his horn with both hands. Then I saw there was blood pouring out of, it seemed, his right eye. I thought he was bleeding directly out of his eye.

"Quadberry?" I called.

He turned around and never said a word to me until I was eighteen. He walked back holding his eye and staggering through the cornstalks. Radcleve had him in the binoculars. Radcleve was trembling . . . but intrigued.

"His mother just screamed. She's running out in the field to get him."

I thought we'd blinded him, but we hadn't. I thought the Quadberrys would get the police or call my father, but they didn't. The upshot of this is that Quadberry had a permanent white space next to his right eye, a spot that looked like a tiny upset crown.

I went from sixth through half of twelfth grade ignoring him and that wound. I was coming on as a drummer and a lover, but if Quadberry happened to appear within fifty feet of me and my most tender, intimate sweetheart, I would duck out. Quadberry grew up just like the rest of us. His father was still a doctor—professor of history—at the town college; his mother was still blond, and a musician. She was organist at an Episcopalian church in Jackson, the big capital city ten miles east of us.

As for Radcleve, he still had no ear for music, but he was there, my buddy. He was repentant about Quadberry, although not so much as I. He'd thrown the mud grenade over the fence only to see what would happen. He had not really wanted to maim. Quadberry had played his tune on the sax, Radcleve had played his tune on the mud grenade. It was just a shame they happened to cross talents.

Radcleve went into a long period of nearly nothing after he gave up violent explosives. Then he trained himself to copy the comic strips, *Steve Canyon* to *Major Hoople*, until he became quite a versatile cartoonist with some very provocative new faces and bodies that were gesturing intriguingly. He could never fill in the speech balloons with the smart words they needed. Sometimes he would pencil in "Err" or "What?" in the empty speech places. I saw him a great deal. Radcleve was not spooked by Quadberry. He even once asked Quadberry what his opinion was of his future as a cartoonist. Quadberry told Radcleve that if he took all his cartoons and stuffed himself with them, he would make an interesting dead man. After that, Radcleve was shy of him too.

When I was a senior we had an extraordinary band. Word was we had outplayed all the big A.A.A. division bands last April in the state contest. Then came news that a new blazing saxophone player was coming into the band as first chair. This person had spent summers in Vermont in music camps, and he was coming in with us for the concert season. Our director, a lovable aesthete named Richard Prender, announced to us in a proud silent moment that the boy was joining us tomorrow night. The effect was that everybody should push over a seat or two and make room for this boy and his talent. I was annoyed. Here I'd been with the band and had kept hold of the taste among the whole percussion section. I could play rock and jazz drum and didn't even really need to be here. I could be in Vermont too, give me a piano and a bass. I looked at the kid on first sax, who was going to be supplanted tomorrow. For two years he had thought he was the star, then suddenly enters this boy who's three times better.

The new boy was Quadberry. He came in, but he was meek, and when he tuned up he put his head almost on the floor, bending over trying to be inconspicuous. The girls in the band had wanted him to be handsome, but Quadberry refused and kept himself in such hiding among the sax section that he was neither handsome, ugly, cute or anything. What he was was pretty near invisible, except for the bell of his horn, the all-but-closed eyes, the Arabian nose, the brown hair with its halo of white ends, the desperate oralness, the giant reed punched into his face, and hazy Quadberry, loving the wound in a private dignified ecstasy.

I say dignified because of what came out of the end of his horn. He was more than what Prender had told us he would be. Because of Quadberry, we could take the band arrangement of

Ravel's *Bolero* with us to the state contest. Quadberry would do the saxophone solo. He would switch to alto sax, he would do the sly Moorish ride. When he played, I heard the sweetness, I heard the horn which finally brought human *talk* into the realm of music. It could sound like the mutterings of a field nigger, and then it could get up into inhumanly careless beauty, it could get among mutinous helium bursts around Saturn. I already loved *Bolero* for the constant drum part. The percussion was always there, driving along with the subtly increasing triplets, insistent, insistent, at last outraged and trying to steal the whole show from the horns and the others. I knew a large boy with dirty blond hair, name of Wyatt, who played viola in the Jackson Symphony and sousaphone in our band—one of the rare closet transmutations of my time—who was forever claiming to have discovered the central *Bolero* one Sunday afternoon over FM radio as he had seven distinct sexual moments with a certain B., girl flutist with black bangs and skin like mayonnaise, while the drums of Ravel carried them on and on in a ceremony of Spanish sex. It was agreed by all the canny in the band that *Bolero* was exactly the piece to make the band soar—now especially as we had Quadberry, who made his walk into the piece like an actual lean Spanish bandit. This boy could blow his horn. He was, as I had suspected, a genius. His solo was not quite the same as the New York Phil's saxophonist's, but it was better. It came in and was with us. It entered my spine and, I am sure, went up the skirts of the girls. I had almost deafened myself playing drums in the most famous rock and jazz band in the state, but I could hear the voice that went through and out that horn. It sounded like a very troubled forty-year-old man, a man who had had his brow in his hands a long time.

The next time I saw Quadberry up close, in fact the first time I had seen him up close since we were eleven and he was bleeding in the cornfield, was in late February. I had only three classes this last semester, and went up to the band room often, to loaf and complain and keep up my touch on the drums. Prender let me keep my set in one of the instrument rooms, with a tarpaulin thrown over it, and I would drag it out to the practice room and whale away. Sometimes a group of sophomores would come up and I would make them marvel, whaling away as if not only deaf but blind to them, although I wasn't at all. If I saw a sophomore girl with exceptional bod or face, I would do miracles of technique I never knew were in me. I would amaze myself. I would be threatening Buddy Rich and Sam Morello. But this time when I went into the instrument room, there was Quadberry on one side, and, back in a dark corner, a small ninth-grade euphonium player whose face was all red. The little boy was weeping and grinning at the same time.

"Queerberry," the boy said softly.

Quadberry flew upon him like a demon. He grabbed the boy's collar, slapped his face, and yanked his arm behind him in a merciless wrestler's grip, the one that made them bawl on TV. Then the boy broke it and slugged Quadberry in the lips and ran across to my side of the room. He said "Queerberry" softly again and jumped for the door. Quadberry plunged across the room and tackled him on the threshold. Now that the boy was under him, Quadberry pounded the top of his head with his fist made like a mallet. The boy kept calling him "Queerberry" throughout this. He had not learned his lesson. The boy seemed to be going into concussion, so I stepped over and touched Quadberry, telling him to quit. Quadberry obeyed and stood up off the boy, who crawled on out into the band room. But once more the boy looked back with a bruised grin, saying "Queerberry." Quadberry made a move toward him, but I blocked it.

"Why are you beating up on this little guy?" I said. Quadberry was sweating and his eyes were wild with hate; he was a big fellow now, though lean. He was, at six feet tall, bigger than me.

"He kept calling me Queerberry."

"What do you care?" I asked.

"I care," Quadberry said, and left me standing there.

We were to play at Millsaps College Auditorium for the concert. It was April. We got on the buses, a few took their cars, and were a big tense crowd getting over there. To Jackson was only a twenty-minute trip. The director, Prender, followed the bus in his Volkswagen. There was a thick fog. A flashing ambulance, snaking the lanes, piled into him head on. Prender, who I would imagine was thinking of *Bolero* and hearing the young horn voices in his band—perhaps he was dwelling on Quadberry's spectacular gypsy entrance, or perhaps he was meditating on the percussion section, of which I was the king—passed into the airs of band-director heaven. We were told by the student director as we set up on the stage. The student director was a senior from the town college, very much afflicted, almost to the point of drooling, by a love and respect for Dick Prender, and now afflicted by a heartbreaking esteem for his ghost. As were we all.

I loved the tough and tender director awesomely and never knew it until I found myself bawling along with all the rest of the boys of the percussion. I told them to keep setting up, keep tuning, keep screwing the stands together, keep hauling in the kettledrums. To just quit and bawl seemed a betrayal to Prender. I caught some girl clarinetists trying to flee the stage and go have their cry. I told them to get the hell back to their section. They obeyed me. Then I found the student director. I had to have my say.

"Look. I say we just play *Bolero* and junk the rest. That's our horse. We can't play *Brighton Beach* and *Neptune's Daughter.* We'll never make it through them. And they're too happy."

"We aren't going to play anything," he said. "Man, to play is filthy. Did you ever hear Prender play piano? Do you know what a cool man he was in all things?"

"We play. He got us ready, and we play."

"Man, you can't play any more than I can direct. You're bawling your face off. Look out there at the rest of them. Man, it's a herd, it's a weeping herd."

"What's wrong? Why aren't you pulling this crowd together?" This was Quadberry, who had come up urgently. "I got those little brats in my section sitting down, but we've got people abandoning the stage, tearful little finks throwing their horns on the floor."

"I'm not directing," said the mustached college man.

"Then get out of here. You're weak, weak!"

"Man, we've got teen-agers in ruin here, we got sorrowville. Nobody can—"

"Go ahead. Do your number. Weak out on us."

"Man, I—"

Quadberry was already up on the podium, shaking his arms.

"We're right here! The band is right here! Tell your friends to get back in their seats. We're doing *Bolero.* Just put *Bolero* up and start tuning. *I'm* directing. I'll be right here in front of you. You look at *me*! Don't you dare quit on Prender. Don't you dare quit on me. You've got to be heard. *I've* got to be heard. Prender wanted me to be heard. I am the star, and I say we sit down and blow."

And so we did. We all tuned and were burning low for the advent into *Bolero,* though we couldn't believe that Quadberry was going to remain with his saxophone strapped to him and conduct us as well as play his solo. The judges, who apparently hadn't heard about Prender's death, walked down to their balcony desks.

One of them called out "Ready" and Quadberry's hand was instantly up in the air, his fingers hard as if around the stem of something like a torch. This was not Prender's way, but it had to do. We went into the number cleanly and Quadberry one-armed it in the conducting. He kept his face, this look of hostility, at the reeds and the trumpets. I was glad he did not look toward me and the percussion boys like that. But he must have known we would be constant and tasteful because I was the king there. As for the others, the soloists especially, he was scaring them into excellence. Prender had never got quite this from them. Boys became men and girls became women as Quadberry directed us through *Bolero*. I even became a bit better of a man myself, though Quadberry did not look my way. When he turned around toward the people in the auditorium to enter on his solo, I knew it was my baby. I and the drums were the metronome. That was no trouble. It was talent to keep the metronome ticking amidst any given chaos of sound.

But this keeps one's mind occupied and I have no idea what Quadberry sounded like on his sax ride. All I know is that he looked grief-stricken and pale, and small. Sweat had popped out on his forehead. He bent over extremely. He was wearing the red brass-button jacket and black pants, black bow tie at the throat, just like the rest of us. In this outfit he bent over his horn almost out of sight. For a moment, before I caught the glint of his horn through the music stands, I thought he had pitched forward off the stage. He went down so far to do his deep oral thing, his conducting arm had disappeared so quickly, I didn't know but what he was having a seizure.

When *Bolero* was over, the audience stood up and made meat out of their hands applauding. The judges themselves applauded. The band stood up, bawling again, for Prender and because we had done so well. The student director rushed out crying to embrace Quadberry, who eluded him with his dipping shoulders. The crowd was still clapping insanely. I wanted to see Quadberry myself. I waded through the red backs, through the bow ties, over the white bucks. Here was the first-chair clarinetist, who had done his bit like an angel; he sat close to the podium and could hear Quadberry.

"Was Quadberry good?" I asked him.

"Are you kidding? These tears in my eyes, they're for how good he was. He was too good. I'll never touch my clarinet again." The clarinetist slung the pieces of his horn into their case like underwear and a toothbrush.

I found Quadberry fitting the sections of his alto in the velvet holds of his case.

"Hooray," I said. "Hip damn hooray for you."

Arden was smiling too, showing a lot of teeth I had never seen. His smile was sly. He knew he had pulled off a monster unlikelihood.

"Hip hip hooray for me," he said. "Look at her. I had the bell of the horn almost smack in her face."

There was a woman of about thirty sitting in the front row of the auditorium. She wore a sundress with a drastic cleavage up front; looked like something that hung around New Orleans and kneaded your heart to death with her feet. She was still mesmerized by Quadberry. She bore on him with a stare and there was moisture in her cleavage.

"You played well."

"Well? Play well? Yes."

He was trying not to look at her directly. Look at *me*, I beckoned to her with full face: I was the *drums*. She arose and left.

"I was walking downhill in a valley, is all I was doing," said Quadberry. "Another man, a wizard, was playing my horn." He locked his sax case. "I feel nasty for not being able to cry like the rest of them. Look at them. Look at them crying."

True, the children of the band were still weeping, standing around the stage. Several moms and dads had come up among them, and they were misty-eyed too. The mixture of grief and superb music had been unbearable.

A girl in tears appeared next to Quadberry. She was a majorette in football season and played third-chair sax during the concert season. Not even her violent sorrow could take the beauty out of the face of this girl. I had watched her for a number of years—her alertness to her own beauty, the pride of her legs in the majorette outfit—and had taken out her younger sister, a second-rate version of her and a wayward overcompensating nymphomaniac whom several of us made a hobby out of pitying. Well, here was Lilian herself crying in Quadberry's face. She told him that she'd run off the stage when she heard about Prender, dropped her horn and everything, and had thrown herself into a tavern across the street and drunk two beers quickly for some kind of relief. But she had come back through the front doors of the auditorium and sat down, dizzy with beer, and seen Quadberry, the miraculous way he had gone on with *Bolero*. And now she was eaten up by feelings of guilt, weakness, cowardice.

"We didn't miss you," said Quadberry.

"Please forgive me. Tell me to do something to make up for it."

"Don't breathe my way, then. You've got beer all over your breath."

"I want to talk to you."

"Take my horn case and go out, get in my car, and wait for me. It's the ugly Plymouth in front of the school bus."

"I know," she said.

Lilian Field, this lovely teary thing, with the rather pious grace of her carriage, with the voice full of imminent swoon, picked up Quadberry's horn case and her own and walked off the stage.

I told the percussion boys to wrap up the packing. Into my suitcase I put my own gear and also managed to steal drum keys, two pairs of brushes, a twenty-inch Turkish cymbal, a Gretsch snare drum that I desired for my collection, a wood block, kettledrum mallets, a tuning harp and a score sheet of *Bolero* full of marginal notes I'd written down straight from the mouth of Dick Prender, thinking I might want to look at the score sheet sometime in the future when I was having a fit of nostalgia such as I am having right now as I write this. I had never done any serious stealing before, and I was stealing for my art. Prender was dead, the band had done its last thing of the year, I was a senior. Things were finished at the high school. I was just looting a sinking ship. I could hardly lift the suitcase. As I was pushing it across the stage, Quadberry was there again.

"You can ride back with me if you want to."

"But you've got Lilian."

"Please ride back with me . . . us. Please."

"Why?"

"To help me get rid of her. Her breath is full of beer. My father always had that breath. Every time he was friendly, he had that breath. And she looks a great deal like my mother." We were interrupted by the Tupelo band director. He put his baton against Quadberry's arm.

"You were big with *Bolero*, son, but that doesn't mean you own the stage."

Quadberry caught the end of the suitcase and helped me with it out to the steps behind the auditorium. The buses were gone. There sat his ugly ocher Plymouth; it was a failed, gay, experimental shade from the Chrysler people. Lilian was sitting in the front seat wearing her shirt and bow tie, her coat off.

"Are you going to ride back with me?" Quadberry said to me.

"I think I would spoil something. You never saw her when she was a majorette. She's not stupid, either. She likes to show off a little, but she's not stupid. She's in the History Club."

"My father has a doctorate in history. She smells of beer."

I said, "She drank two cans of beer when she heard about Prender."

"There are a lot of other things to do when you hear about death. What I did, for example. She ran away. She fell to pieces."

"She's waiting for us," I said.

"One damned thing I am never going to do is drink."

"I've never seen your mother up close, but Lilian doesn't look like your mother. She doesn't look like anybody's mother."

I rode with them silently to Clinton. Lilian made no bones about being disappointed I was in the car, though she said nothing. I knew it would be like this and I hated it. Other girls in town would not be so unhappy that I was in the car with them. I looked for flaws in Lilian's face and neck and hair, but there weren't any. Couldn't there be a mole, an enlarged pore, too much gum on a tooth, a single awkward hair around the ear? No. Memory, the whole lying opera of it, is killing me now. Lilian was faultless beauty, even sweating, even and especially in the white man's shirt and the bow tie clamping together her collar, when one knew her uncomfortable bosoms, her poor nipples. . . .

"Don't take me back to the band room. Turn off here and let me off at my house," I said to Quadberry. He didn't turn off.

"Don't tell Arden what to do. He can do what he wants to," said Lilian, ignoring me and speaking to me at the same time. I couldn't bear her hatred. I asked Quadberry to please just stop the car and let me out here, wherever he was: this front yard of the mobile home would do. I was so earnest that he stopped the car. He handed back the keys and I dragged my suitcase out of the trunk, then flung the keys back at him and kicked the car to get it going again.

My band came together in the summer. We were the Bop Fiends . . . that was our name. Two of them were from Ole Miss, our bass player was from Memphis State, but when we got together this time, I didn't call the tenor sax, who went to Mississippi Southern, because Quadberry wanted to play with us. During the school year the college boys and I fell into minor groups to pick up twenty dollars on a weekend, playing dances for the Moose Lodge, medical-student fraternities in Jackson, teen-age recreation centers in Greenwood, and such as that. But come summer we were the Bop Fiends again, and the price for us went up to $1,200 a gig. Where they wanted the best rock and bop and they had some bread, we were called. The summer after I was a senior, we played in Alabama, Louisiana and Arkansas. Our fame was getting out there on the interstate route.

This was the summer that I made myself deaf.

Years ago Prender had invited down an old friend from a high school in Michigan. He asked me over to meet the friend, who had been a drummer with Stan Kenton at one time and was now a band director just like Prender. This fellow was almost totally deaf and he warned me very sincerely about deafing myself. He said there would come a point when you had to lean over and concentrate all your hearing on what the band was doing and that was the time to quit for a while, because if you didn't you would be irrevocably deaf like him in a month or two. I listened to him but could not take him seriously. Here was an oldish man who had his problems. My ears had ages of hearing left. Not so. I played the drums so loud the summer after I graduated from high school that I made myself, eventually, stone deaf.

We were at, say, the National Guard Armory in Lake Village, Arkansas, Quadberry out in front of us on the stage they'd built. Down on the floor were hundreds of sweaty teen-agers. Four girls in sundresses, showing what they could, were leaning on the stage with broad ignorant lust on their minds. I'd play so loud for one particular chick, I'd get absolutely out of control. The guitar boys would have to turn the volume up full blast to compensate. Thus I went deaf. Anyhow, the dramatic idea was to release Quadberry on a very soft sweet ballad right in the middle of a long ear-piercing run of rock-and-roll tunes. I'd get out the brushes and we would astonish the crowd with our tenderness. By August, I was so deaf I had to watch Quadberry's fingers changing notes on the saxophone, had to use my eyes to keep time. The other members of the Bop Fiends told me I was hitting out of time. I pretended I was trying to do experimental things with rhythm when the truth was I simply could no longer hear. I was no longer a tasteful drummer, either. I had become deaf through lack of taste.

Which was—taste—exactly the quality that made Quadberry wicked on the saxophone. During the howling, during the churning, Quadberry had taste. The noise did not affect his personality; he was solid as a brick. He could blend. Oh, he could hoot through his horn when the right time came, but he could do supporting roles for an hour. Then, when we brought him out front for his solo on something like "Take Five," he would play with such light blissful technique that he even eclipsed Paul Desmond. The girls around the stage did not cause him to enter into excessive loudness or vibrato.

Quadberry had his own girl friend now, Lilian back at Clinton, who put all the sundressed things around the stage in the shade. In my mind I had congratulated him for getting up next to this beauty, but in June and July, when I was still hearing things a little, he never said a word about her. It was one night in August, when I could hear nothing and was driving him to his house, that he asked me to turn off the inside light and spoke in a retarded deliberate way. He knew I was deaf and counted on my being able to read lips.

"Don't . . . make . . . fun . . . of her . . . or me. . . . We . . . think . . . she . . . is . . . in trouble."

I wagged my head. Never would I make fun of him or her. She detested me because I had taken out her helpless little sister for a few weeks, but I would never think there was anything funny about Lilian, for all her haughtiness. I only thought of this event as monumentally curious.

"No one except you knows," he said.

"Why did you tell me?"

"Because I'm going away and you have to take care of her. I wouldn't trust her with anybody but you."

"She hates the sight of my face. Where are you going?"

"Annapolis."

"You aren't going to any damned Annapolis."

"That was the only school that wanted me."

"You're going to play your saxophone on a boat?"

"I don't know what I'm going to do."

"How . . . how can you just leave her?"

"She wants me to. She's very excited about me at Annapolis. William [this is my name], there is no girl I could imagine who has more inner sweetness than Lilian."

I entered the town college, as did Lilian. She was in the same chemistry class I was. But she was rows away. It was difficult to learn anything, being deaf. The professor wasn't a pantomimer—but finally he went to the blackboard with the formulas and the algebra of problems, to my happiness. I hung in and made a B. At the end of the semester I was swaggering around the grade sheet he'd posted. I happened to see Lilian's grade. She'd only made a C. Beautiful Lilian got only a C while I, with my handicap, had made a B.

It had been a very difficult chemistry class. I had watched Lilian's stomach the whole way through. It was not growing. I wanted to see her look like a watermelon, make herself an amazing mother shape.

When I made the B and Lilian made the C, I got up my courage and finally went to see her. She answered the door. Her parents weren't home. I'd never wanted this office of watching over her as Quadberry wanted me to, and this is what I told her. She asked me into the house. The rooms smelled of nail polish and pipe smoke. I was hoping her little sister wasn't in the house, and my wish came true. We were alone.

"You can quit watching over me."

"Are you pregnant?"

"No." Then she started crying. "I wanted to be. But I'm not."

"What do you hear from Quadberry?"

She said something, but she had her back to me. She looked to me for an answer, but I had nothing to say. I knew she'd said something, but I hadn't heard it.

"He doesn't play the saxophone anymore," she said.

This made me angry.

"Why not?"

"Too much math and science and navigation. He wants to fly. That's what his dream is now. He wants to get into an F-something jet."

I asked her to say this over and she did. Lilian really was full of inner sweetness, as Quadberry had said. She understood that I was deaf. Perhaps Quadberry had told her.

The rest of the time in her house I simply witnessed her beauty and her mouth moving.

I went through college. To me it is interesting that I kept a B average and did it all deaf, though I know this isn't interesting to people who aren't deaf. I loved music, and never heard it. I loved poetry, and never heard a word that came out of the mouths of the visiting poets who read at the campus. I loved my mother and dad, but never heard a sound they made. One Christmas Eve, Radcleve was back from Ole Miss and threw an M–80 out in the street for old times' sake. I saw it explode, but there was only a pressure in my ears. I was at parties when lusts were raging and I went home with two girls (I am medium handsome) who lived in apartments of the old two-story 1920 vintage, and I took my shirt off and made love to them. But I have no real idea what their reaction was. They were stunned and all smiles when I got up, but I have no idea whether I gave them the last pleasure or not. I hope I did. I've always been partial to women and have always wanted to see them satisfied till their eyes popped out.

Through Lilian I got the word that Quadberry was out of Annapolis and now flying jets off the *Bonhomme Richard*, an aircraft carrier headed for Vietnam. He telegrammed her that he would set down at the Jackson airport at ten o'clock one night. So Lilian and I were out there waiting. It was a familiar place to her. She was a stewardess and her loops were mainly in the South. She wore a beige raincoat, had red sandals on her feet; I was in a black turtleneck and corduroy jacket, feeling significant, so significant I could barely stand it. I'd already made myself the lead writer at Gordon-Marx Advertising in Jackson. I hadn't seen Lilian in a year. Her eyes were strained, no longer the bright blue things they were when she was a pious beauty. We drank coffee together. I loved her. As far as I knew, she'd been faithful to Quadberry.

He came down in an F-something Navy jet right on the dot of ten. She ran out on the airport pavement to meet him. I saw her crawl up the ladder. Quadberry never got out of the plane. I could see him in his blue helmet. Lilian backed down the ladder. Then Quadberry had the cockpit cover him again. He turned the plane around so its flaming red end was at us. He took it down the runway. We saw him leap out into the night at the middle of the runway going west, toward San Diego and the *Bonhomme Richard*. Lilian was crying.

"What did he say?" I asked.

"He said, 'I am a dragon. America the beautiful, like you will never know.' He wanted to give you a message. He was glad you were here."

"What was the message?"

"The same thing. 'I am a dragon. America the beautiful, like you will never know.' "

"Did he say anything else?"

"Not a thing."

"Did he express any love toward you?"

"He wasn't Ard. He was somebody with a sneer in a helmet."

"He's going to war, Lilian."

"I asked him to kiss me and he told me to get off the plane, he was firing up and it was dangerous."

"Arden is going to war. He's just on his way to Vietnam and he wanted us to know that. It wasn't just him he wanted us to see. It was him in the jet he wanted us to see. He *is* that black jet. You can't kiss an airplane."

"And what are we supposed to do?" cried sweet Lilian.

"We've just got to hang around. He didn't have to lift off and disappear straight up like that. That was to tell us how he isn't with us anymore."

Lilian asked me what she was supposed to do now. I told her she was supposed to come with me to my apartment in the old 1920 Clinton place where I was. I was supposed to take care of her. Quadberry had said so. His six-year-old directive was still working.

She slept on the fold-out bed of the sofa for a while. This was the only bed in my place. I stood in the dark in the kitchen and drank a quarter bottle of gin on ice. I would not turn on the light and spoil her sleep. The prospect of Lilian asleep in my apartment made me feel like a chaplain on a visit to the Holy Land; I stood there getting drunk, biting my tongue when dreams of lust burst on me. That black jet Quadberry wanted us to see him in, its flaming rear end, his blasting straight up into the night at mid-runway—what precisely was he wanting to say in this stunt? Was he saying remember him forever or forget him forever? But I had my own life and was neither going to mother-hen it over his memory nor his old sweetheart. What did he mean, *America the beautiful, like you will never know?* I, William Howly, knew a god-damn good bit about America the beautiful, even as a deaf man. Being deaf had brought me up closer to people. There were only about five I knew, but I knew their mouth movements, the per-spiration under their noses, their tongues moving over the crowns of their teeth, their fingers on their lips. Quadberry, I said, you don't have to get up next to the stars in your black jet to see America the beautiful.

I was deciding to lie down on the kitchen floor and sleep the night, when Lilian turned on the light and appeared in her panties and bra. Her body was perfect except for a tiny bit of fat on her upper thighs. She'd sunbathed herself so her limbs were brown, and her stomach, and the instinct was to rip off the white under-wear and lick, suck, say something terrific into the flesh that you discovered.

She was moving her mouth.

"Say it again slowly."

"I'm lonely. When he took off in his jet, I think it meant he wasn't ever going to see me again. I think it meant he was laughing at both of us. He's an astronaut and he spits on us."

"You want me on the bed with you?" I asked.

"I know you're an intellectual. We could keep on the lights so you'd know what I said."

"You want to say things? This isn't going to be just sex?"

"It could never be just sex."

"I agree. Go to sleep. Let me make up my mind whether to come in there. Turn out the lights."

Again the dark, and I thought I would cheat not only Quad-berry but the entire Quadberry family if I did what was natural.

I fell asleep.

Quadberry escorted B–52s on bombing missions into North Vietnam. He was catapulted off the *Bonhomme Richard* in his suit at 100 degrees temperature, often at night, and put the F–8 on all it could get—the tiny cockpit, the immense long two-million-dollar fuselage, wings, tail and jet engine, Quadberry, the genius master of his dragon, going up to twenty thousand feet to be cool. He'd meet with the big B-52 turtle of the air and get in a position, his cockpit glowing with green and orange lights, and turn on his transistor radio. There was only one really good band, never mind the old American rock-and-roll from Cambodia, and that was Red Chinese opera. Quadberry loved it. He loved the nasal horde in the finale, when the peasants won over the old fat dilettante mayor. Then he'd turn the jet around when he saw the squatty abrupt little fires way down there after the B-52s had dropped their diet. It was a seven-hour trip. Sometimes he slept, but his body knew when to wake up. Another thirty minutes and there was his ship waiting for him out in the waves.

All his trips weren't this easy. He'd have to blast out in daytime and get with the B-52s, and a SAM missile would come up among them. Two of his mates were taken down by these missiles. But Quadberry, as on saxophone, had endless learned technique. He'd put his jet perpendicular in the air and make the SAMs look silly. He even shot down two of them. Then, one day in daylight, a MIG came floating up level with him and his squadron. Quadberry couldn't believe it. Others in the squadron were shy, but Quadberry knew where and how the MIG could shoot. He flew below the cannons and then came in behind it. He knew the MIG wanted one of the B-52s and not mainly him. The MIG was so concentrated on the fat B-52 that he forgot about Quadberry. It was really an amateur suicide pilot in the MIG. Quadberry got on top of him and let down a missile, rising out of the way of it. The missile blew off the tail of the MIG. But then Quadberry wanted to see if the man got safely out of the cockpit. He thought it would be pleasant if the fellow got out with his parachute working. Then Quadberry saw that the fellow wanted to collide his wreckage with the B-52, so Quadberry turned himself over and cannoned, evaporated the pilot and cockpit. It was the first man he'd killed.

The next trip out, Quadberry was hit by a ground missile. But his jet kept flying. He flew it a hundred miles and got to the sea. There was the *Bonhomme Richard*, so he ejected. His back was snapped but, by God, he landed right on the deck. His mates caught him in their arms and cut the parachute off him. His back hurt for weeks, but he was all right. He rested and recuperated in Hawaii for a month.

Then he went off the front of the ship. Just like that, his F-6 plopped in the ocean and sank like a rock. Quadberry saw the ship go over him. He knew he shouldn't eject just yet. If he ejected now he'd knock his head on the bottom and get chewed up in the motor blades. So Quadberry waited. His plane was sinking in the green and he could see the hull of the aircraft carrier getting smaller, but he had oxygen through his mask and it didn't seem that urgent a decision. Just let the big ship get over. Down what later proved to be sixty feet, he pushed the ejection button. It fired him away, bless it, and he woke up ten feet under the surface swimming against an almost overwhelming body of underwater parachute. But two of his mates were in a helicopter, one of them on the ladder to lift him out.

Now Quadberry's back was really hurt. He was out of this war and all wars for good.

Lilian, the stewardess, was killed in a crash. Her jet exploded with a hijacker's bomb, an inept bomb which wasn't supposed to go off, fifteen miles out of Havana; the poor pilot, the poor passengers, the poor stewardesses were all splattered like flesh sparklers over the water just out of Cuba. A fisherman found one seat of the airplane. Castro expressed regrets.

Quadberry came back to Clinton two weeks after Lilian and the others bound for Tampa were dead. He hadn't heard about her. So I told him Lilian was dead when I met him at the airport. Quadberry was thin and rather meek in his civvies—a gray suit and an out-of-style tie. The white ends of his hair were not there—the halo had disappeared—because his hair was cut short. The Arab nose seemed a pitiable defect in an ash-whiskered face that was beyond anemic now. He looked shorter, stooped. The truth was he was sick, his back was killing him. His breath was heavy-laden with airplane martinis and in his limp right hand he held a wet cigar. I told him about Lilian. He mumbled something sideways that I could not possibly make out.

"You've got to speak right at me, remember? Remember me, Quadberry?"

"Mom and Dad of course aren't here."

"No. Why aren't they?"

"He wrote me a letter after we bombed Hué. Said he hadn't sent me to Annapolis to bomb the architecture of Hué. He had been there once and had some important experience—French-kissed the queen of Hué or the like. Anyway, he said I'd have to do a hell of a lot of repentance for that. But he and Mom are separate people. Why isn't *she* here?"

"I don't know."

"I'm not asking you the question. The question is to God."

He shook his head. Then he sat down on the floor of the terminal. People had to walk around. I asked him to get up.

"No. How is old Clinton?"

"Horrible. Aluminum subdivisions, cigar boxes with four thin columns in front, thick as a hive. We got a turquoise water tank; got a shopping center, a monster Jitney Jungle, fifth-rate teeny-boppers covering the place like ants." Why was I being so frank just now, as Quadberry sat on the floor downcast, drooped over like a long weak candle? "It's not our town anymore, Ard. It's going to hurt to drive back into it. Hurts me every day. Please get up."

"And Lilian's not even over there now."

"No. She's a cloud over the Gulf of Mexico. You flew out of Pensacola once. You know what beauty those pink and blue clouds are. That's how I think of her."

"Was there a funeral?"

"Oh, yes. Her Methodist preacher and a big crowd over at Wright Ferguson funeral home. Your mother and father were there. Your father shouldn't have come. He could barely walk. Please get up."

"Why? What am I going to do, where am I going?"

"You've got your saxophone."

"Was there a coffin? Did you all go by and see the pink or blue cloud in it?" He was sneering now as he had done when he was eleven and fourteen and seventeen.

"Yes, they had a very ornate coffin."

"Lilian was the Unknown Stewardess. I'm not getting up."

"I said you still have your saxophone."

"No, I don't. I tried to play it on the ship after the last time I hurt my back. No go. I can't bend my neck or spine to play it. The pain kills me."

"Well, *don't* get up, then. Why am I asking you to get up? I'm just a deaf drummer, too vain to buy a hearing aid. Can't stand to write the ad copy I do. Wasn't I a good drummer?"

"Superb."

"But we can't be in this condition forever. The police are going to come and make you get up if we do it much longer."

The police didn't come. It was Quadberry's mother who came. She looked me in the face and grabbed my shoulders before she saw Ard on the floor. When she saw him she yanked him off the floor, hugging him passionately. She was shaking with sobs. Quadberry was gathered to her as if he were a rope she was trying to wrap around herself. Her mouth was all over him. Quadberry's mother was a good-looking woman of fifty. I simply held her purse. He cried out that his back was hurting. At last she let him go.

"So now we walk," I said.

"Dad's in the car trying to quit crying," said his mother.

"This is nice," Quadberry said. "I thought everything and everybody was dead around here." He put his arms around his mother. "Let's all go off and kill some time together." His mother's hair was on his lips. "You?" he asked me.

"Murder the devil out of it," I said.

I pretended to follow their car back to their house in Clinton. But when we were going through Jackson, I took the North 55 exit and disappeared from them, exhibiting a great amount of taste, I thought. I would get in their way in this reunion. I had an unimprovable apartment on Old Canton Road in a huge plaster house, Spanish style, with a terrace and ferns and yucca plants, and a green door where I went in. When I woke up I didn't have to make my coffee or fry my egg. The girl who slept in my bed did that. She was Lilian's little sister, Esther Field. Esther was pretty in a minor way and I was proud how I had tamed her to clean and cook around the place. The Field family would appreciate how I lived with her. I showed her the broom and the skillet, and she loved them. She also learned to speak very slowly when she had to say something.

Esther answered the phone when Quadberry called me seven months later. She gave me his message. He wanted to know my opinion on a decision he had to make. There was this Dr. Gordon, a surgeon at Emory Hospital in Atlanta, who said he could cure Quadberry's back problem. Quadberry's back was killing him. He was in torture even holding up the phone to say this. The surgeon said there was a seventy-five/twenty-five chance. Seventy-five that it would be successful, twenty-five that it would be fatal. Esther waited for my opinion. I told her to tell Quadberry to go over to Emory. He'd got through with luck in Vietnam, and now he should ride it out in this petty back operation.

Esther delivered the message and hung up.

"He said the surgeon's just his age; he's some genius from Johns Hopkins Hospital. He said this Gordon guy has published a lot of articles on spinal operations," said Esther.

"Fine and good. All is happy. Come to bed."

I felt her mouth and her voice on my ears, but I could hear only a sort of loud pulse from the girl. All I could do was move toward moisture and nipples and hair.

Quadberry lost his gamble at Emory Hospital in Atlanta. The brilliant surgeon his age lost him. Quadberry died. He died with his Arabian nose up in the air.

That is why I told this story and will never tell another.

Ron Hansen

Can I Just Sit Here For a While?

He was called a traveler and that was another thing he loved about the job. If you wanted the hairy truth, Rick Bozack couldn't put his finger on any one thing that made the job such a clincher; it might have been his expense account or the showroom smell of his leased Oldsmobile or the motel rooms: God, the motel rooms, twin double beds and a stainless steel Kleenex dispenser and a bolted-down color TV topped with cellophane-wrapped peppermints which the maid left after she cleaned. He loved the thermos coffee canister the waitress banged down on his table at breakfast, he loved the sweat on his ice-water glass, he loved the spill stains blotting through the turned-over check, and he loved leaving tips of 20 percent even when the girl was slow and sullen and splashed coffee on his newspaper. His sales, his work, his vocation, that was all bonus. The waiting, the handshakes, the lunches, The Close, jeepers, that was just icing.

If you asked Rick Bozack what he did for a living, he wouldn't come out with a song and dance about selling expensive incubators and heart and kidney machines for Doctor's Service Supply Company, Indianapolis. Not off the top of his head he wouldn't. Instead he'd flash on a motel lobby with all the salesmen in their sharp tailored suits, chewing sugarless gum, while the sweet thing behind the counter rammed a roller over a plastic credit card and after-shaves mingled in the air. It was goofy when he thought about it, but walking out through those fingerprinted glass doors, throwing his briefcase onto the red bucket seat, scraping the frost

97

off the windshield, and seeing all those other guys out there in the parking lot with him, grimacing, chipping away at their wipers, blowing on their fingers, sliding their heater controls to Defrost, he felt like a team player again, like he was part of a fighter squadron.

What was this Death of a Salesman crap? he'd say.

What were they feeding everybody about the hard life on the road?

You'd have to be zonkers not to love it.

Then Rick had a real turnaround. A college buddy said something that really clobbered him. Rick and his wife, Jane, had returned to South Bend, his home, for the Notre Dame alumni picnic, and they had collided there with people they hadn't even thought of in years. They sat all night at a green picnic table with baked beans and hot dogs and beer, laughing so much their sides hurt, having a whale of a good time together. They swapped pictures of their kids and Rick drew a diagram of an invention he might get patented, which would rinse out messy diapers for daddies right there in the toilet bowl. He told all comers that he was thirty-four years old and happily married, the father of two girls, and he woke up every morning with a sapsucker grin on his face. Then Mickey Hogan, this terrific buddy in advertising who had just started up his own firm, said you don't know the thrill of business until it's your own, until every sale you make goes directly into your pocket and not to some slob back in the home office.

This guy Hogan wasn't speaking *de profundis* or anything, but Rick was really blown away by what he said. It was one of those fuzzy notions you carry with you for years and then it's suddenly there, it's got shape and bulk and annoying little edges that give you a twinge when you sit down. That's how it was. He and Jane talked about it all the way back to their three-bedroom apartment on Rue Monet in Indianapolis. "How much of what I earn actually makes my wallet any fatter? What do I have besides an income? When am I going to get off my duff and get something going on my own?"

Jane was great about it. She said it was his decision and she loved him and she'd go along with whatever his choice was, but she had watched him waste himself at Doctor's Service Supply Company, Indianapolis. She knew he was a great salesman but he had all the earmarks of a fantastic manager too. She had been hoping he'd come up with something like this but didn't want to influence him one way or the other. "I don't want to push," were her words.

Jane's enthusiasm put a fire under Rick and he began checking things out on the sly: inventory costs, car leases and office space rentals, government withholding tax and F.I.C.A. regulations, and though it seemed dopey and juvenile, the couple decided that they'd both stop smoking, watch their caloric intake, avoid between-meal treats, and exercise regularly. Sure they were mainly concerned with hashing out this new business venture, but how far afield was it to take stock of yourself, your physical condition, to discipline yourself and set goals? That was Rick's comment and Jane thought he was "right on the money."

The two of them let a half-gallon of ice cream melt down in the stainless steel sink, got out the scale and measuring tape, bought matching jogging outfits and they took turns with Tracy and Connor at breakfast while one of them jogged around the block.

And Rick was no slouch when on the road. He jogged in strange cities and on gravel country roads and in parking lots of motels. Other salesmen would run at him in sweatbands and heavy T-shirts and Rick would say, "How's it going?"

"How's it going?" they'd reply.

Rick imagined millions of joggers saying the same things to each other. It felt as good as the days of the Latin Mass, when you knew it was just as incomprehensible in Dusseldorf, West Germany, or Ichikawa, Japan.

On one of his business trips to South Bend, he jogged on the cinder track of Notre Dame's football stadium, where who should he see but Walter Herdzina, a terrific friend of his! Rick was flabbergasted. The guy had aged--who hadn't?--but he remembered Rick like it was only yesterday, even recited some wild dorm incidents that Rick had put the blackboard eraser to. The two men ran an eight-minute mile together and leaned on their knees and wiped their faces on their sweatshirts, and after they had discussed pulse rates, refined sugar, and junk foods, his buddy Walter Herdzina said, "You ought to move back to South Bend."

Jane, bless her heart, kept bringing up South Bend too. It was smack in the middle of his territory, and a natural home base, but he had never really thought about South Bend much before the alumni picnic. When Head Office hired Rick they had naturally assumed he'd want a giant metropolis like Indianapolis to settle in so he could have some jam-packed leisure time, and he had never mentioned his strong links further north. And it wasn't unusual for Rick to spend three or four days in South Bend and not give anyone except his mom a call. But now there was a come-as-you-are feeling, some real hometown warmth there, which he hadn't noticed before.

In September he closed a deal with a gynecological clinic that would earn him six thousand dollars, what salesmen called The Cookies. But instead of driving home for a wingding celebration, he decided to make some business phone contacts, thank you's actually, to ride with his hot streak, see what fell in his lap. And he had an inkling maybe some doctors up there considered him somewhat remote.

So he stopped in the lobby of a downtown bank building to use its plush telephone booths. Then, on an impulse, he asked to see someone in the business loan department. A receptionist said a loan vice president could see him and Rick walked into his office and how's this for coincidence? The banker was Walter Herdzina! You could've knocked Rick over with a feather. "Boy, you're really going places," he said. Walter grinned. "They'll probably wise up and kick me downstairs again before I get the chair warm."

Rick spoke off the top of his head. He had been with Doctor's Service Supply Company, Indianapolis, for six years after three years with Johnson & Johnson. He had built up a pretty good trade representing Indiana and southern Michigan and had offers from industries in Minnesota and California to switch over to a district manager's job and a substantial boost in salary. What he wanted to know was, could a banker like Walter with years of experience and an eye for markets and money potential give him a solid reason why he shouldn't go into business for himself? Start his own distributorship?

The buddy in banking glanced at his watch and suggested they go out for lunch.

Rick figured that meant No. "This is pretty off-the-wall," he said. "I really haven't had time to analyze it or work up any kind of prospectus."

Walter put a hand on his shoulder. "Let's talk about it at lunch."

Mostly they talked about rugby. It had been a maiden sport at Notre Dame when they played it, but now it had taken the school by storm. Why? Because when you got right down to it, men liked seeing what they were made of, what kind of guts they had.

"Lessons like that stick," said Walter. "I get guys coming to me with all kinds of schemes, inventions, brilliant ideas. I can tell right away if they were ever athletes. If they never hurt themselves to win at something, well, I'm a little skeptical."

Walter ordered protein-rich halibut; Rick had the Dieter's Salad.

Rick told the banker traveler stories. He told him anecdotes about sales. He had sold insurance and mutual funds and, for a summer, automobiles, and he had discovered a gimmick, well not that, a *tool*, which hadn't failed him yet. It was called the Benjamin Franklin Close.

"Say you get a couple who're wavering over the purchase of a car. You take them into your office and close the door and say, 'Do you know what Benjamin Franklin would do in situations like this?' That's a toughie for them so you let them off the hook. You take out a tablet and draw a line down the center of the page, top to bottom. 'Benjamin Franklin,' you say, 'would list all the points in favor of buying this car and then he'd list whatever he could against it. Then he'd total things up.' The salesman handles all the benefits. You begin by saying, 'So okay, you've said your old car needs an overhaul. That's point one. You've said you want a station wagon for the kids; that's point two. You've told me that particular shade of brown is your favorite.' And so on. Once you've tabulated your pitches, you flip the tablet around and hand across the pen. 'Okay,' you tell them. 'Now Benjamin Franklin would write down whatever he had *against* buying that car.' And you're silent. As noiseless as you can be. You don't say boo to them. They stare at that blank side of the paper and they get flustered. They weren't expecting this at all. Maybe the wife will say, 'We can't afford it,' and the husband will hurry up and scribble that down. Maybe he'll say, 'It's really more than we need for city driving.' He'll glance at you for approval but you won't even nod your head. You've suddenly turned to stone. Now they're struggling. They see two reasons against and twelve reasons for. You decide to help them. You say, 'Was it the color you didn't like?' Of course not, you dope. You put that down as point three in favor. But the wife will say, 'Oh no, I like that shade of brown a lot.' You sit back in your chair and wait. You wait four or five minutes if you have to, until they're really uncomfortable, until you've got them feeling like bozos. Then you take the tablet from them and make a big show of making the tally. They think you're an idiot anyway; counting out loud won't surprise them. And when you've told them they have twelve points in favor, two points against, you sit back in your chair and let that sink in. You say, 'What do you think Benjamin Franklin would do in this situation?' You've got them cornered and they know it and they can't think of any way out because there's only one way and they never consider it. Pressed against the wall like that the only solution is for the man or woman to say, 'I-- Just-- Don't-- *Feel*-- Like-- It-- Now.' All the salesman can do is recapitulate. If they want to wait, if the vibes don't feel right, if they don't sense it's the appropriate thing to do, they've got him. I just don't feel like it now. There's no way to sell against that."

Walter grinned. He thought Rick might have something. Even in outline the distributorship had real sex appeal.

So that afternoon Rick drove south to Indianapolis with his CB radio turned down so he wouldn't have all the chatter, and he picked up a sitter for his two little roses and took Jane out for dinner that night, claiming he wanted to celebrate the six-thousand-dollar commission. But after they had toasted The Cookies, he sprang the deal on her, explained everything about the lunch and Walter's positive reaction, how it all fit together, fell into place, shot off like a rocket, zoomed. And what it all boiled down to was they could move to South Bend, buy a house, and in two months, three months, a year, maybe he'd have himself a business.

Jane was ecstatic. Jane was a dynamo. While Rick did the dog-and-pony show for his boss and got him to pick up the tab for a move to the heart of Rick's territory, Jane did the real work of selecting their home and supervising the movers. Then Rick walked Tracy and little Connor from house to house down the new block in South Bend, introducing himself and his daughters to their new neighbors. There were five kids the same age on just one side of the street! Rick saw Tracy and Connor as teenagers at a backyard party with hanging lanterns and some of Rick's famous punch, and maybe two thousand four hundred boys trying to get a crack at his girls.

He drank iced tea with a stockbroker who crossed his legs and gazed out the window as Tracy tried to feed earthworms to his spaniel.

"Plenty of playmates," said Rick.

"This place is a population bomb."

"Yeah, but I love kids, don't you? I get home from a week on the road and there's nothing I like better than to roll on the floor a few hours with them."

"But your kids are girls!" the man said. He spit ice cubes back into his glass.

Rick shrugged. "I figure my wife will tell me when I should stop it."

What'd he think? Rick'd be copping feels, pawing them through their training bras? Maybe South Bend had its creepy side after all. Maybe a few of these daddies could bear some scrutiny.

Rick gave a full report to his wife, Jane, as they sat down with beers on the newly carpeted floor of the living room, telling her about all the fascinating people he had met in just a casual swing down the block. She said, "I don't know how you can just go knocking on doors and introducing yourself. I can't think what to converse about when I'm with strangers."

"That's one of the things that comes with being a traveler. You just assume you're welcome until someone tells you otherwise."

But how did that square with the uneasiness Rick Bozack felt with his old chum Mickey Hogan? A year ago Mickey had been an expensive copywriter, but then he had gone out on a limb to take over a smaller house that had been strictly an art and layout jobber and the gamble had paid off in spades. Mickey turned the firm into a real comer in South Bend, what they call in the trade a "hot shop."

But then Mickey had always been a brain. They had been rugby buddies at Notre Dame; they used to shoot snooker together and wear each others tennis shoes and generally pal around like they were in a rowdy television commerical for some brand of beer. Now Mickey was almost skinny and as handsome as Sergio Franchi; and taking full advantage of it, don't let anybody kid you. They had doubled to the Notre Dame/Army game last season and Mickey brought along a knockout who kept sneaking her hand under Mickey's blue leg-warmer. Rick couldn't keep his eyes off her. Even Jane noticed it. "Boy, I bet she put lead in your pencil," she said.

So Rick was delighted, but amazed, when in February Mickey said he'd make the third for a terrific bunch of seats at the Notre Dame/Marquette basketball game. Mickey was even sitting on the snow-shoveled steps of his condominium, like some company president on the skids, when Rick pulled up along the curb. And now Mickey was smoking a black cigarillo as Rick told him how astonished he was these days to see that everyone he met was about his age; they had all risen to positions of authority and he was finding they could do him some good. You always thought it was just your father who could throw a name around. Now Rick was doing it himself. And getting results! "I'm really enjoying my thirties," Rick said, and then smiled. "I've got twenty credit cards in my wallet and I don't get acne anymore."

Mickey looked at him, bored.

"Okay; maybe not twenty credit cards, but my complexion's all cleared-up." Rick had forgotten how much of a jerk Mickey could be.

Rick kept the engine running and shoved The Captain and Tenille in his tape deck so Mickey could nestle with some good tunes, and he pressed the door chimes to a house the Herdzinas had just built: eighty-thousand smackers minimum. A small girl in pink underpants opened the door.

"Hi," said Rick in his Nice Man voice.

The girl shoved a finger up her nose.

Karen Herdzina hugged him hello. The hugging was a phenomenon that was totally new to South Bend and Rick never felt he handled it well. He lingered a bit too long with women and with men he was on the lookout for a quick takedown and two points on the scoreboard.

"I'll put some hustle into Walt," she said. "Tell him to get it in gear."

Walter came out of the bedroom with a new shirt he was ripping the plastic off of. "Mickey in the car?"

Rick nodded. "But it really belts out the heat."

Walter unpinned the sleeves and the cardboards and shoved the trash into a paper sack that had the cellophane wrappers of record albums in it.

"Look at that," he said. "My wife. She goes out spending my hard-earned money on records. The Carpenters, John Denver. I don't know what gets into her sometimes."

"I kind of enjoy John Denver," said Rick.

Walter leaned into Rick as they walked to the thrumming Oldsmobile, fanning three tickets out like a heart-stopping poker hand. "How about these beauties, Richard?"

"Wow. What do I owe ya?"

He frowned, pushed the tickets in his wallet. *"De nada,"* said Walter. "Buy me a beer."

As Rick drove lickety-split to the game, he and Walter talked about their budding families. You could see it was driving Mickey bananas. Here he was a bachelor, giving up a night when he could've probably had some make-out artist in the sack, and all he was hearing was talk about drooling and potties and cutting new teeth. So as he climbed up onto the beltway, Rick introduced the topic of basketball and Walter straddled the hump in the back seat and scrunched forward to talk about the Marquette scoring threat, particularly a couple of spades who'd make All-American, easy. Mickey introduced the topic of Doctor's Service Supply Company, Indianapolis, and asked Walter if he knew Rick was considering his own distributorship.

The banker said, "Heck, I'm the one who put the gleam in his eye." He returned to the back seat and crossed his kid leather gloves in his lap. "I think that's a tremendous opportunity, Rick. Where've you gone with it lately?"

"He's been testing the waters," said Mickey.

"I've had it on the back burner until Jane and the kids get a better lay of the land," said Rick. "I think it might be a pretty good setup though. Almost no time on the road and very little selling. I'll see what it's like to stay around the house and carry those canvas money bags up to a teller window."

Walter said, "I read somewhere that every person who starts a new business makes at least one horrible mistake. Something really staggering. If you get through that and you don't get kayoed, I guess you got it made."

They were quiet for several minutes, as if in mourning for all those bankrupts who had been walloped in the past. The 8–track clicked from 3 to 4. Mickey tapped one of his black cigarillos on a thumbnail.

"You like those things?" Rick asked.

Mickey lit it with the car lighter. "Yep," Mickey said. "I like them a lot."

Rick turned into the Notre Dame parking lot. "Since I gave up smoking, I notice it all the time. This health kick's really made a difference. I'm down two notches on my belt, my clothes don't fit, and I want to screw all the time now." He switched off the ignition. "How's that for a side benefit?"

Mickey said, "You smile a lot, you know that?"

It was an okay game; nothing spectacular as far as Rick was concerned. In fact, if you conked him on the head he might even have said it was boring. Where was the teamwork? Where was the give and take? A couple of black guys were out there throwing up junk shots, making the white guys look like clods, propelling themselves up toward the basket like they were taking stairs three at a time. It went back and forth like that all night, and except for the spine-tingling Notre Dame fight songs, except for the silver flask of brandy they passed up and down the row, he wished he was in a motel room somewhere eating cheese slices on crackers.

At the final buzzer the three men filed out with the crowd, waving to other old buddies and asking them how tricks were. The Oldsmobile engine turned slowly with cold before it fired. Mickey removed The Captain and Tenille from the tape deck. Mister Sophisticated.

Rick took the crosstown and shoved in a tape of Tony Orlando. Walter was paging through one of the catalogues for Doctor's Service Supply Company, Indianapolis, when he noticed a pizza parlor was still open, how did that sound? Rick admitted it didn't blow the top of his head off but he guessed he could give it a whirl. Mickey just sat there like wax.

Rick swerved in next to a souped-up Ford with big rear wheels that looked like boulders. "Secret Storm" was printed in maroon on the fender. As they walked to the entrance, Rick saw the three of them in the reflecting front windows, in blue shirts and rep ties and two-hundred-dollar topcoats, frowns in their eyes and gray threads in their hair and gruesome mortgages on their houses.

Walter stood with Rick at the counter as he ordered a combination pizza. An overhead blower gave them pompadours. "That was fun," said Rick.

"My wife encourages me to go out with the boys. She thinks it'll keep me from chasing tail."

Rick wished he had been somewhere else when Walter said that. It said everything about the guy.

Mickey had walked to the cigarette machine and pressed every button, then, deep in his private Weltschmerz, he wandered past a sign in the restaurant that said "This Section Closed." Rick backed away from the counter with three beers, sloshing some on his coat, and made his way to the forbidden tables where Mickey was sitting.

Mickey frowned. "How long are we going to dawdle here?"

"You got something you wanted to do?"

"There's *always* something to do, Rick."

A girl in a chef's hat seated an elderly couple in the adjoining area. She had pizza menus that she crushed to her breast as she sidestepped around benches toward the drinking buddies, bumping the sign that said "This Section Closed," schoolmarm disapproval in her eyes. Mickey rocked back in his chair. "Can I just sit here for a while? Would it ruin your day if I just sat here?"

The girl stopped and threw everything she had into the question and then shrugged and walked back to the cash register.

Rick almost smacked his forehead, he was that impressed. Mickey could get away with stuff that would land Rick in jail or in small claims court.

Soon he and Walter tore into a combination pizza, achieving at once a glossy burn on the roofs of their mouths. Mickey must not have wanted any. He seemed to have lost the power of speech. After a while Walter asked the two if they had read a magazine article about a recent psychological study of stress.

Rick asked, "How do you find time to read?"

Walter said, "I can't. My wife gets piles of magazines in the mail, though, and gives me digests of them at dinner."

Mickey looked elsewhere as Walter explained that the theory of this particular study was that whenever a person shifted the furniture of his life in any significant way at all, he or she was increasing the chances of serious illness. Change for the better?

Change for the worse? Doesn't matter. If your spouse dies you get a hundred points against you. You get fired, that's fifty. You accomplish something outstanding, really excellent, still you get in the neighborhood of thirty points tacked onto your score. The list went on and on. Mortgages counted, salary bonuses, shifts in eating habits. Walter said, "You collect more than three hundred of these puppies in a year and it's time to consult a shrink."

Neither Walter nor Rick could finish his pizza, so Rick asked the kitchen help for a sack to carry the remains in. Then the three men walked out into the night gripping their collars at their necks, their ears crimped by the cold. It was close to zero. They could hear it in the snow.

There were three boys in the car that was christened "Secret Storm," each dangling cheeze pizza over his mouth.

Rick opened the car door on his side and bumped the trim on the souped-up Ford. He smiled and shrugged his shoulders at the kid on the passenger's side.

The kid called him a son of a bitch.

Mickey immediately walked around the car. "What'd he call you?"

"Nothing, Mickey. He was kidding."

But Mickey was already thumping the kid's car door with his knee. "I want to hear what you called him."

The door bolted open against Mickey's camel's hair coat, soiling it, and a kid bent out unsnapping a Catholic high school letterman's jacket. Before he had the last snap undone, Mickey punched the kid in the neck. The kid grabbed his throat and coughed. Mickey held his fists like cocktail glasses.

Walter stood in the cold with his gloved hands over his ears as Rick tried to pull Mickey away from the fracas. The kid hooked a fist into Rick's ear and knocked him against the car. Mickey tackled the kid and smacked him against the pavement. Dry snow fluffed up and blew. Rick covered his sore ear and Mickey tried to pin the kid's arms with his knees but the other boys were out of the Ford by then and pleading with the kid named Vic to let the guy go. It was at once obvious to Rick that the boys weren't aware they were dealing with three virile males in the prime of their lives, who had once played rugby at Notre Dame in the days when it was just a maiden sport.

Rick and Walter managed to untangle their buddy and haul him inside the car. Rick started the engine and spun his wheels in snow as he gunned the Oldsmobile out of the place. One of the kids kicked his bumper. The others were breathing on their hands.

"I don't believe it," said Rick.

Mickey was huffing; no jogger, he. "You don't believe what?" Mickey said.

"You're thirty-five years old, Mick! You don't go banging high school kids around."

Walter wiped the back window with his glove. "Oh no," he groaned.

Mickey turned around. "Are they following us?"

"Maybe their home's in the same direction," said Rick.

Mickey jerked open the door. Cold air flapped through the catalogues of Doctor's Service Supply Company, Indianapolis. "Let me out," Mickey said.

"Are you kidding?" Rick gave him a look that spoke of his resolute position on the question while communicating his willingness to compromise on issues of lesser gravity.

And yet Mickey repeated, "Let me out."

"What are you going to do?"

"Shut up and let me out of this car."

Walter said, "I think those are *Catholic* kids, Michael."

They were on a potholed residential street of ivied brick homes and one-car garages. There were white globes on eight-foot green streetlamps. Rick made a right-hand turn and so did the other car.

Mickey pushed the door wide open and scraped off the top of a snow pile. He leaned out toward the curb like a sick drunk about to lose it until Rick skidded slantwise on the ice pack and stopped. Then Mickey trotted out and slipped on the ice and sprawled against the right front door of the Ford.

The boy named Vic cracked his noggin on the doorframe trying to get out and he sat back down pretty hard, with tears in his eyes and both hands rubbing his hair.

"All right, you bastard," the driver said, and lurched out, tearing off *his* letterman's jacket. (Rick had worked like hell and never got one. And there weren't any razzle-dazzle black kids around then either.) The third kid got out and put his hand in his jeans pocket. He stripped a stick of gum and folded it in his mouth. Rick walked over to him and the kid's eyes slid. "Bob's going to make mincemeat out of your friend, man."

Mickey and the kid named Bob stepped over a yard hedge and Mickey was now hanging his coat on a clothesline pole. Walter was on the sidewalk stamping snow off his wing tips.

"Can you believe this weather?" Rick asked the kid. "My nose is like an ice cube."

The kid smiled. "Colder than a witch's tit, ain't it?"

The kid was in Rick's pocket. Rick still had the goods, all

right.

Mickey and the boy named Bob were closing in the night-blue back yard like boxers about to touch gloves, when Mickey swung his fist into the kid's stomach and the kid folded up like a card-table chair. "Ow! Oh man, where'd you hit me? Geez, that hurts."

A light went on in an upstairs bathroom.

Vic got out of the car, still holding his head, and the other kid tripped through the snow to help Bob limp to the Ford. "Get me to a hospital quick!"

"Oh, you're okay, Bob," said Vic.

"You don't know, man! I think he might've burst my appendix or something! I think he was wearing a ring!"

Mickey carefully put on his coat and sucked the knuckles of his hand when he sat down inside the car. Rick drove to Mickey's condominium first. Mickey was touching a bump on his forehead, smirking in Rick's direction.

"What made you want to do that, Mick?"

"Are you going to let some punk call you a son of a bitch?"

Rick slapped the steering wheel. "Of course! I do it all the *time*. Is that supposed to destroy you or something?"

Mickey just looked at the floormats or out the window. He jumped out when Rick parked in front of his place, and he didn't say goodbye.

Walter seated himself in the front bucket seat. "Whew! What an evening, huh?"

"I feel like I've run fourteen miles."

Walter crossed his legs and jiggled his shoe until Rick drove onto Walter's driveway whereupon he shook Rick's hand and suggested they do this again sometime and also wished him good luck in getting his business out of the starting gate.

The light was on in the upstairs bedroom of the Bozacks' blue Colonial home. Jane had switched the lights off downstairs. Rick let himself in with the milk box key and hung up his coat. He opened and shut the refrigerator door and then found himself patting his pockets for cigarettes. He went to the dining room breakfront and found an old carton of Salems.

He got a yellow ruled tablet and a pen from the desk and sat down in the living room with a lit cigarette. He printed VENTURE at the top. He drew a line down the center of the paper and numbered the right-hand side from one to twelve. After a few minutes there, Jane came down the stairs in her robe.

"Rick?"

"What?"

"I wanted to know if it was you."

"Who else would it be?"

"Why don't you come up? I'm only reading magazines."

"I think I'd like to just sit here for a while."

"In the *dark*?"

He didn't speak.

"Are you smoking?"

"Yep. I was feeling especially naughty."

She was silent. She stood with both feet on the same step. "You're being awfully mysterious."

"I just want to sit here for a while. Can I do that? Can I just sit here for a while?"

Jane climbed the stairs to their bedroom.

Rick stared at the numbered page. Why quit the team? Why risk the stress? Why give up all those cookies.

If pressed against the wall he'd say, "I just don't feel like it now."

William Kittredge

Thirty-four Seasons of Winter

Ben Alton remembered years in terms of winter. Summers all ran together, each like the last, heat and baled hay and dust. "That was '59," he'd say. "The year I wintered in California." He'd be remembering manure-slick alleys of a feedlot outside Manteca, a flat horizon and constant rain.

Or flood years. "March of '64, when the levees went." Or open winters. "We fed cattle the whole of February in our shirt-sleeves. For old man Swarthout." And then he'd be sad. "One week Art helped. We was done every day by noon and drunk by three." Sad because Art was his stepbrother and dead, and because there'd been nothing but hate between them when Art was killed.

Ben and Art fought only once, when they were thirteen. Ben's father, Corrie Alton, moved in with Art's old lady on her dry-land place in the hills north of Davanero, and the boys bunked together in a back room. The house was yellow white, a frame building surrounded by a fenced dirt yard where turkeys pecked, shaded by three withering peach trees, and the room they shared was furnished with two steel-frame cots and a row of nails where they hung what extra clothing they owned. The first night, while the old people were drinking in town, the boys fought. Ben took a flattened nose and chipped a tooth against one of the cot frames and was satisfied and didn't try again.

The next year Art's mother sold the place for money to drink on, and when that was gone Ben's old man pulled out, heading for Shafter, down out of Bakersfield, going to see friends and work a

111

season in the spuds. Corrie never came back or sent word, so the next spring the boys took a job setting siphons for an onion farmer, doing the muddy and exhausting work of one man, supporting themselves and Art's mother. She died the spring they were seventeen; and Art began to talk about getting out of town, fighting in the ring, being somebody.

So he ran every night, and during the day he and Ben stacked alfalfa bales, always making their thousand a day, twenty bucks apiece, and then in the fall Art went to Portland and worked out in a gym each afternoon, learning to fight, and spent his evenings swimming at the YMCA or watching movies. Early in the winter he began to get some fights, and for at least the first year he didn't lose. People began to know his name in Salem and Yakima and Klamath Falls.

He fought at home only once, a January night in the Peterson barn on the edge of town, snow falling steadily. The barn warmed slowly, losing its odor of harness leather and rotting hay, and under the circle of lights which illuminated the fighters in a blue glare, country people smoked and bet and drank. Circling a sweating and tiring Mexican boy, Art seemed gray white against the darkness of the loft, tapped his gloves and brushed back his thin blond hair with a quick forearm, sure and quiet. Then he moved under an overhand right, ducking in a quick new way he must have learned in Portland, and he was inside, forcing, and flat on his feet, grunting as he followed each short chop with his body. The Mexican backed against one of the rough juniper posts supporting the ring, covered his face, gloves fumbling together as he began sinking and twisting, knees folding, and it ended with the Mexican sprawled and cut beneath one eye, bleeding from the nose, and Art in his corner, breathing easily while he flexed and shook his arms as if he weren't loose yet, and then Art spit the white mouthpiece onto the wet, gray canvas and ducked away under the ropes.

Ben sat that night in the top row of the little grandstand and watched two men drag the other fighter out of the ring and attempt to revive him by pouring water over his head, hugged his knees and watched the crowd settle and heard the silence while everybody watched. Finally, the Mexican boy shook his head and sat up, and the crowd moved in a great sigh.

The next summer Art showed up with Clara, brought her back with him from a string of fights in California. It was an August afternoon, dead hot in the valley hayfields, and dust rose in long spirals from the field ahead where five balers were circling slowly, eating windrows of loose hay and leaving endless and uniform strings of bales. Ben was working the stack, unloading trucks, sweating through his pants every day before noon, shirtless and peeling.

The lemon-colored Buick convertible came across the stubble, bouncing and wheeling hard, just ahead of its own dust, and stopped twenty or thirty yards from the stack, and Art jumped out holding a can of beer over his head. The girl stood beside the convertible in the dusty alfalfa stubble and squinted into the glaring light, moist and sleepy looking. She was maybe twenty, and her sleeveless white blouse was wrinkled from sleeping in the car and sweat-gray beneath the arms. But she was blond and tan and direct in the one-hundred-degree heat of the afternoon. "Ain't she something?" Art said. "She's a kind of prize I brought home." He laughed and slapped her on the butt.

"Hello, Ben," she said. "Art told me about you." They drank a can of beer, iced and metallic tasting, and Art talked about the fighting in California, Fresno, and Tracy, and while he talked he ran his fingers slowly up and down Clara's bare arm. Ben crouched in the shade of the convertible and tried not to watch the girl, and his stomach cramped. Later he lay awake and thought about her, and everything about that meeting seemed too large and real, like some memory of childhood.

Anyway, she was living and traveling with Art. Then the fall he was twenty-five, fighting in Seattle, Art broke his right hand in a way that couldn't be fixed and married Clara and came home to live, driving a logging truck in the summer and drinking in the bars and drawing his unemployment through the winters, letting Clara work as a barmaid when they were broke. The years got away until one afternoon in a tavern called The Tarpaper Shack, when both Ben and Art were thirty-one. Art was sitting with a girl named Marie, and when Ben came in and wandered over to the booth she surprised him by being quiet and nice, with brown eyes and dark hair, not the kind Art ran with on his drunks, and by the end of the summer Marie and Ben were engaged.

Which caused no trouble until Christmas. The stores were open late, but the streets with their decorations were deserted, looking like a carnival at four in the morning, lighted and ready to tear down and move.

"You gonna marry that pig?" Art was drunk. The night barkeeper, a woman called Virgie, was leaning on the counter.

"Yeah," Ben said. "But don't sweat it." Then he noticed Virgie looking past them to the far corner of the vaulted room.

A worn row of booths ran there, beyond the lighted shuffleboard table and bowling machine. Above the last booth he saw the shadowed back of Clara's head. Just the yellow hair and yet certainly her. Art was grinning.

"You see her," he said, talking to Ben. "She's got a problem. She ain't getting any."

Ben finished the beer and eased the glass back to the wooden counter, swirling moisture into rings, wishing he could leave, wanting no more of their trouble. Clara was leaning back, eyes closed and the table in front of her empty except for her clasped hands. She didn't move or look as he approached.

"Hello, Kid," he said. And when she opened her eyes it was the same, like herons over the valley swamps, white against green. Even shadowed beneath the eyes and tired she looked good. "All right if I sit?" he asked. "You want a beer?"

She sipped his, taking the glass without speaking, touching his hand with hers, then smiling and licking the froth from her lips. "Okay," she said, and he ordered another glass and sat beside her.

"How you been? All right?"

"You know," she said, looking sideways at him, never glancing toward Art. "You got a pretty good idea how I been." Then she smiled. "I hear you're getting married."

"Just because you're tied up," he said, and she grinned again, more like her old self. "I mean it," he said. "Guess I ought to tell you once."

"Don't," she said. "For Christ sake. Not with that bastard over there laughing." She drank a little more of the beer, twisting her mouth as if it were sour. "I mean it," she said, after a moment. "Leave me alone."

Ben picked up his empty glass and walked toward the bar, turning the glass in his hand and feeling how it fit his grasp, stood looking at the back of Art's head, the thin hair, fine and blond, and then he wrapped the glass in his fist and smashed it into the hollow of Art's neck, shattering the glass and driving Art's face into the counter. Then he ran, crashing out the door and onto the sidewalk.

His hand was cut and bleeding when he stopped, blocks away. He picked glass from his palm and wrapped his hand in his handkerchief and kept walking, looking in the store windows, bright and lighted for Christmas.

Clara left for Sacramento that night, lived there with her father, worked in a factory southeast of town, making airplane parts and taking care of the old man, not coming back until he died. Sometimes Ben wondered if she would have come back any-

way, even if the old man hadn't died. Maybe she'd just been waiting for Art to come after her. And then one day on the street he
asked, "You and Art going back together?," just hoping he could
get her to talk awhile.

"I guess not," she said. "That's what he told me."

"I'm sorry," Ben said. And funny enough, he was.

"I came back because I wanted," she said. "Guess I lived here
too long."

That spring Ben and Marie were married and began living out
of town, on a place her father owned, and the next fall his father
was killed, crushed under a hillside combine in Washington, just
north of Walla Walla, drunk and asleep at the leveling wheel, dead
when they dug him out. And then the summer Art and Ben turned
thirty-four Marie got pregnant and that winter Art was killed, shot
in the back of the head by a girl named Steffanie Rudd, a thin red-
haired girl just out of high school and, so people said, knocked up
a little. Art was on the end stool in The Tarpaper Shack, his usual
place, when the girl entered quietly and shot before anyone
noticed. He was dead when he hit the floor, face destroyed, blood
splattered and clotting over the mirror and glasses behind the bar.
And all the time music he'd punched was playing on the jukebox.
Trailer for sale or rent, and I can't stop loving you, and time to
bum again, and that's what you get for loving me: Roger Miller,
Ray Charles, Waylon Jennings.

Ben awakened the night of the shooting and heard Marie on
the phone, felt her shake him awake in the dim light of the bedroom. She seemed enormously frightened and continued grasping
with her heavy soft hand, as if to awaken herself. She was eight
months pregnant.

"He's dead." She spoke softly, seeming terrified, as if some
idea she feared had been at last confirmed. "He never had a
chance," she said.

"He had plenty." Ben sat up and put his arm around her,
forced from his shock.

"They never gave him anything." She folded down and began
to cry. Later, nearly morning, after coffee and stumped-out cigarettes, when Marie gave up and went to bed, Ben sat alone at the
kitchen table. He felt sorry for her and wondered if he should.
"Afraid of everything," Art had said. "That's how they are. Every
stinking one."

Ben saw Art drunk and talking like he was ready for anything,
actually involved with nothing but a string of girls like the one

who shot him. And then, somehow, the idea of Art and Marie got hold of Ben. It came from the way she acted, her crying. There was something wrong. Ben knew, sitting there, feeling the knowledge seep around his defense, what it was.

She was in the bedroom, curled under the blankets, crying softly. "What is it?" he asked. "There's something going on." She didn't open her eyes, but the crying seemed to slow a little, hesitate. He waited, standing beside their bed, looking down, all the time wondering, as he became more sure, if it happened in this bed, and all the time knowing it made no difference where it happened. And her fault. Not any fault of Art's. Art was what he was. She could have stopped him. Ben's hands felt strange, as if there was something to be done he couldn't recognize. He asked again, hearing his voice harsh and strained. "What is it?"

She didn't answer. He forced her onto her back, where she couldn't avoid looking at him, held her there, waiting for her to open her eyes, and she struggled silently, twisting her upper body against his grip. His fingers sank into her shoulder and his wrist trembled. They remained like that, forcing against each other. Then she relaxed, turned, and opened her eyes. "What is it?" he asked again. "It was something between you and Art, wasn't it?" Her eyes were changed, shielded.

She shook her head. "No," she said. "No."

"He was screwing you, wasn't he? Is it his kid?"

"It was a long time ago," she said softly.

"My ass." He let go of her shoulder, saw the marks his fingers left. "That's why you're so tore up. Because you ain't getting any more." He walked around the bed, unable for some reason, because of what he was left with, to ask her if it happened here, in this bed. "Isn't that right?" he said.

"It was a long time ago."

"Did you both laugh?"

"It doesn't matter now."

"How come you married me? He turn you down?"

"Because I was afraid of him. I didn't want him. He was just fooling. I wanted you, not him."

Ben slapped her, and she curled quickly again, her hands pressed to her mouth, crying, her shoulders moving. He spun her to face him. "You ain't getting away," he said. "So I was a nice tame dog, and you took me."

"You'll hurt the baby."

"His Goddamned baby."

"It all broke off when I met you," she said. "He told me to go ahead, that you'd be good to me." It had surprised him when they met that she was with Art, but somehow he'd never until now gotten the idea they had anything going on. "It was only a few times after I knew you," she said. "He begged me."

"So I got stuck with the leavings." He cursed her again, at the same time listening to at least a little of what she said. "He begged me." That was sad. Remembering Art those last years, after he came home to stay, Ben believed her.

"So he dumped you off onto me," Ben said. "I wish I could thank him."

"It wasn't like that. He loved you. He said for me to marry you and be happy."

"So you did. And I was stupid enough to go for it."

"He was a little boy. It was fun, but he was a little boy."

"I'm happy," he said. "Things worked out so nice for you." She shook her head and didn't answer. Ben wondered what he should do. It was as if he had never been married, right in always imagining his life as single. He'd watched his friends settle, seen their kids, and it had seemed those were things he was not entitled to, that he was going to grow old in a habit of taverns, rented rooms, separate from the married world. He was still there, outside. And she'd kept it all a secret. "You stinking pig," he said slowly.

"It was a long time ago."

He was tired and his work was waiting. Maybe it was a long time ago and maybe it wasn't. She lay crying while he dressed to go out and feed her father's cattle, and in the afternoon she had the house picked up and a meal waiting. She watched while he ate, but they didn't talk. He asked if she wanted to go to the funeral and she said no and that was all. When he was drinking his coffee, calm and so tired his chest ached, he started thinking about Clara. He wondered if she'd known. Wouldn't have made any difference, he thought. Not after everything else.

Three days later, heading for the burial, he was alone, driving through new snow that softly drifted across the highway, hunched against the wheel, and his hands seemed swollen and dead, fingers thick and numb, the broken cracks in the rough calluses ingrained black. A tire chain ticked a fender, but he kept going. He'd gone out at daylight to feed, a mandatory job that had to be done every day of winter, regardless of other obligations. The rust-streaked Chevrolet swayed on the rutted ice beneath the snow, and the steady and lumbering gait of the team he fed with, two massive frost-coated Belgian geldings, the creaking oceanic motion of the hay wagon, was still with him, more real than this, closer to the

117

speed he was going.

The Derrick County cemetery was just below the road, almost five miles short of town. They were going to bury Art in the open ground reserved for charity burials, away from the lanes of Lombardy poplars and old-time lilacs. By dark the grave would be filled and covered with snow. Ben parked and got out, stood beside the idling Chevrolet, tail pipe spitting fog, and looked down at the hole. The bells of the Catholic church, far away in town, were faintly tolling.

The trail down toward the grave was tromped and hard, frozen into ice, and the first foot of the hole was chiseled and smooth where the frozen earth, embedded with ice, had been chipped out with a bar. Ben stood a moment, then started toward the warm Chevrolet, sat with his hands cupped in his crotch, warming them, then backed slowly out of the graveyard.

Davanero was on the east side of the valley, scattered houses hung with ice, windows sealed against wind by tacked-on plastic sheeting. Forested mountains were indistinguishable from the sky among clouds of storm. The still smoke of house fires rose in dark, slowly dispersing strings. Ben drove between lots heaped with snow-muffled junk, past shacks with open, hanging doors where drifters lived in summer, into the center blocks of town. The stores were open and a few people circulated toward the coffee shops. He felt deserted, cut away from everything, as if this were an island in the center of winter.

The Open sign hung crooked in the front window of The Tarpaper Shack. Ben wondered if Clara was tending bar, if she would go to the funeral. He parked and walked slowly through the snow to the door. The church bells were louder, close and direct. Inside, the tavern was dark and barnlike, empty except for Clara, who was washing glasses in a metal sink. Ben went to the far end, where Art always sat, and eased onto a stool. "I'd take a shot," he said. "A double. Take one yourself."

"I'm closing up," she said. "So there's no use hanging around." She stayed at the sink, hands washing mechanically.

"You going to the funeral? Like a church girl?"

"I'm closing up." Her hands were quiet in the water. "I guess you need a drink," she said. "Go lock the door." She was sitting in one of the booths when he got there. "You ain't going to the funeral?" he asked again. Her face was hard and thin, a contrast to her thickening body.

"What good is that?"

"I guess you feel pretty bad."

"I guess." She drank quickly, like a bird dipping water. "I

would have took anything off him. Any damned thing. And that stupid bitch kills him. I would have given anything for a kid."

Ben sipped the cheap, bitter whiskey. "I don't look at what that girl thought. I don't know."

"He never blamed you over that. Not ever. I seen him cry."

"When he was drunk."

"What the hell—when he was drunk?" She finished her drink.

Ben killed his double, and Clara went for another round. "To hell with their Goddamned funeral," he said. Clara played music, slow country stuff, on the machine, and they danced, staggering against the stools and the shuffleboard table, clutching at each other. She pushed him away after a few rounds. "If you ain't one hell of a dancer," she said. "Art was a pretty dancer." She sat at the booth and reached one arm flat along the table and lay her head beside it, facing the wall. "Goddamn," she said. "I could cry." The music continued.

"I ain't cried since I was a little girl," she said. "Not since then. Not since I was a little girl." Ben wandered through the music of the room, carrying his drink, called his wife on the telephone, fumbling the dial, finally hearing her voice. "You bet your sweet ass I'm drunk," he shouted, without introduction, then hung up.

"Ain't you some hero," Clara said. She drank what whiskey was left in her glass. "You're nothing," she said. "Absolutely nothing."

Outside, the bells had stopped. Nothing. That was what he felt like. Nothing. Like his hands were without strength to steer the car. He sat awhile, half drunk, then drove to the jail, a gray brick building with heavy black wire mesh over the windows. The deputy, a small bald man in military pinks, sat behind a wood desk in the center of the main room, coffee beside him. He smiled when he saw Ben, but didn't say anything. "How's chances of seeing that girl?" Ben asked. He didn't know why he'd come. It was just some idea that because she'd hated Art enough to kill him, because of that, maybe she understood and could tell him, Ben, why he wasn't nothing. He knew, even while he spoke, that it was a stupid, drunk idea.

"Okay," the deputy said, after a minute. "Come on. I guess you got a right."

They went through two heavy locked doors, back into a masonry room without windows, lighted by a long fluorescent tube. Two cells were separated by steel bars six inches apart. The room was warm and in the light seemed to flicker. The girl was sitting on a cot in the left-hand cell, cross-legged, with red hair

119

straight down over her shoulders, wearing a wrinkled blue smock without pockets, looking at her hands, which were folded in her lap. Her eyes, when she looked up, were pale and very large, the whites totally clear. "What now?" she said. Her voice, which seemed forced, was surprisingly loud.

"Ben wanted to see you," the deputy said.

"Like a zoo, ain't it." The girl grinned, gestured with her hands.

"And you're not one bit sorry?" Ben asked. "Just one bit sorry for what you did?"

"Not one bit," the girl echoed. "I've had plenty of time to think about that. I'm not. I'm happy. I feel good."

"He wasn't no bad man," Ben said. "Not really. He never really was."

"He sure as hell wasn't Winston Churchill. He never even tried to make me happy." She refolded her hands in her lap.

"I don't see it," Ben said. "No way I can see you're right. He wasn't that bad."

"The thing I liked about him," she said, "was that he was old enough. He was like you. He was old enough to do anything. He could have been nice if he'd wanted."

The deputy laughed.

"I felt so bad before," the girl said. "Killing him was so easy. The only thing I feel bad about is that I never got down into the center of him and made him crawl around. That's the only thing, I'm sorry about that, but that's all."

"He didn't owe you nothing," Ben said.

The girl looked at the deputy. "Make him leave," she said.

Snow fell again, large and single flakes that dropped straight and wavering through the gray afternoon, and Ben drove slowly home. He could only see the blurred outlines of the trees on either side of the lane toward the house. Marie was in the bedroom sleeping. The dim and wallpapered room was gray and cold, the bed a rumpled island. She was quiet, her shape a mound beneath the blankets, her mouth gaping a little, the pillow damp beside her lips.

After undressing, Ben sat on the edge of the bed. Marie sighed and moved, but didn't waken, and he reached to touch her and then stopped, hovered with his hand extended, his flesh ingrained with dirt and rough over her white skin. Her eyes flickered. "Come," she said, stretching. "Get under the covers."

"In a minute." He went back out and smoked a cigarette, then crawled in bed and put his hand on her belly, waiting to feel the baby flutter, remembering a warm, shirt-sleeve day in February, working with Art and hurrying while they fed a final load of bales to the trailing cattle, eager to get uptown and into the taverns, noontime sun glaring off wind-glazed fields of snow.

John L'Heureux

Departures

The priest is arriving on the train. He is not really a priest, because he is only twenty-five and is still a seminarian, but he wears a Roman collar, and everyone thinks he is a priest, and he thinks of himself as a priest. It is six years since he has visited his parents in their home. They have visited him at the seminary, of course, but this is his first visit to them, and he is very anxious about it.

There is a crazy couple across the aisle, and as the train pulls into the station their anger and excitement come near to hysteria; they have just had—as they keep saying—a scrape with death. "We could have been killed," she says, her voice sharp, abused. "We've had a terrible scrape with death." She only pretends to speak to her husband; actually she is addressing the priest and the couple in front of him and the whole car. Her eyes are glassy and wild and she goes on talking with small gasps and shrieks while her husband—glassy-eyed, too, and in shock—says, "You're right, you're right," and wrestles a red plastic suitcase from the rack overhead. They are still exclaiming as they forge down the aisle, important and proud at being almost dead.

The priest waits. He does not want to be near those crazy people when he greets his parents. This will be a special moment and he wants it to be perfect. These six years have made him ill at ease in public. He cannot stand the noise, the rudeness, the urgency in voices. Emotions spill out of people, they shout in public; anger bristles everywhere, in everyone, in the street, the train station, the train. People chew gum. They belch. They push. He is revolted by the vulgarity, the nakedness of it all. In the seminary there is no emotion, no anger, no urgency—at least not visibly. Everyone keeps inside himself whatever it is he feels.

So the priest stays in his seat until the crazy people have disappeared from the car. Then he gets up, sets his face in a smile—a half-smile—and prepares to meet his parents. As he climbs down the steep iron steps, he is conscious of people on the platform looking. At him? Or just for somebody they are here to meet? Suddenly a woman shrieks and the priest turns to help her, thinking she must be hurt, thinking of Anna Karenina beneath the train wheels. But no. The woman is merely excited and the scream is only delight at seeing a boy, her son probably. "Billy," she says, "Billy baby." She hugs him, kisses him, screams again. The boy is embarrassed and the priest, embarrassed too, turns away. Mother and son, he thinks, a travesty. He has told his parents he will meet them in the waiting room, on the east side, and he joins the crowd moving toward the stairs. Ahead of him he sees another priest, about his own age, red-haired and stout. Sanity, he thinks, an oasis. But as they reach the bottom of the stairs a woman lunges at the red-haired priest, hugging him once and then again, while a man—his father, with the same red hair and fat—slaps him on the back over and over. "Father Joe," they call him, though, by their ages, he has to be their son. The woman puts her arm under Father Joe's and leans into him, her possession.

There is a disturbance now; somebody is shouting, somebody touches his arm. It is the crazy couple, even more hysterical than before, asking him something, insisting he explain to another couple what happened on the train. A little crowd is gathering and the priest, confused, turns from person to person. He is not listening, he merely wants to get away. And then suddenly he sees his mother smiling from beyond the crowd and his father behind her, his hands on her shoulders, smiling. They are a picture of order in all this chaos. The crazy woman tugs at his arm, but he pulls away from her and, moving blindly through the crowd, walks toward his mother and father. Yes, the priest thinks, I will bring order out of chaos.

His mother is beautiful, radiant, and she will not be dead for another fifteen years. She smiles and comes to meet him and he will remember her this way always. He will wake in the night remembering how she is now, what he does to her. Because as she goes to put her arms around him, as she lifts her face to kiss him, he says to her, with a smile made icy by his self-control, "I'll just kiss you on the cheek—don't touch me—and I'll shake hands with

Dad, and then we'll turn and walk out of here." And he bends to kiss her on the cheek, but stops because she has pulled slightly away; she has gone white, and the look of panic on her face is not nearly so terrible as the look of drowning in her eyes.

The priest's father has been dead for five years and now the priest sits by his mother's bedside waiting for her to die. Fifteen years have passed since his train came in and he did not kiss her and she turned her face away. His mother has Parkinson's disease and the benign effects of L-Dopa have worn off, so that she is bent now and trembles violently whenever she tries to do anything for herself. She drools sometimes and sometimes she cannot control her bowels. But the priest has been told it is not Parkinson's which is killing her; it is cancer. The priest thinks a great deal about death and about the things that kill us. He is not surprised, being forty and having seen many people to their deaths, that dying is not only an agony, it is boredom. He has been waiting by her bedside for months now, an hour or two each day, and still she has not died.

His mother is unconscious much of the time. Or barely conscious; it is hard for him to tell. On the occasions when she turns to him and says something, he is astonished that very often it is something he has been thinking himself. A month before he had been remembering his father's quick death, a quick and merciful heart attack—how it had been the death his father would have chosen if he were given choices. "Your father died well," she said, and the priest leaned forward in surprise. He thought she had been unconscious. "Father?" he asked. "He died the way he would have wanted," she said. "Yes," he said, "I was thinking that." She sighed and shook her head, and a tear showed in the corner of her eye. "What?" he asked. "This is not the way I would have chosen," she said. And though he did not say them he thought the words he hated most: "self-pity." So he bit the inside of his lip and said, "Try to sleep, Mother."

Again, a week or so later, he was thinking how he had always taken from them, his mother and father; he had never given them anything. He looked at her lying there, her eyes closed, sweating, and he thought, I'll wet the washcloth and put it on her forehead. But before he could reach the washcloth she said to him, "You've always given to us. You've given us everything." And she looked at him with the drowning look.

This sort of thing has happened several times. He has begun to wonder if he causes her to think of what he is thinking: the exercise of the stronger mind on the weaker. No, it can't be that. And so he sits by her bed reading his Shakespeare—he is completing his Ph.D. in English—and sometimes he adjusts her pillows or wipes her forehead, and when she is able he talks to her. But more and more now it is a matter of waiting for the end. Her medication has been increased; even when she is not unconscious she is so heavily doped against the pain that conversation is impossible. He waits.

The priest's mother is living and the priest is waiting for her to die. He is wanting her to die now that the pain is so bad, now that he cannot bear any longer the suffering, the boredom. But she does not die.

And then finally she does die. But before she dies she wakes and talks to him one last time. He has been thinking of the train, that terrible day when he destroyed everything, when he tried to bring some order out of chaos and said, "Don't touch me" and she turned away from him. He has been thinking of that all day and now she wakes and drugged, confused, looks at him and says, "You're not to worry. When the train comes in, I won't kiss you. I won't touch you." "No!" the priest cries out sharply. "Mother, no." He leans over the bed to kiss her, but as he does she turns from him, saying, "I'll be good. I promise. I'll be good." And with her dying breath, her face still turned from him, she says, "I will."

It is the same day. It is always the same day, except that now he remembers it differently. The priest is leaving on the train, Boston to Springfield, a three-hour trip. He is not really a priest, because he is only twenty-five and is still a seminarian, but he thinks of himself as a priest and so do his parents. His father will not die for another ten years, his mother for fifteen. They will both live to see him ordained.

The train pulls out of the station and the priest begins to read his book, Sartre's *L'existentialisme est un humanisme*. It is boring but good for him. Existentialism is good and humanism is good, and he feels that boredom is just something that goes along with the package. He reads half a page before he realizes he has no idea what he is reading. He is upset about something. What? He doesn't know. Was it getting on the train? Seeing all those people elbowing one another to get ahead, that old woman chewing gum, the man who belched? Partly that. He felt so alien, so removed from them—inhuman. All that pushing and shoving, and there are plenty of empty seats. It makes no sense.

The door between the cars opens and a middle-aged couple come in. She is carrying two shopping bags, one full of presents, wrapped in metallic papers, the other full of something the priest cannot see, because there is a sweater over the top. The man drags an enormous red suitcase, which bumps his leg at every step. It is a warm day and they are both perspiring.

"How about here?" she says, pointing to the seat directly in front of the priest, but then she sees him and says, "No, over here instead," and she backs up, bumping into her husband, who drops the suitcase and curses. "Here," she says. "Yes, this is nice. This side is better. This is fine. Sit down, Freddie. No, let me get next to the window." The man groans and says nothing, giving all his attention to getting the suitcase up into the luggage rack. "This, too," she says, giving him the bag with the presents. "No, I'll keep it at my feet," she says, and takes the bag back. Finally they are settled. The priest has watched them from where he sits, on the other side of the aisle, one seat back, and he continues to watch them. He is surprised to find the taste of acid in his mouth. He wants to spit; he doesn't know why.

Where he has felt uneasy before, he now feels anger. At himself, perhaps. He returns to his book. He is more than a seminarian, he is a Jesuit seminarian, and so he has an obligation to theology and to culture. But after another two pages he decides he does not have an obligation to Sartre and he puts the book in his briefcase. He decides to meditate. Jesuits meditate for at least an hour each day, usually on some incident, some moment, in the life of Christ, and he has never missed meditation once, not even when he lay for a week in the infirmary with a temperature of a hundred and three.

In fact, the infirmary meditation is the nearest he has come to a kind of mystical experience. He had been meditating on the Crucifixion, lying in bed with his scalding temperature, watching what was happening. He saw them drive the nails through the wrists, through the bent feet, saw them lift the heavy cross to the correct angle, until the base thudded into the stone notch that would hold it upright. There was a groan and some blood splattered onto the seamless white tunic they had stripped from him and which now lay at the base of the cross. And then there was blackness. He fell asleep, he supposed, and when he woke, his body soaked with sweat from the fever, he tried to see that white tunic beneath the cross. But he could not see it, he could see only the broad back of a soldier and he could hear the rattle of dice. Then the soldier moved and he could see the others, three of them, taking their turns with the dice, gambling for the tunic and the sandals. And when the last had thrown, one of the soldiers scooped up the dice and held them out to the priest. His hand hung there, offering the dice in his open palm, and while they all stared the priest put out his own hand and slowly, tentatively, took the dice. And then, with the small strength he could muster, he closed his fist around them.

The priest was fevered for three days more, and what he remembered after was that for those three days he held the dice in his hands. It is a meditation the priest can call back at will. He can and he does now, though he does not know why. Not because of the way it makes him feel—because feeling, he knows, has nothing to do with anything. No, he calls it back because it has something to do with *not* feeling, with the reason he is a priest in the first place.

At college his roommate had said to him one day, "Seeing as how you're a Catholic, and the best thing a Catholic can do with his life is be a priest, don't you feel obliged to be a priest?" He laughed, seeing he had struck deep. "I mean, you're smart enough, and you're moral enough—you don't screw or anything—so why not? I mean, aren't you obliged to?" The words were insignificant; it was what they did to him at that particular moment that mattered. Because he had been thinking of the priesthood and wanting, but fearing to ask for, a sign. His roommate's words seemed some kind of sign—no miraculous intervention, just the intervention of pure reason. Not a lightning bolt from heaven, he said to himself, just a slammed door. And the meditation of the dice seemed somehow a confirmation of this sign.

The priest opens his eyes. The train has been stopped for some time, new people have got on, and now it is pulling slowly away from the platform. They are near Worcester somewhere. The priest looks out the window opposite him and can see up ahead a grassy hill where three small boys are waving to the train. On the other side of the aisle the woman is rummaging through her shopping bag, totally absorbed with whatever she has in there. The man is gone—he is at the far end of the car getting a drink of water. The train pulls alongside the little boys and the priest waves to them, but they do not wave back. They throw stones, which fall short of the train—all except one, which strikes the window next to the woman with the shopping bag. It makes a sharp sound and at once there appears on the window a white spot the size of a nickel and, radiating from it, a sunburst of silver cracks. The priest sits forward prepared to do something, but there is nothing to be done. Despite the noise, like a door slamming, the woman does not seem to hear; she continues plunging her hand into the bag and bringing out things he cannot see. The other people around are either sleeping or absorbed in their reading. No one has noticed except him.

The man returns with a cup of water for his wife. She drinks it and they sit in silence looking out the window. "Was that window like that before?" he asks. "Of course," she says. And then she looks at it. "Well, I'm not sure," she says. She puts her finger on the spot of white and traces one of the cracks that radiate from it. "It looks like it's been broken," she says. "Somebody must have thrown a stone," he says, and settles back in his seat. "Well, if it happened while I was sitting here, I could have been hurt—if the glass broke," she says. "It was probably just a stone," he says. "It could have broken. I could have been hurt," she says, "if it was a bullet. I could have been . . ."

She is excited now and leans forward to the couple in front of her. "Did you see this happen? Did you see this window get broken? Right by my head?" But they have seen nothing. She turns to the man across the aisle, to the couple in front of him, to the empty seats behind her. Nobody has seen. The conductor appears and she waves at him, calling, "Look at this, there's been an accident. Somebody broke this window right while I was sitting here."

The conductor looks at the window and at the woman and at the window again. "What?" he says. He looks at the people in front of the couple and across the aisle from them; he looks at the priest. The priest says, "A little boy threw a stone and it hit the window." "Do you see? Do you hear?" the woman says. And she turns to the priest. "Was it a stone? Was I sitting here? Right by the window?" "Yes," the priest says. "I could have been killed," the woman says to the conductor. "Do you hear what the priest said? Would a priest lie? It could have been a bullet." "Damned kids," the conductor says and moves down the aisle. "We've had a narrow escape from death, Freddie," she says, and from here to Springfield her anger and her enthusiasm grow.

The priest is sick. The chaos of life, the chaos of mind. It is all hopeless. Look at that crazy couple. The boredom of lives lived so purposelessly depresses him, sickens him. The emotion, the anger, the public displays.

The train is in Springfield but he waits until the crazy couple get off. He does not want to be near them when he meets his parents. Getting off the train, he hears a woman shriek as she descends upon her son; he sees a fat priest with red hair; he is overwhelmed by the noise, the vulgarity. And then there is a disturbance of some sort. It is the crazy couple. Her husband is tugging at the priest's arm, the woman is trying to draw him into a group that has gathered around her. "The priest saw it all," she is saying. "See that priest? He's living proof. If it weren't for that priest, we wouldn't be here now." But the priest does not hear what she says, because suddenly beyond the crowd he sees his mother, looking beautiful and composed, smiling, and behind her his father. She will not be dead for fifteen years. They will live to see him ordained, his life fulfilled.

He goes to meet them, conscious that he is in public, conscious of a small circle of order in this chaos. And as his mother opens her arms to him, he says, "I'll just kiss you on the cheek—don't touch me—then . . ." But already she has begun to turn away.

The priest is arriving on the train—New York to Boston, a five-hour trip. He has been a priest for many years and, he sometimes thinks, he is a good priest. But what is "good," he thinks. He thinks he does not know that. Sometimes he thinks he does not care. Thinking is his life now and that seems enough. Thinking and seeming. He is fifty-five and will not be dead for another fifteen years. But dying is a moment he does not care to think about.

The priest is coming back from New York, where he attended the wake of his last living relative. There is a peculiar satisfaction in that, a finality he does not fully understand but which he recognizes all the same. He would have said the burial Mass for his aunt but she died on Good Friday, which means the burial cannot take place until Monday, and so the priest is coming back to Boston, where he can be used at midnight tonight in the Easter Vigil services. And then tomorrow the Mass of the Resurrection—whoopee. He is irreverent, sometimes, in the way he thinks; it is his psyche's accommodation to absurdity, or perhaps pain, or bitterness. Anyway, he will be back in Boston in no time, and then he will go to his room and have a good belt of Scotch, and then a couple of hours in bed to recover for the Easter Vigil.

Trains mean nothing to him anymore. He does not see the people who chew gum, who push, who carry on angrily over nothing. He does not care. That is simply how they are, that is how life is, and what can anyone do about it?

His drinking is not a problem, he thinks. It might have become one if he had not, at forty, gone for his Ph.D. in English. That has stabilized him somehow; teaching English is more human than teaching theology. He is grateful for the diversions provided by his Ph.D. He has seen too many priests hit forty and realize nothing else is ever going to happen to them, and he has seen the dodges they take—running off with the school nurse, having affairs with their students' mothers, hitting the bottle. His dodge would have been—would be—hitting the bottle. But it will not happen to him. He is careful, for now. He drinks a fifth of Scotch each week, and if he runs out before the week is over, then he goes without. Of course he does, on occasion, stop by somebody else's room and have a drink from his Scotch. But that is social drinking. That is different. He is handling his after-forty problem very well. He has no regrets, he thinks.

The train pulls into the station and he pushes his way to the front of the car. He is eager to get off and get home. He does not hear the woman who shrieks with pleasure as she descends upon her teenage son. He does not notice the demonstrations of anger and frustration and delight. He does not even smell the rank odor of cigarette butts and urine. He just keeps his eyes cast down and makes his way through the waiting room to the cab stand. Leave the dead to bury the dead, he used to think as he left these depressing public places, but now he does not think about them at all. He is a priest who has left the world to itself, truly.

He is home in his little room and he pours himself a Scotch and drinks it. He showers and stands in front of the long mirror examining the evidence of too much food, too much drink. He will have to cut down. He puts on his yellow pajamas and sets the clock. He has four hours before he must put on vestments for the Easter liturgy; and so he stretches out on the bed and closes his eyes, ready for sleep. But the trip to New York and the aunt's wake and the trip back to Boston swim through his mind and he cannot sleep. He feels good, and he feels guilty for feeling good. The boredom is over, those long hours on trains, the unpleasantness of all those strangers at the wake. Over is good, he thinks. Finality is good. But what is good? Well, he *feels* good and that's something.

The priest wakes from a nightmare. His head aches and he has trouble getting his breath. He is shivering. What was he dreaming? He cannot remember. He is late. He hurries through his shower, shaves, dresses, his mind going back and back to the dream. But always it eludes him. Perhaps it was the soldier dream again. He no longer meditates, but often in his sleep he sees the soldier's back and hears the rattle of dice. The soldier shifts position and the priest sees the others, three of them, taking their turns with the dice. Finally, as always, the last one scoops up the dice and hands them to the priest, who takes them and closes his fist on them and when he looks down—this is the new part, the awful part—he sees that blood is oozing from between his fingers. And then he wakes up. The old meditation, which for years gave him some kind of abstract comfort, has turned to dream and to nightmare. But it was not the soldier dream tonight, it was . . . And again the dream eludes him.

The priest is vested now, saying a brief prayer before leading the procession to the rear of the chapel. The vigil is a long and complicated ritual and in his mind he ticks off the major sections. There is the striking of the new fire—a tricky business, because all the lights are out and you have to fumble around with the flint device. Then the blessing of the new fire, the blessing of the Easter candle, the solemn procession. The singing will be tough, because he has a weak voice. The readings. Then the blessing of the baptismal water . . . Death by drowning, he thinks, and for a second his mind veers to *The Waste Land*, but then he comes back to the vigil. The baptism of the baby—he must check the baby's name before that part of the ceremony—and then the litany and finally, at midnight, Mass. Fire and water. Burning and drowning. Light in the darkness. The water that gives rebirth. It is a symbolism so ancient, so basic, that it must guarantee a reality, he thinks.

And so the ceremony has begun and the priest stands in the vestibule surrounded by the entire community. The lights have been extinguished in the chapel and now the light over the door goes out and they are plunged into complete blackness. They are waiting, all of them, for him to strike flint against flint and start that spark which will be the light shining in the darkness. The flint grates and grates again, and just as he has begun to think he will never get it to work right, there is a flicker and a dot of light and then a flame. The flame catches in the little pot of wax and by its light the priest begins the blessing of the new fire.

"The Lord be with you," he says. And the community responds, "And with your spirit." He breathes easy, because the rest of the prayer he knows by heart. He stares into the fire, reciting the blessing. "Let us pray. O God, through Your Son Jesus Christ, You bestowed the light of Your glory upon the faithful. Sanctify . . ."

But then, in the fire, he recognizes his nightmare. He sees the soldier's back and hears the rattle of dice; the soldier moves and the priest sees not the three other soldiers but his mother; her drowning face is turned away from him and her hand is held out. In her hand are those dice—bloody, eyeless.

"Sanctify . . ." the priest says once more, and now it is time to raise his hand in blessing, but for the moment he cannot, and he continues to stare into the fire. "Sanctify . . ." he says again, staring and staring, still unable to bless, unable to go on or turn away.

"Sanctify . . ."

The word echoes in the darkness and the light flickers until with his bare hands the priest reaches forward and puts the fire out.

131

Leonard Michaels

Murderers

When my uncle Moe dropped dead of a heart attack I became expert in the subway system. With a nickel I'd get to Queens, twist and zoom to Coney Island, twist again toward the George Washington Bridge—beyond which was darkness. I wanted proximity to darkness, strangeness. Who doesn't? The poor in spirit, the ignorant and frightened. My family came from Poland, then never went any place until they had heart attacks. The consummation of years in one neighborhood: a black Cadillac, corpse inside. We should have buried Uncle Moe where he shuffled away his life, in the kitchen or toilet, under the linoleum, near the coffee pot. Anyhow, they were dropping on Henry Street and Cherry Street. Blue lips. The previous winter it was cousin Charlie, forty-five years old. Moe, Charlie, Sam, Adele—family meant a punch in the chest, fire in the arm. I didn't want to wait for it. I went to Harlem, the Polo Grounds, Far Rockaway, thousands of miles on nickels, mainly underground. Tenements watched me go, day after day, fingering nickels. One afternoon I stopped to grind my heel against the curb. Melvin and Arnold Bloom appeared, then Harold Cohen. Melvin said, "You step in dog shit?" Grinding was my answer. Harold Cohen said, "The rabbi is home. I saw him on Market Street. He was walking fast." Oily Arnold, eleven years old, began to urge: "Let's go up to our roof." The decision waited for me. I considered the roof, the view of industrial Brooklyn, the Battery, ships in the river, bridges, towers, and the rabbi's apartment. "All right," I said. We didn't giggle or look to one

132

another for moral signals. We were running.

The blinds were up and curtains pulled, giving sunlight, wind, birds to the rabbi's apartment—a magnificent metropolitan view. The rabbi and his wife never took it, but in the light and air of summer afternoons, in the eye of gull and pigeon, they were joyous. A bearded young man, and his young pink wife, sacramentally bald. Beard and Baldy, with everything to see, looked at each other. From a water tank on the opposite roof, higher than their windows, we looked at them. In psycho-analysis this is "The Primal Scene." To achieve the primal scene we crossed a ledge six inches wide. A half-inch indentation in the brick gave us fingerholds. We dragged bellies and groins against the brick face to a steel ladder. It went up the side of the building, bolted into brick, and up the side of the water tank to a slanted tin roof which caught the afternoon sun. We sat on that roof like angels, shot through with light, derealized in brilliance. Our sneakers sucked hot slanted metal. Palms and fingers pressed to bone on nailheads.

The Brooklyn Navy Yard with destroyers and aircraft carriers, the Statue of Liberty putting the sky to the torch, the dull remote skyscrapers of Wall Street, and the Empire State Building were among the wonders we dominated. Our view of the holy man and his wife, on their living-room couch and floor, on the bed in their bedroom, could not be improved. Unless we got closer. But fifty feet across the air was right. We heard their phonograph and watched them dancing. We couldn't hear the gratifications or see pimples. We smelled nothing. We didn't want to touch.

For a while I watched them. Then I gazed beyond into shimmering nullity, gray, blue, and green murmuring over rooftops and towers. I had watched them before. I could tantalize myself with this brief ocular perversion, the general cleansing nihil of a view. This was the beginning of philosophy. I indulged in ambience, in space like eons. So what if my uncle Moe was dead? I was philosophical and luxurious. I didn't even have to look at the rabbi and his wife. After all, how many times had we dissolved stickball games when the rabbi came home? How many times had we risked shameful discovery, scrambling up the ladder, exposed to their windows—if they looked. We risked life itself to achieve this eminence. I looked at the rabbi and his wife.

Today she was a blonde. Bald didn't mean no wigs. She had ten wigs, ten colors, fifty styles. She looked different, the same, and very good. A human theme in which nothing begat anything and was gorgeous. To me she was the world's lesson. Aryan yellow slipped through pins about her ears. An olive complexion mediated yellow hair and Arabic black eyes. Could one care what she really looked like? What was *really*? The minute you wondered, she looked like something else, in another wig, another style. Without the wigs she was a baldy-bean lady. Today she was a blonde. Not blonde. *A* blonde. The phonograph blared and her deep loops flowed Tommy Dorsey, Benny Goodman, and then the thing itself, Choo-Choo Lopez. Rumba! One, two-three. One, two-three. The rabbi stepped away to delight in blonde imagination. Twirling and individual, he stepped away snapping fingers, going high and light on his toes. A short bearded man, balls afling, cock shuddering like a springboard. Rumba! One, two-three. *Ole!* *Vaya*, Choo-Choo!

> I was on my way to spend some time in Cuba.
> Stopped off at Miami Beach, la-la.
> Oh, what a rumba they teach, la-la.
> Way down in Miami Beach,
> Oh, what a chroombah they teach, la-la.
> Way-down-in-Miami-Beach.

She, on the other hand, was somewhat reserved. A shift in one lush hip was total rumba. He was Mr. Life. She was dancing. He was a naked man. She was what she was in the garment of her soft, essential self. He was snapping, clapping, hopping to the beat. The beat lived in her visible music, her lovely self. Except for the wig. Also a watchband that desecrated her wrist. But it gave her a bit of the whorish. She never took it off.

Harold Cohen began a cocktail-mixer motion, masturbating with two fists. Seeing him at such hard futile work, braced only by sneakers, was terrifying. But I grinned. Out of terror, I twisted an encouraging face. Melvin Bloom kept one hand on the tin. The other knuckled the rumba numbers into the back of my head. Nodding like a defective, little Arnold Bloom chewed his lip and squealed as the rabbi and his wife smacked together. The rabbi clapped her buttocks, fingers buried in the cleft. They stood only on his legs. His back arched, knees bent, thighs thick with thrust, up, up, up. Her legs wrapped his hips, ankles crossed, hooked for constriction. "Oi, oi, oi," she cried, wig flashing left, right, tossing the Brooklyn Navy Yard, the Statue of Liberty, and the Empire State Building to hell. Arnold squealed oi, squealing rubber. His sneaker heels stabbed tin to stop his slide. Melvin said, "Idiot." Arnold's ring hooked a nailhead and the ring and ring finger remained. The hand, the arm, the rest of him, were gone.

We rumbled down the ladder. "Oi, oi, oi," she yelled. In a

freak of ecstasy her eyes had rolled and caught us. The rabbi drilled to her quick and she had us. "OI, OI," she yelled above congas going clop, doom-doom, clop, doom-doom on the way to Cuba. The rabbi flew to the window, a red mouth opening in his beard: "Murderers." He couldn't know what he said. Melvin Bloom was crying. My fingers were tearing, bleeding into brick. Harold Cohen, like an adding machine, gibbered the name of God. We moved down the ledge quickly as we dared. Bongos went tocka-ti-tocka, tocka-ti-tocka. The rabbi screamed, "MELVIN BLOOM, PHILLIP LIEBOWITZ, HAROLD COHEN, MELVIN BLOOM," as if our names, screamed this way, naming us where we hung, smashed us into brick.

Nothing was discussed.

The rabbi used his connections, arrangements were made. We were sent to a camp in New Jersey. We hiked and played volleyball. One day, apropos of nothing, Melvin came to me and said little Arnold had been made of gold and he, Melvin, of shit. I appreciated the sentiment, but to my mind they were both made of shit. Harold Cohen never again spoke to either of us. The counselors in the camp were World War II veterans, introspective men. Some carried shrapnel in their bodies. One had a metal plate in his head. Whatever you said to them they seemed to be thinking of something else, even when they answered. But step out of line and a plastic lanyard whistled burning notice across your ass.

At night, lying in the bunkhouse, I listened to owls. I'd never before heard that sound, the sound of darkness, blooming, opening inside you like a mouth.

Jayne Anne Phillips

Home

I'm afraid Walter Cronkite has had it, says Mom. Roger Mudd always does the news now—how would you like to have a name like that? Walter used to do the conventions and a football game now and then. I mean he would sort of appear, on the sidelines. Didn't he? But you never see him anymore. Lord. Something is going on.

Mom, I say. Maybe he's just resting. He must have made a lot of money by now. Maybe he's tired of talking about elections and mine disasters and the collapse of the franc. Maybe he's in love with a young girl.

He's not the type, says my mother. You can tell *that* much. No, she says, I'm afraid it's cancer.

My mother has her suspicions. She ponders. I have been home with her for two months. I ran out of money and I wasn't in love, so I have come home to my mother. She is an educational administrator. All winter long after work she watches television and knits afghans.

Come home, she said. Save money.

I can't possibly do it, I said. Jesus, I'm twenty-three years old.

Don't be silly, she said. And don't use profanity.

She arranged a job for me in the school system. All day, I tutor children in remedial reading. Sometimes I am so discouraged that I lie on the couch all evening and watch television with her. The shows are all alike. Their laugh tracks are conspicuously similar; I think I recognize a repetition of certain professional laughters. This laughter marks off the half hours.

Finally I make a rule: I won't watch television at night. I will watch only the news, which ends at 7:30. Then I will go to my room and do God knows what. But I feel sad that she sits there alone, knitting by the lamp. She seldom looks up.

Why don't you ever read anything? I ask.

I do, she says. I read books in my field. I read all day at work, writing those damn proposals. When I come home I want to relax.

Then let's go to the movies.

I don't want to go to the movies. Why should I pay money to be upset or frightened?

But feeling something can teach you. Don't you want to learn anything?

I'm learning all the time, she says.

She keeps knitting. She folds yarn the color of cream, the color of snow. She works it with her long blue needles, piercing, returning, winding. Yarn cascades from her hands in long panels. A pattern appears and disappears. She stops and counts; so many stitches across, so many down. Yes, she is on the right track.

Occasionally I offer to buy my mother a subscription to something mildly informative: *Ms., Rolling Stone, Scientific American.*

I don't want to read that stuff, she says. Just save your money. Did you hear Cronkite last night? Everyone's going to need all they can get.

Often, I need to look at my mother's old photographs. I see her sitting in knee-high grass with a white gardenia in her hair. I see her dressed up as the groom in a mock wedding at a sorority party, her black hair pulled back tight. I see her formally posed in her cadet nurse's uniform. The photographer has painted her lashes too lushly, too long; but her deep red mouth is correct.

The war ended too soon. She didn't finish her training. She came home to nurse only her mother and to meet my father at a dance. She married him in two weeks. It took twenty years to divorce him.

When we traveled to a neighboring town to buy my high school clothes, my mother and I would pass a certain road that turned off the highway and wound to a place I never saw.

There it is, my mother would say. The road to Wonder Bar. That's where I met my Waterloo. I walked in and he said, 'There she is. I'm going to marry that girl.' Ha. He sure saw me coming.

Well, I asked, Why did you marry him?

He was older, she said. He had a job and a car. And Mother

was so sick.

My mother doesn't forget her mother.

Never one bedsore, she says. I turned her every fifteen minutes. I kept her skin soft and kept her clean, even to the end.

I imagine my mother at twenty-three; her black hair, her dark eyes, her olive skin and that red lipstick. She is growing lines of tension in her mouth. Her teeth press into her lower lip as she lifts the woman in the bed. The woman weighs no more than a child. She has a smell. My mother fights it continually; bathing her, changing her sheets, carrying her to the bathroom so the smell can be contained and flushed away. My mother will try to protect them both. At night she sleeps in the room on a cot. She struggles awake feeling something press down on her and suck her breath: the smell. When my grandmother can no longer move, my mother fights it alone.

I did all I could, she sighs. And I was glad to do it. I'm glad I don't have to feel guilty.

No one has to feel guilty, I tell her.

And why not? says my mother. There's nothing wrong with guilt. If you are guilty, you should feel guilty.

My mother has often told me that I will be sorry when she is gone.

I think. And read alone at night in my room. I read those books I never read, the old classics, and detective stories. I can get them in the library here. There is only one bookstore; it sells mostly newspapers and *True Confessions* oracles. At Kroger's by the checkout counter I buy a few paperbacks, best sellers, but they are usually bad.

The television drones on downstairs.

I wonder about Walter Cronkite.

When was the last time I saw him? It's true his face was pouchy, his hair thinning. Perhaps he is only cutting it shorter. But he had that look about the eyes—

He was there when they stepped on the moon. He forgot he was on the air and he shouted, 'There . . . there . . : now—We have Contact!' Contact. For those who tuned in late, for the periodic watchers, he repeated: 'One small step . . .'

I was in high school and he was there with the body count. But he said it in such a way that you knew he wanted the war to end. He looked directly at you and said the numbers quietly. Shame, yes, but sorrowful patience, as if all things had passed before his eyes. And he understood that here at home, as well as in starving India, we would pass our next lives as meager cows.

My mother gets *Reader's Digest*. I come home from work, have a cup of coffee, and read it. I keep it beside my bed. I read it when I am too tired to read anything else. I read about Joe's kidney and Humor in Uniform. Always, there are human interest stories in which someone survives an ordeal of primal terror. Tonight it is Grizzly! Two teen-agers camping in the mountains are attacked by a bear. Sharon is dragged over a mile, unconscious. She is a good student loved by her parents, an honest girl loved by her boyfriend. Perhaps she is not a virgin; but in her heart, she is virginal. And she lies now in the furred arms of a beast. The grizzly drags her quietly, quietly. He will care for her all the days of his life . . . Sharon, his rose.

But alas. Already, rescuers have organized. Mercifully, her boyfriend is not among them. He is sleeping en route to the nearest hospital; his broken legs have excused him. In a few days, Sharon will bring him his food on a tray. She is spared. She is not demure. He gazes on her face, untouched but for a long thin scar near her mouth. Sharon says she remembers nothing of the bear. She only knows the tent was ripped open, that its heavy canvas fell across her face.

I turn out my light when I know my mother is sleeping. By then my eyes hurt and the streets of the town are deserted.

My father comes to me in a dream. He kneels beside me, touches my mouth. He turns my face gently toward him.

Let me see, he says. Let me see it.

He is looking for a scar, a sign. He wears only a towel around his waist. He presses himself against my thigh, pretending solicitude. But I know what he is doing; I turn my head in repulsion and stiffen. He smells of a sour musk and his forearms are black with hair. I think to myself, It's been years since he's had an erection—

Finally he stands. Cover yourself, I tell him.

I can't, he says, I'm hard.

On Saturdays I go to the Veterans of Foreign Wars rummage sales. They are held in the drafty basement of a church, rows of collapsible tables piled with objects. Sometimes I think I recognize the possessions of old friends: a class ring, yearbooks, football sweaters with our high school insignia. Would this one have fit Jason?

He used to spread it on the seat of the car on winter nights when we parked by country churches and graveyards. There seemed to be no ground, just water, a rolling, turning, building to a dull pain between my legs.

What's wrong? he said, What is it?

Jason, I can't . . . This pain—

It's only because you're afraid. If you'd let me go ahead—

I'm not afraid of you, I'd do anything for you. But Jason, why does it hurt like this?

We would try. But I couldn't. We made love with our hands. Our bodies were white. Out the window of the car, snow rose up in mounds across the fields. Afterward, he looked at me peacefully, sadly.

I held him and whispered, Soon, soon . . . we'll go away to school.

His sweater. He wore it that night we drove back from the football awards banquet. Jason made All-State but he hated football.

I hate it, he said. So what? he said, that I'm out there puking in the heat? Screaming 'Kill' at a sandbag?

I held his award in my lap, a gold man frozen in midleap. Don't play in college, I said. Refuse the money.

He was driving very slowly.

I can't see, he said, I can't see the edges of the road . . . Tell me if I start to fall off.

Jason, what do you mean?

He insisted I roll down the window and watch the edge. The banks of the road were gradual, sloping off into brush and trees on either side. White lines at the edge glowed up in dips and turns.

We're going to crash, he said.

No, Jason. You've driven this road before. We won't crash.

We're crashing, I know it, he said. Tell me, tell me I'm OK—

Here on the rummage sale table, there are three football sweaters. I see they are all too small to have belonged to Jason. So I buy an old soundtrack, *The Sound of Music*. Air, Austrian mountains. And an old robe to wear in the mornings. It upsets my mother to see me naked; she looks at me so curiously, as though she didn't recognize my body.

I pay for my purchases at the cash register. Behind the desk I glimpse stacks of *Reader's Digests*. The Ladies Auxiliary turns them inside out, stiffens and shellacs them. They make wastebaskets out of them.

I give my mother the record. She is pleased. She hugs me.

Oh, she says, I used to love the musicals. They made me happy. Then she stops and looks at me.

Didn't you do this? she says. Didn't you do this in high

school?

Do what?

Your class, she says. You did *The Sound of Music*.

Yes, I guess we did.

What a joke. I was the beautiful countess meant to marry Captain von Trapp before innocent Maria stole his heart. Jason was a threatening Nazi colonel with a bit part. He should have sung the lead but sports practices interfered with rehearsals. Tall, blond, aged in makeup under the lights, he encouraged sympathy for the bad guys and overshadowed the star. He appeared just often enough to make the play ridiculous.

My mother sits in the blue chair my father used for years.

Come quick, she says. Look—

She points to the television. Flickerings of Senate chambers, men in conservative suits. A commentator drones on about tax rebates.

There, says my mother. Hubert Humphrey. Look at him.

It's true. Humphrey is different, changed from his former toady self to a dessicated old man, not unlike the discarded shell of a locust. Now he rasps into the microphone about the people of these great states.

Old Hubert's had it, says my mother. He's a death mask.

That's what he gets for sucking blood for thirty years.

No, she says. No, he's got it too. Look at him! Cancer. Oh.

For God's sake, will you think of something else for once?

I don't know what you mean, she says. She goes on knitting.

All Hubert needs, I tell her, is a good roll in the hay.

You think that's what everyone needs.

Everyone does need it.

They do not. People aren't dogs. I seem to manage perfectly well without it, don't I?

No, I wouldn't say that you do.

Well, I do. I know your mumbo jumbo about sexuality. Sex is for those who are married, and I wouldn't marry again if it was the Lord himself.

Now she is silent. I know what's coming.

Your attitude will make you miserable, she says. One man after another. I just want you to be happy.

I do my best.

That's right, she says. Be sarcastic.

I refuse to answer. I think about my growing bank account. Graduate school, maybe in California. Hawaii. Somewhere beautiful and warm. I will wear few clothes and my skin will feel the air.

What about Jason, says my mother. I was thinking of him the other day.

Our telepathy always frightens me. Telepathy and beyond. Before her hysterectomy, our periods often came on the same day.

If he hadn't had that nervous breakdown, she says softly, do you suppose—

No, I don't suppose.

I wasn't surprised that it happened. When his brother was killed, that was hard. But Jason was so self-centered. You're lucky the two of you split up. He thought everyone was out to get him. Still, poor thing.

Silence. Then she refers in low tones to the few months Jason and I lived together before he was hospitalized.

You shouldn't have done what you did when you went off to college. He lost respect for you.

It wasn't respect for me he lost—He lost his fucking mind if you remember—

I realize I'm shouting. And shaking. What is happening to me?

My mother stares.

We'll not discuss it, she says.

She gets up. I hear her in the bathroom. Water running into the tub. Hydrotherapy. I close my eyes and listen. Soon, this weekend. I'll get a ride to the university a few hours away and look up an old lover. I'm lucky. They always want to sleep with me. For old time's sake.

I turn down the sound of the television and watch its silent pictures. Jason's brother was a musician; he taught Jason to play the pedal steel. A sergeant in uniform delivered the message two weeks before the State Play-Off games. Jason appeared at my mother's kitchen door with the telegram. He looked at me, opened his mouth, backed off wordless in the dark. I pretend I hear his pedal steel; its sweet country whine might make me cry. And I recognize this silent movie—I've seen it four times. Gregory Peck and his submarine crew escape fallout in Australia, but not for long. The cloud is coming. And so they run rampant in auto races and love affairs. But in the end, they close the hatch and put out to sea. They want to go home to die.

Sweetheart? my mother calls from the bathroom. Could you bring me a towel?

Her voice is quavering slightly. She is sorry. But I never know what part of it she is sorry about. I get a towel from the linen closet and open the door of the steamy bathroom. My mother stands in the tub, dripping, shivering a little. She is so small and thin; she is smaller than I. She has two long scars on her belly, operations of the womb, and one breast is misshapen, sunken, indented near the nipple.

I put the towel around her shoulders and my eyes smart. She looks at her breast.

Not too pretty is it, she says. He took out too much when he removed that lump—

Mom, it doesn't look so bad.

I dry her back, her beautiful back which is firm and unblemished. Beautiful, her skin. Again, I feel the pain in my eyes.

But you should have sued the bastard, I tell her. He didn't give a shit about your body.

We have an awkward moment with the towel when I realize I can't touch her any longer. The towel slips down and she catches it as one end dips into the water.

Sweetheart, she says. I know your beliefs are different than mine. But have patience with me. You'll just be here a few more months. And I'll always stand behind you. We'll get along.

She has clutched the towel to her chest. She is so fragile, standing there, naked, with her small shoulders. Suddenly I am horribly frightened.

Sure, I say, I know we will.

I let myself out of the room.

Sunday my mother goes to church alone. Daniel calls me from D.C. He's been living with a lover in Oregon. Now he is back East; she will join him in a few weeks. He is happy, he says. I tell him I'm glad he's found someone who appreciates him.

Come on now, he says. You weren't that bad.

I love Daniel, his white and feminine hands, his thick chestnut hair, his intelligence. And he loves me, though I don't know why. The last few weeks we were together I lay beside him like a piece of wood. I couldn't bear his touch; the moisture his penis left on my hips as he rolled against me. I was cold, cold. I huddled in blankets away from him.

I'm sorry, I said. Daniel, I'm sorry please—what's wrong with me? Tell me you love me anyway . . .

Yes, he said, Of course I do. I always will. I do.

Daniel says he has no car, but he will come by bus. Is there a place for him to stay?

Oh yes, I say. There's a guest room. Bring some Trojans. I'm a hermit with no use for birth control. Daniel, you don't know what it's like here.

I don't care what it's like. I want to see you.

Yes, I say. Daniel, hurry.

When he arrives the next weekend, we sit around the table with my mother and discuss medicine. Daniel was a medic in Vietnam. He smiles at my mother. She is charmed though she has reservations; I see them in her face. But she enjoys having someone else in the house, a presence; a male. Daniel's laughter is low and modulated. He talks softly, smoothly: a dignified radio announcer, an accomplished anchorman.

But when I lived with him, he threw dishes against the wall. And jerked in his sleep, mumbling. And ran out of the house with his hands across his eyes.

After we first made love, he smiled and pulled gently away from me. He put on his shirt and went to the bathroom. I followed and stepped into the shower with him. He faced me, composed, friendly, and frozen. He stood as though guarding something behind him.

Daniel, turn around. I'll soap your back.

I already did.

Then move, I'll stand in the water with you.

He stepped carefully around me.

Daniel, what's wrong? Why won't you turn around?

Why should I?

I'd never seen him with his shirt off. He'd never gone swimming with us, only wading, alone, down Point Reyes Beach. He wore long-sleeved shirts all summer in the California heat.

Daniel, I said, You've been my best friend for months. We could have talked about it.

He stepped backwards, awkwardly, out of the tub and put his shirt on.

I was loading them on copters, he told me. The last one was dead anyway; he was already dead. But I went after him, dragged him in the wind of the blades. Shrapnel and napalm caught my arms, my back. Until I fell, I thought it was the other man's blood in my hands.

They removed most of the shrapnel, did skin grafts for the burns. In three years since, Daniel made love five times; always in the dark. In San Francisco he must take off his shirt for a doctor; tumors have grown in his scars. They bleed through his shirt, round rust-colored spots.

Face-to-face in bed, I tell him I can feel the scars with my fingers. They are small knots on his skin. Not large, not ugly. But he can't let me, he can't let anyone, look: he says he feels wild, like raging, and then he vomits. But maybe, after they remove the tumors—Each time they operate, they reduce the scars.

We spend hours at the veterans' hospital waiting for appointments. Finally they schedule the operation. I watch the black-ringed wall clock, the amputees gliding by in chairs that tick on the linoleum floor. Daniel's doctors curse about lack of supplies; they bandage him with gauze and layers of Band-Aids. But it is all right. I buy some real bandages. Every night I cleanse his back with a sponge and change them.

In my mother's house, Daniel seems different. He has shaved his beard and his face is too young for him. I can only grip his hands.

I show him the house, the antiques, the photographs on the walls. I tell him none of the objects move; they are all cemented in place. Now the bedrooms, my room.

This is it, I say. This is where I kept my Villager sweaters when I was seventeen, and my dried corsages. My cups from the Tastee Freeze labeled with dates and boy's names.

The room is large, blue. Baseboards and wood trim are painted a spotless white. Ruffled curtains, ruffled bedspread. The bed itself is so high one must climb into it. Daniel looks at the walls, their perfect blue and white.

It's a piece of candy, he says.

Yes, I say, hugging him, wanting him.

What about your mother?

She's gone to meet friends for dinner. I don't think she believes what she says, she's only being my mother. It's all right.

We take off our clothes and press close together. But something is wrong. We keep trying. Daniel stays soft in my hands. His mouth is nervous; he seems to gasp at my lips.

He says his lover's name. He says they aren't seeing other people.

But I'm not other people. And I want you to be happy with her.

I know. She knew . . . I'd want to see you.

Then what?

This room, he says. This house. I can't breathe in here.

I tell him we have tomorrow. He'll relax. And it is so good just to see him, a person from my life.

So we only hold each other, rocking.

Later, Daniel asks about my father.

I don't see him, I say. He told me to choose.

Choose what?

Between them.

My father. When he lived in this house, he stayed in the dark with his cigarette. He sat in his blue chair with the lights and television off, smoking. He made little money; he said he was self-employed. He was sick. He grew dizzy when he looked up suddenly. He slept in the basement. All night he sat reading in the bathroom. I'd hear him walking up and down the dark steps at night. I lay in the dark and listened. I believed he would strangle my mother, then walk upstairs and strangle me. I believed we were guilty; we had done something terrible to him.

Daniel wants me to talk.

How could she live with him, I ask. She came home from work and got supper. He ate it, got up and left to sit in his chair. He watched the news. We were always sitting there, looking at his dirty plates. And I wouldn't help her. She should wash them, not me. She should make the money we lived on. I didn't want her house and his ghost with its cigarette burning in the dark like a sore. I didn't want to be guilty. So she did it. She sent me to college; she paid for my safe escape.

Daniel and I go to the Rainbow, a bar and grill on Main Street. We hold hands, play country songs on the jukebox, drink a lot of salted beer. We talk to the barmaid and kiss in the overstuffed booth. Twinkle lights blink on and off above us. I wore my burgundy stretch pants in here when I was twelve. A senior pinched me, then moved his hand slowly across my thigh, mystified, as though erasing the pain.

What about tonight? Daniel asks. Would your mother go out with us? A movie? A bar? He sees me in her, he likes her. He wants to know her.

Then we will have to watch television.

We pop popcorn and watch the late movies. My mother stays up with us, mixing whiskey sours and laughing. She gets a high color in her cheeks and the light in her eyes glimmers up. She is slipping, slipping back and she is beautiful, oh, in her ankle socks, her red mouth and her armor of young girl's common sense. She has a beautiful laughter. She and Daniel end by mock arm wrestling; he pretends defeat and goes upstairs to bed.

My mother hears his door close. He's nice, she says. You've known some nice people, haven't you?

I want to make her back down.

Yes, he's nice, I say. And don't you think he respects me? Don't you think he truly cares for me, even though we've slept together?

He seems to, I don't know. But if you give them that, it costs them nothing to be friends with you.

Why should it cost? The only cost is what you give, and you

can tell if someone is giving it back.

How? How can you tell? By going to bed with every man you take a fancy to?

I wish I took a fancy oftener, I tell her. I wish I wanted more. I can be good to a man, but I'm afraid—I can't be physical, not really . . .

You shouldn't.

I should. I want to, for myself as well. I don't think—I've ever had an orgasm.

What? she says, Never? Haven't you felt a sort of building up, and then a dropping off . . . a conclusion? like something's over?

No, I don't think so.

You probably have, she assures me. It's not necessarily an explosion. You were just thinking too hard, you think too much.

But she pauses.

Maybe I don't remember right, she says. It's been years, and in the last years of the marriage I would have died if your father had touched me. But before, I know I felt something. That's partly why I haven't . . . since . . . what if I started wanting it again? Then it would be hell.

But you have to try to get what you want—

No, she says. Not if what you want would ruin everything. And now, anyway. Who would want me?

I stand at Daniel's door. The fear is back; it has followed me upstairs from the dead dark bottom of the house. My hands are shaking. I'm whispering . . . Daniel, don't leave me here.

I go to my room to wait. I must wait all night, or something will come in my sleep. I feel its hands on me now, dragging, pulling. I watch the lit face of the clock: three, four, five. At seven I go to Daniel. He sleeps with his pillow in his arms. The high bed creaks as I get in. Please now, yes . . . he is hard. He always woke with erections . . . inside me he feels good, real, and I tell him no, stop, wait . . . I hold the rubber, stretch its rim away from skin so it smooths on without hurting and fills with him . . . now again, here, yes but quiet, be quiet . . . oh Daniel . . . the bed is making noise . . . yes, no, but be careful, she . . . We move and turn and I forget about the sounds. We push against each other hard, he is almost there and I am almost with him and just when it is over I think I hear my mother in the room directly under us—But I am half dreaming. I move to get out of bed and Daniel holds me. No, he says, stay.

We sleep and wake to hear the front door slam.

Daniel looks at me.

There's nothing to be done, I say. She's gone to church.

He looks at the clock. I'm going to miss that bus, he says. We put our clothes on fast and Daniel moves to dispose of the rubber—how? the toilet, no, the wastebasket—He drops it in, bends over, retrieves it. Finally he wraps it in a Kleenex and puts it in his pocket. Jesus, he swears. He looks at me and grins. When I start laughing, my eyes are wet.

I take Daniel to the bus station and watch him out of sight. I come back and strip the bed, bundle the sheets in my arms. This pressure in my chest . . . I have to clutch the sheets tight, tighter—

A door clicks shut. I go downstairs to my mother. She refuses to speak or let me near her. She stands by the sink and holds her small square purse with both hands. The fear comes. I hug myself, press my hands against my arms to stop shaking. My mother runs hot water, soap, takes dishes from the drainer. She immerses them, pushes them down, rubbing with a rag in a circular motion.

Those dishes are clean, I tell her. I washed them last night.

She keeps washing. Hot water clouds her glasses, the window in front of us, our faces. We all disappear in steam. I watch the dishes bob and sink. My mother begins to sob. I move close to her and hold her. She smells as she used to smell when I was a child and slept with her.

I heard you, I heard it, she says. Here, in my own house. Please, how much can you expect me to take? I don't know what to do about anything . . .

She looks into the water, keeps looking. And we stand here just like this.

David Quammen

Walking Out

As the train rocked dead at Livingston he saw the man, in a worn khaki shirt with button flaps buttoned, arms crossed. The boy's hand sprang up by reflex, and his face broke into a smile. The man smiled back gravely, and nodded. He did not otherwise move. The boy turned from the window and, with the awesome deliberateness of a fat child harboring reluctance, began struggling to pull down his bag. His father would wait on the platform. First sight of him had reminded the boy that nothing was simple enough now for hurrying.

They drove in the old open Willys toward the cabin beyond town. The windshield of the Willys was up, but the fine cold sharp rain came into their faces, and the boy could not raise his eyes to look at the road. He wore a rain parka his father had handed him at the station. The man, protected by only the khaki, held his lips strung in a firm silent line that seemed more grin than wince. Riding through town in the cold rain, open topped and jaunty, getting drenched as though by necessity, was—the boy understood vaguely—somehow in the spirit of this season.

"We have a moose tag," his father shouted.

The boy said nothing. He refused to care what it meant, that they had a moose tag.

"I've got one picked out. A bull. I've stalked him for two weeks. Up in the Crazies. When we get to the cabin, we'll build a good roaring fire." With only the charade of a pause, he added, "Your mother." It was said like a question. The boy waited.

149

"How is she?"

"All right, I guess." Over the jeep's howl, with the wind stealing his voice, the boy too had to shout.

"Are you friends with her?"

"I guess so."

"Is she still a beautiful lady?"

"I don't know. I guess so. I don't know that."

"You must know that. Is she starting to get wrinkled like me? Does she seem worried and sad? Or is she just still a fine beautiful lady? You must know that."

"She's still a beautiful lady, I guess."

"Did she tell you any messages for me?"

"She said . . . she said I should give you her love," the boy lied, impulsively and clumsily. He was at once embarrassed that he had done it.

"Oh," his father said. "Thank you, David."

They reached the cabin on a mile of dirt road winding through meadow to a spruce grove. Inside, the boy was enwrapped in the strong syncretic smell of all seasonal mountain cabins: pine resin and insect repellent and a mustiness suggesting damp bathing trunks stored in a drawer. There were yellow pine floors and rope-work throw rugs and a bead curtain to the bedroom and a cast-iron cook stove with none of the lids or handles missing and a pump in the kitchen sink and old issues of *Field and Stream*, and on the mantel above where a fire now finally burned was a picture of the boy's grandfather, the railroad telegrapher, who had once owned the cabin. The boy's father cooked a dinner of fried ham, and though the boy did not like ham he had expected his father to cook canned stew or Spam, so he said nothing. His father asked him about school and the boy talked and his father seemed to be interested. Warm and dry, the boy began to feel safe from his own anguish. Then his father said:

"We'll leave tomorrow around ten."

Last year on the boy's visit they had hunted birds. They had lived in the cabin for six nights, and each day they had hunted pheasant in the wheat stubble, or blue grouse in the woods, or ducks along the irrigation slews. The boy had been wet and cold and miserable at times, but each evening they returned to the cabin and to the boy's suitcase of dry clothes. They had eaten hot food cooked on a stove, and had smelled the cabin smell, and had slept together in a bed. In six days of hunting, the boy had not managed to kill a single bird. Yet last year he had known that, at least once a day, he would be comfortable, if not happy. This year his father planned that he should not even be comfortable. He had said in his last letter to Evergreen Park, before the boy left Chicago but when it was too late for him not to leave, that he would take the boy camping in the mountains, after big game. He had pretended to believe that the boy would be glad.

The Willys was loaded and moving by ten minutes to ten. For three hours they drove, through Big Timber, and then north on the highway, and then back west again on a logging road that took them winding and bouncing higher into the mountains. Thick cottony streaks of white cloud hung in among the mountaintop trees, light and dense dollops against the bulking sharp dark olive, as though in a black-and-white photograph. They followed the gravel road for an hour, and the boy thought they would soon have a flat tire or break an axle. If they had a flat, the boy knew, his father would only change it and drive on until they had the second, farther from the highway. Finally they crossed a creek and his father plunged the Willys off into a bed of weeds.

His father said, "Here."

The boy said, "Where?"

"Up that little drainage. At the head of the creek."

"How far is it?"

"Two or three miles."

"Is that where you saw the moose?"

"No. That's where I saw the sheepman's hut. The moose is farther. On top."

"Are we going to sleep in a hut? I thought we were going to sleep in a tent."

"No. Why should we carry a tent up there when we have a perfectly good hut?"

The boy couldn't answer that question. He thought now that this might be the time when he would cry. He had known it was coming.

"I don't much want to sleep in a hut," he said, and his voice broke with the simple honesty of it, and his eyes glazed. He held his mouth tight against the trembling.

As though something had broken in him too, the boy's father laid his forehead down on the steering wheel, against his knuckles. For a moment he remained bowed, breathing exhaustedly. But he looked up again before speaking.

"Well, we don't have to, David."

The boy said nothing.

"It's an old sheepman's hut made of logs, and it's near where we're going to hunt, and we can fix it dry and good. I thought you might like that. I thought it might be more fun than a tent. But we don't have to do it. We can drive back to Big Timber and buy a tent, or we can drive back to the cabin and hunt birds, like last year. Whatever you want to do. You have to forgive me the kind of ideas I get. I hope you will. We don't have to do anything that you don't want to do."

"No," the boy said. "I want to."

"Are you sure?"

"No," the boy said. "But I just want to."

They bushwhacked along the creek, treading a thick soft mixture of moss and humus and needles, climbing upward through brush. Then the brush thinned and they were ascending an open creek bottom, thirty yards wide, darkened by fir and cedar. Farther, and they struck a trail, which led them upward along the creek. Farther still, and the trail received a branch, then another, then forked.

"Who made this trail? Did the sheepman?"

"No," his father said. "Deer and elk."

Gradually the creek's little canyon narrowed, steep wooded shoulders funneling closer on each side. For a while the game trails forked and converged like a maze, but soon again there were only two branches, and finally one, heavily worn. It dodged through alder and willow, skirting tangles of browned raspberry, so that the boy and his father could never see more than twenty feet ahead. When they stopped to rest, the boy's father unstrapped the .270 from his pack and loaded it.

"We have to be careful now," he explained. "We may surprise a bear."

Under the cedars, the creek bottom held a cool dampness that seemed to be stored from one winter to the next. The boy began at once to feel chilled. He put on his jacket, and they continued climbing. Soon he was sweating again in the cold.

On a small flat where the alder drew back from the creek, the hut was built into one bank of the canyon, with the sod of the hillside lapping out over its roof. The door was a low dark opening. Forty or fifty years ago, the boy's father explained, this hut had been built and used by a Basque shepherd. At that time there had been many Basques in Montana, and they had run sheep all across this ridge of the Crazies. His father forgot to explain what a Basque was, and the boy didn't remind him.

They built a fire. His father had brought sirloin steaks and an onion for dinner, and the boy was happy with him about that. As they ate, it grew dark, but the boy and his father had stocked a large comforting pile of naked deadfall. In the darkness, by firelight, his father made chocolate pudding. The pudding had been his father's surprise. The boy sat on a piece of canvas and added logs to the fire while his father drank coffee. Sparks rose on the heat and the boy watched them climb toward the cedar limbs and the black pools of sky. The pudding did not set.

"Do you remember your grandfather, David?"

"Yes," the boy said, and wished it were true. He remembered a funeral when he was three.

"Your grandfather brought me up on this mountain when I was seventeen. That was the last year he hunted." The boy knew what sort of thoughts his father was having. But he knew also that his own home was in Evergreen Park, and that he was another man's boy now, with another man's name, though this indeed was his father. "Your grandfather was fifty years older than me."

The boy said nothing.

"And I'm thirty-four years older than you."

"And I'm only eleven," the boy cautioned him.

"Yes," said his father. "And someday you'll have a son and you'll be forty years older than him, and you'll want so badly for him to know who you are that you could cry."

The boy was embarrassed.

"And that's called the cycle of life's infinite wisdom," his father said, and laughed at himself unpleasantly.

"What did he die of?" the boy asked, desperate to escape the focus of his father's rumination.

"He was eighty-seven then. Christ. He was tired." The boy's father went silent. Then he shook his head, and poured himself the remaining coffee.

Through that night the boy was never quite warm. He slept on his side with his knees drawn up, and this was uncomfortable but his body seemed to demand it for warmth. The hard cold mountain earth pressed upward through the mat of fir boughs his father had laid, and drew heat from the boy's body like a pallet of leeches. He clutched the bedroll around his neck and folded the empty part at the bottom back under his legs. Once he woke to a noise. Though his father was sleeping between him and the door of the hut, for a while the boy lay awake, listening worriedly, and then woke again on his back to realize time had passed. He heard droplets begin to hit the canvas his father had spread over the sod roof of the hut. But he remained dry.

He rose to the smell of a fire. The tarp was rigid with sleet and frost. The firewood and the knapsacks were frosted. It was that gray time of dawn before any blue and, through the branches above, the boy was unable to tell whether the sky was murky or clear. Delicate sheet ice hung on everything, but there was no wetness. The rain seemed to have been hushed by the cold.

"What time is it?"

"Early yet."

"How early?" The boy was thinking about the cold at home as he waited outside on 96th Street for his school bus. That was the cruelest moment of his day, but it seemed a benign and familiar part of him compared to this.

"Early. I don't have a watch. What difference does it make, David?"

"Not any."

After breakfast they began walking up the valley. His father had the .270, and the boy carried an old Winchester .30–30, with open sights. The walking was not hard, and with this gentle exercise in the cold morning the boy soon felt fresh and fine. Now I'm hunting for moose with my father, he told himself. That's just what I'm doing. Few boys in Evergreen Park had ever been moose hunting with their fathers in Montana, he knew. I'm doing it now, the boy told himself.

Reaching the lip of a high meadow, a mile above the shepherd's hut, they had not seen so much as a magpie.

Before them, across hundreds of yards, opened a smooth lake of tall lifeless grass, browned by September drought and killed by the frosts and beginning to rot with November's rain. The creek was here a deep quiet channel of smooth curves overhung by the grass, with a dark surface like heavy oil. When they had come fifty yards into the meadow, his father turned and pointed out to the boy a large ponderosa pine with a forked crown that marked the head of their creek valley. He showed the boy a small aspen grove midway across the meadow, toward which they were aligning themselves.

"Near the far woods is a beaver pond. The moose waters there. We can wait in the aspens and watch the whole meadow without being seen. If he doesn't come, we'll go up another canyon, and check again on the way back."

For an hour, and another, they waited. The boy sat with his hands in his jacket pockets, bunching the jacket tighter around him, and his buttocks drew cold moisture from the ground. His father squatted on his heels like a country man, rising periodically to inspect the meadow in all directions. Finally he stood up; he fixed his stare on the distant fringe of woods and, like a retriever, did not move. He said, "David."

The boy stood beside him. His father placed a hand on the boy's shoulder. The boy saw a large dark form rolling toward them like a great slug in the grass.

"Is it the moose?"

"No," said his father. "That is a grizzly bear, David. An old male grizzly."

The boy was impressed. He sensed an aura of power and terror and authority about the husky shape, even at two hundred yards.

"Are we going to shoot him?"

"No."

"Why not?"

"We don't have a permit," his father whispered. "And because we don't want to."

The bear plowed on toward the beaver pond for a while, then stopped. It froze in the grass and seemed to be listening. The boy's father added: "That's not hunting for the meat. That's hunting for the fear. I don't need the fear. I've got enough in my life already."

The bear turned and moiled off quickly through the grass. It disappeared back into the far woods.

"He heard us."

"Maybe," the boy's father said. "Let's go have a look at that beaver pond."

A sleek furred carcass lay low in the water, swollen grotesquely with putrescence and coated with glistening blowflies. Four days, the boy's father guessed. The moose had been shot at least eighteen times with a .22 pistol. One of its eyes had been shot out; it had been shot twice in the jaw; and both quarters on the side that lay upward were ruined with shots. Standing up to his knees in the sump, the boy's father took the trouble of counting the holes, and probing one of the slugs out with his knife. That only made him angrier. He flung the lead away.

For the next three hours, with his father withdrawn into a solitary and characteristic bitterness, the boy felt abandoned. He did not understand why a moose would be slaughtered with a light pistol and left to rot. His father did not bother to explain; like the bear, he seemed to understand it as well as he needed to. They walked on, but they did not really hunt.

They left the meadow for more pine, and now tamarack, naked tamarack, the yellow needles nearly all down and going ginger where they coated the trail. The boy and his father hiked along a level path into another canyon, this one vast at the mouth and narrowing between high ridges of bare rock. They crossed and recrossed the shepherd's creek, which in this canyon was a tumbling free-stone brook. Following five yards behind his father, watching the cold, unapproachable rage that shaped the line of the man's shoulders, the boy was miserably uneasy because his father had grown so distant and quiet. They climbed over deadfalls blocking the trail, skirted one boulder large as a cabin, and blundered into a garden of nettles that stung them fiercely through their trousers. They saw fresh elk scat, and they saw bear, diarrhetic with late berries. The boy's father eventually grew bored with brooding, and showed the boy how to stalk. Before dusk that day they had shot an elk.

An open and gently sloped hillside, almost a meadow, ran for a quarter mile in quaking aspen, none over fifteen feet tall. The elk was above. The boy's father had the boy brace his gun in the notch of an aspen and take the first shot. The boy missed. The elk reeled and bolted down and his father killed it before it made cover. It was a five-point bull. They dressed the elk out and dragged it down to the cover of large pines, near the stream, where they would quarter it tomorrow, and then they returned under twilight to the hut.

That night even the fetal position could not keep the boy warm. He shivered wakefully for hours. He was glad that the following day, though full of walking and butchery and oppressive burdens, would be their last in the woods. He heard nothing. When he woke, through the door of the hut he saw whiteness like bone.

Six inches had fallen, and it was still snowing. The boy stood about in the campsite, amazed. When it snowed three inches in Evergreen Park, the boy would wake before dawn to the hiss of sand trucks and the ratchet of chains. Here there had been no warning. The boy was not much colder than he had been yesterday, and the transformation of the woods seemed mysterious and benign and somehow comic. He thought of Christmas. Then his father barked at him.

His father's mood had also changed, but in a different way; he seemed serious and hurried. As he wiped the breakfast pots clean with snow, he gave the boy orders for other chores. They left camp with two empty pack frames, both rifles, and a handsaw and rope. The boy soon understood why his father felt pressure of time: it took them an hour to climb the mile to the meadow. The snow continued. They did not rest until they reached the aspens.

"I had half a mind at breakfast to let the bull lie and pack us straight down out of here," his father admitted. "Probably smarter and less trouble in the long run. I could have come back on snowshoes next week. But by then it might be three feet deep and starting to drift. We can get two quarters out today. That will make it easier for me later." The boy was surprised by two things: that his father would be so wary in the face of a gentle snowfall and that he himself would have felt disappointed to be taken out of the woods that morning. The air of the meadow teemed with white.

"If it stops soon, we're fine," said his father.

It continued.

The path up the far canyon was hard climbing in eight inches of snow. The boy fell once, filling his collar and sleeves, and the gun-sight put a small gouge in his chin. But he was not discouraged. That night they would be warm and dry at the cabin. A half mile on and he came up beside his father, who had stopped to stare down at dark splashes of blood.

Heavy tracks and a dragging belly mark led up to the scramble of deepening red, and away. The tracks were nine inches long and showed claws. The boy's father knelt. As the boy watched, one shining maroon splotch the size of a saucer sank slowly beyond sight into the snow. The blood was warm.

Inspecting the tracks carefully, his father said, "She's got a cub with her."

"What happened?"

"Just a kill. Seems to have been a bird. That's too much blood for a grouse, but I don't see signs of any four-footed creature. Maybe a turkey." He frowned thoughtfully. "A turkey without feathers. I don't know. What I dislike is coming up on her with a cub." He drove a round into the chamber of the .270.

Trailing red smears, the tracks preceded them. Within fifty feet they found the body. It was half-buried. The top of its head had been shorn away, and the cub's brains had been licked out.

His father said "Christ," and plunged off the trail. He snapped at the boy to follow closely.

They made a wide crescent through brush and struck back after a quarter mile. His father slogged ahead in the snow, stopping often to stand holding his gun ready and glancing around while the boy caught up and passed him. The boy was confused. He knew his father was worried, but he did not feel any danger himself. They met the trail again, and went on to the aspen hillside before his father allowed them to rest. The boy spat on the snow. His lungs ached badly.

"Why did she do that?"

"She didn't. Another bear got her cub. A male. Maybe the one we saw yesterday. Then she fought him for the body, and she won. We didn't miss them by much. She may even have been watching. Nothing could put her in a worse frame of mind."

He added: "If we so much as see her, I want you to pick the nearest big tree and start climbing. Don't stop till you're twenty feet off the ground. I'll stay down and decide whether we have to shoot her. Is your rifle cocked?"

"No."

"Cock it, and put on the safety. She may be a black bear and black bears can climb. If she comes up after you, lean down and stick your gun in her mouth and fire. You can't miss."

He cocked the Winchester, as his father had said.

They angled downhill to the stream, and on to the mound of their dead elk. Snow filtered down steadily in purposeful silence. The boy was thirsty. It could not be much below freezing, he was aware, because with the exercise his bare hands were comfortable, even sweating between the fingers.

"Can I get a drink?"

"Yes. Be careful you don't wet your feet. And don't wander anywhere. We're going to get this done quickly."

He walked the few yards, ducked through the brush at streamside, and knelt in the snow to drink. The water was painful to his sinuses and bitterly cold on his hands. Standing again, he noticed an animal body ahead near the stream bank. For a moment he felt sure it was another dead cub. During that moment his father called:

"David! Get up here right now!"

The boy meant to call back. First he stepped closer to turn the cub with his foot. The touch brought it alive. It rose suddenly with a high squealing growl and whirled its head like a snake and snapped. The boy shrieked. The cub had his right hand in its jaws. It would not release.

It thrashed senselessly, working its teeth deeper and tearing flesh with each movement. The boy felt no pain. He knew his hand was being damaged and that realization terrified him and he was desperate to get the hand back before it was ruined. But he was helpless. He sensed the same furious terror racking the cub that he felt in himself, and he screamed at the cub almost reasoningly to let him go. His screams scared the cub more. Its head snatched back and forth. The boy did not think to shout for his father. He did not see him or hear him coming.

His father moved at full stride in a slowed laboring run through the snow, saying nothing and holding the rifle he did not use, crossed the last six feet still gathering speed, and brought his right boot up into the cub's belly. That kick seemed to lift the cub clear of the snow. It opened its jaws to another shrill piggish squeal, and the boy felt dull relief on his hand, as though his father had pressed open the blades of a spring trap with his foot. The cub tumbled once and disappeared over the stream bank, then surfaced downstream, squalling and paddling. The boy looked at his hand and was horrified. He still had no pain, but the hand was unrecognizable. His fingers had been peeled down through the palm like

158

flaps on a banana. Glands at the sides of his jaw threatened that he would vomit, and he might have stood stupidly watching the hand bleed if his father had not grabbed him.

He snatched the boy by the arm and dragged him toward a tree without even looking at the boy's hand. The boy jerked back in angry resistance as though he had been struck. He screamed at his father. He screamed that his hand was cut, believing his father did not know, and as he screamed he began to cry. He began to feel hot throbbing pain. He began to worry about the blood he was losing. He could imagine his blood melting red holes in the snow behind him and he did not want to look. He did not want to do anything until he had taken care of his hand. At that instant he hated his father. But his father was stronger. He all but carried the boy to a tree.

He lifted the boy. In a voice that was quiet and hurried and very unlike the harsh grip with which he had taken the boy's arm, he said:

"Grab hold and climb up a few branches as best you can. Sit on a limb and hold tight and clamp the hand under your other armpit, if you can do that. I'll be right back to you. Hold tight because you're going to get dizzy." The boy groped desperately for a branch. His father supported him from beneath, and waited. The boy clambered. His feet scraped at the trunk. Then he was in the tree. Bark flakes and resin were stuck to the raw naked meat of his right hand. His father said:

"Now here, take this. Hurry."

The boy never knew whether his father himself had been frightened enough to forget for that moment about the boy's hand, or whether his father was still thinking quite clearly. His father may have expected that much. By the merciless clarity of his own standards, he may have expected that the boy should be able to hold onto a tree, and a wound, and a rifle, all with one hand. He extended the stock of the Winchester toward the boy.

The boy wanted to say something, but his tears and his fright would not let him gather a breath. He shuddered, and could not speak. "David," his father urged. The boy reached for the stock and faltered and clutched at the trunk with his good arm. He was crying and gasping, and he wanted to speak. He was afraid he would fall out of the tree. He released his grip once again, and felt himself tip. His father extended the gun higher, holding the barrel. The boy swung out his injured hand, spraying his father's face with blood. He reached and he tried to close torn dangling fingers around the stock and he pulled the trigger.

The bullet entered low on his father's thigh and shattered the knee and traveled down the shin bone and into the ground through his father's heel.

His father fell, and the rifle fell with him. He lay in the snow without moving. The boy thought he was dead. Then the boy saw him grope for the rifle. He found it and rolled onto his stomach, taking aim at the sow grizzly. Forty feet up the hill, towering on hind legs, she canted her head to one side, indecisive. When the cub pulled itself up a snowbank from the stream, she coughed at it sternly. The cub trotted straight to her with its head low. She knocked it off its feet with a huge paw, and it yelped. Then she turned quickly. The cub followed.

The woods were silent. The gunshot still echoed awesomely back to the boy but it was an echo of memory, not sound. He felt nothing. He saw his father's body stretched on the snow and he did not really believe he was where he was. He did not want to move: he wanted to wake. He sat in the tree and waited. The snow fell as gracefully as before.

His father rolled onto his back. The boy saw him raise himself to a sitting position and look down at the leg and betray no expression, and then slump back. He blinked slowly and lifted his eyes to meet the boy's eyes. The boy waited. He expected his father to speak. He expected his father to say *Shinny down using your elbows and knees and get the first-aid kit and boil water and phone the doctor. The number is taped to the dial.* His father stared. The boy could see the flicker of thoughts behind his father's eyes. His father said nothing. He raised his arms slowly and crossed them over his face, as though to nap in the sun.

The boy jumped. He landed hard on his feet and fell onto his back. He stood over his father. His hand dripped quietly onto the snow. He was afraid that his father was deciding to die. He wanted to beg him to reconsider. The boy had never before seen his father hopeless. He was afraid.

But he was no longer afraid of his father.

Then his father uncovered his face and said, "Let me see it."

They bandaged the boy's hand with a sleeve cut from the other arm of his shirt. His father wrapped the hand firmly and split the sleeve end with his deer knife and tied it neatly in two places. The boy now felt searing pain in his torn palm, and his stomach lifted when he thought of the damage, but at least he did not have to look at it. Quickly the plaid flannel bandage began to soak through maroon. They cut a sleeve from his father's shirt to tie over the wound in his thigh. They raised the trouser leg to see the long swelling bruise down the calf where he was hemorrhaging into the bullet's tunnel. Only then did his father realize that he was bleeding also from the heel. The boy took off his father's boot and placed a half-clean handkerchief on the insole where the bullet had exited, as his father instructed him. Then his father laced the boot on again tightly. The boy helped his father to stand. His father tried a step, then collapsed in the snow with a blasphemous howl of pain. They had not known that the knee was shattered.

The boy watched his father's chest heave with the forced sighs of suffocating frustration, and heard the air wheeze through his nostrils. His father relaxed himself with the breathing, and seemed to be thinking. He said,

"You can find your way back to the hut."

The boy held his own breath and did not move.

"You can, can't you?"

"But I'm not. I'm not going alone. I'm only going with you."

"All right, David, listen carefully," his father said. "We don't have to worry about freezing. I'm not worried about either of us freezing to death. No one is going to freeze in the woods in November, if he looks after himself. Not even in Montana. It just isn't that cold. I have matches and I have a fresh elk. And I don't think this weather is going to get any worse. It may be raining again by morning. What I'm concerned about is the bleeding. If I spend too much time and effort trying to walk out of here, I could bleed to death.

"I think your hand is going to be all right. It's a bad wound, but the doctors will be able to fix it as good as new. I can see that. I promise you that. You'll be bleeding some too, but if you take care of that hand it won't bleed any more walking than if you were standing still. Then you'll be at the doctor's tonight. But if I try to walk out on this leg it's going to bleed and keep bleeding and I'll lose too much blood. So I'm staying here and bundling up warm and you're walking out to get help. I'm sorry about this. It's what we have to do.

"You can't possibly get lost. You'll just follow this trail straight down the canyon the way we came up, and then you'll come to the meadow. Point yourself toward the big pine tree with the forked crown. When you get to that tree you'll find the creek again. You may not be able to see it, but make yourself quiet and listen for it. You'll hear it. Follow that down off the mountain and past the hut till you get to the jeep."

He struggled a hand into his pocket. "You've never driven a car, have you?"

The boy's lips were pinched. Muscles in his cheeks ached from clenching his jaws. He shook his head.

"You can do it. It isn't difficult." His father held up a single key and began telling the boy how to start the jeep, how to work the clutch, how to find reverse and then first and then second. As his father described the positions on the floor shift the boy raised his swaddled right hand. His father stopped. He rubbed at his eye sockets, like a man waking.

"Of course," he said. "All right. You'll have to help me."

Using the saw with his left hand, the boy cut a small forked aspen. His father showed the boy where to trim it so that the fork would reach just to his armpit. Then they lifted him to his feet. But the crutch was useless on a steep hillside of deep grass and snow. His father leaned over the boy's shoulders and they fought the slope for an hour.

When the boy stepped in a hole and they fell, his father made no exclamation of pain. The boy wondered whether his father's knee hurt as badly as his own hand. He suspected it hurt worse. He said nothing about his hand, though several times in their climb it was twisted or crushed. They reached the trail. The snow had not stopped, and their tracks were veiled. His father said:

"We need one of the guns. I forgot. It's my fault. But you'll have to go back down and get it."

The boy could not find the tree against which his father said he had leaned the .270, so he went toward the stream and looked for blood. He saw none. The imprint of his father's body was already softened beneath an inch of fresh silence. He scooped his good hand through the snowy depression and was startled by cool slimy blood, smearing his fingers like phlegm. Nearby he found the Winchester.

"The lucky one," his father said. "That's all right. Here." He snapped open the breach and a shell flew and he caught it in the air. He glanced dourly at the casing, then cast it aside in the snow. He held the gun out for the boy to see, and with his thumb let the hammer down one notch.

"Remember?" he said. "The safety."

The boy knew he was supposed to feel great shame, but he felt little. His father could no longer hurt him as he once could, because the boy was coming to understand him. His father could not help himself. He did not want the boy to feel contemptible, but he needed him to, because of the loneliness and the bitterness and the boy's mother; and he could not help himself.

After another hour they had barely traversed the aspen hillside. Pushing the crutch away in angry frustration, his father sat in the snow. The boy did not know whether he was thinking carefully of how they might get him out, or still laboring with the choice against despair. The light had wilted to something more like moonlight than afternoon. The sweep of snow had gone gray, depthless, flat, and the sky warned sullenly of night. The boy grew restless. Then it was decided. His father hung himself piggyback over the boy's shoulders, holding the rifle. The boy supported him with elbows crooked under his father's knees. The boy was tall for eleven years old, and heavy. The boy's father weighed 164 pounds.

The boy walked.

He moved as slowly as drifting snow: a step, then time, then another step. The burden at first seemed to him overwhelming. He did not think he would be able to carry his father far.

He took the first few paces expecting to fall. He did not fall, so he kept walking. His arms and shoulders were not exhausted as quickly as he had thought they would be, so he kept walking. Shuffling ahead in the deep powder was like carrying one end of an oak bureau up stairs. But for a surprisingly long time the burden did not grow any worse. He found balance. He found rhythm. He was moving.

Dark blurred the woods, but the snow was luminous. He could see the trail well. He walked.

"How are you, David? How are you holding up?"

"All right."

"We'll stop for a while and let you rest. You can set me down here." The boy kept walking. He moved so ponderously, it seemed after each step that he had stopped. But he kept walking.

"You can set me down. Don't you want to rest?"

The boy did not answer. He wished that his father would not make him talk. At the start he had gulped for air. Now he was breathing low and regularly. He was watching his thighs slice through the snow. He did not want to be disturbed. After a moment he said, "No."

He walked. He came to the cub, shrouded beneath new snow, and did not see it, and fell over it. His face was smashed deep into the snow by his father's weight. He could not move. But he could breathe. He rested. When he felt his father's thigh roll across his right hand, he remembered the wound. He was lucky his arms had been pinned to his sides, or the hand might have taken the force of their fall. As he waited for his father to roll himself clear, the boy noticed the change in temperature. His sweat chilled him quickly. He began shivering.

His father had again fallen in silence. The boy knew that he would not call out or even mention the pain in his leg. The boy realized that he did not want to mention his hand. The blood soaking the outside of his flannel bandage had grown sticky. He did not want to think of the alien tangle of flesh and tendons and bones wrapped inside. There was pain, but he kept the pain at a distance. It was not *his* hand any more. He was not counting on ever having it back. If he was resolved about that, then the pain was not his either. It was merely pain of which he was aware. His good hand was numb.

"We'll rest now."

"I'm not tired," the boy said. "I'm just getting cold."

"We'll rest," said his father. "I'm tired."

Under his father's knee, the boy noticed, was a cavity in the snow, already melted away by fresh blood. The dark flannel around his father's thigh did not appear sticky. It gleamed.

His father instructed the boy how to open the cub with the deer knife. His father stood on one leg against a deadfall, holding the Winchester ready, and glanced around on all sides as he spoke. The boy used his left hand and both his knees. He punctured the cub low in the belly, to a soft squirting sound, and sliced upward easily. He did not gut the cub. He merely cut out a large square of belly meat. He handed it to his father, in exchange for the rifle.

His father peeled off the hide and left the fat. He sawed the meat in half. One piece he rolled up and put in his jacket pocket. The other he divided again. He gave the boy a square thick with glistening raw fat.

"Eat it. The fat too. Especially the fat. We'll cook the rest farther on. I don't want to build a fire here and taunt Momma."

The meat was chewy. The boy did not find it disgusting. He was hungry.

His father sat back on the ground and unlaced the boot from his good foot. Before the boy understood what he was doing, he had relaced the boot. He was holding a damp wool sock.

"Give me your left hand." The boy held out his good hand, and his father pulled the sock down over it. "It's getting a lot colder. And we need that hand."

"What about yours? We need your hands too. I'll give you my—"

"No, you won't. We need your feet more than anything. It's all right. I'll put mine inside your shirt."

He lifted his father, and they went on. The boy walked.

He moved steadily through cold darkness. Soon he was sweating again, down his ribs and inside his boots. Only his hands and ears felt as though crushed in a cold metal vise. But his father was shuddering. The boy stopped.

His father did not put down his legs. The boy stood on the trail and waited. Slowly he released his wrist holds. His father's thighs slumped. The boy was careful about the wounded leg. His father's grip over the boy's neck did not loosen. His fingers were cold against the boy's bare skin.

"Are we at the hut?"

"No. We're not even to the meadow."

"Why did you stop?" his father asked.

"It's so cold. You're shivering. Can we build a fire?"

"Yes," his father said hazily. "We'll rest. What time is it?"

"We don't know," the boy said. "We don't have a watch."

The boy gathered small deadwood. His father used the Winchester stock to scoop snow away from a boulder, and they placed the fire at the boulder's base. His father broke up pine twigs and fumbled dry toilet paper from his breast pocket and arranged the wood, but by then his fingers were shaking too badly to strike a match. The boy lit the fire. The boy stamped down the snow, as his father instructed, to make a small ovenlike recess before the fire boulder. He cut fir boughs to floor the recess. He added more deadwood. Beyond the invisible clouds there seemed to be part of a moon.

"It stopped snowing," the boy said.

"Why?"

The boy did not speak. His father's voice had sounded unnatural. After a moment his father said:

"Yes, indeed. It stopped."

They roasted pieces of cub meat skewered on a green stick. Dripping fat made the fire spatter and flare. The meat was scorched on the outside and raw within. It tasted as good as any meat the boy had ever eaten. They burned their palates on hot fat. The second stick smoldered through before they had noticed, and that batch of meat fell in the fire. The boy's father cursed once and reached into the flame for it and dropped it and clawed it out, and then put his hand in the snow. He did not look at the blistered fingers. They ate. The boy saw that both his father's hands had gone clumsy and almost useless.

The boy went for more wood. He found a bleached deadfall not far off the trail, but with one arm he could only break up and carry small loads. They lay down in the recess together like spoons, the boy nearer the fire. They pulled fir boughs into place above them, resting across the snow. They pressed close together. The boy's father was shivering spastically now, and he clenched the boy in a fierce hug. The boy put his father's hands back inside his own shirt. The boy slept. He woke when the fire faded and added more wood and slept. He woke again and tended the fire and changed places with his father and slept. He slept less soundly with his father between him and the fire. He woke again when his father began to vomit.

The boy was terrified. His father wrenched with sudden vomiting that brought up cub meat and yellow liquid and blood and sprayed them across the snow by the grayish-red glow of the fire and emptied his stomach dry and then would not release him. He heaved on pathetically. The boy pleaded to be told what was wrong. His father could not or would not answer. The spasms seized him at the stomach and twisted the rest of his body taut in ugly jerks. Between the attacks he breathed with a wet rumbling sound deep in his chest, and did not speak. When the vomiting subsided, his breathing stretched itself out into long bubbling sighs, then shallow gasps, then more liquidy sighs. His breath caught and froth rose in his throat and into his mouth and he gagged on it and began vomiting again. The boy thought his father would choke. He knelt beside him and held him and cried. He could not see his father's face well and he did not want to look closely while the sounds that were coming from inside his father's body seemed so unhuman. The boy had never been more frightened. He wept for himself, and for his father. He knew from the noises and movements that his father must die. He did not think his father could ever be human again.

When his father was quiet, he went for more wood. He broke limbs from the deadfall with fanatic persistence and brought them back in bundles and built the fire up bigger. He nestled his father close to it and held him from behind. He did not sleep, though he was not awake. He waited. Finally he opened his eyes on the beginnings of dawn. His father sat up and began to spit.

"One more load of wood and you keep me warm from behind and then we'll go."

The boy obeyed. He was surprised that his father could speak. He thought it strange now that his father was so concerned for himself and so little concerned for the boy. His father had not even asked how he was.

The boy lifted his father, and walked.

Sometime while dawn was completing itself, the snow had resumed. It did not filter down soundlessly. It came on a slight wind at the boy's back, blowing down the canyon. He felt as though he were tumbling forward with the snow into a long vertical shaft. He tumbled slowly. His father's body protected the boy's back from being chilled by the wind. They were both soaked through their clothes. His father was soon shuddering again.

The boy walked. Muscles down the back of his neck were sore from yesterday. His arms ached, and his shoulders and thighs, but his neck hurt him most. He bent his head forward against the weight and the pain, and he watched his legs surge through the snow. At his stomach he felt the dull ache of hunger, not as an appetite but as an affliction. He thought of the jeep. He walked.

He recognized the edge of the meadow but through the snow-laden wind he could not see the cluster of aspens. The snow became deeper where he left the wooded trail. The direction of the wind was now variable, sometimes driving snow into his face, sometimes whipping across him from the right. The grass and snow dragged at his thighs, and he moved by stumbling forward and then catching himself back. Twice he stepped into small overhung fingerlets of the stream, and fell violently, shocking the air from his lungs and once nearly spraining an ankle. Farther out into the meadow, he saw the aspens. They were a hundred yards off to his right. He did not turn directly toward them. He was afraid of crossing more hidden creeks on the intervening ground. He was not certain now whether the main channel was between him and the aspen grove or behind him to the left. He tried to project from the canyon trail to the aspens and on to the forked pine on the far side of the meadow, along what he remembered as almost a straight line. He pointed himself toward the far edge, where the pine should have been. He could not see a forked crown. He could not even see trees. He could see only a vague darker corona above the curve of white. He walked.

He passed the aspens and left them behind. He stopped several times with the wind rasping against him in the open meadow, and rested. He did not set his father down. His father was trembling uncontrollably. He had not spoken for a long time. The boy wanted badly to reach the far side of the meadow. His socks were soaked and his boots and cuffs were glazed with ice. The wind was chafing his face and making him dizzy. His thighs felt as if they had been bruised with a club. The boy wanted to give up and set his father down and whimper that this had gotten to be very unfair; and he wanted to reach the far trees. He did not doubt which he would do. He walked.

He saw trees. Raising his head painfully, he squinted against the rushing flakes. He did not see the forked crown. He went on, and stopped again, and craned his neck, and squinted. He scanned a wide angle of pines, back and forth. He did not see it. He turned his body and his burden to look back. The snow blew across the meadow and seemed, whichever way he turned, to be streaking into his face. He pinched his eyes tighter. He could still see the aspens. But he could not judge where the canyon trail met the meadow. He did not know from just where he had come. He looked again at the aspens, and then ahead to the pines. He considered the problem carefully. He was irritated that the forked ponderosa did not show itself yet, but not worried. He was forced to estimate. He estimated, and went on in that direction.

When he saw a forked pine it was far off to the left of his course. He turned and marched toward it gratefully. As he came nearer, he bent his head up to look. He stopped. The boy was not sure that this was the right tree. Nothing about it looked different, except the thick cakes of snow weighting its limbs, and nothing about it looked especially familiar. He had seen thousands of pine trees in the last few days. This was one like the others. It definitely had a forked crown. He entered the woods at its base.

He had vaguely expected to join a trail. There was no trail. After two hundred yards he was still picking his way among trees and deadfalls and brush. He remembered the shepherd's creek that fell off the lip of the meadow and led down the first canyon. He turned and retraced his tracks to the forked pine.

He looked for the creek. He did not see it anywhere near the tree. He made himself quiet, and listened. He heard nothing but wind, and his father's tremulous breathing.

"Where is the creek?"

His father did not respond. The boy bounced gently up and down, hoping to jar him alert.

"Where is the creek? I can't find it."

"What?"

"We crossed the meadow and I found the tree but I can't find the creek. I need you to help."

"The compass is in my pocket," his father said.

He lowered his father into the snow. He found the compass in his father's breast pocket, and opened the flap, and held it level. The boy noticed with a flinch that his right thigh was smeared with fresh blood. For an instant he thought he had a new wound. Then he realized that the blood was his father's. The compass needle quieted.

"What do I do?"

His father did not respond. The boy asked again. His father said nothing. He sat in the snow and shivered.

The boy left his father and made random arcs within sight of the forked tree until he found a creek. They followed it onward along the flat and then where it gradually began sloping away. The boy did not see what else he could do. He knew that this was the wrong creek. He hoped that it would flow into the shepherd's creek, or at least bring them out on the same road where they had left the jeep. He was very tired. He did not want to stop. He did not care any more about being warm. He wanted only to reach the jeep, and to save his father's life.

He wondered whether his father would love him more generously for having done it. He wondered whether his father would ever forgive him for having done it.

If he failed, his father could never again make him feel shame, the boy thought naively. So he did not worry about failing. He did not worry about dying. His hand was not bleeding, and he felt strong. The creek swung off and down to the left. He followed it, knowing that he was lost. He did not want to reverse himself. He knew that turning back would make him feel confused and desperate and frightened. As long as he was following some pathway, walking, going down, he felt strong.

That afternoon he killed a grouse. He knocked it off a low branch with a heavy short stick that he threw like a boomerang. The grouse fell in the snow and floundered and the boy ran up and plunged on it. He felt it thrashing against his chest. He reached in and it nipped him and he caught it by the neck and squeezed and wrenched mercilessly until long after it stopped writhing. He cleaned it as he had seen his father clean grouse and built a small fire with matches from his father's breast pocket and seared the grouse on a stick. He fed his father. His father could not chew. The boy chewed mouthfuls of grouse, and took the chewed gobbets in his hand, and put them into his father's mouth. His father could swallow. His father could no longer speak.

The boy walked. He thought of his mother in Evergreen Park, and at once he felt queasy and weak. He thought of his mother's face and her voice as she was told that her son was lost in the woods in Montana with a damaged hand that would never be right, and with his father, who had been shot and was unconscious and dying. He pictured his mother receiving the news that her son might die himself, unless he could carry his father out of the woods and find his way to the jeep. He saw her face change. He heard her voice. The boy had to stop. He was crying. He could not control the shape of his mouth. He was not crying with true sorrow, as he had in the night when he held his father and thought his father would die; he was crying in sentimental self-pity. He sensed the difference. Still he cried.

He must not think of his mother, the boy realized. Thinking of her could only weaken him. If she knew where he was, what he had to do, she could only make it impossible for him to do it. He was lucky that she knew nothing, the boy thought.

No one knew what the boy was doing, or what he had yet to do. Even the boy's father no longer knew. The boy was lucky. No one was watching, no one knew, and he was free to be capable.

The boy imagined himself alone at his father's grave. The grave was open. His father's casket had already been lowered. The boy stood at the foot in his black Christmas suit, and his hands were crossed at his groin, and he was not crying. Men with shovels stood back from the grave, waiting for the boy's order for them to begin filling it. The boy felt a horrible swelling sense of joy. The men watched him, and he stared down into the hole. He knew it was a lie. If his father died, the boy's mother would rush out to Livingston and have him buried and stand at the grave in a black dress and veil squeezing the boy to her side like he was a child. There was nothing the boy could do about that. All the more reason he must keep walking.

Then she would tow the boy back with her to Evergreen Park. And he would be standing on 96th Street in the morning dark before his father's cold body had even begun to grow alien and decayed in the buried box. She would drag him back, and there would be nothing the boy could do. And he realized that if he returned with his mother after the burial, he would never again see the cabin outside Livingston. He would have no more summers and no more Novembers anywhere but in Evergreen Park.

The cabin now seemed to be at the center of the boy's life. It seemed to stand halfway between this snowbound creek valley and the train station in Chicago. It would be his cabin soon.

The boy knew nothing about his father's will, and he had never been told that legal ownership of the cabin was destined for him. Legal ownership did not matter. The cabin might be owned by his mother, or sold to pay his father's debts, or taken away by the state, but it would still be the boy's cabin. It could only forever belong to him. His father had been telling him *Here, this is yours. Prepare to receive it.* The boy had sensed that much. But he had been threatened, and unwilling. The boy realized now that he might be resting warm in the cabin in a matter of hours, or he might never see it again. He could appreciate the justice of that. He walked.

He thought of his father as though his father were far away from him. He saw himself in the black suit at the grave, and he heard his father speak to him from aside: *That's good. Now raise your eyes and tell them in a man's voice to begin shoveling. Then turn away and walk slowly back down the hill. Be sure you don't cry. That's good.* The boy stopped. He felt his glands quiver, full of new tears. He knew that it was a lie. His father would never be there to congratulate him. His father would never know how well the boy had done.

He took deep breaths. He settled himself. Yes, his father

would know somehow, the boy believed. His father had known all along. His father knew.

He built the recess just as they had the night before, except this time he found flat space between a stone back and a large fallen cottonwood trunk. He scooped out the snow, he laid boughs, and he made a fire against each reflector. At first the bed was quite warm. Then the melt from the fires began to run down and collect in the middle, forming a puddle of wet boughs under them. The boy got up and carved runnels across the packed snow to drain the fires. He went back to sleep and slept warm, holding his father. He rose again each half hour to feed the fires.

The snow stopped in the night, and did not resume. The woods seemed to grow quieter, settling, sighing beneath the new weight. What was going to come had come.

The boy grew tired of breaking deadwood and began walking again before dawn and walked for five more hours. He did not try to kill the grouse that he saw because he did not want to spend time cleaning and cooking it. He was hurrying now. He drank from the creek. At one point he found small black insects like winged ants crawling in great numbers across the snow near the creek. He stopped to pinch up and eat thirty or forty of them. They were tasteless. He did not bother to feed any to his father. He felt he had come a long way down the mountain. He thought he was reaching the level now where there might be roads. He followed the creek, which had received other branches and grown to a stream. The ground was flattening again and the drainage was widening, opening to daylight. As he carried his father, his head ached. He had stopped noticing most of his other pains. About noon of that day he came to the fence.

It startled him. He glanced around, his pulse drumming suddenly, preparing himself at once to see the long empty sweep of snow and broken fence posts and thinking of Basque shepherds fifty years gone. He saw the cabin and the smoke. He relaxed, trembling helplessly into laughter. He relaxed, and was unable to move. Then he cried, still laughing. He cried shamelessly with relief and dull joy and wonder, for as long as he wanted. He held his father, and cried. But he set his father down and washed his own face with snow before he went to the door.

He crossed the lot walking slowly, carrying his father. He did not now feel tired.

The young woman's face was drawn down in shock and revealed at first nothing of friendliness.

"We had a jeep parked somewhere, but I can't find it," the boy said. "This is my father."

They would not talk to him. They stripped him and put him before the fire wrapped in blankets and started tea and made him wait. He wanted to talk. He wished they would ask him a lot of questions. But they went about quickly and quietly, making things warm. His father was in the bedroom.

The man with the face full of dark beard had telephoned for a doctor. He went back into the bedroom with more blankets, and stayed. His wife went from room to room with hot tea. She rubbed the boy's naked shoulders through the blanket, and held a cup to his mouth, but she would not talk to him. He did not know what to say to her, and he could not move his lips very well. But he wished she would ask him some questions. He was restless, thawing in silence before the hearth.

He thought about going back to their own cabin soon. In his mind he gave the bearded man directions to take him and his father home. It wasn't far. It would not require much of the man's time. They would thank him, and give him an elk steak. Later he and his father would come back for the jeep. He could keep his father warm at the cabin as well as they were doing here, the boy knew.

While the woman was in the bedroom, the boy overheard the bearded man raise his voice:

"He what?"

"He carried him out," the woman whispered.

"What do you mean, carried him?"

"Carried him. On his back. I saw."

"Carried him from where?"

"Where it happened. Somewhere on Sheep Creek, maybe."

"Eight miles?"

"I know."

"*Eight miles?* How could he do that?"

"I don't know. I suppose he couldn't. But he did."

The doctor arrived in half an hour, as the boy was just starting to shiver. The doctor went into the bedroom and stayed five minutes. The woman poured the boy more tea and knelt beside him and hugged him around the shoulders.

When the doctor came out, he examined the boy without speaking. The boy wished the doctor would ask him some questions, but he was afraid he might be shivering too hard to answer in a man's voice. While the doctor touched him and probed him and took his temperature, the boy looked the doctor directly in the eye, as though to show him he was really all right.

The doctor said:

"David, your father is dead. He has been dead for a long time. Probably since yesterday."

"I know that," the boy said.

Mary Robison

Pretty Ice

I was up the whole night before my fiancé was due to arrive from the East—drinking coffee, restless and pacing, my ears ringing. When the television signed off, I sat down with a packet of the month's bills and figured amounts on a lined tally sheet in my checkbook. Under the spray of a high-intensity lamp, my left hand moved rapidly over the touch tablets of my calculator.

Will, my fiancé, was coming from Boston on the six-fifty train—the dawn train, the only train that still stopped in the small Ohio city where I lived. At six-fifteen I was still at my accounts; I was getting some pleasure from transcribing the squarish green figures that appeared in the window of my calculator. "Schwab Dental Clinic," I printed in a raveled backhand. "Thirty-eight and 50/100."

A car horn interrupted me. I looked over my desktop and out the living-room window of my rented house. The saplings in my little yard were encased in ice. There had been snow all week, and then an ice storm. In the glimmering driveway in front of my garage, my mother was peering out of her car. I got up and turned off my lamp and capped my ivory Mont Blanc pen. I found a coat in the semidark in the hall, and wound a knitted muffler at my throat. Crossing the living room, I looked away from the big pine mirror; I didn't want to see how my face and hair looked after a night of accounting.

My yard was a frozen pond, and I was careful on the walkway. My mother hit her horn again. Frozen slush came through the toe of one of my chukka boots, and I stopped on the path and frowned at her. I could see her breath rolling away in clouds from the cranked-down window of her Mazda. I have never owned a car nor learned to drive, but I had a low opinion of my mother's compact. My father and I used to enjoy big cars, with tops that came down. We were both tall and we wanted what he called "stretch room." My father had been dead for fourteen years, but I resented my mother's buying a car in which he would not have fitted.

"Now what's wrong? Are you coming?" my mother said.

"Nothing's wrong except that my shoes are opening around the soles," I said. "I just paid a lot of money for them."

I got in on the passenger side. The car smelled of wet wood and Mother's hair spray. Someone had done her hair with a minty-white rinse, and the hair was held in place by a zebra-striped headband.

"I think you're getting a flat," I said. "That retread you bought for the left front is going."

She backed the car out of the drive, using the rear-view mirror. "I finally got a boy I can trust, at the Exxon station," she said. "He says that tire will last until hot weather."

Out on the street, she accelerated too quickly and the rear of the car swung left. The tires whined for an instant on the old snow and then caught. We were knocked back in our seats a little, and an empty Kleenex box slipped off the dash and onto the floor carpet.

"This is going to be something," my mother said. "Will sure picked an awful day to come."

My mother had never met him. My courtship with Will had all happened in Boston. I was getting my doctorate there, in musicology. Will was involved with his research at Boston U., and with teaching botany to undergraduates.

"You're sure he'll be at the station?" my mother said. "Can the trains go in this weather? I don't see how they do."

"I talked to him on the phone yesterday. He's coming."

"How did he sound?" my mother said.

To my annoyance, she began to hum to herself.

I said, "He's had rotten news about his work. Terrible, in fact."

"Explain his work to me again," she said.

"He's a plant taxonomist."

"Yes?" my mother said. "What does that mean?"

"It means he doesn't have a lot of money," I said. "He studies grasses. He said on the phone he's been turned down for a research grant that would have meant a great deal to us. Apparently the work he's been doing for the past seven or so years is irrelevant or outmoded. I guess 'superficial' is what he told me."

"I won't mention it to him, then," my mother said.

We came to the expressway. Mother steered the car through some small windblown snow dunes and down the entrance ramp. She followed two yellow salt trucks with winking blue beacons that were moving side by side down the center and right-hand lanes.

"I think losing the grant means we should postpone the wedding," I said. "I want Will to have his bearings before I step into his life for good."

"Don't wait too much longer, though," my mother said.

After a couple of miles, she swung off the expressway. We went past some tall high-tension towers with connecting cables that looked like staff lines on a sheet of music. We were in the decaying neighborhood near the tracks. "Now I know this is right," Mother said. "There's our old sign."

The sign was a tall billboard, black and white, that advertised my father's dance studio. The studio had been closed for years and the building it had been in was gone. The sign showed a man in a tuxedo waltzing with a woman in an evening gown. I was always sure it was a waltz. The dancers were nearly two stories high, and the weather had bleached them into phantoms. The lettering—the name of the studio, my father's name—had disappeared.

"They've changed everything," my mother said, peering about. "Can this be the station?"

We went up a little drive that wound past a cinderly lot full of flatbed trucks and that ended up at the smudgy brownstone depot.

"Is that your Will?" Mother said.

Will was on the station platform, leaning against a baggage truck. He had a duffle bag between his shoes and a plastic cup of coffee in his mittened hand. He seemed to have put on weight, girlishly, through the hips, and his face looked thicker to me, from temple to temple. His gold-rimmed spectacles looked too small.

My mother stopped in an empty cab lane, and I got out and called to Will. It wasn't far from the platform to the car, and Will's pack wasn't a large one, but he seemed to be winded when he got to me. I let him kiss me, and then he stepped back and blew a cold breath and drank from the coffee cup, with his eyes on my face.

Mother was pretending to be busy with something in her handbag, not paying attention to me and Will.

"I look awful," I said.

"No, no, but I probably do," Will said. "No sleep, and I'm fat. So this is your town?"

He tossed the coffee cup at an oil drum and glanced around at the cold train yards and low buildings. A brass foundry was throwing a yellowish column of smoke over a line of Canadian Pacific boxcars.

I said, "The problem is you're looking at the wrong side of the tracks."

A wind whipped Will's lank hair across his face. "Does your mom smoke?" he said. "I ran out in the middle of the night on the train, and the club car was closed. Eight hours across Pennsylvania without a cigarette."

The car horn sounded as my mother climbed from behind the wheel. "That was an accident," she said, because I was frowning at her. "Hello. Are you Will?" She came around the car and stood on tiptoes and kissed him. "You picked a miserable day to come visit us."

She was using her young-girl voice, and I was embarrassed for her. "He needs a cigarette," I said.

Will got into the back of the car and I sat beside my mother again. After we started up, Mother said, "Why doesn't Will stay at my place, in your old room, Belle? I'm all alone there, with plenty of space to kick around in."

"We'll be able to get him a good motel," I said quickly, before Will could answer. "Let's try that Ramada, over near the new elementary school." It was odd, after he had come all the way from Cambridge, but I didn't want him in my old room, in the house where I had been a child. "I'd put you at my place," I said, "but there's mountains of tax stuff all over."

"You've been busy," he said.

"Yes," I said. I sat sidewise, looking at each of them in turn. Will had some blackish spots around his mouth—ballpoint ink, maybe. I wished he had freshened up and put on a better shirt before leaving the train.

"It's up to you two, then," my mother said.

I could tell she was disappointed in Will. I don't know what she expected. I was thirty-one when I met him. I had probably dated fewer men in my life than she had gone out with in a single year at her sorority. She had always been successful with men.

"William was my late husband's name," my mother said. "Did Belle ever tell you?"

"No," Will said. He was smoking one of Mother's cigarettes.

"I always liked the name," she said. "Did you know we ran a

177

dance studio?"

I groaned.

"Oh, let me brag if I want to," my mother said. "He was such a handsome man."

It was true. They were both handsome—mannequins, a pair of dolls who had spent half their lives in evening clothes. But my father had looked old in the end, in a business in which you had to stay young. He had trouble with his eyes, which were bruised-looking and watery, and he had to wear glasses with thick lenses.

I said, "It was in the dance studio that my father ended his life, you know. In the ballroom."

"You told me," Will said, at the same instant my mother said, "Don't talk about it."

My father killed himself with a service revolver. We never found out where he had bought it, or when. He was found in his warm-up clothes—a pullover sweater and pleated pants. He was wearing his tap shoes, and he had a short towel folded around his neck. He had aimed the gun barrel down his mouth, so the bullet would not shatter the wall of mirrors behind him. I was twenty then—old enough to find out how he did it.

My mother had made a wrong turn and we were on Buttles Avenue. "Go there," I said, pointing down a street beside Garfield Park. We passed a group of paper boys who were riding bikes with saddlebags. They were going slow, because of the ice.

"Are you very discouraged, Will?" my mother said. "Belle tells me you're having a run of bad luck."

"You could say so," Will said. "A little rough water."

"I'm sorry," Mother said. "What seems to be the trouble?"

Will said, "Well, this will be oversimplifying, but essentially what I do is take a weed and evaluate its structure and growth and habitat, and so forth."

"What's wrong with that?" my mother said.

"Nothing. But it isn't enough."

"I get it," my mother said uncertainly.

I had taken a mirror and a comb from my handbag and I was trying for a clean center-part in my hair. I was thinking about finishing my bill paying.

Will said, "What do you want to do after I check in, Belle? What about breakfast?"

"I've got to go home for a while and clean up that tax jazz, or I'll never rest," I said. "I'll just show up at your motel later. If we ever find it."

"That'll be fine," Will said.

Mother said, "I'd offer to serve you two dinner tonight, but I think you'll want to leave me out of it. I know how your father and I felt after he went away sometimes. Which way do I turn here?"

We had stopped at an intersection near the iron gates of the park. Behind the gates there was a frozen pond, where a single early-morning skater was skating backward, expertly crossing his blades.

I couldn't drive a car but, like my father, I have always enjoyed maps and atlases. During automobile trips, I liked comparing distances on maps. I liked the words *latitude, cartography, meridian*. It was extremely annoying to me that Mother had gotten us turned around and lost in our own city, and I was angry with Will all of a sudden, for wasting seven years on something superficial.

"What about up that way?" Will said to my mother, pointing to the left. "There's some traffic up by that light, at least."

I leaned forward in my seat and started combing my hair all over again.

"There's no hurry," my mother said.

"How do you mean?" I asked her.

"To get William to the motel," she said. "I know everybody complains, but I think an ice storm is a beautiful thing. Let's enjoy it."

She waved her cigarette at the windshield. The sun had burned through and was gleaming in the branches of all the maples and buckeye trees in the park. "It's twinkling like a stage set," Mother said.

"It is pretty," I said.

Will said, "It'll make a bad-looking spring. A lot of shrubs get damaged and turn brown, and the trees don't blossom right."

I put my comb away and smiled back at Will. For once I agreed with my mother. Everything was in place, the way it was supposed to be, quiet and holding still.

Jean Thompson

Applause, Applause

Poor Bernie, Ted thought, as rain thudded against the car like rotten fruit. Watching it stream and bubble on the windshield he promised himself not to complain about it lest Bernie's feelings be hurt. He was anxious to impress this on his wife. Poor Bernie, he said aloud. Things never work out the way he plans.

His wife nodded. Ted could see from her unsmiling, preoccupied face that it would be difficult to coax her into a conspiracy. In fact, she was probably blaming him for it: his friend, his weekend, therefore, his rain. Look, Ted said. He went to so much trouble setting this up. I'd hate to have him think we weren't enjoying it, whatever happens.

Lee, his wife, turned her chin toward him. He used to call her the Siennese Madonna because of that narrow face, long cheeks and haughty blue eyes. Easy to see her reduced to two-dimensional paint. She had never heard of Sienna. Now she said All right, I won't sulk. But I'll save the vivaciousness till later, OK?

He was a little hurt that she saw no need to be charming for him, but he said nothing. After all, she hadn't complained. He burrowed his hands in his pockets for warmth and looked out the smeared window.

The car was parked in a clearing of pebbled yellow clay. On all sides were dark sapping pine trees, impenetrable, suffocating. It made him a little dizzy to think of how limitless those trees were, how many square miles they covered. The clearing contained two gas pumps and a trading post that sold moccasins, orange pop, and insect repellant. If you turned your back on the building it was easy to believe the world contained only the pines and the implacable rain.

Poor Bernie. He wondered at what point the friends of one's youth acquire epithets. When do we begin to measure their achievements against their ambitions?

Ten years ago he and Bernie Doyle were in college. Ten years ago they sat in bars, Bernie's pipe smoke looped around their heads. Or perhaps on the broken-spined, cat-perfumed sofa that was always reincarnated in their succession of apartments. How they had talked: God, he had never talked that seriously, that openly, to a woman. Perhaps it was something one outgrew. Like the daydreams of the dusky, moody photographs that would appear on one's book jackets. The experimentation with names. Theodore Valentine? T. R. Valentine? T. Robert Valentine? The imaginary interviews. ("Valentine is a disarmingly candid, intensely personal man whose lean, somber features belie his formidable humor. The day I met him he wore an old black turtleneck, Levis and sandals, a singularly unpretentious yet becoming costume...")

Yes, he had admitted all these fantasies to Bernie, and Bernie admitted he shared them. How vulnerable they had been to each other, still were, he supposed. Behind the naive vanities, the daydreams, they had very badly wanted to be writers. Had wanted it without knowing at all what it was they wanted, their fervor making up for their ignorance. His older self was cooler, more noncommittal, for he had learned that to publicize your goals means running the risk of falling short of them.

Ten years of letters, of extravagant alcoholic phone calls. The continual measure they took of each other. Their vanished precocity, reluctantly cast aside at age twenty-five or so. Ten years which established Ted's increasingly self-conscious, increasingly offhand reports of publications, recognitions. Bernie had kept up for a few years, had even talked about getting a book together. After that he responded to Ted's letters with the same grave formula: he wasn't getting a lot done but he hoped to have more time soon. Ted was sure he'd given it up entirely. He knew how easy it was to let your discipline go slack. You had to drive yourself continually, not just to get the work done but to keep faith. Faith that what you were doing was worth the hideous effort you put into it. Easier, much easier, to let it go. The whole process of writing was a road as quirky and blind as the one they had driven this morning to the heart of the Adirondacks, this weekend, and the epithet, Poor Bernie.

Was he himself a success? He wasn't able to say that, not yet at least. Three years ago a national magazine printed a story. The smaller quarterlies published him with some regularity, paid him less frequently. His was one of the names an extremely well-read person might frown at and say Yes, I think I've heard of him. It was like being one of those Presidents no one can ever remember, Polk or Millard Fillmore. Of course you wanted more than that.

But he'd made progress. He hadn't given up. These were the important things. And he dreaded the inevitable discussions with Bernie when their younger incarnations would stand in judgment of them. How could he manage to be both tactful and truthful, feeling as he did that uncomfortable mixture of protectiveness and contempt. Yes, he admitted it, the slightest touch of contempt . . .

Is this them, Lee asked as an orange VW station wagon, its rain-slick paint lurid against the pines, slowed at the clearing. Ted squinted. Maybe . . . The car stopping. Yeah, I think so. The window on the passenger's side was rolled down and a woman's face bobbed and smiled at him. He had an impression of freckles, skin pink as soap. Paula? Ted grinned and pantomimed comprehension.

We're supposed to follow, he told Lee, and eased the car onto the road. Again the dripping trees closed over them. They were climbing now, trailing the VW along a tight spiral. It was impossible to see more than twenty yards ahead. At times they passed mailboxes, or shallow openings in the woods that indicated roads, but for the most part there was only the green-black forest, the thick pudding rain.

Where's that college he teaches at, asked Lee. Ted looked at her and tried to unravel the history of her thoughts for the last silent half-hour. She still wore her languid, neutral expression. The Madonna attends a required meeting of the Ladies' Auxiliary.

Sixty miles away. No, farther. Eighty. It was another thing he wondered about, Bernie's precarious instructor job. Four sections of composition. Abortion, Pro and Con. My First Date. Topic sentences. Footnotes.

And he married one of his students?

Ted nodded. It was hard for him to imagine Bernie as a figure of authority or some little girl regarding him with the reverence and hysteria of student crushes. But it had happened.

Lee pointed. The VW's bumper was winking at them and Ted slowed, ready to turn. Now it was scarcely a road they followed but a dirt lane. Milder, deciduous trees interlaced above them and screened the rain somewhat. They rocked along the muddy ruts for half a mile.

Then the sudden end of the lane, the cabin of dark brown shingles with Bernie already waving from the porch. Ted was out of the car almost before it had stopped, was shaking Bernie's hand and saying something like Son of a Gun, and grinning. Bernie said Valentine, you lout, and reached up to pound him on the back.

The women drifted after them. Hey, Paula, come shake hands with Ted. And this is Lee. Bernie, Paula. Ted found himself appraising Lee as she climbed the steps, took satisfaction in her length of leg, her severely beautiful face now softened with a smile. The four of them stood nodding at each other for a moment. Like two sets of dolls built to different scale, Ted thought, the Doyles so small, he and Lee an angular six inches taller. Furious exercise had kept Ted in shape, and he knew the faint line of sunburn under his eyes was becoming. He realized he was standing at attention, and cursed his vanity.

Bernie looked more than ever like a Swiss toymaker as imagined by Walt Disney. Small bones and white supple hands. His gray eyes unfocused behind rimless glasses. The ever-present pipe which, when inserted, drew his whole face into a preoccupied, constipated look. He had grown a dark manicured beard.

And Paula? He knew her to be at least twenty-four, but she could have passed for sweet eighteen. Snub little nose. Smiling mouth like the squiggle painted on a china doll. Green eyes in that pink transparent skin. Yes, she would be something to take notice of in a stuffy classroom.

Even as he absorbed and ordered his impressions the group broke, Bernie pushing the front door open, Paula talking about food. He followed Bernie ·into a paneled room and the damp, bone-deep cold that would accompany the whole weekend first seized him. He heard Lee's lightly inflected voice keeping her promise: What a lovely fireplace. We can tell ghost stories around it.

You bet, said Bernie, and squatted before it, poking the grate. There's even dry wood on the porch.

Looking at him, Ted experienced the uneasy process of having to square his observations with his memories. As if this was not really Bernie until he conformed with Ted's image of him. How long had it been, three years? He began to be more sure of himself as he noted familiar mannerisms surfacing. Bernie's solemnity; he discussed firewood in the same tone another man might use for religion. The deftness of his hands wielding the fireplace tools. Ted imagined him shaping chunks of pine into cuckoo clocks, bears, and monkeys . . .

Now stop that, he warned himself. It was a writer's curse, this verbal embroidery. Never seeing anything as it was, always analyzing and reformulating it. Maybe the entire habit of observation, the thing he trained himself in, was just a nervous tic, a compulsion. He shook his head and joined Lee in her exploration of the cabin.

The main room was high-ceilinged, dark. In hot weather he imagined its shadows would bless the skin, but now the bare floors made his feet ache with cold. There were two bedrooms, one on each side of the main room. The furniture was a mixture of wicker and raw wood. In the rear were a trim new kitchen and bathroom. They stepped out the back door and Ted whistled.

Even in the rain the blue-gray bowl of the lake freshened his eyes. Its irregular shoreline formed bays, coves, little tongues of land, all furred with silent pine. He could not see the opposite shore. There was an island just where he might have wished for one, a mound of brush and rock. The air smelled clean and thin.

Lee spoke to Bernie, who had joined them. It's incredible. Just too lovely.

Bernie grinned, as if the lake were a treat he had prepared especially for them. And Ted felt all his discomfort drop away as he saw his friend's happiness, his desire to make them happy. God bless Bernie; he'd forget all this gloomy nonsense about artistic accomplishment. Are there many cabins up here, he asked.

Quite a few. But the lake is so big and the trees so thick we have a lot of privacy. He pointed with his pipe. There's the boathouse. And dock. No beach I'm afraid, it's all mud.

They stood in the shelter of the porch, rain hanging like lace from the gutters. Then Lee said Too cold out here for me, and they all went inside.

Paula was rummaging through groceries in the kitchen. Here, said Lee. Let me do something useful. A little cluster of polite words filled the air, Paula demurring, Lee insisting. Ted hoped that for once Lee would be graceful about helping in the kitchen, leave him and Bernie alone without getting sarcastic later about Man-Talk and Woman's Work. He tried to catch her eye but she was pulling her blonde hair into a knot and asking Paula about the mayonnaise.

Bernie offered him a beer and they drifted to the living room. Sitting down Ted had a moment of apprehension, like the beginning of a job interview. Bernie frowned and coaxed his pipe into life. How often had he used it as a prop; Ted knew his shyness. At last the bowl reddened. So tell me, Bernie said. How goes it with you?

Ted realized how much he'd rehearsed his answer: Not too bad. But I'll never be rich.

Bernie chuckled. Poor but honest.

Poor but poor. With Lee's job we get by. And I do some free-lancing, write ad copy for a car dealer, that sort of thing. He shrugged. And how about you?

Ted was aware he had shifted too quickly, had seemed to brush off Bernie's question in an attempt to be polite, reciprocal. Damn. He'd have to watch that.

Ah, Bernie said. The pastoral life of a college instructor. It's like being a country priest, really, with your life revolving around the feast days. Registration. Final exams. Department meetings on First Fridays.

You're getting tired of it?

It's a job, Ted. Like anything else it has its ups and downs. Actually I'm glad it's not excessively glamorous. This way I don't feel tied to it, committed. I can stay fluid, you know?

What would you do instead?

Sell hardware. Open a museum. I don't know. Paula wants to work as a photographer. She's pretty good. And I wouldn't mind getting back to the writing. It's been simmering in me for a long time.

That hint of justification. Ted felt the same prepared quality in Bernie's answer as in his own. He risked his question: Have you been able to get anything done?

Any writing, you mean? Dribs and drabs. I decided what I needed was to remove myself from pressure, you know? Work at my own pace without worrying about marketing a finished product. Of course I know that's not the way you go about it.

Yeah. It's out of the typewriter and into the mails.

You still work on a schedule?

Absolutely. Seems to be the only way I get anything done. Lee covers for me. I have tantrums if the phone rings.

You must really throw yourself into the thing.

The implied sympathy, the chance to speak of his frustrations with someone who would understand them, was a luxury. Jesus, he said. You spend hours wrestling with yourself, trying to keep your vision intact, your intensity undiminished. Sometimes I have to stick my head under the tap to get my wits back. And for what? You know what publishing is like these days. Paper costs going up all the time. Nothing gets printed unless it can be made into a movie. Everything is media. Crooked politicians sell their unwritten memoirs for thousands. I've got a great idea for a novel. It's about a giant shark who's possessed by a demon while swimming in the Bermuda Triangle. And the demon talks in CB lingo, see? There'll be recipes in the back.

Bernie laughed and Ted continued. Then the quarterlies, the

185

places you expect to publish serious writing. They're falling all over themselves trying to be trendy, avant-garde. If you write in sentence fragments and leave plenty of blank space on the page, you're in. Pretentiousness disguised as trail-blazing. All the editors want to set themselves up as interpreters of a new movement. I hope they choke on their own jargon. Anti-meta-post-contemporary-surfictional literature. Balls.

He stopped for breath. I'm sorry, he said. Didn't mean to get carried away.

Not at all. It does me good to hear a tirade now and then. Reminds me of college, makes me feel ten years younger.

Still. He should not have spoken with such bitterness. It sounded like he was making excuses. Ted smiled, lightening his tone. The artist takes his lonely stand against the world.

As well he ought to. But really, Valentine, don't you get tired of beating your head against all that commercialism? Trying to compete with it? I mean, of course you do, but do you think it affects what you write?

Was it Bernie's solemnity that always made his questions sound so judgmental? Ted knew it was more than an issue of mannerisms. Bernie pondered things, thought them through; you respected his sincerity. Ted gave the only answer pride allowed: No, because the work can't exist in a vacuum. It has to get out there in the world, and reach people. Ted drained his beer and ventured to define the issue between them. You're saying it's better to be an Emily Dickinson, a violet by a mossy stone half-hidden to the eye, that sort of thing. Keep it in shoeboxes in the closet so you can remain uncorrupted.

Bernie turned his hands palms upward and managed to express dissent by spreading his white fingers. Just that it's possible to lose sight of what you set out to do. Even get too discouraged.

How quickly we've moved into position, Ted thought. Each of us defending our lives. He remembered his earlier resolution to speak tactfully, cushion any comparison between their accomplishments. And here was Bernie seeming to demand such comparison. How easy it would be to make some mention of his publications, play up some of the things he's muted in his letters, insist on Bernie's paying tribute to them. He even admitted to himself that beneath everything he'd wanted his success acknowledged. Like the high school loser who dreams of driving to the class reunion in a custom-made sports car. As if only those who knew your earlier weakness could verify your success.

But he would not indulge himself. Partly because, like his earlier outburst, it would threaten to say too much, and partly because he wanted this meeting to be without friction. Couldn't they rediscover their younger, untried selves? It was a kind of nostalgia. So he said I don't know, Bernie. You may be right. But the only way for me to accomplish anything is by competing with the market.

Bernie considered this, seemed to accept it as a final statement. He dumped his pipe into the fireplace. Ted noticed the beginning of a tonsure, a doorknob-sized patch of naked scalp. The sight enabled him to recapture all his tenderness. Shall we join the ladies, Bernie asked, rising.

They were sitting at the kitchen table with mugs of coffee. Well, Ted said, resting a hand on Lee's shoulder. I hope you haven't been bored. He meant it half as apology, half as warning: you'd better not be.

Au contraire, Lee answered. We've been trying to reconcile post-Hegelian dogma with Jamesian pragmatism. But she grinned.

And Paula said Actually, we were telling raunchy jokes. Give us ten more minutes.

He liked her. Her pinkness, plumpness. Like a neat little bird, all smooth lines and down. Her round good-humored chin. And Lee seemed to be doing all right with her.

I think it's quit raining, said Bernie. If you've got sturdy enough shoes we could take a hike.

It was still very wet under the trees. A careless tug at a branch might flip cold rainbow-edged drops down your back. And the sky was gray as concrete. But they enjoyed the silence, the soft sucking ground matted with last year's needles. They perched on a fallen tree at the lake's edge and chunked stones into the crisp water. Bernie explained it was too early, too cool for the black flies whose bites made bloody circles just beneath the skin.

How often do you get up here, Ted asked. Bernie told him about every other weekend when the weather was right. Ted launched into abundant, envious speech: They were lucky sons-of-bitches, did they know that back in Illinois there were only tame little man-made lakes, tidy parks, lines of Winnebagoes like an elephant graveyard, right Lee? As if complimenting this part of Bernie's life might restore some balance between them.

They walked back single file along the sunken trail. Ted was at the rear. Lee's blondeness looked whiter, milkier out here. Perhaps it was the heaviness of the dark green air, like the light just before a thunderstorm which plays up contrasts. Bernie and Paula's heads were the same shade of sleek brown, slipping in and out of his vision. It struck him that once again he was observing and being conscious of himself as an observer. It was a habit he'd fallen into, not necessarily a bad one. But he'd been working very hard at the writing lately (Lee had insisted on this vacation; he rather begrudged the time spent away from his desk) and this heightened self-awareness was a sign of strain. As if he couldn't really escape his work or the persona that went with it.

The Artist's impressions of a walk in the woods. The Artist's view on viewing. The Artist on Art. How do you get your ideas for stories, Mr. Valentine? Well, I simply exploit everything I come into contact with. One ended, of course, by losing all spontaneity. You saw people as characters, sunsets as an excuse for similes—

Bernie called a warning over his shoulder just as Ted felt a drop of rain slide down his nose. They quickened their pace to a trot as the rain fell, first in fat splatters that landed as heavily as frogs, then finer, harder. By the time they reached the porch their clothes were dark and dripping.

Fire, said Bernie. Coffee and hot baths, said Paula. The movement, the busyness, cheered them as much as the dry clothes. When at last they sat on each side of the stone fireplace, the odor of smoke working into their skins and hair, they all felt the same sense of shelter.

Damn, said Bernie. I wanted to take you fishing. But he looked comfortable, his pipe bobbing in his mouth.

Maybe tomorrow, said Paula. The rain had polished her skin, now the fire was warming it, bringing out different tints: apricot, cameo. She and Bernie made a peaceful, domestic couple. He could imagine them sitting like this, on either side of the fire, for the next thirty years. The retired Swiss toymaker and his wife.

But was Bernie happy? Did he feel, as Ted would have in his place, a sense of failure, of goals having shrunk. You never knew. Or, this visit would probably not allow him to learn. The time was too short to break down much of the politeness that passed between them as guest and host. Recapturing their former intimacy, that intensity, seemed as difficult as remembering what virginity had felt like. They should have left the wives behind, just come up here for a messy bachelor weekend of drinking and cards. This impulse moved him to ask if anyone wanted a whiskey.

They did. He passed glasses, leaned back into his chair. Well, said Lee. It's too early to tell ghost stories.

Ted and I could talk about our misspent youth.

She wants something ghostly, Doyle, not ghastly.

Oh go ahead, Lee urged Bernie. Tell me something that can be used against him. She was at her most animated, perhaps from the first bite of the liquor. The Madonna is photographed for a Seagram's commercial. Go ahead, she repeated.

Tell her I was a football hero.

If you won't tell Paula about that indecent exposure thing.

Agreed. Ted gulped at his drink to induce the mood of nostalgia. One thing I'll always remember. You and me taking a bottle of strawberry wine up on the roof of the humanities building.

Did you really, said Paula.

We thought we were Bohemians, Bernie explained. Artistic, not ethnic.

We pretended it was absinthe.

A rooftop in Paris at the turn of the century.

I was James Joyce.

I was Oscar Wilde.

We were going to be paperback sensations.

We were full of shit.

I don't know, Ted objected. I mean, certainly we were naive. Who isn't at twenty? But you have to begin with wild idealism, dreams of glory. It's the raw fuel that gets you through the disappointments.

You mean the brute facts of editors, publishing.

Ted nodded. The manuscripts that come back stained with spaghetti sauce. The places that misspell your name. All the ambiguities of success. If we'd known what was actually involved in writing, we probably never would have attempted it.

When we leave here, Lee put in, we have to go to New York and talk with Ted's agent. You wouldn't believe the nastiness and wheeler-dealer stuff that goes on in that New York scene. It's like a court in Renaissance Italy. Intrigues within intrigues.

Bernie raised his eyebrows above the rim of his glasses. You have an agent now?

Yes. Since last November. He's trying to place the novel for me.

And you've finished the novel? Paula, do we have champagne? I've been hearing about this book for years.

Well, I've finished the draft. If it's accepted I'll no doubt have to do rewrites. Damn Lee for bringing up the agent; it would only make Bernie more aware of the gap between their achievements. He searched for some way to de-escalate things. You should be glad you've escaped all this messiness so far. Retained your youthful innocence.

The bottom log of the fire, which had been threatening to burn through, now collapsed. Red winking sparks flew up the black column of the chimney as the fire assumed a new pattern. Bernie squatted in front of it raking the embers into place. He spoke without turning around.

You know, I read that piece you had in—what was it—the one about the schizophrenic?

"The Lunatic." He sat up a little straighter in his chair, adopted the carefully pleasant expression with which he received criticism.

Ted was very happy with that piece, Lee informed everyone. And the magazine did a good production job. She beamed at him, sweetly proud of making a contribution to the discussion. He wished she hadn't spoken, had left him free to frame his reply after listening to Bernie. But she was only repeating what she'd heard him say.

That's it, "The Lunatic." I admire the language use, the control in the thing. The way you managed to milk images. But—

that terrible pause—

I felt there was a kind of slickness in the thing, almost glibness. I mean, you're talking about a man who's having a mental breakdown. And you treat that rather flippantly. Perhaps you intended it, but I wondered why.

There were a number of replies he could make. He settled for the most general: The story is something of a satire, Bernie. Think of all the literature that's dealt with madness. It's an extremely well-trodden path. You simply can't write about the subject straightforwardly anymore. People expect something new.

Bernie frowned and rubbed his jaw under the dense beard. Ted knew, watching him, that Bernie had thought his argument through. Had prepared it carefully, step by step, like he did everything.

I thought, Bernie continued, that your complaint against avant-garde fiction was its emphasis on form over content. Blank space on the page, tortured syntax, that sort of thing. The writing screaming for attention. Aren't you agreeing with them now? Saying, in effect, rather than exploring the individuality of this character or situation, I'll dress it up in a different package. Pretend not to take it seriously.

Both women were watching rather helplessly, as if they realized their little store of soothing words and social graces would be of no use. And the defense that came to Ted's mind (Nobody writes like Henry James anymore. Or, more crudely, Your aesthetic is outdated) sounded like a small boy's taunts. So he said I do take the character and situation seriously. That doesn't mean one can't experiment with form, depart from rigid storytelling conventions. Otherwise you wind up repeating what's already been done. Repeating yourself too.

Bernie shook his head. Again that gesture of judgment. I'm

sorry, but I see it as a response to the market. The thing I was talking about earlier. You tailor the writing to what the editors are buying. Maybe unconsciously. You're certainly not writing about the giant sharks. But it's still a form of corruption.

And what, in particular, is being corrupted?

I hope I can put this right. It's like, that increased self-consciousness, that authorial presence that's always thrusting itself between the reader and the page—see, I'm telling this story, you're reading it, I'll try to amuse you, watch this—is rather paralyzing. What you're doing, a general you (a parenthetical smile), is making disclaimers for the piece, covering your tracks. I'll play this a little tongue-in-cheek so I won't be called to account for it.

You might as well dispute abstraction in painting, Bernie. Form can't be entirely neglected in favor of content. Otherwise we might still be seeing those Victorian pictures of blind children and noble hounds.

It runs the danger of shallowness, Ted.

Well, I suppose the only way to avoid the dangers is not to write anything at all.

He hadn't realized how angry he was until he heard himself speak. Damn the whiskey, damn his own thin-skinned hatred of criticism. He was too quick to take things as insults. Now, having said the one unforgivable thing, there was no retreat. The four of them sat without looking at each other. Bernie plunged into a fury of pipe-cleaning, tamping, lighting, as another man might have cracked his knuckles. The rain filled the silence, gusting against the windows and shrinking the warmth of the fire.

Finally Paula said I'm going to see what there is for dinner. Ted stood up as soon as she did, muttering about another drink. He paused in the kitchen only long enough to slosh the liquor in his glass. Paula opened the refrigerator and said Hm, fried chicken maybe? He said Fine and walked out the back door.

The rain had brought an early blue darkness. He could still make out the shoreline, the agitation of the lake as the rain pocked its surface. Far away on his left shone one point of light, a white feeble thing that he could not imagine indicated human companionship, laughter, warmth. Even though he stood under the ledge, moisture beaded his clothes like dew. He gave himself over completely to the melancholy of it all. The only consolation he could find was the thought that argument was a form of intimacy.

When he came back inside both women were busy in the kitchen. Can I peel potatoes or something, he asked. They sat him at the kitchen table with a bowl of strawberries to hull. A little boy hiding behind women. He didn't want to go back to the living room where he knew Bernie would be sitting. Lee and Paula seemed determined to speak of nothing more serious than gravy making. He watched Lee as she moved between stove and sink, a little surprised at her vivacity. As if she had formed some alliance without his being aware of it. Her hair had dried in soft waves with a hint of fuzziness; a looser style than she usually wore. Although she spoke to him occasionally, she did not meet his eye. It didn't seem that she was avoiding him; rather, she was busy, he was extraneous, incidental . . .

But he was projecting his injured feeling onto her, his gloom and self-pity. Snap out of it, he told himself. You're going to be here another thirty-six hours.

That realization must have been shared, must have been what got them through the evening. The act of sitting down to food together restored some tenuous rhythm. Afterward Paula suggested Monopoly. They let the bright cardboard, the little mock triumphs and defeats, absorb them. Ted thought how harmless all greed and competition were when reduced to this scale, then he berated himself for facile irony.

At midnight Bernie yawned and said I'm down to thirty dollars and Marvin Gardens. Somebody buy me out.

Who's ahead? Add it up, Paula suggested.

It turned out to be Ted, who felt hulking and foolish raking in his pile of paper money. Flimsy pastel trophies. He was duly congratulated. He did a parody of the young Lindbergh acknowledging cheers. Modestly tugging his forelock. The tycoon needs some rest, he said, and they all agreed.

Goodnight. Goodnight, and if you need extra blankets they're at the top of the closet. I'm sure we'll be fine. Bernie latched the door and said Maybe it'll clear up tomorrow.

It took Ted a moment to realize he was speaking of the rain.

He waited until everyone was settled before he used the bathroom. No use risking more sprightly greetings. When he got back Lee was in bed, her fair hair spilling from the rolled sheets like corn silk.

He wanted her to start talking first, but her eyes were squeezed shut against the bed-side lamp. Well, he said. Too neutral, inadequate.

Would you turn that light off?

He reached, produced darkness. She sighed and said Much better. He lay for a moment accustoming himself to the black stillness, the smell of the rough pine boards. The mattress was sparse, lopsided. It seemed to have absorbed the dank cold of the cabin.

He burrowed into its thin center. Then the even sound of Lee's breathing told him she was falling asleep. Almost angry, he shook her shoulder.

What? She was more irritated than sleepy.

Don't fall asleep. I wanted to talk to you.

Go ahead.

He waited a moment to control himself. You're not making it very easy.

She twisted inside the sheets until she rested on one elbow, facing him. All right, I'll make it easy. What the hell were you arguing about? I hate it when you start talking like that. All that rhetoric. You take it so seriously. Was any of it worth snapping at him like that?

Of course I take it seriously. He was accusing me of shallowness. Corruption.

Oh boy. Lee drawled her sarcasm. And you couldn't forget your literary reflexes for one minute.

No. I guess I couldn't.

Her hand emerged from the darkness and gave his shoulder a series of small tentative pats. Poor Ted. Her voice was kinder. The pats continued, light but persistent, as if a moth were battering itself against him. He supressed the impulse to brush it away.

Why poor Ted?

Because sometimes I think you don't enjoy what you're doing at all. The writing I mean. You get so upset.

Don't be silly.

I know. The Agony and the Ecstasy. She yawned. Well I hope you two make up. They're nice folks.

Her lips, seeming disembodied in the blind darkness, found his chin, his mouth. Good night.

Good night.

He waited until she was asleep or pretending to be asleep. He got up, put on his pants and sweater, and padded into the kitchen. Turned on the fluorescent light over the sink.

Her cruelest words spoken in her softest voice. Her revenge, thinking or unthinking, for all the times he'd shut himself away from her. He'd had his work to do. His sulks and tantrums. His insistence on the loftiness of his purpose, the promise of his future. His monstrous self-importance. The whole edifice threatened.

He didn't enjoy it.

Of course you were gratified at the high points. The little recognitions and deference. Of course you made a point of bemoaning the labor involved. Saying it drove you mad with frustration. That was expected. But enjoyment? Where was the enjoyment?

The pines still rattled in the wind. The rain was a dim silver fabric without seam or edge, unrolling from the sky. He thought of walking into it, losing himself in all that fragrant blackness, in the thick gunmetal lake. Oh he was tired of his cleverness, his swollen sensitivity. Better to crouch under a rock in the rain and reduce yourself to nerve, skin, and muscle. But his self-consciousness would not allow this either. It told him it would be melodramatic, a petulant gesture. Bad form.

Something, some weight, passed over the floorboards behind him and he turned, his nostrils cocked. It was the ticklish perfume of pipe smoke that reached him first.

H'lo, he said, and Bernie's mouth curved around the polished wooden stem of his pipe. He managed to walk to where Ted was standing by the back door without seeming to advance in a straight line.

Foul weather, he said nodding. He too had resumed his clothes.

I'll say. They watched the faint movement of water on water. Then Bernie said Drink?

Sure.

While there was still tension perceptible in their cautious responses, in Bernie's stiff-wristed pouring of drinks, it seemed a formality. The simple fact of coming together like this was a promise of reconciliation. When Bernie was seated across from him, Ted began with the obvious. I'm sorry about tonight. I was way out of line.

I guess I provoked you, Ted. I'm jealous. I admit it.

And I am insecure and narcissistic.

Would it be too maudlin to wish we were kids again?

Ted shook his head. In some ways I think I'm still twenty. The prize student who's always fawning for approval, pats on the head.

You're too hard on yourself.

Yes. I am. He blinked at the checked tablecloth, trying to get his eyes to focus on its pattern.

And I'm not hard enough. Bernie smiled. Such confessions.

They're necessary. Who else can absolve us of our sordid pasts?

Now the room has the contours and atmosphere of all rooms in which people stay awake talking. The fluorescent light is grainy, staring. The clutter on the kitchen table—ketchup bottle, sagging butter dish, tin of Nestle's Quik, the rowdy crudded ashtray—the world is narrowed into these, a little universe that the eyes return to again and again. Now it begins, the sorting and testing of words.

194

Remember that words are not symbols of other words. There are words which, when tinkered with, become honest representatives of the cresting blood, the fine living net of nerves. Define rain. Or even joy. It can be done.

Stephanie Vaughn

Able, Baker, Charlie, Dog

When I was twelve years old, my father was tall and awesome. I can see him walking across the parade ground behind our quarters. The wind blew snow into the folds of his coat and made the hem swoop around his legs. He did not lower his head, he did not jam his hands into the pockets. He was coming home along a diagonal that would cut the parade ground into perfect triangles, and he was not going to be stopped by any snowstorm. I stood at the kitchen door and watched him through a hole I had rubbed in the steamy glass.

My grandmother and mother fidgeted with pans of food that had been kept warm too long. It was one o'clock on Saturday and he had been expected home at noon.

"You want to know what this chicken looks like?" said my grandmother. "It looks like it died last year."

My mother looked into the pan but didn't say anything.

My grandmother believed my mother should have married a minister, not an Army officer. Once my mother had gone out with a minister, and now he was on the radio every Sunday in Ohio. My grandmother thought my father had misrepresented himself as a religious man. There was a story my mother told about their first date. They went to a restaurant and my father told her that he was going to have twelve sons and name them Peter, James, John, et cetera. "And I thought, Twelve sons!" said my mother. "Boy, do I pity your poor wife." My mother had two miscarriages and then she had me. My father named me Gemma, which my grandmother

196

believed was not even a Christian name.

"You want to know what this squash looks like?" said my grandmother.

"It'll be fine," said my mother.

Just then the wind gusted on the parade ground, and my father veered to the left. He stopped and looked up. How is it possible you have caught me off guard, he seemed to ask. Exactly where have I miscalculated the velocities, how have I misjudged the vectors?

"It looks like somebody peed in it," my grandmother said.

"Keep your voice low," my father told me that day as we ate the ruined squash and chicken. "Keep your voice low and you can win any point."

We were living in Fort Niagara, a little Army post at the juncture of the Niagara River and Lake Ontario. We had been there through the fall and into the winter, as my father, who was second in command, waited for his next promotion. It began to snow in October. The arctic winds swept across the lake from Canada and shook the windows of our house. Snow drifted across the parade ground, and floes of ice piled up against each other in the river, so that if a person were courageous enough, or foolhardy enough, and also lucky, he could walk the mile across the river to Canada.

"And always speak in sentences," he told me. "You have developed a junior-high habit of speaking in fragments. Learn to come to a full stop when you complete an idea. Use semicolons and periods in your speech."

My mother put down her fork and knife. Her hands were so thin and light they seemed to pass through the table as she dropped them in her lap. "Zachary, perhaps we could save some of the lecture for dessert?" she said.

My grandmother leaned back into her own heaviness. "The poor kid never gets to eat a hot meal," she said. She was referring to the rule that said I could not cut my food or eat while I was speaking or being spoken to, and I was always being spoken to. My father used mealtimes to lecture on the mechanics of life, the how-tos of a civilized world. Normally, I was receptive to his advice, but that day I was angry with him.

"You know, Dad," I said, "I don't think my friends are going to notice a missing semicolon."

I thought he would give me a fierce look, but instead he winked. "And don't say 'you know,'" he said.

He never said "you know," never spoke in fragments, never slurred his speech, even years later when he had just put away a fifth of Scotch and was trying to describe the Eskimo custom of chewing up the meat before it was given to the elders, who had no teeth. He spoke with such calculation and precision that his sentences hung over us like high vaulted ceilings, or rolled across the table like ornaments sculptured from stone. It was a huge cathedral of a voice, full of volume and complexity.

He taught me the alphabet. Able, Baker, Charlie, Dog. It was the alphabet the military used to keep "B"s separate from "V"s and "I"s separate from "Y"s. He liked the music of it, the way it sounded on his fine voice. I was four years old and my grandmother had not come to live with us yet. We were stationed in Manila, and living in a house the Army had built on squat stilts to protect us from the insects. There was a typhoon sweeping inland, and we could hear the hoarse sound of metal scraping across the Army's paved street. It was the corrugated roof of the house next door.

"Don't you think it's time we went under the house?" my mother said. She was sitting on a duffelbag that contained our tarps and food rations. The house had a loose plank in the living-room floor, so that if the roof blew away, or the walls caved in, we could escape through the opening and sit in the low space between the reinforced floor and the ground until the military rescue bus came.

My father looked at me and said, "Able, Baker, Charlie, Dog. Can you say it, Gemma?"

I looked up at the dark slope of our own metal roof.

"Can you say it?"

"Able, Baker, Charlie, Dog," I said.

The metal rumbled on the road outside. My mother lifted the plank.

"We will be all right," he said. "Easy, Fox, George, How."

"Anybody want to join me?" said my mother.

"Easy," I said.

"Rachel, please put that plank back."

"Easy, Fox, George, How," I said.

My mother replaced the plank and sat on the floor beside me. The storm grew louder, the rain fell against the roof like handfuls of gravel.

"Item, Jig, King." My father's voice grew lower, fuller. We sat under the sound of it and felt safe. "Love, Mike, Nan."

But then we heard another sound—something that went *whap-whap*, softly, between the gusts of rain. We tilted our heads toward the shuttered windows.

"Well," said my father, standing up to stretch. "I think we are losing a board or two off the side of the house."

"Where are you going?" said my mother. "Just where do you think you're going?"

He put on his rain slicker and went into the next room. When he returned, he was carrying a bucket of nails and a hammer. "Obviously," he said, "I am going fishing."

We moved back to the States when I was six, and he taught me how to play parcheesi, checkers, chess, cribbage, dominoes, and twenty questions. "When you lose," he told me, "don't cry. When you win, don't gloat."

He taught me how to plant tomatoes and load a shotgun shell. He showed me how to gut a dove, turning it inside out as the Europeans do, using the flexible breastbone for a pivot. He read a great many books and never forgot a fact or a technical description. He explained the principles of crop rotation and the flying buttress. He discussed the Defenestration of Prague.

When I was in elementary school, he was sent abroad twice on year-long tours—once to Turkey and once to Greenland, both strategic outposts for America's Early Warning System. I wanted to, but could not write him letters. His came to me every week, but without the rhythms of his voice the words seemed pale and flat, like the transparent shapes of cells under a microscope. He did not write about his work, because his work was secret. He did not send advice, because that he left to my mother and grandmother in his absence. He wrote about small things—the smooth white rocks he found on a mountainside in Turkey, the first fresh egg he ate in Greenland. When I reread the letters after he died, I was struck by their grace and invention. But when I read them as a child, I looked through the words—"eggs . . . shipment . . . frozen"—and there was nothing on the other side but the great vacuum of his missing voice.

"I can't think of anything to say," I told my mother the first time she urged me to write to him. He had already been in Turkey for three months. She stood behind me at the heavy library table and smoothed my hair, touched my shoulders. "Tell him about your tap lessons," she said. "Tell him about ballet."

"Dear Dad," I wrote. "I am taking tap lessons. I am also taking ballet." I tried to imagine what he looked like. I tried to put a face before my face, but it was gray and featureless, like the face of a statue worn flat by wind and rain. "And I hope you have a Happy Birthday next month," I concluded, hoping to evade the necessity of writing him again in three weeks.

The autumn I turned twelve, we moved to Fort Niagara, which was the administrative base for the missile sites strung along the Canadian border between Lake Erie and Lake Ontario. It was a handsome post, full of oak trees, brick buildings, and history. The French had taken the land from the Indians and built the original fort. The British took the fort from the French, and the Americans took it from the British. My father recounted the battles for us as we drove there along the wide sweep of the Niagara River, past apple orchards and thick pastures. My grandmother sat in the back seat and made a note of each red convertible that passed. I was supposed to be counting the white ones. When we drove through the gate and saw the post for the first time—the expanses of clipped grass, the tall trees, the row of Colonial houses overlooking the river—my grandmother put down her tablet and said, "This is some post." She looked at my father admiringly, the first indication she had ever given that he might be a good match for my mother after all. She asked to be taken to the far end of the post, where the Old Fort was. It sat on a point of land at the juncture of the lake and river, and looked appropriately warlike, with its moat and tiny gun windows, but it was surprisingly small—a simple square of yellow stone. "Is this all there is?" I said as my grandmother and I posed for pictures on the drawbridge near two soldiers dressed in Revolutionary War costumes. It was hard to imagine that chunks of a vast continent had been won and lost within the confines of a fortress hardly bigger than Sleeping Beauty's castle at Disneyland. Later, as we drove back along the river, my father said in his aphoristic way, "Sometimes the biggest battles are the smallest ones."

The week after we settled in our quarters, we made the obligatory trip to the Falls. It was a sultry day—Indian summer—and our eyes began to water as we neared the chemical factories that surround the city of Niagara Falls. We stopped for iced tea and my father explained how the glaciers had formed the escarpment through which the Falls had cut a deep gorge. "Escarpment"—that was the term he used, instead of "cliff." It skidded along the roof of his mouth and entered the conversation with a soft explosion.

We went to the Niagara Falls Museum and examined the containers people had used successfully to go over the Falls early in the century, when there was a thousand-dollar prize given to survivors. Two were wooden barrels strapped with metal bands. One was a giant rubber ball reinforced with a steel cage. A fourth was a long steel capsule. On the walls were photographs of each survivor and plaques explaining who had been injured and how.

The steel capsule was used by a man who had broken almost every bone in his body. The plaque said that he was in the hospital for twenty-three weeks and then took his capsule around the world on a speaking tour. One day when he was in New Zealand, he slipped on an orange peel, broke his leg, and later died of complications.

We went next to Goat Island and stood on the open back to watch the leap and dive of the white water. My mother held her handbag close to her breasts. She had a habit of always holding things this way—a stack of dinner plates, the dish towel, some mail she had brought in from the porch; she hunched over slightly, so that her body seemed at once to be protective and protected. "I don't like the river," she said. "I think it wants to hypnotize you." My father put his hands in his pockets to show how at ease he was, and my grandmother went off to buy an ice-cream cone.

At the observation point, we stood at a metal fence and looked into the frothing water at the bottom of the gorge. We watched bits and pieces of rainbows appear and vanish in the sunlight that was refracted off the water through the mist. My father pointed to a black shape in the rapids above the Horseshoe Falls. "That's a river barge," he said. He lowered his voice so that he could be heard under the roar of the water. "A long time ago, there were two men standing on that barge waiting to see whether in the next moment of their lives they would go over."

He told us the story of the barge then—how it had broken loose from a tug near Buffalo and floated down-river, gathering speed. The two men tore at the air, waved and shouted to people on shore, but the barge entered the rapids. They bumped around over the rocks, and the white water rose in the air. One man—"He was the thinking man," said my father—thought they might be able to wedge the barge among the rocks if they allowed the hull to fill with water. They came closer to the Falls—four hundred yards, three hundred—before the barge jerked broadside and stopped. They were there all afternoon and night, listening to the sound of the water pounding into the boulders at the bottom of the gorge. The next morning, they were rescued, and one of the men, the thinking man, told the newspapers that he had spent the night playing poker in his head. He played all the hands, and he bluffed himself. He drew to inside straights. If the barge had torn loose from the rocks in the night, he was going to go over the Falls saying, "Five-card draw, jacks or better to open." The other man had sat on the barge, his arms clasped around his knees, and watched the mist blow back from the edge of the Falls in the moonlight. He could not speak.

"The scream of the water entered his body," said my father.

He paused to let us think about that.

"Well, what does that mean?" my grandmother said at last.

My father rested his arms on the fence and gazed pleasantly at the Falls. "He went insane."

The river fascinated me. I often stood between the yellow curtains of my bedroom and looked down upon it and thought about how deep and swift it was, how black under the glittering surface. The newspaper carried stories about people who jumped over the Falls, fourteen miles upriver from our house. I thought of their bodies pushed along the soft silt of the bottom, tumbling silently, huddled in upon themselves like fetuses—jilted brides, unemployed factory workers, old people who did not want to go to rest homes, teen-agers who got bad grades, young women who fell in love with married men. They floated invisibly past my bedroom window, out into the lake.

That winter, I thought I was going to die. I thought I had cancer of the breasts. My mother had explained to me about menstruation, she had given me a book about the reproductive systems of men and women, but she had not told me about breasts and how they begin as invisible lumps which become tender and sore.

I thought the soreness had begun in a Phys. Ed. class one day in December when I was hit in the chest with a basketball. I didn't worry about it, and it went away by New Year's. In January, I found a pamphlet at the bus stop. I was stamping my feet in the cold, looking down at my boots, when I saw the headline—"CANCER: SEVEN WARNING SIGNALS." When I got home, I went into the bathroom and undressed. I examined myself for enlarged moles and small wounds that wouldn't heal. I was systematic. I sat on the edge of the tub with the pamphlet by my side and began with my toenails, looking under the tips of them. I felt my soles, arches, ankles. I worked my way up my body and then I felt the soreness again, around both nipples. At dinner that night I didn't say anything all through the meal. In bed I slept on my back, with my arms stiff against my sides.

The next Saturday was the day my father came home late for lunch. The squash sat on the back of the stove and turned to ochre soup. The chicken fell away from the bones. After lunch he went into the living room and drank Scotch and read a book. When I came down for supper, he was still sitting there, and he told my mother he would eat later. My grandmother, my mother, and I ate silently at the kitchen table. I took a long bath. I scrubbed my chest hard.

I went straight to my bedroom, and after a while my mother came upstairs and said, "What's wrong?"

I didn't say anything.

She stood in front of me with her hands clasped in front of her. She seemed to lean toward her own hands. "But you've been acting, you know"—and here she laughed self-consciously, as she used the forbidden phrase—"you know, you've been acting different. You were so quiet today."

I went to my chest of drawers and took the pamphlet out from under a stack of folded underpants and gave it to her.

"What's this?"

"I think I have No. 4," I said.

She must have known immediately what the problem was, but she didn't smile. She asked me to raise my nightgown and she examined my chest, pressing firmly, as if she were a doctor. I told her about the soreness. "Here?" she said. "And here? What about here, too?" She told me I was beginning to "develop." I knew what she meant, but I wanted her to be precise.

"You're getting breasts," she said.

"But I don't *see* anything."

"You will."

"You never told me it would hurt."

"Oh, dear. I just forgot. When you're grown up you just forget what it was like."

I asked her whether, just to be safe, I could see a doctor. She said that of course I could, and I felt better, as if I had had a disease and already been cured. As she was leaving the room, I said, "Do you think I need a bra?" She smiled. I went to sleep watching the snow fall past the window. I had my hands cupped over my new breasts.

When I awoke, I did not recognize the window. The snow had stopped and moonlight slanted through the glass. I could not make out the words, but I heard my father's voice filling up the house. I tiptoed down the back staircase that led to the kitchen and stood in the slice of shadow near the doorjamb. My grandmother was telling my mother to pack her bags. He was a degenerate, she said—she had always seen that in him. My mother said, "Why, Zachary, why are you doing this?"

"Just go pack your bags," my grandmother said. "I'll get the child."

My father said conversationally, tensely, "Do I have to break your arms?"

I leaned into the light. He was holding on to a bottle of Scotch with one hand, and my mother was trying to pull it away with both of hers. He jerked his arm back and forth, so that she was drawn into a little dance, back and forth across the linoleum in front of him.

"The Lord knows the way of righteousness," said my grandmother.

"Please," said my mother. "Please, please."

"And the way of the ungodly shall perish," said my grandmother.

"Whose house is this?" said my father. His voice exploded. He snapped his arm back, trying to take the bottle from my mother in one powerful gesture. It smashed against the wall, and I stepped into the kitchen. The white light from the ceiling fixture burned across the smooth surfaces of the refrigerator, the stove, the white Formica counter tops. It was as if an atom had been smashed somewhere and a wave of radiation was rolling through the kitchen. I looked him in the eye and waited for him to speak. I sensed my mother and grandmother on either side of me, in petrified postures. At last, he said, "Well." His voice cracked. The word split in two. "Wel-el." He said it again. His face took on a flatness.

"I am going back to bed," I said. I went up the narrow steps, and he followed me. My mother and grandmother came along behind, whispering. He tucked in the covers, and sat on the edge of the bed, watching me. My mother and grandmother stood stiff against the door. "I am sorry I woke you up," he said finally, and his voice was deep and soothing. The two women watched him go down the hall, and when I heard his steps on the front staircase I rolled over and put my face in the pillow. I heard them turn off the lights and say good night to me. I heard them go to their bedrooms. I lay there for a long time, listening for a sound downstairs, and then it came—the sound of the front door closing.

I went downstairs and put on my hat, coat, boots. I followed his footsteps in the snow, down the front walk and across the road to the riverbank. He did not seem surprised to see me next to him. We stood side by side, hands in our pockets, breathing frost into the air. The river was filled from shore to shore with white heaps of ice, which cast blue shadows in the moonlight.

"This is the edge of America," he said, in a tone that seemed to answer a question I had just asked. There was a creak and crunch of ice as two floes below us scraped each other and jammed against the bank.

"You knew all week, didn't you? Your mother and your grandmother didn't know, but I knew that you could be counted on to know."

I hadn't known until just then, but I guessed the unspeakable thing—that his career was falling apart—and I knew. I nodded. Years later, my mother told me what she had learned about the incident, not from him but from another Army wife. He had called a general a son of a bitch. That was all. I never knew what the issue was or whether he had been right or wrong. Whether the defense of the United States of America had been at stake, or merely the pot in a card game. I didn't even know whether he had called the general a son of a bitch to his face or simply been overheard in an unguarded moment. I only knew that he had been given a "7" instead of a "9" on his Efficiency Report and then passed over for promotion. But that night I nodded, not knowing the cause but knowing the consequences, as we stood on the riverbank above the moonlit ice. "I am looking at that thin beautiful line of Canada," he said. "I think I will go for a walk."

"No," I said. I said it again. "No." I wanted to remember later that I had told him not to go.

"How long do you think it would take to go over and back?" he said.

"Two hours."

He rocked back and forth in his boots, looked up at the moon, then down at the river. I did not say anything.

He started down the bank, sideways, taking long graceful sliding steps, which threw little puffs of snow in the air. He took his hands from his pockets and hopped from the bank to the ice. He tested his weight against the weight of the ice, flexing his knees. I watched him walk a few yards from the shore and then I saw him rise in the air, his long legs scissoring the moonlight, as he crossed from the edge of one floe to the next. He turned and waved to me, one hand making a slow arc.

I could have said anything. I could have said "Come back" or "I love you." Instead, I called after him, "Be sure and write!" The last thing I heard, long after I had lost sight of him far out on the river, was the sound of his laugh splitting the cold air.

In the spring he resigned his commission and we went back to Ohio. He used his savings to invest in a chain of hardware stores with my uncle. My uncle arranged the contracts with the builders and plumbers, and supervised the employees. My father controlled the inventory and handled the books. He had been a logistics officer, and all the skills he might have used in supervising the movement of land, air, and sea cargoes, or in calculating the disposition of several billion dollars' worth of military supplies, were instead brought to bear on the deployment of nuts and bolts, plumbers' joints and nipples, No. 2 pine, Con-Tact paper, acrylic paint, caulking guns, and rubber dishpans. He learned a new vocabulary—traffic builders, margins, end-cap displays, perfboard merchandisers, seasonal impulse items—and spoke it with the ostentation and faint amusement of a man who has just mastered a foreign language.

"But what I really want to know, Mr. Jenkins," I heard him tell a man on the telephone one day, "is why you think the Triple Gripper Vegetable Ripper would make a good loss-leader item in midwinter." He had been in the hardlines industry, as it was called, for six months, and I was making my first visit to his office, and then only because my mother had sent me there on the pretext of taking him a mid-morning snack during a busy Saturday. I was reluctant to confront him in his civilian role, afraid I would find him somehow diminished. In fact, although he looked incongruous among the reds, yellows, and blues which the previous owner had used to decorate the office, he sounded much like the man who had taught me to speak in complete sentences.

"Mr. Jenkins, I am not asking for a discourse on coleslaw."

When he hung up, he winked at me and said, "Your father is about to become the emperor of the building and housewares trade in Killbuck, Ohio."

I nodded and took a seat in a red-and-blue chair.

Then he looked at his hands spread upon the spotless ink blotter and said, "Of course, you know that I do not give a damn about the Triple Gripper Vegetable Ripper."

I had skipped a grade and entered high school. I saw less and less of him, because I ate dinner early, so that I could go to play rehearsals, basketball games, dances. In the evenings he sat in a green chair and smoked cigarettes, drank Scotch, read books—the same kinds of books, year after year. They were all about Eskimos and Arctic explorations—an interest he had developed during his tour in Greenland. Sometimes, when I came in late and was in the kitchen making a snack, I watched him through the doorway. Often he looked away from the book and gazed toward the window. He would strike a match and let it burn to his thumb and fingertip, then wave it out. He would raise the glass but not drink from it. I think he must have imagined himself to be in the Arctic during those moments, a warrior tracking across the ice for bear or seal. Sometimes he was waiting for me to join him. He wanted to tell me about the techniques the Eskimos had developed for survival, the way they stitched up skins to make them water-tight vessels. He became obsessive on the subject of meat. The Eskimo diet was nearly all protein. "Eat meat," he said. Two professors at

Columbia had tested the value of the Eskimo diet by eating nothing but caribou for a year and claimed they were healthier at the end of the experiment than they had been before.

Later, when I went to college, he developed the habit of calling me long distance when my mother and grandmother had gone to bed and he was alone downstairs with a drink. "Are you getting enough protein?" he asked me once at three in the morning. It was against dorm rules to put through calls after midnight except in cases of emergency, but his deep, commanding voice was so authoritative ("This is Gemma Jackson's father, and I must speak with her immediately") that it was for some time believed on my corridor that the people in my family were either accident-prone or suffering from long terminal illnesses.

He died the summer I received my master's degree. I had accepted a teaching position at a high school in Chicago, and I went home for a month before school began. He was over-weight and short of breath. He drank too much, smoked too many cigarettes. The doctor told him to stop, my mother told him, my grandmother told him.

My grandmother was upstairs watching television and my mother and I were sitting on the front porch. He was asleep in the green chair, with a book in his lap. I left the porch to go to the kitchen to make a sandwich, and as I passed by the chair I heard him say, "Ahhhh. Ahhhhhh." I saw his fist rise to his chest. I saw his eyes open and dilate in the lamplight. I knelt beside him. "Are you O.K.?" I said. "Are you dreaming?"

We buried him in a small cemetery near the farm where he was born. In the eulogy he was remembered for having survived the first wave of the invasion of Normandy. He was admired for having been the proprietor of a chain of excellent hardware stores.

"He didn't have to do this," my mother said after the funeral. "He did this to himself."

"He was a good man," said my grandmother. "He put a nice roof over our heads. He sent us to Europe twice."

Afterward I went alone to the cemetery. I knelt beside the heaps of wilted flowers—mostly roses and gladiolas, and one wreath of red, white, and blue carnations. Above me, the maple pods spun through the sunlight like wings, and in the distance the corn trumpeted green across the hillsides. I touched the loose black soil at the edge of the flowers. Able, Baker, Charlie, Dog. I could remember the beginning of the alphabet, up through Mike and Nan. I could remember the end. X-Ray, Yoke, Zebra. I was his only child, and he taught me what he knew. I wept then, but not because he had gone back to Ohio to read about the Eskimos and sell the artifacts of civilized life to homeowners and builders. I wept because when I was twelve years old I had stood on a snowy riverbank as he became a shadow on the ice, and waited to see whether he would slip between the cracking floes into the water.

Joy Williams

Train

Inside, the Auto-Train was violet. Both little girls were pleased because it was their favorite color. Violet was practically the only thing they agreed on. Danica Anderson and Jane Muirhead were both ten years old. They had traveled from Maine to Washington, D.C., by car with Jane's parents and were now on the train with Jane's parents and one hundred nine other people and forty-two automobiles on the way to Florida where they lived. It was September. Danica had been with Jane since June. Danica's mother was getting married again and she had needed the summer months to settle down and have everything nice for Dan when she saw her in September. In August, her mother had written Dan and asked what she could do to make things nice for Dan when she got back. Dan replied that she would like a good wall-hung pencil sharpener and satin sheets. She would like cowboy bread for supper. Dan supposed that she would get none of these things. Her mother hadn't even asked her what cowboy bread was.

The girls explored the entire train, north to south. They saw everyone but the engineer. Then they sat down in their violet seats. Jane made faces at a cute little toddler holding a cloth rabbit until he started to cry. Dan took out her writing materials and began writing to Jim Anderson. She was writing him a postcard.

"Jim," she wrote, "I miss you and I will see you any minute. When I see you we will go swimming right away."

"That is real messy writing," Jane said. "It's all scrunched together. If you were writing to anyone other than a dog, they

209

wouldn't be able to read it at all."

Dan printed her name on the bottom of the card and embellished it all with X's and O's.

"Your writing to Jim Anderson is dumb in about twelve different ways. He's a *golden retriever,* for Godssakes."

Dan looked at her friend mildly. She was used to Jane yelling at her and expressing disgust and impatience. Jane had once lived in Manhattan. She had developed certain attitudes. Jane was a treasure from the city of New York currently on loan to the state of Florida where her father, for the last two years, had been engaged in running down a perfectly good investment in a marina and dinner theater. Jane liked to wear scarves tied around her head. She claimed to enjoy grapes and brown sugar and sour cream for dessert more than ice cream and cookies. She liked artichokes. She *adored* artichokes. She *adored* the part in the New York City Ballet's *Nutcracker Suite* where the Dew Drops and the candied Petals of Roses dance to the "Waltz of the Flowers." Jane had seen the *Nutcracker* four *times,* for godssakes.

Dan and Jane and Jane's mother and father had all lived with Jane's grandmother in her big house in Maine all summer. The girls hadn't seen that much of the Muirheads. The Muirheads were always "cruising." They were always "gunk-holing," as they called it. Whatever that was, Jane said, for Godssakes. Jane's grandmother had a house on the ocean and knew how to make pizza and candy and sail a canoe. She called pizza *'za.* She sang hymns in the shower. She sewed sequins on their jeans and made them say grace before dinner. After they said grace, Jane's grandmother would ask forgiveness for things done and left undone. She would, upon request, lie down and chat with them at night before they went to sleep. Jane was crazy about her grandmother and was quite a nice person in her presence. One night, at the end of summer, Jane had had a dream in which men dressed in black suits and white bathing caps had broken into her grandmother's house and taken all her possessions and put them in the road. In Jane's dream, rain fell on all her grandmother's things. Jane woke up weeping. Dan had wept too. Jane and Dan were friends.

The train had not yet left the station even though it was two hours past the posted departure time. An announcement had just been made that said that a two-hour delay was built into the train's schedule.

"They make up the time at night," Jane said. She plucked the postcard from Dan's hand. "This is a good one," she said. "I think you're sending it to Jim Anderson just so you can save it yourself." She read aloud, "This is a photograph of the Phantom

Dream Car crashing through a wall of burning television sets before a cheering crowd at the Cow Palace in San Francisco."

At the beginning of the summer, Dan's mother had given her one hundred dollars, four packages of new underwear and three dozen stamped postcards. Most of the cards were plain but there were a few with odd pictures on them. Dan's mother wanted to hear from her twice weekly throughout the summer. She had married a man named Jake, who was a carpenter. Jake had already built Dan three bookcases. This seemed to be the extent of what he knew how to do for Dan.

"I only have three left now," Dan said, "but when I get home, I'm going to start my own collection."

"I've been through that phase," Jane said. "It's just a phase. I don't think you're much of a correspondent. You wrote, 'I got sunburn. Love, Dan' . . . 'I bought a green Frisbee. Love, Dan' . . . 'Mrs. Muirhead has swimmer's ear. Love, Dan' . . . 'Mr. Muirhead went water-skiing and cracked his rib. Love, Dan' . . . When you write to people you should have something to say."

Dan didn't reply. She had been Jane's companion for a long time, and was wearying of what Jane's mother called her "effervescence."

Jane slapped Dan on the back and hollered, "Danica Anderson, for Godssakes! What is a clod like yourself doing on this fabulous journey!"

Together, the girls made their way to the Starlight Lounge in Car 7 where Mr. and Mrs. Muirhead told them they would be enjoying cocktails. They hesitated in the car where the train's magician was with his audience, watching him while he did the magic silks trick, the cut and restored handkerchief trick, the enchanted salt shaker trick, and the dissolving quarter trick. The audience, primarily retirees, screamed with pleasure.

"I don't mind the tricks," Jane whispered to Dan, "but the junk that gets said drives me crazy."

The magician was a young man with a long spotted face. He did a lot of card forcing. Again and again, he called the card that people chose from a shuffled deck. Each time that the magician was successful, the audience participant yelled and smiled and in general acted thrilled. Jane and Dan passed on through.

"You don't really choose," Jane said. "He just makes you think you choose. He does it all with his pinky." She pushed Dan forward into the Starlight Lounge where Mrs. Muirhead was on a banquette staring out the window at a shed and an unkempt bush which was sliding slowly past. She was drinking a martini. Mr. Muirhead was several tables away talking to a young man wearing jeans and a yellow jacket. Jane did not sit down. "Mummy," she said, "can I have your olive?"

"Of course not," Mrs. Muirhead said, "it's soaked in gin."

Jane, Dan in tow, went to her father's table. "Daddy," Jane demanded, "why aren't you sitting with Mummy? Are you and Mummy having a fight?"

Dan was astonished at this question. Mr. and Mrs. Muirhead fought continuously and as bitterly as vipers. Their arguments were baroque, stately, and although frequently extraordinary, never enlightening. At breakfast, they would be quarreling over an incident at a cocktail party the night before or a dumb remark made fifteen years ago. At dinner, they would be howling over the fate, which they called by many names, which had given them one another. Forgiveness, charity and cooperation were qualities unknown to them. They were opponents *pur sang*. Dan was sure that one morning, Jane would be called from her classroom and told as gently as possible by Mr. Mooney, the school principal, that her parents had splattered one another's brains all over the lanai.

Mr. Muirhead looked at the children sorrowfully and touched Jane's cheek.

"I am not sitting with your mother because I am sitting with this young man here. We are having a fascinating conversation."

"Why are you always talking to young men?" Jane asked.

"Jane, honey," Mr. Muirhead said, "I will answer that." He took a swallow of his drink and sighed. He leaned forward and said earnestly, "I talk to so many young men because your mother won't let me talk to young women." He remained hunched over, patting Jane's cheek for a moment, and then leaned back.

The young man extracted a cigarette from his jacket and hesitated. Mr. Muirhead gave him a book of matches. "He does automobile illustrations," Mr. Muirhead said.

The young man nodded. "Belly bands. Pearls and flakes. Flames. All custom work."

Mr. Muirhead smiled. He seemed happier now. Mr. Muirhead loved conversations. He loved "to bring people out." Dan supposed that Jane had picked up this pleasant trait from her father and distorted it in some perversely personal way.

"I bet you have a Trans Am yourself," Jane said.

"You are so-o-o right," the young man said. "It's ice-blue. You like ice-blue? Maybe you're too young." He extended his hand showing a large gaudy stone in a setting that seemed to be gold. "Same color as this ring," he said.

Dan nodded. She could still be impressed by adults. Their mysterious, unreliable images still had the power to attract and confound her, but Jane was clearly not interested in the young man. She demanded much of life. She had very high standards when she wanted to. Mr. Muirhead ordered the girls ginger ales and the young man and himself another round of drinks. Sometimes the train, in the mysterious way of trains, would stop, or even reverse, and they would pass unfamiliar scenes once more. The same green pasture filled with slanty light, the same row of clapboard houses, each with the shades of their windows drawn against the heat, the same boats on their trailers, waiting on dry land. The moon was rising beneath a spectacular lightning and thunder storm. People around them were commenting on it. Close to the train, a sheen of dark birds flew low across a dirt road.

"Birds are only flying reptiles, I'm sure you're all aware," Jane said suddenly.

"Oh my God, what a horrible thought!" Mr. Muirhead said. His face had become a little slack and his hair had become somewhat disarranged.

"It's true, it's true," Jane sang. "Sad but true."

"You mean like lizards and snakes?" the young man asked. He snorted and shook his head.

"*Glorified* reptiles, certainly," Mr. Muirhead said, recovering a bit of his sense of time and place.

Dan suddenly felt lonely. It was not homesickness, although she would have given anything at that moment to be poking around in her little aluminum boat with Jim Anderson. She wouldn't even be living any longer in the place she thought of as "home." The town was the same but the place was different. The house where she had been a little tiny baby and had lived her whole life belonged to someone else now. Over the summer, her mother and Jake had bought another house which Jake was going to fix up.

"Reptiles have scales," the young man said, "or else they are long and slimy."

Dan felt like bawling. She could feel the back of her eyes swelling up like cupcakes. She was surrounded by strangers saying crazy things, and had been for quite some while. Even her own mother said crazy things in a reasonable way that made Dan know she was a stranger too. Dan's mother told Dan everything. Her mother told her she wouldn't have to worry about having brothers or sisters. Her mother discussed the particular nature of the problem with her. Half the things Dan's mother told her, Dan didn't want to know. There would be no brothers and sisters. There would be Dan and her mother and Jake, sitting around the house together, caring deeply for one another, sharing a nice life together, not making any mistakes.

Dan excused herself and started toward the lavatory on the level below. Mrs. Muirhead called to her as she approached and handed her a folded piece of paper. "Would you be kind enough to give this to Mr. Muirhead?" she asked. Dan gave Mr. Muirhead the note and went down to the lavatory. She sat on the little toilet as the train rocked along and cried.

After a while, she heard Jane's voice saying, "I hear you in there, Danica Anderson. What's the matter with you?"

Dan didn't say anything.

"I know it's you," Jane said. "I can see your stupid shoes and your stupid socks."

Dan blew her nose, pushed the button on the toilet and said, "What did the note say?"

"I don't know," Jane said. "Daddy ate it."

"He ate it!" Dan exclaimed. She opened the door of the stall and went to the sink. She washed her hands and splashed her face with water. She giggled. "He really ate it?"

"Everybody is looped in that Starlight Lounge," Jane said. Jane patted her hair with a hairbrush. Jane's hair was full of tangles and she never brushed hard enough to get them out. She looked at Dan by looking in the mirror. "Why were you crying?"

"I was thinking about your grandma," Dan said. "She said that one year she left the Christmas tree up until Easter."

"Why were you thinking about my grandma!" Jane yelled.

"I was thinking about her singing," Dan said, startled. "I like her singing."

In her head, Dan could hear Jane's grandmother singing about Death's dark waters and sinking souls, about Mercy Seats and the Great Physician. She could hear the voice rising and falling through the thin walls of the Maine house, borne past the dark screens and into the night.

"I don't want you thinking about my grandma," Jane said, pinching Dan's arm.

Dan tried not to think of Jane's grandma. Once, she had seen her fall coming out of the water. The beach was stony. The stones were round and smooth and slippery. Jane's grandmother had skinned her arm and bloodied her lip.

The girls went into the corridor and saw Mrs. Muirhead standing there. Mrs. Muirhead was deeply tanned. She had put her hair up in a twist and a wad of cotton was noticeable in her left ear. The three of them stood together, bouncing and nudging against one another with the motion of the train.

"My ear is killing me," Mrs. Muirhead said. "I think there's something they're not telling me. It crackles and snaps in there. It's like a bird breaking seeds in there." She touched the bone between cheekbone and ear. "I think the doctor I was seeing should lose his license. He was handsome and competent, certainly, but on my last visit, he was vacuuming my ear and his secretary came in to ask him a question and she put her hand on his neck. She stroked his neck, his secretary! While I was sitting there having my ear vacuumed!" Mrs. Muirhead's cheeks were flushed.

The three of them gazed out the window. The train must have been clipping along, but things outside, although gone in an instant, seemed to be moving slowly. Beneath a street light, a man was kicking his pick up truck.

"I dislike trains," Mrs. Muirhead said. "I find them depressing."

"It's the oxygen deprivation," Jane said, "coming from having to share the air with all these people."

"You're such a snob, dear," Mrs. Muirhead sighed.

"We're going to supper now," Jane said.

"Supper," Mrs. Muirhead said. "Ugh."

The children left her looking out the window, a disconsolate, pretty woman wearing a green dress with a line of frogs dancing around it.

The dining car was almost full. The windows reflected the eaters. The countryside was dim and the train pushed through it.

Jane steered them to a table where a man and woman silently labored over their meal.

"My name is Crystal," Jane offered, "and this is my twin sister, Clara."

"Clara!" Dan exclaimed. Jane was always inventing drab names for her.

"We were triplets," Jane went on, "but the other died at birth. Cord got all twisted around his neck or something."

The woman looked at Jane and smiled.

"What is your line of work?" Jane persisted brightly.

There was silence. The woman kept smiling, then the man said, "I don't do anything, I don't have to do anything. I was injured in Vietnam and they brought me to the base hospital and worked on reviving me for forty-five minutes. Then they gave up. They thought I was dead. Four hours later, I woke up in the mortuary. The Army gives me a good pension." He pushed his chair away from the table and left.

Dan looked after him, astonished, a cold roll raised halfway to her mouth. "Was your husband really dead for all that while?" she asked.

"My husband, ha!" the woman said. "I'd never laid eyes on

that man before the 6:30 seating."

"I bet you're a professional woman who doesn't believe in men," Jane said slyly.

"Crystal, how did you guess! It's true, men are a collective hallucination of women. It's like when a group of crackpots get together on a hilltop and see flying saucers." The woman picked at her chicken.

Jane looked surprised, then said, "My father went to a costume party once wrapped from head to foot in aluminum foil."

"A casserole," the woman offered.

"No! A spaceman, an alien astronaut!"

Dan giggled, remembering when Mr. Muirhead had done that. She felt that Jane had met her match with this woman.

"What do you do!" Jane fairly screamed. "You won't tell us!"

"I do drugs," the woman said. The girls shrank back. "Ha," the woman said. "Actually, I test drugs for pharmaceutical companies. And I do research for a perfume manufacturer. I am involved in the search for human pheromones."

Jane looked levelly at the woman.

"I know you don't know what a pheromone is, Crystal. To put it grossly, a pheromone is a smell that a person has that can make another person do or feel a certain thing. It's an irresistible signal."

Dan thought of mangrove roots and orange groves. Of the smell of gas when the pilot light blew out on Jane's grandmother's stove. She liked the smell of the Atlantic Ocean when it dried upon your skin and the smell of Jim Anderson's fur when he had been rained upon. There were smells that could make you follow them, certainly.

Jane stared at the woman, tipping forward slightly in her seat.

"Relax, will you, Crystal, you're just a child. You don't even *have* a smell yet," the woman said. "I test all sorts of things. Sometimes I'm part of a control group and sometimes I'm not. You never know. If you're part of the control group, you're just given a placebo. A placebo, Crystal, is something that is nothing, but you don't know it's nothing. You think you're getting something that will change you or make you feel better or healthier or more attractive or something, but you're not really."

"I know what a placebo is, " Jane muttered.

"Well that's terrific, Crystal, you're a prodigy." The woman removed a book from her handbag and began to read it. The book had a denim jacket on it which concealed its title.

"Ha!" Jane said, rising quickly and attempting to knock over a glass of water. "My name's not Crystal!"

Dan grabbed the glass before it fell and hurried after her. They returned to the Starlight Lounge. Mr. Muirhead was sitting with another young man. This young man had a blond beard and a studious manner.

"Oh, this is a wonderful trip!" Mr. Muirhead said exuberantly. "The wonderful people you meet on a trip like this! This is the most fascinating young man. He's a writer. Been everywhere. He's putting together a book on cemeteries of the world. Isn't that some subject? I told him anytime he's in our town, stop by our restaurant, be my guest for some stone crab claws."

"Hullo," the young man said to the girls.

"We were speaking of Père-Lachaise, the legendary Parisian cemetery," Mr. Muirhead said. "So wistful. So grand and romantic. Your mother and I visited it, Jane, when we were in Paris. We strolled through it on a clear crisp autumn day. The desires of the human heart have no boundaries, girls. The mess of secrets in the human heart are without number. Witnessing Père-Lachaise was a very moving experience. As we strolled, your mother was screaming at me, Jane. Do you know why, honey-bunch? She was screaming at me because back in New York, I had garaged the car at the place on East 84th Street. Your mother said that the people in the place on East 84th Street never turned the ignition all the way off to the left and were always running down the battery. She said that there wasn't a soul in all of New York City who didn't know that the people running the garage on East 84th Street were idiots who were always ruining batteries. Before Père-Lachaise, girls, this young man and I were discussing the Panteón, just outside of Guanajuato in Mexico. It so happens that I am also familiar with the Panteón. Your mother wanted some tiles for the foyer so we went to Mexico. You stayed with Mrs. Murphy, Jane. Remember? It was Mrs. Murphy who taught you how to make egg salad. In any case, the Panteón is a walled cemetery, not unlike the Campo Santo in Genoa, Italy, but the reason everybody goes there is to see the mummies. Something about the exceptionally dry air in the mountains has preserved the bodies and there's a little museum of mummies. It's grotesque of course, and it certainly gave me pause. I mean it's one thing to think we will all gather together in a paradise of fadeless splendor like your grandma thinks, lamby-lettuce, and it's another thing to think as the Buddhists do that latent possibilities withdraw into the heart at death, but do not perish, thereby allowing the being to be reborn, and it's one more thing, even, to believe like a Goddamn scientist in one of the essential laws of physics which states that no energy is ever lost. It's one thing to think any of those things, girls, but it's quite another to be standing in that little museum looking at those miserable mummies. The horror and indignation were in their faces still. I almost cried aloud, so vivid was my sense of the fleetingness of this life. We made our way into the fresh air of the courtyard and I bought a package of cigarettes at a little stand which sold postcards and films and such. I reached into my pocket for my lighter and it appeared that my lighter was not there. It seemed that I had lost my lighter. The lighter was a very good one that your mother had bought me the Christmas before, Jane, and your mother started screaming at me. There was a very gentle, warm rain falling, and there were bougainvillea petals on the walks. Your mother grasped my arm and reminded me that the lighter had been a gift from her. Your mother reminded me of the blazer she had bought for me. I spilled buttered popcorn on it at the movies and you can still see the spot. She reminded me of the hammock she bought for my fortieth birthday, which I allowed to rot in the rain. She recalled the shoulder bag she bought me, which I detested, it's true. It was somehow left out in the yard and I mangled it with the lawnmower. Descending the cobbled hill into Guanajuato, your mother recalled every one of her gifts to me, offerings both monetary and of the heart. She pointed out how I had mishandled and betrayed every one."

No one said anything. "Then," Mr. Muirhead continued, "there was the Modena Cemetery in Italy."

"That hasn't been completed yet," the young man said hurriedly. "It's a visionary design by the architect Aldo Rossi. In our conversation, I was just trying to describe the project to you."

"You can be assured," Mr. Muirhead said, "that when the project is finished and I take my little family on a vacation to Italy, as we walk, together and afraid, strolling through the hapless landscape of the Modena Cemetery, Jane's mother will be screaming at me."

"Well, I must be going," the young man said. He got up.

"So long," Mr. Muirhead said.

"Were they really selling postcards of the mummies in that place?" Dan asked.

"Yes they were, sweetie-pie," Mr. Muirhead said. "In this world there is a postcard of everything. That's the kind of world this is."

The crowd was getting boisterous in the Starlight Lounge. Mrs. Muirhead made her way down the aisle toward them and with a deep sigh, sat beside her husband. Mr. Muirhead gesticulated and formed words silently with his lips as though he was talking to the girls.

"What?" Mrs. Muirhead said.

"I was just telling the girls some of the differences between men and women. Men are more adventurous and aggressive with greater spatial and mechanical abilities. Women are more consistent, nurturent and aesthetic. Men can see better than women, but women have better hearing," Mr. Muirhead said.

"Very funny," Mrs. Muirhead said.

The girls retired from the melancholy regard Mr. and Mrs. Muirhead had fixed upon one another, and wandered through the cars of the train, occasionally returning to their seats to fuss in the cluttered nests they had created there. Around midnight, they decided to revisit the game car where earlier, people had been playing backgammon, Diplomacy, anagrams, crazy eights and Clue. They were still at it, variously throwing down queens of diamonds, moving troops through Asia Minor and accusing Colonel Mustard of doing it in the conservatory with a wrench. Whenever there was a lull in the playing, they talked about the accident.

"What accident?" Jane demanded.

"Train hit a Buick," a man said. "Middle of the night." The man had big ears and a tattoo on his forearm.

"There aren't any good new games," a woman complained. "Haven't been for years and years."

"Did you fall asleep?" Jane said accusingly to Dan.

"When could that have happened?" Dan said.

"We didn't see it," Jane said, disgusted.

"Two teenagers escaped without a scratch," the man said. "Lived to laugh about it. They are young and silly but it's no joke to the engineer. The engineer has a lot of paperwork to do after he hits something. The engineer will be filling out forms for a week." The man's tattoo said MOM AND DAD.

"Rats," Jane said.

The children returned to the darkened dining room where *Superman* was being shown on a small television set. Jane instantly fell asleep. Dan watched Superman spin the earth backward so he could prevent Lois Lane from being smothered in a rock slide. The train shot past a group of old lighted buildings. SEWER KING, a sign said. When the movie ended, Jane woke up.

"When we lived in New York," she said muzzily, "I was sitting in the kitchen one afternoon doing my homework and this girl came in and sat down at the table. Did I ever tell you this? It was the middle of the winter and it was snowing. This person just came in with snow on her coat and sat right down at the table."

"Who was she?" Dan asked.

"It was me, but I was old. I mean I was about thirty years old or something."

"It was a dream," Dan said.

"It was the middle of the afternoon, I tell you! I was doing my homework. She said, 'You've never lifted a finger to help me.' Then she asked me for a glass with some ice in it."

After a moment, Dan said, "It was probably the cleaning lady."

"Cleaning lady! Cleaning lady for Godssakes, what do you know about cleaning ladies!"

Dan felt her hair bristle as though someone were running a comb through it back to front, and realized she was mad, madder than she'd been all summer, for all summer she'd only felt humiliated when Jane was nasty to her.

"Listen up," Dan said, "don't talk to me like that any more."

"Like what," Jane said cooly.

Dan stood up and walked away, leaving Jane sitting there, not realizing what had happened to her. Jane was saying, "The thing I don't understand is how she ever got into that apartment. My father had about a dozen locks on the door."

Dan sat in her seat in the quiet, dark coach and looked out at the dark night. She tried to recollect how it seemed dawn happened. Things just sort of rose out, she guessed she knew. There was nothing you could do about it. She thought of Jane's dream in which the men in white bathing caps were pushing all her grandma's things out of the house and into the street. The inside became empty and the outside became full. Dan was beginning to feel sorry for herself. She was alone, with no friends and no parents, sitting on a train between one place and another, scaring herself with someone else's dream in the middle of the night. She got up and walked through the rocking cars to the Starlight Lounge for a glass of water. After 4 A.M. it was no longer referred to as the Starlight Lounge. They stopped serving drinks and turned off the electric stars. It became just another place to sit. Mr. Muirhead was sitting there, alone. He must have been on excellent terms with the stewards because he was drinking a Bloody Mary.

"Hi, Dan!" he said.

Dan sat opposite him. After a moment she said, "I had a very nice summer. Thank you for inviting me."

"Well, I hope you enjoyed your summer, sweetie," Mr. Muirhead said.

"Do you think Jane and I will be friends forever?" Dan asked.

Mr. Muirhead looked surprised. "Definitely not. Jane will not have friends. Jane will have husbands, enemies and lawyers." He cracked ice noisily with his white teeth. "I'm glad you enjoyed your summer, Dan, and I hope you're enjoying your childhood. When you grow up, a shadow falls. Everything's sunny and then this big goddamn *wing* or something passes overhead."

"Oh," Dan said.

"Well, I've only heard that's the case actually," Mr. Muirhead said. "Do you know what I want to be when I grow up?" He waited for her to smile. "When I grow up I want to become an Indian so I can use my Indian name."

"What is your Indian name?" Dan asked, smiling.

"My Indian name is 'He Rides a Slow Enduring Heavy Horse.' "

"That's a nice one," Dan said.

"It is, isn't it?" Mr. Muirhead said, gnawing ice.

Outside, the sky was lightening. Daylight was just beginning to flourish on the city of Jacksonville. It fell without prejudice on the slaughter houses, Dairy Queens and courthouses, on the car lots, sabal palms and a billboard advertisement for pies.

The train went slowly around a long curve, and looking backward, past Mr. Muirhead, Dan could see the entire length of it moving ahead. The bubble-topped cars were dark and sinister in the first flat and hopeful light of the morning.

Dan took the three postcards she had left out of her bookbag and looked at them. One showed Thomas Edison beneath a banyan tree. One showed a little tar-paper shack out in the middle of the desert in New Mexico where men were supposed to have invented the atomic bomb. One was a "quicky" card showing a porpoise balancing a grapefruit on the top of his head.

"Oh, I remember those," Mr. Muirhead said, picking up the "quicky" card. "You just check off what you want." He read aloud, *"How are you? I am fine( ) lonesome ( ) happy ( ) sad ( ) broke ( ) flying high ( ) "* Mr. Muirhead chuckled. He read, *"I have been good ( ) no good ( ). I saw The Gulf of Mexico ( ) The Atlantic Ocean ( ) The Orange Groves ( ) Interesting Attractions ( ) You in My Dreams ( )."*

"I like this one," Mr. Muirhead said, chuckling.

"You can have it," Dan said. "I'd like you to have it."

"You're a nice little girl," Mr. Muirhead said. He looked at his glass and then out the window. "What do you think was on that note Mrs. Muirhead had you give me?" he asked. "Do you think there's something I've missed?"

Richard Yates

Oh, Joseph, I'm So Tired

When Franklin D. Roosevelt was President-elect there must have been sculptors all over America who wanted a chance to model his head from life, but my mother had connections. One of her closest friends and neighbors, in the Greenwich Village courtyard where we lived, was an amiable man named Howard Witman who had recently lost his job as a reporter on the *New York Post*. And one of Howard's former colleagues from the *Post* was now employed in the press office of Roosevelt's New York headquarters. That would make it easy for her to get in—or, as she said, to get an entrée—and she was confident she could take it from there. She was confident about everything she did in those days, but it never quite disguised a terrible need for support and approval on every side.

She wasn't a very good sculptor. She had been working at it for only three years, since breaking up her marriage to my father, and there was still something stiff and amateurish about her pieces. Before the Roosevelt project her specialty had been "garden figures"—a life-size little boy whose legs turned into the legs of a goat at the knees and another who knelt among ferns to play the pipes of Pan; little girls who trailed chains of daisies from their upraised arms or walked beside a spread-winged goose. These fanciful children, in plaster painted green to simulate weathered bronze, were arranged on homemade wooden pedestals to loom around her studio and to leave a cleared space in the middle for the modeling stand that held whatever she was working on in clay.

Her idea was that any number of rich people, all of them gracious and aristocratic, would soon discover her: they would want her sculpture to decorate their landscaped gardens, and they would want to make her their friend for life. In the meantime, a little nationwide publicity as the first woman sculptor to "do" the President-elect certainly wouldn't hurt her career.

And, if nothing else, she had a good studio. It was, in fact, the best of all the studios she would have in the rest of her life. There were six or eight old houses facing our side of the courtyard, with their backs to Bedford Street, and ours was probably the show-place of the row because the front room on its ground floor was two stories high. You went down a broad set of brick steps to the tall front windows and the front door; then you were in the high, wide, light-flooded studio. It was big enough to serve as a living room too, and so along with the green garden children it contained all the living-room furniture from the house we'd lived in with my father in the suburban town of Hastings-on-Hudson, where I was born. A second-floor balcony ran along the far end of the studio, with two small bedrooms and a tiny bathroom tucked away upstairs; beneath that, where the ground floor continued through to the Bedford Street side, lay the only part of the apartment that might let you know we didn't have much money. The ceiling was very low and it was always dark in there; the small windows looked out underneath an iron sidewalk grating, and the bottom of that street cavity was thick with strewn garbage. Our roach-infested kitchen was barely big enough for a stove and sink that were never clean, and for a brown wooden icebox with its dark, ever-melting block of ice; the rest of that area was our dining room, and not even the amplitude of the old Hastings dining-room table could brighten it. But our Majestic radio was in there too, and that made it a cozy place for my sister Edith and me: we liked the children's programs that came on in the late afternoons.

We had just turned off the radio one day when we went out into the studio and found our mother discussing the Roosevelt project with Howard Whitman. It was the first we'd heard of it, and we must have interrupted her with too many questions because she said "Edith? Billy? That's enough, now. I'll tell you all about this later. Run out in the garden and play."

She always called the courtyard "the garden," though nothing grew there except a few stunted city trees and a patch of grass that never had a chance to spread. Mostly it was bald earth, interrupted here and there by brick paving, lightly powdered with soot and scattered with the droppings of dogs and cats. It may have been six or eight houses long, but it was only two houses wide, which gave it a hemmed-in, cheerless look; its only point of interest was a dilapidated marble fountain, not much bigger than a birdbath, which stood near our house. The original idea of the fountain was that water would drip evenly from around the rim of its upper tier and tinkle into its lower basin, but age had unsettled it; the water spilled in a single ropy stream from the only inch of the upper tier's rim that stayed clean. The lower basin was deep enough to soak your feet in on a hot day, but there wasn't much pleasure in that because the underwater part of the marble was coated with brown scum.

My sister and I found things to do in the courtyard every day, for all of the two years we lived there, but that was only because Edith was an imaginative child. She was eleven at the time of the Roosevelt project, and I was seven.

"Daddy?" she asked in our father's office uptown one afternoon. "Have you heard Mommy's doing a head of President Roosevelt?"

"Oh?" He was rummaging in his desk, looking for something he'd said we might like.

"She's going to take his measurements and stuff here in New York," Edith said, "and then after the Inauguration, when the sculpture's done, she's going to take it to Washington and present it to him in the White House." Edith often told one of our parents about the other's more virtuous activities; it was part of her long, hopeless effort to bring them back together. Many years later she told me she thought she had never recovered, and never would, from the shock of their breakup: she said Hastings-on-Hudson remained the happiest time of her life, and that made me envious because I could scarcely remember it at all.

"Well," my father said. "That's really something, isn't it." Then he found what he'd been looking for in the desk and said, "Here we go; what do you think of these?" They were two fragile perforated sheets of what looked like postage stamps, each stamp bearing the insignia of an electric light bulb in vivid white against a yellow background, and the words "More light."

My father's office was one of many small cubicles on the twenty-third floor of the General Electric building. He was an assistant regional sales manager in what was then called the Mazda Lamp Division—a modest job, but good enough to have allowed him to rent into a town like Hastings-on-Hudson in better times—and these "More light" stamps were souvenirs of a recent sales convention. We told him the stamps were neat—and they were—but expressed some doubt as to what we might do with them.

"Oh, they're just for decoration," he said. "I thought you

could paste them into your schoolbooks, or—you know—whatever you want. Ready to go?" And he carefully folded the sheets of stamps and put them in his inside pocket for safekeeping on the way home.

Between the subway exit and the courtyard, somewhere in the West Village, we always walked past a vacant lot where men stood huddled around weak fires built of broken fruit crates and trash, some of them warming tin cans of food held by coat-hanger wire over the flames. "Don't stare," my father had said the first time. "All those men are out of work, and they're hungry."

"Daddy?" Edith inquired. "Do you think Roosevelt's good?"

"Sure I do."

"Do you think all the Democrats are good?"

"Well, most of 'em, sure."

Much later I would learn that my father had participated in local Democratic Party politics for years. He had served some of his political friends—men my mother described as dreadful little Irish people from Tammany Hall—by helping them to establish Mazda Lamp distributorships in various parts of the city. And he loved their social gatherings, at which he was always asked to sing.

"Well, of course, you're too young to remember Daddy's singing," Edith said to me once after his death in 1942.

"No, I'm not; I remember."

"But I mean really remember," she said. "He had the most beautiful tenor voice I've ever heard. Remember 'Danny Boy'?"

"Sure."

"Ah, God, that was something," she said, closing her eyes. "That was really—that was really something."

When we got back to the courtyard that afternoon, and back into the studio, Edith and I watched our parents say hello to each other. We always watched that closely, hoping they might drift into conversation and sit down together and find things to laugh about, but they never did. And it was even less likely than usual that day because my mother had a guest—a woman named Sloane Cabot who was her best friend in the courtyard, and who greeted my father with a little rush of false, flirtatious enthusiasm.

"How've you been, Sloane?" he said. Then he turned back to his former wife and said "Helen? I hear you're planning to make a bust of Roosevelt."

"Well, not a bust," she said. "A head. I think it'll be more effective if I cut it off at the neck."

"Well, good. That's fine. Good luck with it. Okay, then." He gave his whole attention to Edith and me. "Okay. See you soon.

How about a hug?"

And those hugs of his, the climax of his visitation rights, were unforgettable. One at a time we would be swept up and pressed hard into the smells of linen and whiskey and tobacco; the warm rasp of his jaw would graze one cheek and there would be a quick moist kiss near the ear; then he'd let us go.

He was almost all the way out of the courtyard, almost out in the street, when Edith and I went racing after him.

"Daddy! Daddy! You forgot the stamps!"

He stopped and turned around, and that was when we saw he was crying. He tried to hide it—he put his face nearly into his armpit as if that might help him search his inside pocket—but there is no way to disguise the awful bloat and pucker of a face in tears.

"Here," he said. "Here you go." And he gave us the least convincing smile I had ever seen. It would be good to report that we stayed and talked to him—that we hugged him again—but we were too embarrassed for that. We took the stamps and ran home without looking back.

"Oh, aren't you excited, Helen?" Sloane Cabot was saying. "To be meeting him, and talking to him and everything, in front of all those reporters?"

"Well, of course," my mother said, "but the important thing is to get the measurements right. I hope there won't be a lot of photographers and silly interruptions."

Sloane Cabot was some years younger than my mother, and strikingly pretty in a style often portrayed in what I think are called Art Deco illustrations of that period: straight dark bangs, big eyes, and a big mouth. She too was a divorced mother, though her former husband had vanished long ago and was referred to only as "that bastard" or "that cowardly son of a bitch." Her only child was a boy of Edith's age named John, whom Edith and I liked enormously.

The two women had met within days of our moving into the courtyard, and their friendship was sealed when my mother solved the problem of John's schooling. She knew a Hastings-on-Hudson family who would appreciate the money earned from taking in a boarder, so John went up there to live and go to school, and came home only on weekends. The arrangement cost more than Sloane could comfortably afford, but she managed to make ends meet and was forever grateful.

Sloane worked in the Wall Street district as a private secretary. She talked a lot about how she hated her job and her boss, but the good part was that her boss was often out of town for extended periods: that gave her time to use the office typewriter in pursuit of her life's ambition, which was to write scripts for the radio.

She once confided to my mother that she'd made up both of her names: "Sloane" because it sounded masculine, the kind of name a woman alone might need for making her way in the world, and "Cabot" because—well, because it had a touch of class. Was there anything wrong with that?

"Oh, Helen," she said. "This is going to be wonderful for you. If you get the publicity—if the papers pick it up, and the news-reels—you'll be one of the most interesting personalities in America."

Five or six people were gathered in the studio on the day my mother came home from her first visit with the President-elect.

"Will somebody get me a drink?" she asked, looking around in mock helplessness. "Then I'll tell you all about it."

And with the drink in her hand, with her eyes as wide as a child's, she told us how a door had opened and two big men had brought him in.

"Big men," she insisted. "Young, strong men, holding him up under the arms, and you could see how they were straining. Then you saw this *foot* come out, with these awful metal braces on the shoe, and then the *other* foot. And he was sweating, and he was panting for breath, and his face was—I don't know—all bright and tense and horrible." She shuddered.

"Well," Howard Whitman said, looking uneasy, "he can't help being crippled, Helen."

"Howard," she said impatiently, "I'm only trying to tell you how *ugly* it was." And that seemed to carry a certain weight. If she was an authority on beauty—on how a little boy might kneel among ferns to play the pipes of Pan, for example—then surely she had earned her credentials as an authority on ugliness.

"*Any*way," she went on, "they got him into a chair, and he wiped most of the sweat off his face with a handkerchief—he was still out of breath—and after a while he started talking to some of the other men there; I couldn't follow that part of it. Then finally he turned to me with this smile of his. Honestly, I don't know if I can describe that smile. It isn't something you can see in the newsreels; you have to be there. His eyes don't change at all, but the corners of his mouth go up as if they're being pulled by pup-pet strings. It's a frightening smile. It makes you think: This could be a dangerous man. This could be an evil man. Well anyway, we started talking, and I spoke right up to him. I said 'I didn't vote for you, Mr. President.' I said 'I'm a good Republican and I voted for President Hoover.' He said 'Why are you here, then?' or some-thing like that, and I said 'Because you have a very interesting head.' So he gave me the smile again and he said 'What's interesting about it?' And I said 'I like the bumps on it.' "

By then she must have assumed that every reporter in the room was writing in his notebook, while the photographers got their flashbulbs ready; tomorrow's papers might easily read:

GAL SCULPTOR TWITS FDR
ABOUT "BUMPS" ON HEAD

At the end of her preliminary chat with him she got down to business, which was to measure different parts of his head with her calipers. I knew how that felt: the cold, trembling points of those clay-encrusted calipers had tickled and poked me all over during the times I'd served as model for her fey little woodland boys.

But not a single flashbulb went off while she took and recorded the measurements, and nobody asked her any questions; after a few nervous words of thanks and good-bye she was out in the corridor again among all the hopeless, craning people who couldn't get in. It must have been a bad disappointment, and I imagine she tried to make up for it by planning the triumphant way she'd tell us about it when she got home.

"Helen?" Howard Whitman inquired, after most of the other visitors had gone. "Why'd you tell him you didn't vote for him?"

"Well, because it's true. I *am* a good Republican; you know that."

She was a storekeeper's daughter from a small town in Ohio; she had probably grown up hearing the phrase "good Republican" as an index of respectability and clean clothes. And maybe she had come to relax her standards of respectability, maybe she didn't even care much about clean clothes anymore, but "good Republican" was worth clinging to. It would be helpful when she met the customers for her garden figures, the people whose low, courteous voices would welcome her into their lives and who would almost certainly turn out to be Republicans too.

"I believe in the aristocracy!" she often cried, trying to make herself heard above the rumble of voices when her guests were discussing communism, and they seldom paid her any attention. They liked her well enough: she gave parties with plenty of liquor, and she was an agreeable hostess if only because of her touching eagerness to please; but in any talk of politics she was like a shrill, exasperating child. She believed in the aristocracy.

She believed in God, too, or at least in the ceremony of St. Luke's Episcopal Church, which she attended once or twice a year. And she believed in Eric Nicholson, the handsome middle-aged

Englishman who was her lover. He had something to do with the American end of a British chain of foundries: his company cast ornamental objects into bronze and lead. The cupolas of college and high-school buildings all over the East, the lead-casement windows for Tudor-style homes in places like Scarsdale and Bronxville—these were some of the things Eric Nicholson's firm had accomplished. He was always self-deprecating about his business, but ruddy and glowing with its success.

My mother had met him the year before, when she'd sought help in having one of her garden figures cast into bronze, to be "placed on consignment" with some garden-sculpture gallery from which it would never be sold. Eric Nicholson had persuaded her that lead would be almost as nice as bronze and much cheaper; then he'd asked her out to dinner, and that evening changed our lives.

Mr. Nicholson rarely spoke to my sister or me, and I think we were both frightened of him, but he overwhelmed us with gifts. At first they were mostly books—a volume of cartoons from *Punch*, a partial set of Dickens, a book called *England in Tudor Times* containing tissue-covered color plates that Edith liked. But in the summer of 1933, when our father arranged for us to spend two weeks with our mother at a small lake in New Jersey, Mr. Nicholson's gifts became a cornucopia of sporting goods. He gave Edith a steel fishing rod with a reel so intricate that none of us could have figured it out even if we'd known how to fish, a wicker creel for carrying the fish she would never catch, and a sheathed hunting knife to be worn at her waist. He gave me a short axe whose head was encased in a leather holster and strapped to my belt—I guess this was for cutting firewood to cook the fish—and a cumbersome net with a handle that hung from an elastic shoulder strap, in case I should be called upon to wade in and help Edith land a tricky one. There was nothing to do in that New Jersey village except take walks, or what my mother called good hikes; and every day, as we plodded out through the insect-humming weeds in the sun, we wore our full regalia of useless equipment.

That same summer Mr. Nicholson gave me a three-year subscription to *Field and Stream,* and I think that impenetrable magazine was the least appropriate of all his gifts because it kept coming in the mail for such a long, long time after everything else had changed for us: after we'd moved out of New York to Scarsdale, where Mr. Nicholson had found a house with a low rent, and after he had abandoned my mother in that house—with no warning—to return to England and to the wife from whom he'd never really been divorced.

But all that came later; I want to go back to the time between Franklin D. Roosevelt's election and his Inauguration, when his head was slowly taking shape on my mother's modeling stand.

Her original plan had been to make it life-size, or larger than life-size, but Mr. Nicholson urged her to scale it down for economy in the casting, and so she made it only six or seven inches high. He persuaded her too, for the second time since he'd known her, that lead would be almost as nice as bronze.

She had always said she didn't mind at all if Edith and I watched her work, but we had never much wanted to; now it was a little more interesting because we could watch her sift through many photographs of Roosevelt cut from newspapers until she found one that would help her execute a subtle plane of cheek or brow.

But most of our day was taken up with school. John Cabot might go to school in Hastings-on-Hudson, for which Edith would always yearn, but we had what even Edith admitted was the next best thing: we went to school in our bedroom.

During the previous year my mother had enrolled us in the public school down the street, but she'd begun to regret it when we came home with lice in our hair. Then one day Edith came home accused of having stolen a boy's coat, and that was too much. She withdrew us both, in defiance of the city truant officer, and pleaded with my father to help her meet the cost of a private school. He refused. The rent she paid and the bills she ran up were already taxing him far beyond the terms of the divorce agreement; he was in debt; surely she must realize he was lucky even to have a job. Would she ever learn to be reasonable?

It was Howard Whitman who broke the deadlock. He knew of an inexpensive, fully accredited mail-order service called The Calvert School, intended mainly for the homes of children who were invalids. The Calvert School furnished weekly supplies of books and materials and study plans; all she would need was someone in the house to administer the program and to serve as a tutor. And someone like Bart Kampen would be ideal for the job.

"The skinny fellow?" she asked. "The Jewish boy from Holland or wherever it is?"

"He's very well educated, Helen," Howard told her. "And he speaks fluent English, and he'd be very conscientious. And he could certainly use the money."

We were delighted to learn that Bart Kampen would be our tutor. With the exception of Howard himself, Bart was probably our favorite among the adults around the courtyard. He was twenty-eight or so, young enough so that his ears could still turn red when he was teased by children; we had found that out in teasing him once or twice about such matters as that his socks didn't match. He was tall and very thin and seemed always to look startled except when he was comforted enough to smile. He was a violinist, a Dutch Jew who had emigrated the year before in the hope of joining a symphony orchestra, and eventually of launching a concert career. But the symphonies weren't hiring then, nor were lesser orchestras, so Bart had gone without work for a long time. He lived alone in a room on Seventh Avenue, not far from the courtyard, and people who liked him used to worry that he might not have enough to eat. He owned two suits, both cut in a way that must have been stylish in the Netherlands at the time: stiff, heavily padded shoulders and a nipped-in waist; they would probably have looked better on someone with a little more meat on his bones. In shirtsleeves, with the cuffs rolled back, his hairy wrists and forearms looked even more fragile than you might have expected, but his long hands were shapely and strong enough to suggest authority on the violin.

"I'll leave it entirely up to you, Bart," my mother said when he asked if she had any instructions for our tutoring. "I know you'll do wonders with them."

A small table was moved into our bedroom, under the window, and three chairs placed around it. Bart sat in the middle so that he could divide his time equally between Edith and me. Big, clean, heavy brown envelopes arrived in the mail from The Calvert School once a week, and when Bart slid their fascinating contents onto the table it was like settling down to begin a game.

Edith was in the fifth grade that year—her part of the table was given over to incomprehensible talk about English and History and Social Studies—and I was in the first. I spent my mornings asking Bart to help me puzzle out the very opening moves of an education.

"Take your time, Billy," he would say. "Don't get impatient with this. Once you have it you'll see how easy it is, and then you'll be ready for the next thing."

At eleven each morning we would take a break. We'd go downstairs and out to the part of the courtyard that had a little grass. Bart would carefully lay his folded coat on the sidelines, turn back his shirt cuffs, and present himself as ready to give what he called airplane rides. Taking us one at a time, he would grasp one wrist and one ankle; then he'd whirl us off our feet and around and around, with himself as the pivot, until the courtyard and the buildings and the city and the world were lost in the dizzying blur of our flight.

231

After the airplane rides we would hurry down the steps into the studio, where we'd usually find that my mother had set out a tray bearing three tall glasses of cold Ovaltine, sometimes with cookies on the side and sometimes not. I once overheard her telling Sloane Cabot she thought the Ovaltine must be Bart's first nourishment of the day—and I think she was probably right, if only because of the way his hand would tremble in reaching for his glass. Sometimes she'd forget to prepare the tray and we'd crowd into the kitchen and fix it ourselves; I can never see a jar of Ovaltine on a grocery shelf without remembering those times. Then it was back upstairs to school again. And during that year, by coaxing and prodding and telling me not to get impatient, Bart Kampen taught me to read.

It was an excellent opportunity for showing off. I would pull books down from my mother's shelves—mostly books that were the gifts of Mr. Nicholson—and try to impress her by reading mangled sentences aloud.

"That's wonderful, dear," she would say. "You've really learned to read, haven't you."

Soon a white and yellow "More light" stamp was affixed to every page of my Calvert First Grade Reader, proving I had mastered it, and others were accumulating at a slower rate in my arithmetic workbook. Still other stamps were fastened to the wall beside my place at the school table, arranged in a proud little white and yellow thumb-smudged column that rose as high as I could reach.

"You shouldn't have put your stamps on the wall," Edith said.

"Why?"

"Well, because they'll be hard to take off."

"Who's going to take them off?"

That small room of ours, with its double function of sleep and learning, stands more clearly in my memory than any other part of our home. Someone should probably have told my mother that a girl and boy of our ages ought to have separate rooms, but that never occurred to me until much later. Our cots were set foot-to-foot against the wall, leaving just enough space to pass along-side them to the school table, and we had some good conversations as we lay waiting for sleep at night. The one I remember best was the time Edith told me about the sound of the city.

"I don't mean just the loud noises," she said, "like the siren going by just now, or those car doors slamming, or all the laughing and shouting down the street; that's just close-up stuff. I'm talking about something else. Because you see there are millions and millions of people in New York—more people than you can possibly imagine, ever—and most of them are doing something that makes a sound. Maybe talking, or playing the radio, maybe closing doors, maybe putting their forks down on their plates if they're having dinner, or dropping their shoes if they're going to bed—and because there are so many of them, all those little sounds add up and come together in a kind of hum. But it's so faint—so very, very faint—that you can't hear it unless you listen very carefully for a long time."

"Can you hear it?" I asked her.

"Sometimes. I listen every night, but I can only hear it sometimes. Other times I fall asleep. Let's be quiet now, and just listen. See if you can hear it, Billy."

And I tried hard, closing my eyes as if that would help, opening my mouth to minimize the sound of my breathing, but in the end I had to tell her I'd failed. "How about you?" I asked.

"Oh, I heard it," she said. "Just for a few seconds, but I heard it. You'll hear it too, if you keep trying. And it's worth waiting for. When you hear it, you're hearing the whole city of New York."

The high point of our week was Friday afternoon, when John Cabot came home from Hastings. He exuded health and normality; he brought fresh suburban air into our bohemian lives. He even transformed his mother's small apartment, while he was there, into an enviable place of rest between vigorous encounters with the world. He subscribed to both *Boy's Life* and *Open Road for Boys,* and these seemed to me to be wonderful things to have in your house, if only for the illustrations. John dressed in the same heroic way as the boys shown in those magazines, corduroy knickers with ribbed stockings pulled taut over his muscular calves. He talked a lot about the Hastings high-school football team, for which he planned to try out as soon as he was old enough, and about Hastings friends whose names and personalities grew almost as familiar to us as if they were friends of our own. He taught us invigorating new ways to speak, like saying "What's the diff?" instead of "What's the difference?" And he was better even than Edith at finding new things to do in the courtyard.

You could buy goldfish for ten or fifteen cents apiece in Woolworth's then, and one day we brought home three of them to keep in the fountain. We sprinkled the water with more Woolworth's granulated fish food than they could possibly need, and we named them after ourselves: "John," "Edith," and "Billy." For a week or two Edith and I would run to the fountain every morning, before Bart came for school, to make sure they were still alive and to see if they had enough food, and to watch them.

"Have you noticed how much bigger Billy's getting?" Edith asked me. "He's huge. He's almost as big as John and Edith now. He'll probably be bigger than both of them."

Then one weekend when John was home he called our attention to how quickly the fish could turn and move. "They have better reflexes than humans," he explained. "When they see a shadow in the water, or anything that looks like danger, they get away faster than you can blink. Watch." And he sank one hand into the water to make a grab for the fish named Edith, but she evaded him and fled. "See that?" he asked. "How's that for speed. Know something? I bet you could shoot an arrow in there, and they'd get away in time. Wait." To prove his point he ran to his mother's apartment and came back with the handsome bow and arrow he had made at summer camp (going to camp every summer was another admirable thing about John); then he knelt at the rim of the fountain like the picture of an archer, his bow steady in one strong hand and the feathered end of the arrow tight against the bowstring in the other. He was taking aim at the fish named Billy. "Now, the velocity of this arrow," he said in a voice weakened by his effort, "is probably more than a car going eighty miles an hour. It's probably more like an airplane, or maybe even more than that. Okay; watch."

The fish named Billy was suddenly floating dead on the surface, on his side, impaled a quarter of the way up the arrow with parts of his pink guts dribbled along the shaft.

I was too old to cry, but something had to be done about the shock and rage and grief that filled me as I ran from the fountain, heading blindly for home, and half-way there I came upon my mother. She stood looking very clean, wearing a new coat and dress I'd never seen before and fastened to the arm of Mr. Nicholson. They were either just going out or just coming in—I didn't care which—and Mr. Nicholson frowned at me (he had told me more than once that boys of my age went to boarding school in England), but I didn't care about that either. I bent my head into her waist and didn't stop crying until long after I'd felt her hands stroking my back, until after she had assured me that goldfish didn't cost much and I'd have another one soon, and that John was sorry for the thoughtless thing he'd done. I had discovered, or rediscovered, that crying is a pleasure—that it can be a pleasure beyond all reckoning if your head is pressed in your mother's waist and her hands are on your back, and if she happens to be wearing clean clothes.

There were other pleasures. We had a good Christmas Eve in our house that year, or at least it was good at first. My father was there, which obliged Mr. Nicholson to stay away, and it was nice to see how relaxed he was among my mother's friends. He was shy, but they seemed to like him. He got along especially well with Bart Kampen.

Howard Whitman's daughter Molly, a sweet-natured girl of about my age, had come in from Tarrytown to spend the holidays with him, and there were several other children whom we knew but rarely saw. John looked very mature that night in a dark coat and tie, plainly aware of his social responsibilities as the oldest boy.

After a while, with no plan, the party drifted back into the dining-room area and staged an impromptu vaudeville. Howard started it: he brought the tall stool from my mother's modeling stand and sat his daughter on it, facing the audience. He folded back the opening of a brown paper bag two or three times and fitted it onto her head; then he took off his suit coat and draped it around her backwards, up to the chin; he went behind her, crouched out of sight, and worked his hands through the coat-sleeves so that when they emerged they appeared to be hers. And the sight of a smiling little girl in a paper-bag hat, waving and gesturing with huge, expressive hands, was enough to make everyone laugh. The big hands wiped her eyes and stroked her chin and pushed her hair behind her ears; then they elaborately thumbed her nose at us.

Next came Sloane Cabot. She sat very straight on the stool with her heels hooked over the rungs in such a way as to show her good legs to their best advantage, but her first act didn't go over.

"Well," she began, "I was at work today—you know my office is on the fortieth floor—when I happened to glance up from my typewriter and saw this big old man sort of crouched on the ledge outside the window, with a white beard and a funny red suit. So I ran to the window and opened it and said 'Are you all right?' Well, it was Santa Claus, and he said 'Of course I'm all right; I'm used to high places. But listen, miss: can you direct me to number seventy-five Bedford Street?' "

There was more, but our embarrassed looks must have told her we knew we were being condescended to; as soon as she'd found a way to finish it she did so quickly. Then, after a thoughtful pause, she tried something else that turned out to be much better.

"Have you children ever heard the story of the first Christmas?" she asked. "When Jesus was born?" And she began to tell it in the kind of hushed, dramatic voice she must have hoped might be used by the narrators of her more serious radio plays.

" . . . And there were still many miles to go before they

reached Bethlehem," she said, "and it was a cold night. Now, Mary knew she would very soon have a baby. She even knew, because an angel had told her, that her baby might one day be the saviour of all mankind. But she was only a young girl"—here Sloane's eyes glistened, as if they might be filling with tears—"and the traveling had exhausted her. She was bruised by the jolting gait of the donkey and she ached all over, and she thought they'd never, ever get there, and all she could say was 'Oh, Joseph, I'm so tired.' "

The story went on through the rejection at the inn, and the birth in the stable, and the manger, and the animals, and the arrival of the three kings; when it was over we clapped a long time because Sloane had told it so well.

"Daddy?" Edith asked. "Will you sing for us?"

"Oh, well, thanks, honey," he said, "but no; I really need a piano for that. Thanks anyway."

The final performer of the evening was Bart Kampen, persuaded by popular demand to go home and get his violin. There was no surprise in discovering that he played like a professional, like something you might easily hear on the radio; the enjoyment came from watching how his thin face frowned over the chin rest, empty of all emotion except concern that the sound be right. We were proud of him.

Some time after my father left a good many other adults began to arrive, most of them strangers to me, looking as though they'd already been to several other parties that night. It was very late, or rather very early Christmas morning, when I looked into the kitchen and saw Sloane standing close to a bald man I didn't know. He held a trembling drink in one hand and slowly massaged her shoulder with the other; she seemed to be shrinking back against the old wooden icebox. Sloane had a way of smiling that allowed little wisps of cigarette smoke to escape from between her almost-closed lips while she looked you up and down, and she was doing that. Then the man put his drink on top of the icebox and took her in his arms, and I couldn't see her face anymore.

Another man, in a rumpled brown suit, lay unconscious on the dining-room floor. I walked around him and went into the studio, where a good-looking young woman stood weeping wretchedly and three men kept getting in each other's way as they tried to comfort her. Then I saw that one of the men was Bart, and I watched while he outlasted the other two and turned the girl away toward the door. He put his arm around her and she nestled her head in his shoulder; that was how they left the house.

Edith looked jaded in her wrinkled party dress. She was reclining in our old Hastings-on-Hudson easy chair with her head tipped back and her legs flung out over both the chair's arms, and John sat cross-legged on the floor near one of her dangling feet. They seemed to have been talking about something that didn't interest either of them much, and the talk petered out altogether when I sat on the floor to join them.

"Billy," she said, "do you realize what time it is?"

"What's the diff?" I said.

"You should've been in bed hours ago. Come on. Let's go up."

"I don't feel like it."

"Well," she said, "I'm going up, anyway," and she got laboriously out of the chair and walked away into the crowd.

John turned to me and narrowed his eyes unpleasantly. "Know something?" he said. "When she was in the chair that way I could see everything."

"Huh?"

"I could see everything. I could see the crack, and the hair. She's beginning to get hair."

I had observed these features of my sister many times—in the bathtub, or when she was changing her clothes—and hadn't found them especially remarkable; even so, I understood at once how remarkable they must have been for him. If only he had smiled in a bashful way we might have laughed together like a couple of regular fellows out of *Open Road for Boys,* but his face was still set in that disdainful look.

"I kept looking and looking," he said, "and I had to keep her talking so she wouldn't catch on, but I was doing fine until you had to come over and ruin it."

Was I supposed to apologize? That didn't seem right, but nothing else seemed right either. All I did was look at the floor.

When I finally got to bed there was scarcely time for trying to hear the elusive sound of the city—I had found that a good way to keep from thinking of anything else—when my mother came blundering in. She'd had too much to drink and wanted to lie down, but instead of going to her own room she got into bed with me. "Oh," she said. "Oh, my boy. Oh, my boy." It was a narrow cot and there was no way to make room for her; then suddenly she retched, bolted to her feet, and ran for the bathroom, where I heard her vomiting. And when I moved over into the part of the bed she had occupied my face recoiled quickly, but not quite in time, from the slick mouthful of puke she had left on her side of the pillow.

For a month or so that winter we didn't see much of Sloane because she said she was "working on something big. Something really big." When it was finished she brought it to the studio, looking tired but prettier than ever, and shyly asked if she could read it aloud.

"Wonderful," my mother said. "What's it about?"

"That's the best part. It's about us. All of us. Listen."

Bart had gone for the day and Edith was out in the courtyard by herself—she often played by herself—so there was nobody for an audience but my mother and me. We sat on the sofa and Sloane arranged herself on the tall stool, just as she'd done for telling the Bethlehem story.

"There is an enchanted courtyard in Greenwich Village," she read. "It's only a narrow patch of brick and green among the irregular shapes of very old houses, but what makes it enchanted is that the people who live in it, or near it, have come to form an enchanted circle of friends.

"None of them have enough money and some are quite poor, but they believe in the future; they believe in each other, and in themselves.

"There is Howard, once a top reporter on a metropolitan daily newspaper. Everyone knows Howard will soon scale the journalistic heights again, and in the meantime he serves as the wise and humorous sage of the courtyard.

"There is Bart, a young violinist clearly destined for virtuosity on the concert stage, who just for the present must graciously accept all lunch and dinner invitations in order to survive.

"And there is Helen, a sculptor whose charming works will someday grace the finest gardens in America, and whose studio is the favorite gathering place for members of the circle."

There was more like that, introducing other characters, and toward the end she got around to the children. She described my sister as "a lanky, dreamy tomboy," which was odd—I had never thought of Edith that way—and she called me "a sad-eyed, seven-year-old philosopher," which was wholly baffling. When the introduction was over she paused a few seconds for dramatic effect and then went into the opening episode of the series, or what I suppose would be called the "pilot."

I couldn't follow the story very well—it seemed to be mostly an excuse for bringing each character up to the microphone for a few lines apiece—and before long I was listening only to see if there would be any lines for the character based on me. And there were, in a way. She announced my name—"Billy"—but then instead of speaking she put her mouth through a terrible series of contortions, accompanied by funny little bursts of sound, and by the time the words came out I didn't care what they were. It was true that I stuttered badly—I wouldn't get over it for five or six more years—but I hadn't expected anyone to put it on the radio.

"Oh, Sloane, that's marvelous," my mother said when the reading was over. "That's really exciting."

. And Sloane was carefully stacking her typed pages in the way she'd probably been taught to do in secretarial school, blushing and smiling with pride. "Well," she said, "it probably needs work, but I do think it's got a lot of potential."

"It's perfect," my mother said. "Just the way it is."

Sloane mailed the script to a radio producer and he mailed it back with a letter typed by some radio secretary, explaining that her material had too limited an appeal to be commercial. The radio public was not yet ready, he said, for a story of Greenwich Village life.

Then it was March. The new President promised that the only thing we had to fear was fear itself, and soon after that his head came packed in wood and excelsior from Mr. Nicholson's foundry.

It was a fairly good likeness. She had caught the famous lift of the chin—it might not have looked like him at all if she hadn't—and everyone told her it was fine. What nobody said was that her original plan had been right, and Mr. Nicholson shouldn't have interfered: it was too small. It didn't look heroic. If you could have hollowed it out and put a slot in the top, it might have made a serviceable bank for loose change.

The foundry had burnished the lead until it shone almost silver in the highlights, and they'd mounted it on a sturdy little base of heavy black plastic. They had sent back three copies: one for the White House presentation, one to keep for exhibition purposes, and an extra one. But the extra one soon toppled to the floor and was badly damaged—the nose mashed almost into the chin—and my mother might have burst into tears if Howard Whitman hadn't made everyone laugh by saying it was now a good portrait of Vice President Garner.

Charlie Hines, Howard's old friend from the *Post* who was now a minor member of the White House staff, made an appointment for my mother with the President late on a weekday morning. She arranged for Sloane to spend the night with Edith and me; then she took an evening train down to Washington, carrying the sculpture in a cardboard box, and stayed at one of the less expensive Washington hotels. In the morning she met Charlie Hines in some crowded White House anteroom, where I guess they disposed of the cardboard box, and he took her to the waiting room outside the Oval Office. He sat with her as she held the naked head in her lap, and when their turn came he escorted her in to the President's desk for the presentation. It didn't take long. There were no reporters and no photographers.

Afterwards Charlie Hines took her out to lunch, probably because he'd promised Howard Whitman to do so. I imagine it wasn't a first-class restaurant, more likely some bustling, no-nonsense place favored by the working press, and I imagine they had trouble making conversation until they settled on Howard, and on what a shame it was that he was still out of work.

"No, but do you know Howard's friend Bart Kampen?" Charlie asked. "The young Dutchman? The violinist?"

"Yes, certainly," she said. "I know Bart."

"Well, Jesus, there's *one* story with a happy ending, right? Have you heard about that? Last time I saw Bart he said 'Charlie, the Depression's over for me,' and he told me he'd found some rich, dumb, crazy woman who's paying him to tutor her kids."

I can picture how she looked riding the long, slow train back to New York that afternoon. She must have sat staring straight ahead or out the dirty window, seeing nothing, her eyes round and her face held in a soft shape of hurt. Her adventure with Franklin D. Roosevelt had come to nothing. There would be no photographs or interviews or feature articles, no thrilling moments of newsreel coverage; strangers would never know of how she'd come from a small Ohio town, or of how she'd nurtured her talent through the brave, difficult, one-woman journey that had brought her to the attention of the world. It wasn't fair.

All she had to look forward to now was her romance with Eric Nicholson, and I think she may have known even then that it was faltering—his final desertion came the next fall.

She was forty-one, an age when even romatics must admit that youth is gone, and she had nothing to show for the years but a studio crowded with green plaster statues that nobody would buy. She believed in the aristocracy, but there was no reason to suppose the aristocracy would ever believe in her.

And every time she thought of what Charlie Hines had said about Bart Kampen—oh, how hateful; oh, how hateful—the humiliation came back in wave on wave, in merciless rhythm to the clatter of the train.

She made a brave show of her homecoming, though nobody was there to greet her but Sloane and Edith and me. Sloane had fed us, and she said "There's a plate for you in the oven, Helen," but my mother said she'd rather just have a drink instead. She was then at the onset of a long battle with alcohol that she would ultimately lose; it must have seemed bracing that night to decide on a drink instead of dinner. Then she told us "all about" her trip to Washington, managing to make it sound like a success. She talked of how thrilling it was to be actually inside the White House; she repeated whatever small, courteous thing it was that President Roosevelt had said to her on receiving the head. And she had brought back souvenirs: a handful of note-size White House stationery for Edith, and a well-used briar pipe for me. She explained that she'd seen a very distinguished-looking man smoking the pipe in the waiting room outside the Oval Office; when his name was called he had knocked it out quickly into an ashtray and left it there as he hurried inside. She had waited until she was sure no one was looking; then she'd taken the pipe from the ashtray and put it in her purse. "Because I knew he must have been somebody important," she said. "He could easily have been a member of the Cabinet, or something like that. Anyway, I thought you'd have a lot of fun with it." But I didn't. It was too heavy to hold in my teeth and it tasted terrible when I sucked on it; besides, I kept wondering what the man must have thought when he came out of the President's office and found it gone.

Sloane went home after a while, and my mother sat drinking alone at the dining-room table. I think she hoped Howard Whitman or some of her other friends might drop in, but nobody did. It was almost our bedtime when she looked up and said "Edith? Run out in the garden and see if you can find Bart."

He had recently bought a pair of bright tan shoes with crepe soles. I saw those shoes trip rapidly down the dark brick steps beyond the windows—he seemed scarcely to touch each step in his buoyancy—and then I saw him come smiling into the studio, with Edith closing the door behind him. "Helen!" he said. "You're back!"

She acknowledged that she was back. Then she got up from the table and slowly advanced on him, and Edith and I began to realize we were in for something bad.

"Bart," she said, "I had lunch with Charlie Hines in Washington today."

"Oh?"

"And we had a very interesting talk. He seems to know you very well."

"Oh, not really; we've met a few times at Howard's, but we're not really—"

"And he said you'd told him the Depression was over for you because you'd found some rich, dumb, crazy woman who was paying you to tutor her kids. Don't interrupt me."

But Bart clearly had no intention of interrupting her. He was backing away from her in his soundless shoes, retreating past one stiff green garden child after another. His face looked startled and pink.

"I'm not a rich woman, Bart," she said, bearing down on him. "And I'm not dumb. And I'm not crazy. And I can recognize ingratitude and disloyalty and sheer, rotten viciousness and *lies* when they're thrown in my face."

My sister and I were halfway up the stairs jostling each other in our need to hide before the worst part came. The worst part of these things always came at the end, after she'd lost all control and gone on shouting anyway.

"I want you to get out of my house, Bart," she said. "And I don't ever want to see you again. And I want to tell you something. All my life I've hated people who say 'Some of my best friends are Jews.' Because *none* of my friends are Jews, or ever will be. Do you understand me? *None* of my friends are Jews, or ever will be."

The studio was quiet after that. Without speaking, avoiding each other's eyes, Edith and I got into our pajamas and into bed. But it wasn't more than a few minutes before the house began to ring with our mother's raging voice all over again, as if Bart had somehow been brought back and made to take his punishment twice.

" . . . And I said '*None* of my friends are Jews, or ever will be . . .' "

She was on the telephone, giving Sloane Cabot the highlights of the scene, and it was clear that Sloane would take her side and comfort her. Sloane might know how the Virgin Mary felt on the way to Bethlehem, but she also knew how to play my stutter for laughs. In a case like this she would quickly see where her allegiance lay, and it wouldn't cost her much to drop Bart Kampen from her enchanted circle.

When the telephone call came to an end at last there was silence downstairs until we heard her working with the ice pick in the icebox: she was making herself another drink.

There would be no more school in our room. We would probably never see Bart again—or if we ever did, he would probably not want to see us. But our mother was ours; we were hers; and we lived with that knowledge as we lay listening for the faint, faint sound of millions.